Rhys Thomas lives in Wales. He is in his early thirties. *The Suicide Club* is his first novel.

Find out more at www.thesuicideclub.com

The
Suicide Club

Rhys Thomas

BLACK SWAN

TRANSWORLD PUBLISHERS
61–63 Uxbridge Road, London W5 5SA
A Random House Group Company
www.rbooks.co.uk

THE SUICIDE CLUB
A BLACK SWAN BOOK: 9780552774970

First published in Great Britain
in 2009 by Doubleday
an imprint of Transworld Publishers
Black Swan edition published 2010

Addresses for Random House Group Ltd companies outside the UK
can be found at: www.randomhouse.co.uk
The Random House Group Ltd Reg. No. 954009

Penguin Random House is committed to a sustainable future for
our business, our readers and our planet. This book is made from
Forest Stewardship Council® certified paper.

MIX
Paper from
responsible sources
FSC® C018179

Printed and bound in Great Britain by Clays Ltd, Elcograf S.p.A.

Typeset in 12/14.25pt Bembo by Falcon Oast Graphic Art Ltd.
2 4 6 8 10 9 7 5 3 1

For Mum and Dad

The vast bulk of humanity is irredeemably mediocre.
  – Ronald Hayman describing Friedrich Nietzsche's beliefs

Do not go gentle into that good night . . .
Rage, rage against the dying of the light.

– Dylan Thomas

1

Call me Ishmael. Apparently, you have to have a good line to start a book so I stole that one from *Moby-Dick*, which is a book about a whale that I've never read. You know when I said call me Ishmael? Well, call me Richard Joseph Henry Harper because that's my name. Yes, it's a stupid name, I know. This book is about me and my friends and it gets a bit messy later on, I have to warn you. Only in terms of raw human emotion though. But I digress. It all started with Freddy.

I remember it well, the first time that we met. Mrs Kenna was telling us about the champion British miler, Roger Bannister. Mrs Kenna was an elderly lady with whom I had a mild fascination (if that's not too oxymoronic). Her husband and son had both died of a rare brain cancer so her whole existence was coated in tragedy. And I love people with a tragedy, genuinely *love* them. There's something about those emotions at the end of the spectrum that really gets me. And this woman had them in spades, poor thing. She always spoke with eloquence, as though a blanket of words had been pulled over her grief, smoothing the bumps, iron-ing out all that furious emotion, and for that I admired her because I have my very own furious emotion. Boiling inside me like acid. But only sometimes. And not really.

Anyhoo, I was listening to the lesson. Apparently Roger

Bannister, who was the first man to run a mile in under four minutes – big wow – was also a brilliant doctor. I'm sorry, I didn't mean 'big wow' just then, I was just showing off. I always do that – say something that I don't mean just to show off. I know it's a bad thing though. Being the first man to do *anything* is good, but running a mile in under four minutes for the first time must have been a pretty big thing. You know, back in the fifties.

I'm going to say something a bit weird now, but don't worry because it's important that I tell you this early on. Sometimes a mental image, like a photograph, will explode in my brain and it's the most horrendous thing you can imagine. For no reason, it just shoots into my head and there it is, unblinking, deadly: c, the Worst Case Scenario ('c' stands for 'constant' by the way because a Worst Case Scenario is always constant). Let me give you an example of what I mean.

My Worst Case Scenario for Mrs Kenna is she's sitting at the side of her dead husband and son's graves and somebody comes over and rapes her, then kills her right there on her husband's tombstone. So not only does she die but the guy who kills her robs her of her dignity too. She's naked and bloody on the grave. I know it's awful, that's why it's a Worst Case Scenario. That image always came to me in history class and I hated it because it's not healthy.

It's sort of like a gift I have, imagining these sorts of things, though it is equally a curse (God, that's cheesy – in truth it's just a curse). No matter how well something is going I can always imagine something terrible out of nowhere, all black and arachnoid, first of all blurring the edges like a creeping cataract and then consuming the whole thing like carbon monoxide petrified and leaden with mass. W–C–S.

It doesn't matter if it's the first or the hundredth time you've thought about it, it never becomes more or less shocking because it is not mutable – that's why it's a Worst Case Scenario. It's the worst possible thing that can possibly happen. I told you it was a bit weird but, as you'll see later on, it's important that you know I have these Worst Case Scenarios.

Then, all of a sudden, Craig Bartlett-Taylor started saying something from the back of the class. Lots of kids in my school have double-barrelled surnames because I go to a *very* good school.

'Miss,' is what he said.

We all turned round to look at him – he always sat at the back of every class because he was a bit of a freak. Today, Craig Bartlett-Taylor looked pale as hell. He looked like he was wearing make-up or something, but that's fine because loads of my friends wear some sort of make-up for the image, but Craig looked like he didn't know he was wearing make-up. He looked like a porcelain doll.

'I've just taken a whole bottle of pills, Miss.'

It was really weird when he said that. He said it so crisp and clear, like a snowflake. You know? Mrs Kenna was floundering, I could tell. Just more tragedy for her. Honestly, the tragedy was bursting at the seams, seeping through the pores for Mrs Kenna. She clearly didn't know what to do, even though she said, as she ran over to Craig, 'Show me the bottle.'

She looked funny running. Old people do. Their legs need WD-40.

Suddenly, Bartlett-Taylor fell off his chair on to the floor. The other kids gasped with the drama of it all. My heart was going mad. I sat up a little in my seat to see if he was frothing at the mouth – that's always a bad sign. But his mouth looked pretty dry. There didn't seem to be a pill bottle anywhere and we all said later that he must have taken the pills at the end of lunch or something.

Craig didn't even start having a fit or anything like that.

11

He just lay there, his eyes half open like he was just drifting off to sleep. *A sleep from which he will never awake*, a stupid Count Dracula voice said inside my head. I was worried for Craig but trying not to show it. I'd grown up with him and seeing him like that made my skin crawl a little. I wanted to do something, but I didn't know what. So I just sat there like a moron.

And that was the first time I saw Freddy. Frederick Spaulding-Carter. He was out of his chair straight away and running over to Craig like the wind. His chair upped itself on to two legs and then fell to the floor in a swirl of drama.

People always say that when dramatic things happen time slows down and everything goes in slow motion. I'd never really known anything truly dramatic so I wasn't sure if it was true. But I swear to God when Freddy ran to save Craig the world didn't slow down at all. It happened at the exact same speed that I'd lived the whole of my life.

He reached Bartlett–Taylor and slipped his arm under his body, lifting him on to his side. Then he grabbed his other arm and pulled it across his chest. I can't remember it exactly but he was doing what's called the Recovery Position. You do it if someone's out cold. I don't know what it does, maybe it straightens your windpipe into your lungs so you can access air more easily. I'm not sure.

'Call an ambulance,' he said. It came out as both quiet and loud. His black hair had flopped in front of his eyes. I had never seen this boy before so why the hell was he sat at the back of my classroom?

Mrs Kenna shouted to me to go and get the headmaster and tell him what had happened. Me. Why did it have to be me? I was good in class and I did my homework most of the time so why should I miss out? By the time I finished having this thought I was halfway down the corridor because in

12

truth I was a little bit terrified that Craig was in real trouble. I'm not disaffected or anything like that. I'm a normal kid, and I have a good soul.

As I ran I Worst Case Scenarioed the fate of Bartlett-Taylor. It was pretty bad. At his funeral, his dad, who was about seventy because they had Craig when they were too old, was crying. It was terrible because parents who have kids who die never, ever recover. It's impossible to recover from it because it's Not Natural. We as human beings are a Natural phenomenon and when things that are Not Natural happen, like a kid dying before their parents, you can't get over it properly because it's against the normal grain of the universe, right? So anyway, his old dad was crying as he lowered his boy's coffin into the ground. It was raining and the mud at the graveside was slippery. The old man, who had a frail skeleton, couldn't keep his footing because he was just an old man, and he fell over. The coffin slumped to one side and made a horrible thud as it smacked against the walls of the grave before dropping into the pit and cracking. The coffin came to a stop and everyone knew that the boy's corpse was inside the casket, lying deathly still, nothing more than a slab of meat. Bartlett-Taylor had lost his dignity and it was all because his old man was too old and weak.

Suddenly I remembered something. A memory from when I was little. Craig and I had been playing bows and arrows. We were in the same team. It was one of those long summer days that you only really have when you're a kid. We were hiding behind this weird grass hummock in the woods. We were on our backs, our heads lying against the grass, watching the branches of the trees swaying overhead. It was so still. We had never been the greatest of friends and in truth I had teased him a little bit along with the other kids, but I had still known him since I was three and that counts for a lot. I'd forgotten all about that day in the woods, but now there it was, in my head, making my heart beat with fear.

I smacked on the headmaster's door but he was on the phone when I burst in. He looked at me like I had just committed some terrible crime. His face was turning red and I thought that when he was through with his phone call he was actually going to murder me. He didn't like me much. I think it's because I sometimes used to get in trouble but still did well in examinations because I'm naturally intelligent. If I applied myself I reckon it's possible I could do well in life and I think, later on, I *will* apply myself and do good things for other people.

'Sir,' I shouted. Too loud.

His eyes bulged like the guy at the end of *Total Recall* when he goes out into the Martian atmosphere and the pressure basically crushes his skull.

'Sir, Mrs Kenna sent me. There's been the most terrible incident.' It was a ridiculous thing to say but sometimes I can't help saying ridiculous things to people I consider ridiculous. 'Craig Bartlett-Taylor's taken an overdose and he's collapsed off his chair.' The words spewed out fast and clear. I knew that I had to get the message out quick – the clock was ticking.

He didn't take his eyes off me as he cut his call short and dialled for an ambulance. When he was finished he asked which room Craig was in and walked out of the office. He sort of ran but he sort of walked too. Like a few steps and then a skip so that he didn't look like he was too concerned. Even though a child could be potentially dying right now.

This wasn't the first time that Craig Bartlett-Taylor had done something like this. He's got this thing in his head where he just hates everything. At least, that's the impression I get. When he's being nice, he's too nice, you know? Like it doesn't mean anything and he's just going through the motions. I think he'd had a nervous breakdown. You never recover from one of those because it's Not Natural.

Once, when we were kids, we were making fun of him. So he said he was going to throw himself in the river and end it all. He strode off down the street and around the corner. We knew he wouldn't go through with it though. He was feeling bad because his mother had just had a stroke and one of the older kids had stolen his ice cream and thrown it at the church. We were only about ten at the time. Anyway, he came back five minutes later. We asked him why he was still alive and he said, and this is completely true, that he'd forgotten his bathers.

Then he tried to kill himself again when he was thirteen, but this attempt was more serious. He threw himself out of his bedroom window. But only broke a leg. His parents must have been cartwheeling with worry. That was around the time when I stopped making fun of him.

For some reason I started wondering if my MCR album had turned up from Play. My Chemical Romance are a band that I really like. They're punkish but they get slated and called emo a lot, though that's not really what they are. Sometimes they are a bit though. Lots of people don't get it, but that's not my fault. I love them. Play is the Internet shop where I get most of my albums. It's my parents' account but they let me use it as long as I tell them. It delivers for free and the albums are cheaper than anywhere else I can find in the *real* world. Even cheaper than Tesco, and they're pretty good. Sometimes I'll still go into HMV to get an album, but they're more expensive – I just go there because sometimes I like going into record shops because there's always a good feeling in those places. In truth I probably started thinking about the album to distract myself from Craig. I do that a lot. But now I've totally lost the thread of the story so I'd better get back to it.

We were all outside because we'd been told to wait in the

yard. The flashing blue lights of the ambulance were shining off all the walls – you can see them from around corners they are so powerful. The drama of it all made some of the girls cry and you can't blame them: death's an awful thing.

One of my best friends, a girl called Clare, who has really black hair and wears pretty cool clothes which she designs herself, was stood on her own. It was strange for her because she was one of the most popular girls in school and always surrounded by an entourage of other girls. I was with a couple of my friends, but she looked so pretty stood all on her own that I wanted to talk to her, so I went over.

'I hope he's OK,' I said, as if I was full of worry and concern. Which I was.

'What the hell was he trying to do anyway?' she said.

Clare was pretty great because if she was just hanging around the streets she'd wear jeans, studded belt and some hoody, but when she went out she'd wear skirts and look awesome. She liked the same sort of music as me but, just like me, she wasn't into it so much that she was like a goth or anything. You could say we were emo, which is short for emotional. It's sort of a term used for more sensitive kids who like music and films more than sport, I guess you could say simply, but it's a word I don't really like because I don't think you can put people into groups so easily, and I'm not really emo anyway, only a little bit, but I guess if you had to stick a label on me then it would be the closest thing. Maybe I'm a hybrid of emo and indie. Clare was more emo than me. But only just. Although extremely pretty she was one of those girls who you've known for so long you don't really think *like that* about them but sometimes you also do, you know?

'I guess it all got too much for him,' I said sarcastically, to cover up my fear.

'You really do say some weird stuff sometimes, Richie.'

16

'Thank you.'

'No, thank you.'

We both looked at one another and tried not to laugh. There was a small red blotch next to her nose that I guessed was the start of a spot, which was strange for Clare because her skin wasn't like that.

'He probably did it as a plea for attention.' I said 'plea for attention' because that's what morons would say.

'You shouldn't joke about it – he must be pretty fucked up to do that. He could *die*.'

When she said that, some weird distant thought climbed inside my head, which I didn't want to think about in case I started doing something stupid, like crying. I had to change the subject. It was best to think about something else entirely so I tried my best to pack the thought of Craig up into a box and lock it away.

'Are you going out tonight?' I said.

I felt bad because I was picturing her naked, even though she thought I was just her friend. That made me feel sleazy. She didn't realize that I sometimes thought of her in that way. When I spoke to her I was sometimes getting something out of it that she didn't know about, because she thought we were friends, and that's not the right thing to do.

She shrugged and looked at me with that wicked twinkle in her eye, as if she knew what I was thinking.

'Why don't you just ask me out?'

'Yeah, right.'

'I'm serious.' She took a step closer to me. We always played stupid little games like this. 'You like me, I like you. We could do stuff.'

I thought she might actually grab me and get off with me right there, but she didn't.

'You've got an overinflated sense of ego,' I quipped.

'You just don't want to admit how you feel.'

'Who the hell was that kid who put him in the Recovery Position anyway?' I asked. I wasn't changing the subject because I had just seen the same kid out of the corner of my eye and it was a natural progression for the conversation. He was dressed quite strangely because instead of wearing the school blazer he wore a sweater.

My school is a very good school. It is eclectic, which means it has a nice mix of people. Rich people. Firstly, it's a private school, so you have to pay to go here. My dad's an air traffic controller and my mother's a private doctor so we have a lot of money in my family. Both my parents inherited a lot too. It's not a fair system but it's nothing to do with me. I didn't choose to go to the school – my parents sent me.

Secondly, the school is right next to an American airbase so there are a lot of American kids who go here which means we have a fairly transatlantic vibe going on. Whatever's big in America comes to my school first.

Thirdly, because it's such a good school, lots of parents from all over Britain want to send their kids here and so it is also a boarding school, which means that some of the kids actually *live* here, which is a concept beyond my understanding.

But don't think for a second that my school is like one of those old buildings with old trees and leafy paths because it's not like that at all. You've got wholly the wrong idea if you thought that. Many of the buildings at my school were put up in the seventies and are quite hideous.

'He's a new kid,' said Clare, hooking her arm under mine and leaning her head on my shoulder. 'It's his first day. Did you see him? He was awesome.'

I had to admit that he did handle the situation well. He may well have saved the boy's life, which was quite a thing to do on one's first day at a new school.

'He's really good-looking,' she said.

Another fact that I had to corroborate. He had Chiselled Features, which I realize is cheesy, but it was true. He was one of those people whose hair always looked cool. It was quite long, nearly down to his shoulders, but he definitely wasn't a goth because it was healthy and curled intellectually away at the ends, like my little brother's. I'm not bad-looking at all but he was much better-looking than me.

'Have you met him?' I said.

She was staring at him, not even listening to me. If I'd known then what I know now about Freddy, I'd have told her to snap out of it. It was like she was in a trance. I dread to think what was going through her mind – it was probably pretty dirty. She's done some wild stuff. I always tell her that it's because she hates herself and we have a good laugh about it. We laugh at psychotherapy because we consider it to be a pseudo-science.

Anyway, all of a sudden a gurney was being rolled out of the front door, on top of which lay Craig Bartlett-Taylor. He had a drip in his arm but we could all tell that he was alive. For a second there I started feeling a little bit dizzy. All of my excuse thoughts drained away and my worry about Craig returned. I was suddenly struck with a feeling of inconsolable sadness. I started wondering how his parents would feel when they found out that their son had tried to kill himself. Again. Then I started to think that Craig Bartlett-Taylor was a selfish little shit. He always wore long sleeves, even in summer, because he used to cut himself. He wasn't trying to hide his cuts out of shame; everyone knew that long sleeves in summer was a sure sign of a self-mutilator. He *wanted* people to know because it's kind of cool to do that stuff, not that I ever would. It appeals to intelligent teenagers because we understand drama and romanticism, but have fucked-up hormones.

The paramedics hoisted him into the ambulance and I felt

Clare's head lift from my shoulder. We looked at each other and smiled a little in a rubbish attempt at reassurance that Craig would be OK. I unhooked her arm and put mine around her. She rested her head back on my shoulder and we didn't say anything as the ambulance pulled out of the yard and started up its chilling sirens.

Soon it was gone and the teachers were saying things like 'OK, everybody back inside' but Clare and I waited for a moment, staring at the autumn leaves scuttling and hopping across the dry ground. I shifted my eyes to the kid who had saved Craig. He was on his own with his hands in his pockets. Suddenly my gaze was being returned and we stared at each other from across the yard. I smiled to him and nodded my head and he smiled back. There was a brief moment between us and I found myself pulling Clare closer to me. Then Freddy went inside.

2

I walked home on my own that night. I was conflicted. On the one hand I was happy and excited at the prospect of receiving my new My Chemical Romance album from Play, but on the other, Craig Bartlett-Taylor had tried to commit suicide.

Although I felt bad for Craig, what he had done had annoyed me more and more as the afternoon had passed. If he wanted to kill himself then fine but he should have thought about his parents. Imagine it. Imagine going home and finding your mother dead on the floor. You'd always thought she loved you but how could she if she was prepared to leave you? If you're a parent reading this, imagine being told that your son was dead – and through his own choice. It would be like having metal rods at the centre of your skeleton and having them ripped out by a giant magnet. Yes, I felt sorry for Craig, you don't do something like that lightly, it's just . . . I don't know.

I checked the post but my MCR album hadn't turned up. I heard noises coming from the kitchen and as I walked along the hallway I tried not to think about Craig.

My house is like a typical suburban English house. My mum likes to keep it neat and tidy, although my room is a bit of a mess as she's not allowed in there (even though I know she goes in there because she stacks my mess into neat little piles). We're lucky because the rooms are quite big but other than that it's just normal. Actually, I have an en suite bathroom in my room which I guess is not normal, but hey-ho. Apart from that though the only big difference between my house and other houses is that the fairly long hallway is full of books. Not just a few books, I mean *hundreds* of books. My mother's obsessed with them.

I like books and I don't like books. Books are certainly good as storytelling devices because you can get really involved with one. But people whose houses are lined with books I think should spend more time living and less time reading, you know? It's like they have books instead of walls and they think it's really impressive, but it doesn't impress me. I'd rather be fooling around with a girl than reading a book.

In the kitchen, my nine-year-old brother Toby was sat at the big pine table. The sun had nearly set because it was October. As usual, Toby was drawing a picture with his coloured pencils. All he did all day was draw pictures and write poetry. He didn't have any interest in sports whatsoever.

'All right, Tobe?' I asked. I noticed that his feet didn't get to within a foot of the floor because he was so short.

He looked up. He had blond hair that curled at the ends like Freddy. It wasn't curly, apart from at the ends.

'Hiya, Rich,' he squealed.

The trouble with Toby was that he was just so tiny. His body was so frail that if he ever got hit by a car he wouldn't stand a chance.

I spent a lot of my time worrying about him getting killed in an accident. I WCSed it all the time, but I won't go into it here. It's awful. But I knew that it would happen. I could just tell that he was the type of kid who would get himself killed somehow – one of those people who you can imagine being gone from the world with a bang of tragedy. Some people you can't imagine being not there – but some people you can. When I was out with Toby I always kept an eye on him.

'What are you drawing?' I said.

'Oh, it's just a Christmas picture that I've knocked up.' He spoke with a maturity beyond his years, he really did.

I went over to the table. His picture was actually pretty good. It was a bird's-eye view of a lake that had iced over. Snow-covered pines grew all around it. And on the lake were lots of tiny little people, each of them meticulously laid out with colourful little hats and scarves. Some were throwing snowballs, some were skating and one guy in a corner was actually ice fishing!

'Oh my God, Tobe. This is awesome.'

He beamed. He loved it when I said nice things to him, and I always said nice things to him when he deserved it, which was a lot of the time.

'Thanks, Rich.'

'I'm not kidding. This is really, really good. Have you shown it to Mum yet?'

'She's not home.'

'You keep this up and you could be an artist when you're older. How'd you like that?'

Toby shrugged.

'You could hang in the Louvre.'

'I'm not *that* good yet.'

I sucked in air through my teeth.

'I don't know,' I said. 'This is a nice piece.'

'I know you're joking.'

'You just stick to your dreams, Tobe. If you put your mind to it, you can accomplish anything.' And I ruffled his hair. I was trying to be inspirational. I swept out of the room, deliberately leaving my pearls of wisdom dripping off the air.

I went to my room, got undressed, had a shower, went back to my room, locked my door (I felt so much more secure behind a locked door), turned on my laptop. Clare was already on MSN (which is a free software package from Microsoft called Messenger that allows you to talk to your friends online in real time which is VITAL), along with my best friend, Matthew, so I asked them what they were doing:

Smackdown Kid [Me] says:	**Zup peeps.**
Little SubPop [Clare] says:	**You're home then.**
Smackdown Kid says:	**Yeah, just got home.**

I waited. Matthew was typing a message. He always took ages. I swear to God I don't know what he was doing on his end. Just then, my phone beeped with a text message. Weirdly it was Clare: *Can I come over yours tonight?*

I quickly tapped into the computer.

Smackdown Kid says:	**What r u doin?**
Little SubPop says:	**Just play along.**

It was strange because Matthew obviously had no idea what the last two lines meant. Finally:

Matt says:	**I'm completely fucked. My parents are going crazy on me because they think I shouldn't go out every night. r u lot out tonight?!?**

I was already replying to Clare's text: *Wot time?* I don't actually like abbreviating messages because it's not good grammar but sometimes there's just no time. We first started using text speak to mock people who used it non-ironically, but we used it so much that in the end it just became normal, which is quite depressing really. The minute I sent the text, another one came through: *Soon . . .* Then I was back at my keyboard because I don't like predictive texts as much as typing.

Smackdown Kid says: Why r u doing this Clare?

Matthew, as usual, spent ages writing his reply. Just as the message flashed up my phone bleeped again.

Matt says:	**What r u 2 on about?!?!?!?**
Smackdown Kid says:	**Meet at the war memorial at 7.30?**
Matt says:	**I'm there.**

I looked at my phone. *I just want it to be me and you. No Matt.*

My heart started thumping. All of a sudden I didn't know what to do. I felt bad for Matthew being left out of all this, and because I was about to fob him off for a girl. Nowadays boys hang around with girls all the time – it's not like it used to be – but it's still bad to sly on a friend. Clare always came over to my house and I always went over to hers, but something was different this time. I texted her back: *I'll call you in a minute.*

I logged off without even saying goodbye, which made me feel guilty. I might have texted him later, but I didn't. Then, seconds later, Little SubPop went offline as well, which must have looked incredibly suspicious because we had both come off at the same time. Matthew must have been sat in his room feeling ostracized to hell because he knew what was going on – he was just as clever as everyone else in our group.

I turned my computer off, picked up the house phone, and called Clare.

'Hi, it's me,' she said. She sounded out of breath.

'Hi. So what's going on?'

'I'll tell you later.'

'Why can't you tell me now?'

She got annoyed at this, in that way that girls do.

'God, I said I'd tell you later.'

There was a pause. I could hear 'Planet Telex', an old Radiohead song, playing in the background. Clare had excellent music taste because she had an older brother who taught her everything.

'You're a really good friend,' she said at last. You know that feeling when at the other end of the line the voice sounds tinny and resounds with silence and drama? Her voice was like that.

I knew what was happening. It was Craig. Back in the yard when I had my arm around her had meant as much to her as it had to me.

I could feel a bond of friendship burning gloriously out of the ether and into life; a shared experience and feeling that connected us. Whenever I make a bond with somebody I imagine a golden rope running out of my chest and into theirs, connecting the two souls. It burns up out of nothing and is just there, linking you to that person, your two souls glowing white-blue in bright orbs. The rope thrums with energy and makes your whole body tingle. It's amazing how people can react to one another, you know, the feelings that come from it.

'You can come over whenever you want,' I said quietly. It was one of those times when you know the other person is feeling the exact same thing as you. It's the best thing in the world when bonds are forged, don't you think? It lasts for ever if you do it right.

The end strains of 'Planet Telex' were washing into the line, that bit which sounds like an alien message, or radio static. It was really bizarre.

'I'll be there soon.' And she hung up.

I got changed into my jeans and pulled on my white Lost Prophets T-shirt. This was a band who all the Californian Girls loved because they were really big in LA at the time. I looked OK in my T-shirt.

I'm quite lucky because I have an athletic frame. I'm not muscly, but I'm not skinny either. I have brown hair that's a little bit wavy and which I grow quite long on top but quite short on the back and sides. My friend Matthew says that my hair looks a bit like a bicycle helmet, a cruel criticism, but one I accept with both grace and dignity. People tell me that my face is 'cute' or 'mischievous' but really it looks like it doesn't quite fit on my skull, but in a not-bad way, I guess. It's my big eyes that make people think I'm cute but sometimes they get too big, like when I'm surprised, and then I just look like a spaz. All in all I'm pretty happy with the way I look, which is an oddity for teenagers.

I could hear my parents downstairs but I didn't want to see them. They must have heard about what Craig Bartlett-Taylor had done by now and I really didn't have the energy to speak to them about it – my parents have this uncanny knack of bringing my true feelings up and it freaks me out a bit. On my CD player I started playing my Damien Rice album, which I love. It's a bit depressing but it's perfect for times of reflection.

My parents split up when I was thirteen. It was THE most terrible thing that could have happened. In the months leading up to it they would scream at each other late at night. They thought I was asleep, but I wasn't. Sometimes I would get up early on a Saturday morning and hear them downstairs, already going at it hammer and tongs.

'You never even fucking loved me,' she would scream, her voice all warbly. It is such a shocking thing to hear your own mother using the F word.

27

Then my dad would say something calmly which was too muffled to decipher and then you'd hear a mug smash or something and my mother would be crying, shouting, 'I hate it here. I fucking hate it.' She'd say the F word quietly sometimes.

She'd run out and I'd hear her car drive off and when I got up nothing would be mentioned. I still don't know why they split up. I think my mother thought my father was having an affair, but I know that he'd never do that. Not to me.

The emotions I went through at the time were all over the place. But I never thought it was my fault, which can happen sometimes; the kids think it's their fault. My tutor at school would say, 'It's not your fault,' and I'd say, 'But they were happy before they had me,' because I was making fun of him.

Of course I felt bad for my parents. I hated seeing them so unhappy. But I also wanted them to stay together and in that respect I was conflicted – I wanted them to stay together but it was their staying together that was making them unhappy, you know?

Anyway, one night my dad came into my room and sat at the end of my bed. He gave me a long speech about how they'd decided to go their separate ways and that it wasn't my fault. I snapped a little bit and told him to stay, not to leave. I was crying my eyes out like a baby, I really was. And I meant every tear. I was being torn apart.

By morning I felt a little better and in less than a week I had concluded that it would be better this way because their happiness was the most important thing. The next feeling I had was embarrassment and it was far worse than the original grief. In school, I felt like a leper or something. Everybody knew what had happened and nobody said a word. It was just the most awful thing. Nothing was ever mentioned, not even amongst my best friends. The only person I spoke to about it was Matthew. It really was embarrassing. I don't think I ever really recovered from my parents' split, even though they got back together a year later. I developed a lovely little fear of commitment – and I was only fourteen!

There was a knock at my door. It was Clare. I made sure that the back of my jeans dragged on the floor underneath my bare feet because I thought it looked cool.

'Hey,' I said.

'Why have you got your door locked?'

'Because I was—' I almost said something really crass but I hemmed it back in just in time. It would have been inappropriate. We always said shocking things like, 'Jesus Christ, I hope your parents get cancer,' but we didn't mean it. We're just pushing against a tide of political correctness. When you can't say anything at all, sometimes it all comes flooding out when nobody's around. Floodgates and all that. But saying something crass then seemed out of place.

We were lying on my bed, her head on my chest, and I was playing with her hair. We always did stuff like this – it didn't mean anything. We were watching television on silent whilst listening to Damien Rice. It was like a perfect moment in heaven.

'I saw the way you were looking at me in the yard today,' she said softly. She's got a brilliant accent. Quite posh, but also lazy, like she doesn't care.

I didn't reply.

She turned her body over and in an instant, like she had been there all along, she was straddling me. Her face came in towards mine, her black hair blocking out the light, and she kissed my cheek.

This was strange. Clare was very capable of playing cruel games with boys and I didn't know what she was doing. All I really knew at that moment was that my body was telling

29

me that it wanted to have sex with her. That was my base feeling.

Her hair was touching my face. She kissed my forehead, and then my nose, and then my lips. Gently, softly, like in a novel. But it was real. She brought her hand up and, with index and middle finger, placed her flopping hair expertly behind her ear, tracing the line from her temple to the back of her neck. Silhouetted against my bedroom light was the outline of an out-of-focus landscape — a jawline leading to a dark, blurry ear.

She wasn't getting off with me, she was just kissing me. She pulled back a little and her eyes were massive with dark-purple eye liner that was simply perfect. And then she said something in a quiet voice that came out just right.

'You're gorgeous,' she said.

I couldn't bear it if she was playing with me. I had no reason to think it, but something at the back of my mind was saying, You be careful now, Rich.

She started kissing my face again and with her right hand she grabbed the top of my arm, sliding up underneath my T-shirt. I started thinking about the birthmark on the back of her neck that nobody ever mentioned — the aesthetic taboo. I loved that she had it because it meant that she was vulnerable and I love that in people, especially girls. Her touch was amazingly smooth.

This wasn't my first time with a girl. I'd been with a few girls to varying levels of sexual activity which I don't like to divulge because it's crass, but I had never actually had sexual intercourse. And I knew that I wouldn't be having it tonight either. It just wouldn't be right.

I didn't kiss her back, I just lay there. With her free hand she went for my belt but I grabbed her wrist.

'What?' she said, her eyes closed. 'I want to see what I'm doing to you.'

I turned my head dramatically to one side. The truth is, I didn't want her to see what she was doing to me. We were friends.

'I don't think I can do this with you,' I said.

Her eyes opened and I thought she was going to take my face off with a cleaver. She would have if she'd had one. And then, with extreme undercurrents of violence, she stabbed at the air with her finger, pointing at me.

'You are a . . .' She mouthed the next two words as if to emphasize her anger. '*Fucking prick.*' There was a noise actually, but it was so quiet you could barely hear it.

And then she did something that I could not believe. It had never happened before and I didn't actually believe that things like this happened in real life, but here was the living proof. She stormed out the room! Left the house! I couldn't believe it. I was completely dumbstruck by the sheer, audacious DRAMA of the girl. It was glorious.

A sudden swell of guilt came into me but I don't know why because I had done nothing wrong. I was being a good person by stopping it because it could have jeopardized our friendship and, at that moment, I didn't really know what was going on. It had all happened so fast that the screen doors went up. Clare hated herself anyway. That's why she tried to give herself to me. She always went too far with boys who liked her. She used to think that if a boy liked her she'd have cold sexual intercourse with him and then leave him. She lost her virginity when she was thirteen. Thirteen! That's insane. And she was never sexually abused by her father or anything either. She was just weird like that.

The next thing I did was a bit off. To be honest, I wasn't actually handling things as well as I would have liked. I hate the way I let people get to me because I wish I could be aloof. I like to think that I could have risen above the whole Clare thing, but she had penetrated my walls. She was in. And that was bad because I like to think that my defence mechanism (ha) is pretty sturdy. I admit that my mind was scrambled and the next thing I did was not the smartest. I picked up my phone and texted her: *You're a weirdo.* Apostrophes, the lot.

3

As soon as Clare left the phone started ringing, which jolted me back to reality. I wanted to pretend that I didn't feel hurt and so I answered it enthusiastically.

'Holoha,' I shouted, even though the call could easily have been for my mum or dad. Which it wasn't. It was Johnny, a boy with whom I had gone to primary school. After we left I went to private school and he went to the regular comprehensive. We stayed in touch, but not very often. It was always something I regretted, but that's life.

He was calling because his band, Atticus, were playing in the local pub. It was pretty much the only time I got to see him nowadays so I said I'd be there, although inside I got that creeping feeling of worry in my gut. I didn't like going into pubs. I was too young and it was quite obvious. Lots of kids my age got really drunk every weekend, but I didn't feel the need to do this. I don't hate drinking or anything, I like it. I just don't want to get off my face *all* the time.

Also, some of the kids from the comprehensive school would be there. They hated us private-school snobs and loved to pick fights on us.

And I hate fighting. I'm pretty good at it because I'm a good sportsman with lots of coordination and I never lose my head. I've had a lot of fights in my time and I put up a pretty good show for the most part. But I hate punching people in the face. I know from experience how much it hurts and inflicting that sort of pain on other people bothers me.

But you can't live your life in fear and that's why I said I'd go.

When I hung up, I immediately went back to thinking about Clare. I kept re-running the events in my head thinking how it *could* have gone. I should have had sex with her. It would have been easier. My world would be different if I'd done that. But I didn't. I didn't love her enough to have sex anyway. Not yet.

At seven I went downstairs. My parents were in the living room, out of sight. 'Mum,' I called.

'Hi, honey,' she said with a massive smile. She was holding a spoon.

'Hi. Good day at work?'

'Yes, thank you,' she replied.

'Do you know if a CD was delivered today, by any chance?'

'I don't think so.'

Then her brow furrowed. I could see that she was about to say something about Craig. I had to get away.

'OK. I'm going out.' I headed for the front door.

'You haven't had your tea.'

'Don't want any.' And I was out.

It was quite a walk to town, about a quarter of a mile, but I didn't mind making it. I'd stick my headphones in and lose myself completely.

I love music, probably more than anything else in the whole world. It's about the only thing that can really get inside me and rummage around. What gets me about it, I reckon, is not the actual music, but what's left at the end, when everything else has been stripped away, when all the music has gone and all that's left is what the bands *mean*. A lot of the time you strip everything away and there's nothing left and the music is soulless but sometimes, when there's something special, the meaning is the exact same thing that drives the very centre of you, that tiny pearl of energy that's so delicate that even if you just *think* about it you get the shivers. Sometimes you connect with music on such a deep level that you can't really describe it in words, you know? It's just there, in you. It's like the bands pop their heads around a curtain and say, 'Hello, your soul. You're not alone.' And that's the sort of music I'm into. The stuff that ties itself around my life.

Anyhoo, when me and my friends go out, we always meet at the war monument. It has steps all around it and we can sit there and mess around. Because it was winter, the sky was pitch black apart from the stars twinkling on and off, and the shop lights beamed out on to the pavements like they were full of angels or something – colours all over the place.

There weren't many people there, just Matthew, his American girlfriend Jenny, and someone with their back to me and hood up. Jenny had moved to the airbase a few years ago and had been going out with Matthew pretty much from the second month she got here. She was such a sweet girl. Being from California she had a big, bright, wide-eyed optimism for the world that some people hated for being so in-your-face, but I loved it.

I took out my headphones and sat down on the lowest step, trying to get a look at who was under the hood. To my horror it was Clare. She was staring vacantly at the passing cars, assumedly ignoring me.

'Hello, Matthew,' I said. I was the only person who called him that. Most people just called him Matt.

'Richard,' he replied.

'Hi, Richie,' said Jenny cheerily, in her American accent.

I smiled at her. 'Hiya.'

'Don't I get a hello?' said Clare suddenly, her head turning towards me, the vacant look washed clean away, replaced by a fake smile, as if she'd just made a decision. She was trying to act like she hadn't almost just had sex with me.

I looked at her.

'Hi,' I answered awkwardly.

'You'll never guess who's out.'

I thrust my hands into the pockets of my hoody. 'Who?' I asked, really amiably.

'Freddy.'

I didn't know who Freddy was at this point.

'The new boy who saved Craig's life,' she said, like it was obvious and it was actually offensive that I wouldn't know his name.

'Oh,' I said. 'Where is he?'

'He's gone to the shops.'

I looked at her. Although we were in the middle of a mental battle, I noticed, not for the first time that day, just how devastatingly pretty she was. I think maybe I was starting to fall in love. Or maybe not. Who knows?

'Isn't he a boarder?' Boarders weren't allowed out of the school on Fridays after ten, even though at that point it was only half seven.

'Yeah, so?' she said. Her words were suddenly barbed, like a switch had been flicked, and the normality that she had just shown was gone. I'm sure Matthew and Jenny picked up on the tension.

I caught Clare's eye for a second but she looked away. Awkward. I needed to speak to her, on her own, to try and explain.

I'd like to say that at that point a cold wind suddenly swept down the high street and the air changed, the clouds rolled in front of the moon and everything went dark. Then I could say as soon as it happened Freddy came into my life. But none of that stuff did happen. The world stayed the same when I met Frederick Spaulding-Carter properly for the very first time.

It was dark but we all saw him as he bounded across the road to us, nipping between the car headlights like a spectre or something. And he had the Californian Girls with him – a definite tick in the right box. These were the attractive girls from the airbase that hung around in one beautiful group. They weren't all from California, despite their nickname – they had just always been called that. They weren't very nice people and were often bitchy but I guess the way they did it was so over the top that it was quite funny, as long as they weren't targeting you. They rarely befriended the boarders though, who tended to be a little *too* upper-class English, even for us. We kept it real. As if. So for them to have latched on to Freddy was strange.

'Freddy!' called Clare, beckoning him over.

'Yeah?' He came over, full of energy. His shoulders were heaving up and down because he was slightly out of breath.

My cynical side told me that I didn't like him because there was something off with him, like his mind and his body didn't quite match up. You know how binoculars can sometimes show two different images because the distance between the two lenses isn't right for your eyes? Well, Freddy's body and mind were a bit like that – not quite flush.

However, I try not to listen to my cynical side because it's negative, and being negative is complex and intricate, and if you want to live a happy, normal life there's no room for cynicism. Cynicism doesn't sit well on the human soul.

Clare was introducing Freddy to Matthew, who jerked his head backwards as an approving acknowledgement.

'And this,' she said, not even looking at me, 'is Richard.'

As our eyes met a beam of light swept over him from a passing car. His cheeks had gone red in the cold but the rest of his face was very pale. I always thought there was something romantic about the way some people go pale in the cold. He had small bags under his eyes that were also a little red, which looked immensely cool, like he was exhausted and running on fumes. The skin was tight on his face so that you could see the shape of his skull and in truth I felt a little jealous at how his little face-eccentricities made him look better not worse.

'Hi,' I said. 'That was awesome what you did this afternoon.'

He laughed a little. 'Thanks,' he said.

'Oh my God,' said one of the Californian Girls. 'I couldn't believe how brave that was.' And she touched his arm.

'I wouldn't exactly say it was *brave*,' I said. 'It was *good*, but it was hardly pulling him out of a burning oil rig, was it?' It came out really harsh-sounding, but that's not how I meant it. Many of my jokes misfire and I end up sounding really arrogant and horrible. There was an awkward silence.

But then something happened. Freddy laughed. And I suddenly connected with him, all my doubts obliterated like an exploding planet. If he got my jokes, he must have been up on my level. As far as I was concerned, he was now my friend.

'Don't laugh at him,' said one of the girls, who was insanely good-looking, just ridiculous. 'He's not funny.'

'Hey,' I said, genuinely hurt. I hated how the Californian Girls were so hurtful to people. 'What the hell is that supposed to mean?'

She tilted her head to one side and pulled a face like a smile, even though it was definitely NOT a smile.

★

We wandered up the long high street towards the pub where Johnny's band were playing, past all the bright shop-fronts that always seem so light when the dark nights first close in.

My town is an old market town where farmers used to take their animals, though that part of its history is long gone. But the pretty, higgledy-piggledy houses with old bricks and alleyways running through to windy back streets are still there. They've been converted into these ornate little shops with big, wooden-framed bay windows and hanging baskets and general community-spiritedness. Most of the shops are old antique shops or bookshops or flower shops or coffee shops or clothes shops that sell things like corduroy trousers and tweed jackets – you know the sort of thing.

There's a little bridge about halfway down the high street which goes over this small, shallow brook and in the summer people throw bread to the ducks that hang around there.

It's the sort of place that people come to from miles around wearing their comfiest, nicest clothes. They wander around and have a cup of coffee and then go back home and say, 'Oh what a lovely day we've had.' I've never really understood this because yes, it's a nice enough place, but it's incredibly boring.

I hung back as we made our way to the pub, partly because I wanted to avoid Clare, and partly because Jenny and Freddy were bringing up the rear of our little group and I was interested to learn more about him. It was icy cold but I loved it as that type of air makes the world come alive. The sky was completely clear and you could see the stars up in the sky very clearly. I was half a step behind Jenny and Freddy. Her blonde hair looked really smooth and awesome.

'So what were you thinking when you saw Craig like that?' she said. Jenny has one of those really sweet-sounding

American accents and it's not too nasal, like most of the other Californian Girls, whose voices are quite grotesque. She wasn't really like them at all, apart from she was from the same country as them.

'I don't know,' I heard him say. 'I just saw him and then I was up and next to him. It was a bit weird really.' I couldn't place Freddy's accent. It was the sort of accent that could have come from anywhere.

'You probably saved his life.'

'I don't know about that.' I could see the breath coming out of his mouth. 'Why do you think he did it?'

Jenny shrugged.

'I hardly know the guy. Richie knows him much better than I do.' She turned her head around a little, bringing me into the conversation. 'What do you think?'

'I don't know,' I said honestly. 'It's weird to think that I used to know him really well and I've been in some of his classes and stuff, but I just haven't *really* known him at all for years. It's like I don't know anything about him any more. And never did, you know?'

'I know exactly what you mean,' said Freddy. 'Kids who you know when you're young just drift away and you don't even realize.'

What an odd remark to say out loud, I thought. And yet very eloquent.

'Yeah,' I sort of stuttered.

'Do many people like him?'

'Not really,' I said. 'He's a bit of a freak.'

'Rich!' Jenny shrieked, slapping my arm.

Freddy smiled.

'I don't mean in a bad way,' I retorted, defending myself. 'Now that it's happened I guess it was obvious. Before, you'd never have known how fucked up he was.'

'Ah, hindsight,' said Freddy, out of the blue, and in a

mock-dramatic tone. 'The cruel mistress who arrived too late.'

Jenny and I laughed loudly. The mood was very light all of a sudden.

'So,' Jenny started. I noticed her cheeks were all rosy from the cold. 'How are you finding boarding school?'

I loved the way she was always so interested in everything. She had this great way of being really nice but not in a creepy way, if you know what I mean. Like now, with this conversation. If it had been just me and Freddy talking it would have been far more awkward but it wasn't; it was very easy. Her little blonde presence was like an aura that surrounded you.

'It's great,' he shrugged.

'Where were you before?'

'In my local school, back home. My father's always worked away but my mother got a new job in London, in publishing. She wasn't going to take it but I said she had to – she's always wanted to go into it – and I sort of wanted to go to boarding school anyway.'

'You *wanted* to go? Wow.' Her eyes went wide and round.

I noticed the sound of the cars whooshing past, their headlights splashing on to the dark road in front of them.

'Sure. I love the idea of boarding school. It's like in the films, you know? Anyway, we're all in the same boat up there. We just stick together.'

'No offence,' I said, 'but I don't think I could handle it; being around strangers all the time.'

'I guess you get used to it. It's still a bit weird, you're right. I've only been here a week though so I can't really say. There're a few freaks up there, and some bullies, but most of them are OK. You should come up.'

'Yeah, defo,' beamed Jenny. 'I've never been up there before.'

'You're kidding.'

'No. I try and get Matt to take me but you know what he's like,' she said, looking at me. She lifted her shoulders like a hulk and went, 'Murgh,' pretending to be a zombie version of Matthew.

I laughed at her.

'So have you seen the school lake?'

Jenny shook her head.

'I know it's there,' she offered.

Freddy paused uncertainly for a moment, like he didn't want to overstep the mark.

'We could go up there later. If you want. I went there the other night when the moon was out and it's amazing. I found this really cool place—'

'This is *so* going to happen,' interrupted Jenny excitedly.

I said nothing as I don't like to commit to something that I'm not definitely going to do.

'Do you think you'll get homesick?' I said, changing the subject for no real reason.

'I don't know. I don't think so. My room-mate does. He's only eleven and he hates it.'

This struck a chord with me. Freddy had his own version of my Toby.

'What's his name?'

'Anthony.'

We all laughed.

'He's a class little kid but he misses home. I feel pretty sorry for him.' He smiled, thinking of something. 'He's great though. He calls his parents at like, three o'clock in the morning. He told me the teachers tell him off for doing it but he does it anyway. They'll probably end up taking his phone off him.'

'Aww. He sounds adorable,' Jenny cooed.

'It's their own fault anyway,' he said, not listening.

'They shouldn't have sent him away in the first place.'

He said it bitterly, like there was a crack in him. A prickle came up on my neck and I wondered if Jenny felt it too. There was a little barb, a little of that untamed anger that I sometimes get (but only very rarely). This is what I meant when I said about the binocular lenses not quite matching up.

We had arrived at the pub and I could see a doorman standing outside. He looked decidedly unimpressed with the group of fifteen-year-old kids coming his way.

'Good evening,' I said to him.

He looked down at me, amused.

'Good evening to you,' he said.

I went to walk past him but he stood in my way.

'Excuse me, please,' I said. We were only bantering. There was no way he was letting me past.

'Come on, mate. How old are you? Six?'

'Twelve, actually,' I retorted, and stepped back.

I texted Johnny, my friend who was in the band, who came out to meet us, but we still weren't allowed in and so Johnny went and got the owner, who said it was all right for us to go in as long as we didn't try to get served alcohol.

As I walked past the doorman I said, 'Thanks.'

And he said, 'You're welcome.'

Our entrance wasn't quite as cool as I would have liked but at least we were in. And we had a secret bottle of vodka, which we slipped into the Cokes we bought.

I feel I should explain about the Egg and Train pub because it's quite unusual. There are two sides to it, left and right. On the right-hand side, there's a big pool room with a jukebox where all the young people go. On weekends a DJ comes in, the lights go down and it all gets pretty sordid. The left-hand side of the pub is the family-friendly side where people of all ages go. I prefer the young-people side because, and I hate to say this because it's bound to come out wrong, I love sleaziness. And you can *smell* the hormones on the dark side.

Johnny's band were playing on the nice side because the local kids from the comprehensive school would definitely leave if there was a loud band playing on their side. They just don't get it. And anyway, the band members' parents could support their kids when they played on the light side.

I found myself a corner with Matthew, Jenny and Freddy. We had been in the pub for around an hour. I didn't want to stand in the middle of the floor in case the barman saw I was tipsy, and chucked me out. I watched the people walking past, back and forth to the bar, saying 'Excuse me' to the people in their way, and I felt warm inside. Across the room I saw a group of my friends from school. I hung around with quite a few different groups because I liked talking to people. It was fun. One of the boys caught my eye and waved to me so I raised my glass to him.

'Do you think that if people were nicer to him,' said Jenny, 'that he wouldn't have done it?'

'I don't know,' said Freddy. 'I think some people are just *like* that.'

'What do you mean?' said Matthew. His eyes were looking in two separate directions because he was drunk. His eyes went funny when he drank.

'Just that, I don't know . . . actually, I have no idea what I'm talking about!'

We all laughed.

'Richard Harper!' somebody called from over Freddy's shoulder.

I peered over and saw my friend Phil.

'Hello, mate,' I said.

Phil came over. He was tall and quite awkward, with a bit of a belly.

'Here to see the band?'

He looked up towards the stage, where the drummer was tightening some bolts on his kit, or whatever it is they do.

'It's your mate, isn't it?'

'Yeah.'

I saw Phil glance nervously across to Freddy out of the corner of his eye.

'Phil, this is Freddy,' I offered.

'Hi,' Phil said.

'Hi.' They both shook hands, which for some reason struck me as funny.

'That was pretty cool, what you did,' he said.

'Cheers.'

'You've actually saved somebody's life.'

Freddy smiled. 'I don't know about that.'

'I don't know what Craig was doing,' interrupted Phil. 'Still, I guess it's a story to tell.' He took a slurp from his can of Coke. 'Not a great story though.'

I chuckled. Phil was funny.

'Alex is looking for you, Rich.' Alex being the boy I sat next to in geography.

'What for?'

He shrugged. 'Dunno.'

Out of nowhere I started to have terrible visions of Craig lying in bed with his parents at his side in a quiet Friday-night hospital ward whilst I was in the pub getting drunk. Phil had turned his attention to the others about homework or something. My head started to feel light with the alcohol. I wanted to do something to help Craig but I had no idea what. I felt a WCS coming on. My throat started to feel heavy for Craig.

Out of the corner of my eye I saw Clare walking past and instinctively yanked her jumper. She turned to me and I smiled drunkenly. I was sort of trying to apologize for whatever it was I had done, but it must have looked pretty pathetic when all I could think to do was smile.

She spoke first.

'Do you know what I'm going to write in my diary tonight?' she said.

'I didn't know you had a diary,' I slurred.

'Yes, I have a diary and I write *everything* in there.'

I gulped loudly. But only symbolically, not really.

'And do you know what I'm going to write about you?'

I shook my head.

'Enlighten me,' I said, trying to compose myself.

'I'm going to write that you're a really good friend.'

Oh, I thought.

'Listen,' I started, not really knowing what the hell I was going to say. But my head was starting to clear. My WCS was on the wane. 'I didn't want it to go any further than it did because . . . you know . . .' I looked at the floor to add meaning. 'We're friends and I don't think I could handle it if that changed. I don't want things to be weird between us.'

There was a long, long pause. I could feel her eyes on me. She leaned in and gave me a peck on the cheek.

'It was a test,' she said suddenly.

I knew that by saying it was a test she was trying to get out of the fact that she had been rejected.

'A test for what?' Although I knew what she meant.

'I know what I look like to boys. I *know* that guys go crazy for me. And I wanted to find out why you were so nice to me.'

I nodded, watching the guitarist tune his guitar, which was gleaming in the light, giving me white blotches on my field of vision.

'And you passed,' she said.

I sighed. For her.

46

'I might keep a diary,' I said.

'Yeah, right.'

'Yeah . . . right,' I retorted.

'You're a boy.'

'So?'

'So it would be gay.'

'Don't be stupid. I could keep a diary because I'm *sensitive*.'

'You're about as sensitive as a cripple's spine.'

You see what I mean about us saying shocking things? I felt that when Clare said that it was wholly inappropriate and she went down in my estimation because saying something like that when having a normal conversation is exceptionally crass.

'Why do you say stuff like that?'

'It's not so bad.'

My head was spinning a little bit.

'It is bad. You shouldn't say stuff like that. It's really un-ladylike.'

'Whatever. Look, I was trying to explain myself to you—'

'You say something like that because you can't say you're sorry without adding something shocking to take away the bite of the apology.'.

I was making fun of her by saying that and she shared the joke – we were pretending to be like the kids out of that TV show *Dawson's Creek* where everything is life or death. We always do it. We get really angry at each other, have a massive argument, the argument dissolves into drama, we start play-acting and forget that we were ever angry at each other in the first place.

'And I could keep a diary.'

She laughed.

'You couldn't keep a diary.'

'Could.'

'Couldn't.'

I took a sip on my Coke, which tasted like that acrid dandelion milk with all the vodka that was in it. But the drink felt good. I was so happy to have got it all out in the open with Clare so that we could get back to normal. Inwardly I smiled and then I pulled the most exceptionally arrogant face that you can imagine.

'Could.'

4

'Come through here,' he said, the wind in his hair.

We were in the school grounds, having already walked all the way back from the pub. It was me, Clare, Matthew, Jenny and Freddy. The dorms were a good half a mile away from the school proper and up here the buildings were exactly as you would expect from a private boarding school. Unlike the main school, which was a mixture of old and new, this whole place was aged; old buildings, old trees, old ivy growing over old lumps of stone. I rarely came up here because I didn't really hang out with the boarders, but it was a spectacular place. You'd expect to see floppy-haired poets in blazers and scarves reciting Blake or one of those old English chaps, not the wannabe gangsta idiots that mostly lived up there.

Freddy was ushering us into some dense bushes that lined the long driveway up to the dorms. It was pretty cool how Freddy, the talk of the whole school, had somehow managed to latch on to us.

I had seen the school lake a few times, but never at night.

'Where are we going, Freddy?' Jenny asked.

'Just follow me,' is what he said softly. *Just follow me*. His eyes were sparkling in the moonlight. Freddy was strange. I detected some weird, indefinable sadness in him. On the surface he was excited because he had made new friends and he had coaxed us all the way up here. In that manner he was like a little boy but behind that there was definitely something up. All of a sudden I had a compulsion to throw my arms around him and give him a big hug, tell him that everything was going to be OK. I had been drinking, yes, but it was more than that. There was definitely something about him.

We followed him through the bushes, which were quite thick, in near-enough pitch blackness, all five of us. Five went in, five came out, but it wasn't as simple as that. Those bushes were like the wardrobe in Narnia; when we came out the other side we were in a whole different world.

We were stood at the top of a gentle grassy hill. I was looking at my feet when I came out but, as my eyes rose up towards the sky, the grass ran away to a vast silver lake that glimmered in the bright moonlight. I was instantly hit with awe. It was like something out of a picture book.

'You've got to see this place I found.' Freddy was beckoning us on, so excited by whatever it was he was about to show us.

It was strange but also endearing how he was speaking to us as if we were old friends, as if we hadn't just met that day.

'This place is like, so beautiful,' Jenny whispered in her very over-the-top American way.

But she wasn't wrong. Dare I say it, the place had a historic majesty about it. You could feel the souls of past students presiding over the lake and its secrets. Well, not really, but you know what I mean.

The grass was wet underfoot as Freddy led us all the way down to the water's edge to a gravel path that wound around the shore. I can remember that the air was freezing, so cold it felt like needles were pricking my face.

'I found this yesterday.' Freddy was looking over his shoulder as he walked, as if he knew the path like the back of his hand. I watched his breath curl up into the night sky and listened to the soft sound of the lake gently lapping the shore. I liked the way that he had saved somebody's life earlier on that day but now here he was acting like everything was normal, like he hadn't done something amazing.

Presently, we came to a rise in the land where the path strayed away from the lake slightly. There were a few trees in this raised area growing on either side of the path, making it much darker.

It was in these trees that Freddy stopped.

'Ta-da.' He was gesturing away from the lake towards what I guess would be called a stone folly.

It was perfect, like something out of ancient Greece or something. It was a kind of stone shelter, made from big old bricks with a flat roof covered in ivy that hung down like a fringe. It must have been at least a hundred years old.

Inside was a stone bench, which we all sat on and which turned our backsides to ice. From this vantage point we could see the lake. It was perfectly framed by two tall trees, whose canopies interlinked overhead. A thin layer of mist had formed on the surface, as if some of the water had got curious and decided to take a look at us. For a few moments we just sat there and stared at it.

Freddy sighed. 'I guess it's not so bad coming to live here.'

I felt for him when he said that. It sounded like he had been thrown into this situation without a choice and here he was opening up to us because he didn't have anyone else to talk to.

I looked at Clare sat next to me, our legs touching. I knew she would say something. Her pale face was glowing silvery.

'You didn't want to come here?'

Freddy paused.

'I don't know. A part of me is glad because it's a big

51

adventure and stuff and I'm out on my own in the world, but . . . I don't know.'

We didn't push it any further. I didn't want to mention that what he was saying didn't exactly match up with what he had told me and Jenny earlier that night when he said he saw boarding school as an adventure.

The view from here was stunning, clearer still in the cold winter air.

'I wish I could spend my whole life doing things like this,' I said, my emotions running away as they so often do. My head was buzzing pleasantly from the alcohol I had consumed.

'I intend to,' Freddy said. 'This is how I'm going to live my whole life. When I leave school I'm going to do this sort of thing all the time.'

I looked out at the silver lake and wondered if it was possible to live a life where all you did was magical things, like huddle on a stone bench with your friends in the middle of the night.

'I'm not going to let anything get me down. It's this idea I have. Like, I'm never going to get a job unless I like the job.' He sucked some spit in off his bottom lip, carefree. 'It makes no sense to work if you hate it. We only get one life so what's the point in wasting big chunks of it doing things that you don't want to?' He was speaking so softly, like he was in a daydream. His speech was slightly slurred, but not so much that what he was saying didn't seem heartfelt.

'There are so many people in the world doing things that they don't want to do, and it's depressing.' He leaned forward from the stone bench and looked at us all, his eyes glittering. 'I never want to be like that. I'm never ever going to let the weight of the world crush me.' He paused and again I got the feeling that he was trying to tell us something. After a few seconds he decided to go on. 'My mum always says that I used to be really sensitive when I was a little kid. But I still feel that way now. Nothing's changed inside me. I don't think it ever will. I *want* to feel like this because people get old and they just, sort of, harden. I don't want to be like that.'

I was shocked by his outright honesty, the way he seemed to trust us enough to speak like this.

'I want my life to be one big romantic adventure. A journey towards paradise. I want to be part of a world inside a world. See, I think that there are lots of people like us.'

'What do you mean?' asked Jenny. '"Like us"?'

'You know.' Freddy nodded out to the lake. 'People who like doing things like this. When I was back home, my friends wouldn't come to a place like this if I asked them. They'd tell me to fuck off. They'd want to try and get into a club or something. But I'd much prefer to come to somewhere like this and just talk.'

I smiled. I preferred things like this as well; we all did. It wasn't just going to the lake, it was far more than that. I had always felt like I was different from most of the kids at my school. They all seemed so normal, they fitted in so well. I was popular in school, but I felt like I was lying. I felt like I had to act different to how I was so that I could fit in.

'I know it doesn't seem like it sometimes, and sometimes I think the world has got something really wrong with it, but I just *know* that there are other people like us, who feel the same way as us, all over the place. Do you know what I mean?'

I did know. I knew exactly what he meant. Nobody said anything.

'They probably feel really cut off, but they're not. It just feels that way because there's a big distance between us. That's what special is – being rare, right? But I want to find people like that and hold on to them. Don't you think that would be great? Like if there was a sort of club?'

53

'A club for lost souls?' I said dramatically.

'Yes! And we'll find each other and when we do we'll make sure we live our lives to the absolute limit. All of the people who refuse to give up on their dreams will go together into the unknown, wherever it may take us, and leave everyone else behind.'

I thought for a moment about my dream of writing cartoons for kids and wondered if I would ever give up on that. The way things were looking I'd go to university and study something that would give me a safe career because that was what my parents wanted. I didn't want to do it, but I certainly felt the pressure.

Freddy brushed his hand through his hair. It looked like he may have been getting upset – it was hard to tell.

'I see adults walking around and I think, What happened to you? Why did you give up? I've actually said this to my dad and he just said, "You'll learn."'

I didn't know if he was still talking to us at this point, but we were certainly still listening.

'Well, I don't really want to learn that lesson. It doesn't sound like much of a thing to learn – how to collapse. People always said that I'd stop liking this or stop liking that when I got older, but it's never happened so far. I still have my *Phantom Menace* figures! One of my teachers asked me if I wanted to drive a nice car when I'm older and I said that that sort of thing doesn't really interest me and he told me that it will when I see my friends driving around in them.' He leaned forward and looked at us. 'But I don't believe that. I don't think I ever will.'

'My parents always say that to me!' Matthew exclaimed. 'I know what you mean!' I was surprised how urgently he said it; he was usually so sceptical about this sort of dreamy-talking. I noticed that he had his arm around Jenny. She was looking out across the lake, not saying anything.

54

Her parents were probably the strictest out of all of us.

'I think we just have to hang on. That's the secret. Like as if we're in a tree and life is trying to shake us out. Nearly everyone will fall off but I think a few people can stick it out if they have each other for support. People like us.' He swallowed. 'That's what I mean.'

'But it's not that easy, is it?' said Matthew. 'It's nice to talk about it, sure, but you have to get a job eventually.'

'Yeah, but not doing something you hate. That's what I mean. You don't want to have a miserable life.'

Clare sat up.

'I want to hear more about this adventure.'

Freddy's tone changed suddenly. The serious side of him had suddenly left and a playful side had taken its place.

'It's an adventure, that's all. For the people who never let go. Like, tomorrow we'll stop off in a forest glade, drink wine and recite poetry about unrequited love.'

The picture burned up in my mind with incredible clarity. It was tongue in cheek but it was still very strong.

'Can we wear scarves?' I asked.

Freddy raised an eyebrow.

'My dear Richard, scarves are an imperative.'

'My God,' cooed Clare. 'That sounds ace. I'll bring a picnic hamper.'

Then Jenny cottoned on.

'And I'll take pictures of the whole thing.'

'Black-and-white, of course,' Freddy said with a smile. He stopped and looked at us again. 'I think I'm glad I've met you.' Reaching inside his coat he pulled out a packet of Marlboro Lights. 'Let's smoke cigarettes.' He looked at us as if we were naughty children about to break the rules. Which, I suppose, is exactly what we were. Matt declined but the rest of us accepted.

'We need to smoke a *lot* on our grand adventure,' Freddy

said. 'And make love in bedsits on cloudy afternoons.'

'Freddy!' Clare's eyes opened wide in *faux* shock.

'I'm sorry,' he protested, 'but it's true. We can't deny ourselves *anything*. That's the point of the whole philosophy.' He sat back on the slab and leaned against the wall. 'To live like that.'

His hair looked blue in the moonlight. I lit my cigarette and blew out some smoke. I couldn't tell where the smoke ended and my condensed breath began. My insides were humming. I had had my feelings articulated into words with perfection. Somebody understood me. I had found someone. There was a comfortable silence, the atmosphere happy and light as we shared the remainder of the vodka and smoked away in the freezing-cold folly whilst the snow-white lake shone only for us.

5

When my parents got back together, they asked me how I would feel about their having another baby – a new member of the family. I said absolutely not, went crazy, threw a lot of things that I owned and slammed my door. My parents never did have another kid and my job was done. But now when I try to remember it I get the worst human feeling – that one where you know you've done something very wrong and which you can never undo.

When I think back on that time, I feel awful for what I did. The reason my parents wanted a new baby was because it would set a marker for their relationship – out of something bad would come something good. The new baby would have really brought them close – which they are now, but not like it was before. They'll never get back to the way it was because something happened to their relationship which was Not Natural. And you never come back from something like that.

It was during that time that I went off the rails in a big way. I had just turned fourteen and over those few months I went nuts. Crazy. I shouldn't have been like that – most people in that situation would be relieved that their life was back on track. But not me. For some stupid adolescent reason, I wanted revenge. I wanted my parents to go through the hell that I went through. I know that sounds ridiculous, and I don't know why I reacted so irrationally, but that's what happened. I wish I could have been stronger but I wasn't. I am trying to change that now though.

I used to stay out late, get drunk, smoke cannabis in my bedroom, misbehave in school, the lot. I really was a little bastard. On one occasion an eminent doctor, and father of one of my friends, had to take me home in the back of his minivan (people carrier – we call them minivans because that's what the American kids in school call them) because I got out of my skull on vodka in his basement. My parents were horrified and were tearing their hair out. They kept telling me that I had problems but I didn't listen. Then I did something bad. I did something very, very bad, my Bad Thing, which I will never forget but won't go into here. Many people still remember it because old people have difficulty forgiving, but I don't think I deserve my reputation as a hell-raiser because I try to be a good boy nowadays, I really do. Probably the worst thing about my Bad Thing was that it didn't stop me. I had been so angry at the time that the incident hadn't made me see the light. I carried on the way I was, getting lower and lower.

But there's always a turning point eventually, and for me it was something awful I did to Toby, my little brother. I told him that I'd take him into the city to visit the cinema and have lunch. We had done it once before and he'd really loved it, being out with his older brother. We had taken the train, had breakfast, walked around, gone to the museum to kill time (he loved that), had lunch, and gone to the cinema. I have to admit that it was a brilliant day. So Tobe was really looking forward to this next trip. Saturday morning came and he was banging on my door at nine o'clock. As you know, I have a lock on my door and there was no way in hell I was getting up. It was too early and I was hungover. At fourteen. He kept knocking. I knew that he was waiting on the other side even though he didn't say anything, he just kept knocking. Toby never shouts through doors, or through walls. If he wants to communicate with somebody in another room he'll get up and go and speak to them. He's like a civilized gent, you know? So he kept knocking, never louder, never longer. He knocked five times every two minutes for – guess how long. Nearly an hour. I finally crawled out of bed at around noon to answer a phone call from one of my friends.

My mother didn't say anything to me at first, just gave me a laser glare.

'Are you going to take your brother into the city?' she said eventually and reproachfully, the phone held limply in her hand.

'Get off my back,' I said. 'I'm going out with my friends. I can't take him. You go.'

'You've let him down again. I don't know why he loves you so much,' she hissed.

'Gimme the phone.'

Anyway I took the call and went through to the kitchen where Toby was sat at the table drawing one of his pictures (he really does spend most of his time there, I'm not stylizing). And that was the moment that everything changed for me. Seeing him in the kitchen sat at the table like he hadn't had his dreams shattered because of his big brother who he idolized was heart-breaking. I had shattered his dreams and I'll tell you how I know this. Because the stupid little idiot was wearing a shirt and tie! And he was eight! He was looking forward to the trip so much that he had put on a shirt and tie. He'd slicked his hair across his forehead with water and I'll tell you now that my heart ached. I still didn't take him into town because I would have lost too much face, but after that I was a different person. All because of Tobe the old-man Poet Laureate.

But enough of my past. Let's get on with the show, right?

The next day, Matthew came over to my house to play some computer golf.

Matthew and I had known each other since we were three. Our mothers are good friends and we had spent a lot of time together in our childhood. He's a solid chap, with good grades and a pretty girlfriend – an all-round nice guy. He's basically a much better person than me because he doesn't have the bad thoughts in his head that I have. At least I don't think he does. He's just a really good person.

I'll tell you a funny story about how we became friends. I was a very shy toddler. Throughout the first year of school, even though I could speak fluently, I didn't say a word. I don't know why, I just didn't. So because I didn't speak, I didn't really have any friends. Until one day, that is. I remember it quite clearly. I was walking back to the classroom after playtime and suddenly Matthew accidentally fell into step by my side. We were both walking at the same pace and it was quite awkward. If I sped up he sped up and if I slowed down he slowed down, like our brains were connected. Then, all of a sudden . . . we were holding hands! We just started holding hands. Now I think back on it, it was hilarious.

Anyway, it was sunny outside and the sky was blue. I felt a little guilty being inside when it was such a nice day. I was glad Matthew had come over though because I wanted to talk to him. He was sitting on the floor at the foot of my bed and I was lying on my duvet, on my stomach. This had been the seating arrangement for computer games since I'd first known him. When I went to his house it was exactly the same, apart from I was on the floor and he was on his bed.

'What do you think of Freddy?' I said.

His face was blank, engrossed in the screen.

'Man's a hero.'

'I'm serious.'

The little golf man on the screen putted his ball but just missed on the right, because Matthew doesn't understand the idea of tilting greens and hits it directly at the hole every time.

'I liked what he said by the lake.'

'Yeah.'

He lined up his next putt. 'But it's never going to happen. I'm going to university to do engineering and that's that. There's no way my parents would let me leave school to go and live in the woods.'

I laughed inwardly at how the conversation had been bent around inside his head. But what he was saying made sense, I guess. It was a bit of a dream.

'Jenny kept talking about it on the way home though,' he said. 'You know what she's like. She can't wait until she doesn't have to go to school any more. She hates it. Do you know that she gets so stressed about school that she gets sick? I mean, her parents are so strict that she's simply not allowed to fail. My parents are bad, but hers . . . get in the hole!' His golf man was lifting the ball out of the cup and throwing his cap in the air.

'Nice one, Matthew,' I said. 'A nine.'

'I'm going into the city with her this afternoon. And the Californian Girls.'

'Oh God,' I moaned. And then added, 'Can I come?'

I love the city on a Saturday afternoon. It's always alive with energy; people going about their lives, buying things and making themselves feel good. The glass is shiny and the lights lift my spirits. It's like nothing's real *anywhere* but it's good fake, not bad.

Jenny spent most of the afternoon snapping away happily at passers-by with her camera. She loved photography. She was really artistic. And when she showed you her photos they were always excellent, not the run-of-the-mill photos that all girls took. Some of her pictures were on display outside the art department, and she loved that.

There was something vaguely sexy about the way she adjusted the focus on the lens between her middle finger and thumb. Her lithe forearms were working in perfect harmony with the skeleton of her hand – all cartilage and muscles working synchronously like a machine.

She was really pretty in a cute, Californian way. She wasn't like Clare. Jenny had blonde hair and a tan, and whilst Clare had sharp features (yuk, what a thing to say), Jenny's nose and cheeks were more roundy and smoothed. Jenny wasn't like most of the other Americans, who had a tendency to act adult-like, which came out as plain embarrassing.

One of the Californian Girls started telling us about a party that she had been invited to. Some of the older American kids who were doing their baccalaureates (which are internationally recognized examinations that our school does instead of the lesser A levels), had booked out the cricket pavilion and were planning on having a Halloween party. It sounded like a great idea.

'I hope Freddy will be there,' said one of the girls, the only one with brown hair.

'Yeah, me too,' I said. 'He's so handsome it's obscene.'

She looked at me in genuine disgust.

I felt I needed to explain. 'I'm only joking.'

'You can never tell with you. You're weird.'

'No I'm not.' The way she said it was so cold it hurt a little and I instantly lost all respect for her because doing that was easier than getting upset.

'Yes you are.'

'He's not weird, he's special,' chirped Matthew.

'Thank you, Matthew.' I considered storming off, getting

62

some drama into the scene, but thought better of it because they wouldn't get it. 'Why call me weird?' I said to the girl, by this time genuinely offended. I thought for a second that I was going to start crying.

'Why did you say you think Freddy's handsome?'

'Charlotte,' said Jenny in a high voice. 'Leave Richie alone.'

'I was making a joke,' I said.

'Oh yeah? What joke?'

'You know. Like I was gay.'

'And what's wrong with being gay?' She made one of those American faces.

I sighed. 'Nothing. It's just – it's funny.'

'I don't think being gay's funny.'

I couldn't believe this. 'No, nor me.'

'You're homophobic. That's great, Matty, you've got a great best friend.'

'Yeah,' I said quickly. 'He has. Actually.'

The other Californian Girls were loving the completely uncalled-for attack. I wasn't really used to people having a go at me and I could feel myself blushing.

'I was being facetious. If you even know what that means.'

You know what? There's nothing worse than somebody who thinks they're more intelligent than they are. I was getting angry, but not like I was when I was fourteen and went a bit nuts. Just normal angry. I paused, shaking a little bit. I hate the way I let people get to me.

'You know what?' I said, pointing at her. 'I wish you were gay. Then you could go fuck yourself.' That was too good *not* to storm off. So I did.

I was laughing my head off. Not out loud, of course; outside I was just smiling to myself. I hollered a right into an arcade and there, not forty feet away, and coming my way, was Craig Bartlett-Taylor. I instantly jumped into a shop so that he wouldn't see me. I don't know why I did that. In reality I should have escaped, but the world is never like reality, is it? Bartlett–Taylor came straight into the shop, lolloping along like a fucking moron. I'm sorry I just said that but I'm still wound up by that Californian Girl, just thinking about her.

'Hey, Craig,' I called from across the aisle. My arms were in the air.

He was wearing an Iron Maiden T-shirt so the bandages on his arms were perfectly visible. 'That's a great look for your slash marks, you crazy bastard,' I said loudly. I felt instantly sick. This wasn't me. I was almost shaking because of the Californian Girl and I had just taken my anger out on Craig. I had been worried about him all weekend and thinking that I wanted to do something to help and then when I finally saw him I said something like that because I can't control myself.

A couple of people looked at me and I felt awful because I was being like a typical teenager. He sauntered over to me and stopped. His eyes looked all empty, like he was on drugs. He probably was; to, you know, curb his madness. He wasn't laughing at my joke. I didn't realize that a suicidal mood is not tinged with irony. There is no room for jokes with something like that.

'Jesus, Craig, I'm sorry for saying that.' I put my hand on his upper arm. 'How are you?'

He shrugged. 'I'm OK.'

'Um, should you be . . . you know . . . out and about . . . on your own, I mean?'

'My parents are queuing for food over there.' He gave the barest of gestures with his free arm.

My heart went out to him. He was really upset. I could feel his energy coming into me and it was just terrible.

'So. What now?'

'I have to go back to school.' The way he was talking was

really scary. It was like he wasn't actually speaking to me at all. It was more like he was just going through the motions of a conversation without meaning it.

I knew full well that if he went back to school he would get torn apart. I could see his parents over at the food place. His dad was wearing a wool sweater with a shirt and tie and his mother was wearing a long dress and a blouse with baggy arms – they were so old it was sickeningly depressing. They both wore glasses and I thought that I was going to cry. I pictured the old man removing his spectacles, taking a freshly pressed handkerchief from his pocket and cleaning the flecks of dust off the lenses. I couldn't even start to imagine what it must have been like in the evenings for Craig. He must have sat in their living room with patterned carpet and crappy TV watching something indescribably terrible.

'Listen,' I said. 'One of the American kids is having a party on Halloween in the cricket pavilion. Do you want to go?'

'I don't know.'

'Come on, it'll be great. You can stay with me all night, I won't leave your side.'

'I don't know.'

'It's OK,' I said. 'Don't say yes or no now. I've got your number. I'll give you a call closer to the time. OK?'

'OK,' he said. It was bizarre, like he didn't seem to be having any sort of emotional response to me at all. This suicide thing runs deep, I tell you.

We walked out of the shop together and I took him back over to his parents.

'There you are,' said his dad. 'And you've brought a friend.' He smiled massively at me.

'Hello,' I answered politely, my heart splintering.

His voice was quite nasal, like his nose was full of hair. But he was such a kindly soul. I tried to gauge how he was feeling towards his son. This poor man; he'd worked his whole life, had just retired and now his son put him through *this*. He should have been enjoying his twilight years but his child was stopping it. I could see him hoisting his legs up over the side of his bed at night, having laid his slippers neatly side by side. He'd take hold of his wife's hand and whisper in her ear, 'It'll be OK, my darling.' He would notice a tear glistening at the corner of her eye, which she would wipe clear with a handkerchief. Then he would tighten his grip on her other hand and give her a peck on the cheek. 'He's a good kid really.'

6

And so things went on. After that night I guess you could say we became Freddy's circle of friends. I sometimes wonder exactly what happens when a kid arrives at a new school. Is the group that they latch on to just a coincidence? Or is there an inbuilt ability that allows us to seek out our own?

It was strange because before Freddy came along we didn't have such a rigidly formed gang. It was almost like that night in the folly looking out over the school lake had set us apart. It was as though we loved Freddy and wanted to keep him to ourselves, our own little secret that we didn't want to share with anybody.

It became clear quite quickly that Freddy was good at schoolwork. In much the same way as me he was able to understand things he was told straight off the bat, not like some of the other kids, who used to struggle. But there was far more to him than academia. He was funny, but not like a clown, nice, but not overly nice, serious when he wanted to be, and stupid when he wanted to be.

Two weeks had passed and it was the night of the Halloween party. History class had just ended and as we filed out I pushed ahead of a few kids because I wanted to talk to Craig. I caught up with him and grabbed hold of his arm.

'Hey,' I said.

'Oh,' he sighed when he saw me, though his facial expression didn't change.

'That party's tonight. I can call for you at about seven.'

'I'm not going.'

'What? Not going? What are you talking about?'

I really wanted him to go. The past two weeks must have been awful for Craig. Everybody was talking about him and some of the more teenagerish kids had said some disgraceful things. If you ask me, he should never have been allowed back to school – not with all those *teenagers*. We can be nasty creatures when provoked. And a suicide attempt counts as provocation. But not for me. My heart went out to him and I was sure I could feel a bond burning to life between us. The golden rope that would join us was translucent at the moment and I needed it to solidify. Which meant making some sort of connection with Craig.

'I don't want to go. But thanks for asking, it's really kind of you,' he said. His voice was flat; there was no meaning behind his words. Even his eyes were still glazed. This boy was a mess.

'I'm coming over to your house at seven o'clock, right? I'm not going to make you go to the party, but I just want you to know that I really want to go. And if you don't go, I don't go. And I wouldn't think that you were that selfish.' I was treading on eggshells.

Craig just looked at the floor when I said this. Still no connection.

'Rich!' somebody called from behind. It was Freddy. His hair was flopping in front of his face but not like a goth.

'Freddy, will you tell Craig that he has to come to this party tonight?'

Freddy looked at Craig with quite realistic seriousness.

'Do you want to go?'

'Not really.'

'You do what you want.' He took a step closer to Craig. 'Are you OK?'

I really hoped that Freddy wouldn't swan in and make the connection that I had been working towards. That would have been unbearable – it was me who was the most concerned. Genuinely.

But he didn't. Craig just shrugged.

All of a sudden one of the kids in the year above noticed Craig. An American kid, which was the worst part.

'Hey, Craig. Craig!' Craig looked up. 'Way to try and kill yourself, man.' And then he started laughing. One of his friends actually high-fived him. Which I thought was just plain ridiculous. We high-fived ironically but the American kids did it for real because Americans can be like that sometimes.

I felt disgusted at the remark. I took a step towards them, when something happened that I didn't expect.

Freddy got involved.

'Hey,' he called.

The corridor was jam-packed and the American kid, who was a big boy, didn't hear Freddy.

'Hey,' he called again. 'Fuck-face.'

This time the American stopped. I swear I saw his ears twitch. He turned back to Freddy. He didn't look angry or anything – I think he was more shocked.

'Take that back,' said Freddy. I was right on his shoulder.

'Take what back?'

'Take it back or I'm going to smack your fucking head in.' The way he said it was chilling. In that moment I saw something genuinely *menacing* in his face, that same balled-up anger that I had. We didn't normally let it show but when it occasionally bubbled over into the real world it was unsettling. Something in the darker places of me was glad to see this aspect of him. Knowing that Freddy had this side to him meant one thing – he really was like me. I knew it had been there all along, just knew it.

The American looked at Freddy in disbelief. My heart was thumping – it was going to happen, I could tell. It was all going to go crazy.

The American kid took a step through the crowd of kids towards us. We were like rocks in a river sticking out above the surface, looking at each other.

'Craig's really upset and you think it's OK to make things worse by saying stuff like that to him just so you can get a laugh.' I couldn't tell if he was being ironic. I think he might have been serious.

I hate the feeling of *knowing* that comes just before a fight – an apocalypse at the window.

The American kid took another two steps forward and was practically on us. I was thinking about making the first move. My plan was to lift my arm up high so that any momentum I could get up wouldn't be blocked by the crowd.

'Listen,' said the American kid. There was a weird look in his eye that didn't suit the situation somehow. I then realized that he wasn't talking to me or Freddy, he was looking past us. He was talking to Craig. 'I didn't mean anything, man,' he said. 'I was only kidding around, right?'

I looked at Craig. He just shrugged. He really did do a lot of shrugging.

I noticed that a couple of attractive girls that I had never seen before were looking at us all. They were in awe of us. Of Freddy anyway.

Freddy and the American kid made eye contact and you know what? You know what happened? They made a bond between them. It burned up crisp and clear right in front of me – a rope of gold came up out of nowhere.

Suddenly things went back to normal and it was all over. Just like that.

I smacked Craig on the shoulder.

'I'm still calling for you at seven.'

When I got home from school my mother was hanging up some bats that she had made out of paper.

'You're home early,' I said, like one of those sons whose parents can't believe how lucky they are to have such a delightful, grounded child.

'I love Halloween,' she said.

'I know. What could be better than a celebration centred entirely around evil?'

'Thank you for the insight, Richard.'

I made my way up the stairs.

'We'll be eating at seven tonight,' she called.

'Not me. I'm going out.' And I locked my bedroom door.

There was still no sign of my MCR album in the post. Play have a policy whereby they won't look into missing parcels until they've been missing for fourteen days. And their time was up. I was surprised, to be honest – this had never happened to me before. Usually the stuff I ordered came straight away.

I logged on and, before writing them an email, checked the order status on their website. I was surprised to see that my order now read: *Temporarily out of stock. Your order will be dispatched as soon as it arrives.*

I'm pretty patient and I was prepared to wait – they hadn't let me down before. I knew deep down that the CD would turn up in the end.

After that I checked my emails. Nothing. And nobody was on MSN either. Strange. I showered and when I got back to my computer there was still nobody online. I was a bit annoyed because I wanted to make plans for meeting up with everyone for the party in the pavilion.

At half six I left my house.

I love Halloween. We celebrate it in my town because the Americans absolutely lap it up. There're always tons of little kids running around dressed up as monsters and stuff and all the older American kids get drunk and go to the graveyard to scare themselves.

As I made my way over to Craig's house there were literally hundreds of kids dressed up in fancy-dress costumes. The best one I saw was a kid of about seven who was dressed all in black (as if black clothes somehow constitute Halloween clothing) and his only piece of actual costume was a Frankenstein mask. It cracked me up. He walked splay-footed with a big bucketful of sweets that he had been given, all three feet of him, like the lord of the manor. Hilarious.

I got over to Craig's house and knocked the door just as a pile of little kids came tinkling up the path.

'Trick or treat,' they called to me.

I turned round. 'Don't mess with me, kids,' I said. A gust of wind blew up the path. 'I . . . am the devil.'

The door opened. It was Craig's father and he was dressed up like Count Dracula. My heart melted for this old guy. He just seemed to love life so much. So much that he must have taken his son's share, I thought. He had dyed his hair jet black and his wife must have put white make-up on him because he looked gaunt. He gave the kids some sweets (everybody has a big bowl of sweets in their house on Halloween for the kids) and ushered me in.

'I must say,' he said. 'My wife and I really appreciate your efforts.'

I had rung Craig a few times over the last fortnight – that's what he meant by 'efforts'. I noticed that he was looking at the way I was dressed. I had on a red hoody, light-blue jeans, and my Converses. I looked like an older version of Elliott out of *ET*, a look I often try to emulate.

As he led me upstairs I couldn't help but conjure a Worst Case Scenario for him losing his footing and falling down the steps to his death. I don't mean for them to be as extreme as they are but there's this thing in my head that always makes my thoughts run away. The more I try to hem them in the wilder they get, and so I usually just let them go, just wait for them to pass before getting back to normal.

Craig's house was typical of old people. All old and creaky and quiet. His room was at the far end of a long corridor. I suddenly remembered the house from when I was a kid and started feeling a little bit guilty that I hadn't been there for so many years.

Craig's father used to be high up in the Army. He still worked now once in a while over at the airbase as a consultant or something. I think he was something to do with weapons. *Meh.* (That's a noise for indifference.)

He knocked on the door and pushed it open.

'Craig, love,' he said, which sounded weird. 'Your friend is here to see you.'

I smiled at the old man.

'Thanks,' I said.

'I'll bring you some tea,' he said.

'I don't drink tea,' I lied, for no reason. No reason whatsoever.

'Really? How odd.' He looked genuinely confused. 'Well, I'll leave you to it,' he said and shut the door behind him.

Craig was lying spreadeagled on his bed, staring at the ceiling of his room. He didn't even have any music on or anything. I was still trying to get to grips with the fact that he was totally fucked up.

His room was really bare. There was a desk with a new PC on it, a bookshelf with about five books that clearly hadn't been moved in years, an old radio sat on top of the book-shelf, and a lamp that was switched off. There was also a chest of drawers, a wardrobe, and some of his clothes were scattered on the floor. On the wall was one poster – a dog-eared photo of a colourful parrot. And that was it. Apart from, in the corner of the room, a stack of *National Geographic* magazines on the floor. One of them, I noticed, was actually on a small bedside table. On the cover was a photograph of a green lizard with a red stripe running up its back. It was a very unteenagerish bedroom. I think it was then, when I saw how weird his room was, that I realized just how far gone Craig really was. He must have come home from school every night, trudged up to his room and lain on his bed flipping through the *National Geographics*. I felt sick with the thought of how boring it must have been. He didn't have any friends and so never would have gone out.

Up until his suicide attempt two weeks ago, you would not really have known that he was such a mess. He tried to mix in with us all but never really got anywhere. He was always too nice; there was something not quite right with him. A lot of kids were really horrible to him, and I may have been one of them from time to time.

When I went through my difficult patch I once told him that his parents would be dead before he was twenty because they had him too late and he was probably genetically retarded. I now felt the worst guilt ever for having said something so *evil* but I can hardly make a time machine and go back, can I? And even if I could, I would probably choose to go back to dinosaur times instead.

Inside he had been drowning but outside he was just slightly weird. Now though, since his 'attempt', he was nothing, not even the 'nice boy' that he had perfected for society. He was a Shell of a Man. I guess this was the real him. He must have hated trying to be normal when all he really wanted to do was lie on his bed and read his magazines.

Every now and again there's a pocket of tragedy in the world so sad that it's not even funny.

'Come on, you,' I said. 'We're late.'

'I'm not going,' he said.

'Yes you are.' I went over to the bed, grabbed his wrist, and started to yank him off the sheets.

'Hey,' he called. And then my heart started singing like a bird because . . . he was laughing. Craig Bartlett-Taylor was laughing.

I caught his joy and pulled even harder at his arm.

'Come on, you bastard,' I shrieked. This was euphoria. I was *saving* his *soul*.

'All right, all right,' he said, 'I'll go.'

He sat on the edge of his bed. He had stopped laughing and the happy atmosphere had somehow been sucked out of the room again in an instant and he was his old depressed self. It had been a strange moment, like he had forgotten that he was supposed to be mentally ill for a second. But I didn't care. I had found a chink in the armour. I had made first contact.

7

The cricket pavilion is set back off the road by about a mile and you have to walk down this dark, oak-tree-lined dirt track to get to it. It's totally hemmed in by a river and a forest and if ever a psychopath was going to attack a gang of teenagers cut off from civilization, this was his chance. That didn't happen, obviously. Inside, I was curious as to where the others were. Nobody had tried contacting me, which was strange, and nobody had been online, but my brain refused to entertain the idea that they might have been doing things without me.

Inside the American guys had gone to NO lengths to give the party a Halloween theme. There were no candles, no pumpkins, no paper cut-out skeletons hung on strings, none of that stuff. It was just mounted cricket bats and boards telling you the captains of yesteryear.

I could tell that Craig was terrified being there so I said to him, 'It'll be OK.' This was the first time he had been 'out' since his suicide attempt. The music was mellow and the room was full of smoke. Loads of kids were kissing in dark corners and it was stunningly sleazy.

I took one look around the room and my heart instantly slumped about a foot downwards. My mouth dried out and a pang of desperation cracked into my ribs. Over there in the corner, sat in four chairs. The four of them. They had arranged the chairs so that it was like they were cut off from everybody else. Including me. I hadn't been invited. I was stuck in my tracks, not knowing if I should go over to them or leave the room quickly and pretend I hadn't seen them. I knew that they had planned something like this. That's why nobody had been on MSN, but I had denied it to myself.

I just felt so offended all of a sudden. How could they do this to me? Matthew and Jenny, and Freddy and Clare were in their own little world, laughing their heads off.

Suddenly rage got a little bit of a hold of me and I went over, just managing to stop myself exploding as I arrived.

'Hi, guys,' I said, as if there was nothing wrong.

It was clearly awkward. I felt so jealous of them. They looked so settled and balanced together. I WCSed them sat around a dinner table when they were forty, all black roll-neck sweaters and thick-rimmed glasses. 'Oh, remember that boy, what was his name? Richard Harper. I wonder what he's doing now. Oh ha ha ha, how delightful.' FUCKING BASTARDS.

'Richie,' said Clare. 'What are you doing here?' She was wearing a big, baggy sweater, like Kurt Cobain.

I nodded my head and pursed my lips. 'I came down here to bone my new bat in.'

'Yeah, but I thought you said you were staying in with Craig tonight.'

I laughed like I was saying what the hell are you talking about. I even lifted my hand, turned it palm-upwards as I did it. 'What are you talking about?'

Clare had on her aloof voice.

'You said you weren't coming unless Craig was coming and Craig said he didn't want to go.'

'Oh,' I said, suddenly realizing something. 'So this' – I gestured in circles – 'is all *your* doing. I should have known.'

'Oh you should have known,' she said, doing an impression of me, which was *very* annoying.

I noticed Freddy looking at his shoes, clearly embarrassed. How dare Clare put him in such an awkward situation. 'Yeah, I should have.'

'Well, maybe if you didn't treat me like I wasn't there all the time.'

I knew what she was doing – she was trying to drag our argument into the Drama, where we have an over-the-top fake argument, and I wasn't having that.

'You can forget it, Clare. This is serious.'

'This is serious,' she said again in my voice.

'Stop doing that.'

Suddenly, Freddy said, 'Rich, I don't think Clare—'

'You stay out of it, Freddy,' I snapped, losing control.

As I said it I looked at his face and thought that I may have, just for a second, seen a smirk. My brain suddenly accelerated and my insecure side had a massive WCS wherein Freddy was talking about me behind my back. 'Hey, let's go to the Halloween party, just the four of us,' he said. 'But what about Rich?' Matthew asked. 'No, just us.'

'I'm sorry,' he said.

I made sure I didn't say anything for the next five seconds because I knew without doubt that if I did speak then I would say something incredibly bad.

'I'm sorry,' I said at last.

'We're all sorry,' Clare chipped in sarcastically.

As soon as she said it I got angry again. She always had a knack of knowing exactly how to really annoy me. I pointed my finger at her, just about to unleash the big secret about how she had made a move on me in my bedroom and how I had turned her down.

She knew it was coming so she got in first.

'Well, you're here now.' She looked at Craig and gave him this massive smile. 'I'm so glad you came, honey.'

I don't think he was even listening. He was just staring at the wall. I'm glad he didn't seem to hear because I was sure she was being patronizing.

I looked at her for a moment, to see if there was anything else she was going to say.

'I'm going to get a drink,' I mumbled.

I took Craig over to the long table at the back of the room where there was a keg of beer and poured two cups.

'Can you believe they came here without us?'

'Did you ask them to meet us?' he said flatly.

'Well, no, but—' I turned to face him. He had spoken! He had listened to what I had said and formed an answer inside his head that he had then popped into his mouth and spoken out loud. 'That's a good point!' I exclaimed. They do say that mental people have insight, don't they. I handed him his drink.

'Does this have alcohol in it?' he asked.

I looked into his cup. It was clearly beer. 'Er, yes,' I said.

'I'm not allowed it.'

'Go on,' I said. 'One won't hurt.'

'No, I mean I can't have it. I'm on pills.'

Oh God, I thought. I was such an inconsiderate idiot. I looked at the table and noticed a bottle of Coke, which I guess people were using to mix with things like vodka and gin.

'Shit, sorry, Craig.' I grabbed a fresh cup and poured him some of the Coke. 'Here you go,' I said. It actually felt really good, being there with Craig. The conversation was extremely basic but at least it was a conversation.

One of the American kids walked past. I saw that he didn't have a drink.

'Adam,' I called to him.

He stopped.

'Whassup, Ricardo?' This was what the American kids called me.

'Drink?' I offered him Craig's beer, which he took gladly.

'Thanks, man.' And then he walked off.

I looked back over to Clare and the others. As soon as I did I caught Freddy's eye. He lifted his eyebrows and called me over. The rage that I had felt had already pretty much evaporated, thanks to Craig. And Freddy had that excited look on his face. I tried to force into my head that the WCS I had had about him just now was a complete figment of my imagination. I often get them mixed up with reality, like when you wake up after a dream that you were sure had happened.

'Come on, Craig, let's go back over there.'

There was music playing in the background and as I walked through the smoky air I felt like I was in a film. I grabbed two chairs and we sat down.

'Clare says you don't believe in psychology,' said Freddy.

I laughed when he said it. 'It's bullshit, isn't it?' I looked at Clare. Her eyes were glazed. I hadn't noticed before but she was clearly drunk. 'We always play-act scenarios where we talk to one another with psychobabble. Oh, you're just angry at your dad, that sort of thing. Don't we?'

Clare smiled at me, keeping her eyes on mine, and nodded.

Freddy took a sip of his beer. 'It's the whole "motivation" thing in general. I don't believe in motivation, in people doing things purely because of something that happened in their past. You know, like cause and effect. I just don't think it's true when it comes to human beings. People say, oh you're more competitive because your parents split up.'

'Did your parents split up?' I chirped quickly.

'Er, no, it's an example.' There was a pause. 'But I don't want to believe that.' His words were slightly slurred. 'I can understand it with science, explaining things like earth-quakes through science. But not people. You can't explain people with common sense. It's not that simple.' In this dim light, his eyes looked big and black. 'Surely we can't just be explained away like that. It's so . . . cold, I guess. Do you know what I mean?'

He had a lovely way with words. He didn't speak like he had opinions and those opinions were CORRECT, he just offered up ideas gently and romantically.

'It's like, there's got to be *something* special about us that can't be defined. It's this whole idea of motivation. You hear it in English all the time – the character was motivated by this or that. If not, then it doesn't ring true. Rubbish! I don't want everything I do to be motivated by something that happened in my past. If I see a pretty girl and tell her I love her, I don't want that to be because of the way I was brought up, I want it to be because I love her.'

'Like on your romantic adventure,' I said. I must have come across as being sarcastic, but I wasn't.

He smiled at me. 'Yeah.'

There was a pause. I had inadvertently killed the conversation.

'I've got a question,' said Freddy, changing the subject. 'What are those two birds in the sports field?'

'Burlington and Bertie?' said Matthew.

'They're the school mascots,' I said.

'Is that what they are?'

'They're the fastest birds on the planet.'

'Well, I think they're bent.'

I laughed out loud recklessly. It was so shocking to hear Freddy say that after his little speech.

'Burlington and Bertie? You think they're . . . gay?'

'Yes. Yes I do. I think that they are two male eagles and that they are in love.'

'Hmm. And what, pray tell,' I said, 'do you propose we do about this situation?'

We were both putting on posh English accents.

'I think that if this scandal were to get out, it would spell the end of our fine institution.'

'Over four hundred years of history ended in a second.'

'I deem that something must be done.'

I saw Jenny and Matthew look at each other and smile at our little joke.

'Go on.'

He stopped talking in the accent now and returned to being normal Freddy.

'I say we kidnap them.'

'What?' Jenny gasped and put her hand over her mouth.

'Come on. How pretentious can you get, keeping two peregrine falcons? We can set them free. We'll be taking them from the real world and bringing them on our big romantic adventure. They can be our first project.' He grinned.

An odd sensation entered me; an old feeling that I used to get when I knew that I was about to do something bad. A rush. It was as if Freddy was knocking at the door of the monster who lived inside me, and asking if he wanted to come out to play. Was he being serious? I didn't know if his actions would match his words.

I mulled over his idea of setting the birds free. I didn't want to get into something like this because my troubled days were behind me. But that odd sensation, creeping up . . . it was very persuasive.

'I think it's a great idea,' I said.

★

Actually, do you mind if I quickly jump out of the story and say something here? I get the feeling that the things I'm writing must make me sound like a disaffected youth or something. I think I should point out that that's not like me at all. All of my friends, everyone I've ever met, in fact, is like me to a greater or lesser extent. I'm not mental at all. I know I keep referring back to my past when I did something bad and went a bit off the rails but that was only for a few months and it was a knee-jerk reaction to my parents splitting up. There was my Bad Thing, but that was a one-off. I'll never do something like that again as long as I live. I promise. Please please please don't start assuming that I'm like some sort of anti-hero, a kid who's kicking against the world. Because I'm not that. I love the world. I love all the people in this great big melting pot. I'm just like ALL of my friends. It is imperative that I say this to you now. I admit that what happened afterwards is far from normal but up until all that happened I was as average as any teenager. You know what it's like, it's a time when Things Are Changing, to coin a phrase from those moronic sex-education lessons. But it's true. We're all like this when we're young. A little bit. Right?

The party started to drag and so Jenny came up with the idea of going to the graveyard. I'd always wanted to go to a grave-yard on Halloween because it's such a cool thing to do, so I enthusiastically backed her plans. We made our way up the long, tree-sheltered lane from the pavilion in pitch blackness, all six of us holding hands so that we didn't fall. As we went I imagined our hands were a line of golden rope, burning bright, one.

We arrived at the gates of the graveyard and stopped. The tombstones were glowing in the silvery light of the moon, which by this time had broken through the clouds and was sat in the sky as a beautiful white giant orb. There were some tall trees in the grounds that had lost all but the last stragglers of leaves, which hissed at us like cats. The shadows were sweeping all around us, moving, changing, shifting. They weren't actually, of course, that was all in my head. The clipped lawn beneath my feet was wet and the ivy that burrowed its way out the ground and over some of the older graves seemed to suck light into its leaves. I tried to drink in the gothic atmosphere of the place, to let it all seep into my bones through osmosis so that I would always remember it.

In silence, we passed through the gates. None of us said a word as we wended our way between the graves. I could imagine zombie hands bursting up through the soil like in that old Michael Jackson video.

There were dead people all around me. They just didn't know it yet.

'Shouldn't we hold a seance or something?' said Matthew at last.

Mist was coming out of our mouths – we must have looked like a human power factory chugging away in there.

'I have a better idea,' said Freddy, and he took a step towards Matthew.

It was menacing but Matthew stayed where he was. Another step forward. Then another. I was holding my breath. This was horrible. What was Freddy doing? Suddenly he lashed out and pushed Matthew hard in the chest. Time stopped. It was freaky as hell. Chilling, even.

And then Freddy spoke. 'Tag,' he said, and ran away.

We all stayed where we were for a second. Then, as one, we took a step back from Matthew like a flock of birds with hive mind. You know, distributed intelligence. And we ran.

We heard Freddy shouting.

'Next one to get tagged is frozen,' he called.

I started laughing. Frozen meant that you had to stand

where you were tagged, legs apart. You could only re-enter the game when someone crawled between your legs to free you. I headed for a cluster of tall graves that looked like a decent hiding spot.

Whenever I used to play tag I liked to stay in one place and see the danger coming rather than run around like a headless chicken. I looked out from my hiding place. I hadn't realized it but I had run up a small incline and could see out over the entire cemetery. Freddy was doing the same as me; hiding. Jenny was running around the centre, Matthew toying with her. Craig was sat on a grave, clearly not playing. I felt a bite of sorrow in my ribs.

I heard a noise behind me and swung round. It was Clare. She looked so small in her massive Nirvana sweater, which was a red-and-black-striped woollen thing that she knitted herself. Her white skin was glowing in the dark. And her smile was just amazing.

'Come with me,' she said. She grabbed me by the arm and pulled me up. With my wrist in her hand she started running around the inside of the graveyard's outer wall, ducking down all the while.

'Where are we going?' I said.

'I've got an idea.'

It was just me and her and, to tell you the truth, I didn't really know what she was doing: one minute she was being horrible to me and the next she was being like this. We came around to the main gates at the front of the cemetery.

Hanging off them was a set of wind chimes. She picked up a stick and started running it over the metal pipes that tinkled quietly against the night. I was suddenly struck with an overwhelming urge to grab her and start kissing her really hard.

She stopped the wind chimes and looked at me. 'Can we have a secret team?' she whispered.

'A what?' I whispered back.

'Me and you. We could be a secret team.'

'What?'

Her face had a childlike excitement. 'Like, if we're in the same room together, even if we're on opposite sides, we can look at each other and give a quick nod because we're in the team. Just me and you. No matter what anyone throws at us, we can use each other for support. It'll be our secret. Nobody will know.'

Her nose was red and her frame looked tiny under her clothes. I think I was really starting to fall for her. After all those years it was finally happening. But was it now? Or had it actually started back on that day when Craig had tried to kill himself? I remembered putting my arm around her thinking that Craig was dead, and saying to myself, I hope *you* never die, Clare.

'How long have you been thinking about this?' I said, barely audible, mist coming out of my mouth like I was in a film.

She looked at me and took my hands in hers. 'I think I'm falling in love with you.'

I genuinely almost fainted. We looked at each other for a second. Her face was like, well, I can't even describe it. I went to speak but just as I did the edges of her mouth curled up. Just for a second.

I suddenly got it. Drama. Although disappointed, I had to play along because otherwise I would lose face because I had let my guard down.

Falling to my knees, I whispered quickly, 'You have to marry me. Let's go to Paris. Meet me in the railroad café at six o'clock tomorrow morning.'

Then she fell to her knees.

'You're so amazing,' she swooned. Bitch.

Sometimes I wished we hadn't set up such intricate rules

for our relationship. It was like walking on a tightrope your whole life. We could *never* say what we truly meant. It was Self-destructive, blah, blah, blah.

I so much wish she had been serious when she told me she loved me. Maybe she was but then resented it because it would have meant *her* guard had been let down so she had to change tack and pretend that she was being dramatic all along. It really was that complicated.

Upset, I said, 'Let's split up. We'll get caught if we stay together.'

She looked at me long and hard, and shrugged.

'Whatever,' she said, as if I had just done something in-credibly offensive. And she ran off. I sighed. Why do I always have to spoil things?

I padded stealthily back up the hill to my original hiding spot and looked out. Jenny was running along a line of graves and suddenly, from nowhere, Matthew lunged at her, sending her sprawling across a patch of grass. To be honest, it seemed a bit rough. She lay on the ground, back against the turf. Laughing like a hooligan. Matthew pulled her to her feet and they looked at one another. Then he was gone and Jenny remained where she was, legs apart like a triangle, frozen. She was so great.

As Matthew ran off, hurdling the graves as he went, Freddy came out of the shadows and freed Jenny. They both set off. I looked back to the direction in which Matthew had run but he had disappeared. I watched Freddy and Jenny split up and then I heard a noise behind me. I spun round but it was too late. Matthew dived at me and grabbed me round the waist. I slipped backwards and the back of my legs bumped into a low headstone. Over I went and I still can't believe I didn't break my back.

'Agh. You bastard,' I hissed.

He got up and smiled.

'Tag,' he said. And he was off. I got to my feet and dusted myself down. Condensation on the grass left my clothes soggy and cold. I spread my legs, hoping that someone would come save me.

'Psst,' I heard.

I looked behind me. There was a scary-as-hell crypt that I hadn't seen before. At the side I could see Clare's sweater.

'Free me,' I whispered. 'Matthew's over the other side. Come on.'

She stepped out from her hiding place. The bottoms of her jeans were soaked. She was smiling at me. With her moon-beam skin she looked like a sylph. I don't mean to be melodramatic about her appearance, but I was falling in love with her and you see everything through a soft-focus filter when that happens. She moved towards me like she was floating. There was a smile like the Mona Lisa's on her face. Her eyes were catching the moonlight.

'Come on, free me,' I said again.

Without taking her eyes off me, as if to emphasize the gravity of what she was doing, she took a side-step away from me. She kept moving away, putting distance between me and her, fully intending me to understand her symbolism. Which I did. Loud and clear. But it only made me want her more because maybe I'm a bit Self-destructive. I nodded knowingly as she slipped away into the darkness.

8

A crack of yellow light cut a swathe across the horizon. Dawn was coming from the east although most of the sky was still dark. I had called my parents to say I was sleeping over at Matthew's house when in truth we had stayed out all night. We'd even persuaded Craig to call his parents, which was great because, even though he wasn't showing it, he must have been enjoying himself. Freddy was going to get in trouble but he didn't care, said this was what he had meant by not being restricted by anybody.

And now here we were, on the edge of the school grounds, peering over the low wooden fence. Mist was coming up off the lawn, the air was cold and you could hear the crows cawing in the bare trees.

None of us were saying anything because we were so exhausted, but we had one thing to do before we could go home. Kidnap a peregrine falcon.

'Listen,' I said to Clare quietly. 'I have to ask, it's been bugging me all night.' I took a deep breath. 'Where did you go before the party?' I had to ask, even if it did mean giving her the upper hand in our little game.

'Over Matt's.'

She came right out with it, like she hadn't been hiding it at all. Which she had. 'So . . .' I felt so pathetic saying this. 'Why didn't you call me?'

She couldn't look at me when she answered. 'Because we thought you were over Craig's.'

I knew it was rubbish.

'Anyway,' she added, 'what do you care?'

'OK,' Freddy interrupted. 'Let's do this.'

I suddenly caught Clare looking at Freddy like he was a god.

The six of us clambered over the fence and ran across the lawn. It was probably around six in the morning. We thrashed over the outer defences and I pretended we were about to storm the keep. I had a sick feeling in my gut because I knew that I would get in trouble for doing something stupid like this, but my monster was getting the better of me. Anyway, it was exactly like Freddy had said — keeping falcons as mascots was plain pretentious.

The aviary was next to the school gym. The falcons were enclosed in a small paddock at which we were now stood. I could see their cage up against the wall. We waited on the fence, trying to get up some courage.

The plan was to get the smaller one, Bertie. After we had him we'd keep him somewhere safe and send death threats to the headmaster using letters cut out of newspapers. It was quite evil I know but we weren't actually going to harm the bird itself, so what did it matter?

'I don't know about this,' said Matthew. 'If my parents find out, it'll be the end of me.'

The two girls remained silent. Craig, as usual, wasn't saying anything either. Freddy and I tried to coax Matthew round, but he had made his mind up before we had even reached the school. He wasn't coming. And that first dissent led to more. Jenny and, to my dismay, Clare both backed out.

So it was going to be down to me and Freddy. Operation Free as a Bird. Deep down I was actually glad it was just me and Freddy. This was the first time that it had been just us doing something. I could feel the golden rope of a bond forming between our souls.

We snuck across the lawn like a couple of cat burglars and as we went I clearly remember thinking about him. Running across that grass, the back of his head bobbing up and down in front of me, might as well have been in slow motion. I had never met anyone like him before. I remember thinking that in the short time we had been friends he had saved Craig's life, taken us to the school lake under the white light of a full moon, taken us to the graveyard to play tag, and now, here we were about to kidnap the school falcon. It was as if my life had shifted up a gear in fun since we had met.

Added to this, I loved his philosophy. I know at our age lots of people spout their teenage musings, and there was an element of that to Freddy, but it didn't dampen the impact of what he said. What he believed rang true in me. He saw the world as a beautiful, poetic place where anything was possible, just as long as you didn't let anything get you down. If you looked into his tunnel of belief you didn't have to worry about what was going on to the right and the left. There was no room for explanation, for science, for coldness. Humans couldn't be explained.

I needed to believe that. I had always felt the exact same way but had never been able to put it into words. Freddy had done that for me. When he had told us about how he wanted to make a connection between all of the lost souls, and about how he never wanted to succumb to the world, he might as well as have put his hand down my throat, ripped out my hardwire, held it above his head and said, 'Here is what Richard Harper believes and wants more than anything. Let me read it to you.'

And it wasn't just me. The others were enraptured as well. I think we all got the sense that we were holding on to his coat-tails to see where we would go. Yes, I remember having all of these thoughts as we crossed the paddock to the falcons' cage.

Those were the good days. Those were the days that I remember with great affection. I often wonder if things could have gone differently, or if it was all pre-ordained from the start. Was there anything any of us could have done somewhere along the line that could have sent our course in a different direction? Or were our stars always aligned for what happened?

It was all going to change. That yellow line of dawn could just as easily have been a line drawn between everything that went before and everything that went after.

The cage was on a set of waist-high stilts. We got closer and I caught the first glimpse of the greyish down of the birds. They were so silent, sat amongst their straw beds. I had held the birds in my first year but I was wearing one of those big leather gloves so I had never actually touched them. Their feathers were apparently amazingly soft.

We were in front of the wire mesh.

'Look how beautiful they are,' Freddy whispered, in a trance, his eyes fixed on them.

I nudged him to snap him out of it.

'OK,' he said. 'You pull the hatch open and I'll grab it.'

'Got it.'

My heart was off, beating hard. Bertie's head was bobbing back and forth. His little round eyes looked like they had the wisdom of ages in them. I whipped the door open and Freddy lunged in. All I saw was an explosion of feathers in his face. I jumped round to the front of the cage.

'Grab him,' Freddy called, laughing. Bertie was in my face, flapping like crazy. His eyes were glaring at me but he didn't try to peck my face off or anything.

'Get a hold of him, Rich,' I heard Freddy call again.

The other bird, Burlington, had his head up against the

mesh and was squawking in panic. I was laughing like mad at the whole scenario. The flapping of Bertie's wings was creating a wind that washed through my face like a fresh ocean storm.

Freddy grabbed Bertie from behind and took him out of my hands. He calmed down immediately when Freddy held him. The wind from his wings was gone. We had captured the bird! I opened my mouth in silent glee, really chuffed with our little prank. Inside the cage, Burlington fell silent. I pictured the headmaster's face when our first joke death threat arrived on his desk. But then Freddy turned his body away from the others, who were watching from behind the fence about forty feet away. His body was also turning away from me and I just about caught the grimace that flashed across his face. But he didn't turn far enough away that I couldn't see what he did next. Which was to take the bird's neck in his hands and snap it in two.

9

We were in an aeroplane and the doors had suddenly blown off. The pilot came on the PA screaming, 'Everybody brace! We're going down!' All the air was being sucked out. I closed my eyes. Freddy had killed the bird.

Not flapping any more, Bertie was limp in his hands. Dead.

I took a step backwards and opened my mouth. Not because I was being dramatic, but because I didn't know what else to do. I couldn't believe what I had just seen. I was sort of totally horrified by what was happening. That poor bird.

But then Freddy realized that I had seen what he had done. His face went blank and his whole body became incredibly still. There was a deep, deep silence.

'I think he's dead,' he whispered. 'I think I killed him.'

'Yeah,' I said timidly. I didn't want to give away that I knew he had done it deliberately. I was scared of what he might do to me.

'You don't think I did it on purpose?' He looked like he was about to burst into tears.

'What?' I said.

He was biting his lip now and the blood had drained from his face.

'Hey.' Clare was calling us, sort of whispering, sort of shouting. 'What's happening?'

'Nothing,' I called. 'It's fine.'

'What are we going to do?' said Freddy. He looked really upset now, like he was about to flip out.

I didn't know what to do. We had just killed one of the school falcons. No, *Freddy* had just killed the falcon. But I had helped him. I had tried to grab the bird when it was getting away. If *I* hadn't got in the way it would have escaped and it would still be alive. I was equally responsible. I swallowed hard.

'We'll put him back,' I said a little too coolly for my liking. My mind wasn't tumbling any more. I was calm and it was awful. I didn't want to react to such horror with such placidity.

'Put him back?' He was whispering fast. 'How can you be so cool about this? The poor fucker's dead.'

Yeah, I thought, you killed it.

'Well, what do you suggest, *Frederick*?'

He nodded quickly.

'OK, let's get it back in the cage.'

We turned away from the others so they couldn't see.

'Hey, what's happening?' Clare scowled.

Turning my head to face them I saw Craig looking blankly at us. He didn't care what was going on. But, and there was no mistaking it, he was looking at the dead bird.

I am suddenly at the school gates, eleven years old, my first day at school. My new uniform feels heavy, my blazer a little too big for me. A beautiful day. Nerves tingling in my belly. A white flash.

I'm in the paddock, leather glove on my hand. Mr Thatcher, the man who looks after the falcons, his hand on my shoulder. The smell of grass. The sudden explosion of wings beating. A silhouette of a figure in flight against the sun. My arm suddenly heavy, I'm re-adjusting my weight to stop from falling over. Serenity. The falcon on my arm; still, proud. A white flash.

I stared at Bertie's corpse. Freddy placed it heavy-handedly back in the cage and closed the door. Burlington hopped over to Bertie and prodded him with his beak but Bertie's body didn't move.

Freddy looked me in the eye.

'I'm sorry,' he said.

My calmness was leaving me again and a different feeling impacted my chest hard. It was heavy and evil. It was guilt. I felt a little better because I was reacting in a more human way but it didn't help much.

'Let's get away from here,' I said.

We weren't trying to be clever or dramatic or ironic any more. All that was stripped away and we were left exposed, our emotions naked.

We sprinted across the paddock and vaulted the fence.

'Run,' Freddy said to the others.

I didn't even look at them; I was going home. My lungs were on fire as I ran, eating up the grass and the roads with my legs as they rolled beneath me, the light of a new day coming over the edge of the curved earth, catching up with me all the way, screaming at me that I was a bad person, evil. The guilt was consuming me like a worm in an apple but by the time I was halfway home it was taken over by yet another feeling: fear. Fear that, by the time I got to my front door, had ballooned into terror.

Terror of what would happen to me if I got caught, of course, but more than that, terror of the act in which I had been involved – terror at what I had done and who I was. Oh God, the monster was coming.

The vision of the murder replayed in my head. The way Freddy had done it was so cold. It was like he wasn't even human any more, just a fleshy machine going through the motions. He was looking straight at the bird as he wrung its neck, no expression on his face whatsoever. The expression you have when you do your shoelaces up? That's what Freddy looked like when he killed the bird. In fact, it was even weirder than that, it was like another face's skin had been pulled taut over his own and you simply didn't know what was happening underneath it. That was the very first time I saw that nothing expression on his face and it stays with me even now.

How could he have done that? I had felt like I knew him, but I can't have. I was being torn up inside because I thought I had met someone who could show me the direction in which I had to go in my life. He had murdered a helpless animal. That's kind of what psychopaths do.

But then, after he had done it, it looked as if he was going to cry. The enormity of the situation, his blurred emotions, my blurred emotions were too much for me to comprehend. I had done some bad things in my life, my Bad Thing, but I would never have done something like that. Perhaps he wasn't so much like me after all. Perhaps I was wrong.

I got my keys from my pocket and ran inside my house. The grandfather clock in our hallway said it was just gone seven. I snuck up the stairs with as much stealth as I could manage and got to my bedroom. Shutting the door quietly I slid the lock across and lay on my bed, staring up at the ceiling just like Craig Bartlett-Taylor had been doing when I called for him. I think I started to know how he felt – what it was like to be trapped with no way out. My chest heaved up and down like a wave out at sea.

I didn't feel like throwing up and I didn't feel like crying – the two feelings I would have said somebody would have if I was writing a book about somebody who wasn't *real*. In truth, now that I was home and lying on my bed, locked away from the world, all I felt was tired. I crawled over my bed, reached my CD player, put on Damien Rice, and clambered under my sheets, still fully clothed, the bottoms of my jeans still cold and wet from the grass over which I had run so fast.

10

I once wrote a story for my English teacher as part of an assignment. My story was about a French artist called Pascal. He was a landscape painter, and he was very good. But he was never good enough to be great. His trouble was that he could never get the colour of the sky quite right. He fretted over this for years, but no matter how much he mixed his paints he could never get the right blue. So he asked his muse for advice. She thought for a moment and declared that the perfect hue was in his eyes. Pascal had the most beautiful blue eyes, and his muse said that, whenever she looked into them, they reminded her of the sky. So Pascal set to work trying to get a blue that would mirror his eyes. But still he failed. His life fell apart and he went mad. His muse left him and he became a recluse. In the end, nobody saw him for weeks. They broke into his studio and found him dead next to his easel. Mounted on the stand was the most beautiful landscape that anybody had ever seen. The sky was perfect – Pascal had done it. The irony was that in his mad state Pascal had cut out his eyes and painted them into the canvas and so had never actually seen his life's masterpiece.

My teacher loved the story and said that he would enter it in the next inter-schools competition that came up.

My friends asked me how Pascal could see what he was painting if he didn't have any eyes, which left me in the unenviable position of having to tell them that they just didn't understand.

A few weeks later a competition came up and my English teacher entered the story, just as he said he would. He said it was bound to win. But then my parents split up and I started going off the rails. I did something very bad, the worst thing I've ever done, got caught, and do you know what happened? They withdrew my entry. I'll never know what would have happened if I'd won that competition. The headmaster said that I was going down the Wrong Track and that I needed to be stopped. I believe that that competition could have done me real good in my recuperation, but they took it away from me. They wanted me saved and the only thing that could have saved me was that which they took away. A story about irony. That's sort of ironical, isn't it?

I woke up at eleven. At first I thought it had all been a dream, I really did. It actually took me a while to realize that it was all too true. Those few moments when I was unsure as to what had happened were wonderful. They were the segments of time in which my mind told me I was innocent. But I wasn't, was I? I went to my en suite and washed my face. My head was going crazy.

I almost jumped out of my skin when my phone started buzzing in my pocket. It was Clare. I didn't want to speak to anybody, but I also really wanted to speak to her, which does make sense to me.

'Hi,' I said.

'You killed Bertie,' she said matter-of-factly.

'Clare, please,' I began. Oh my God, my voice was breaking. 'Can you . . .' I moved the phone away from my mouth so she wouldn't know that I had almost started crying. I got myself together. 'Can you come over?' I managed.

There was silence on the line; I think she knew how upset I was.

'I'll be over as soon as I can. Are you OK?'

I hung up because I needed to lie down and do something very weak. I started crying. I had spent so long trying to be a good boy and lying to myself that I was anything but a nasty little shit who thinks he's better than other people. My fake world that I had built was about to come crashing down around me. My reality was slipping. Soon I would be that horrible person that I knew I really was. I wanted some way to kill that part of me, the bad part, but I just didn't know how to do it.

I knew that I would never tell anybody that it was Freddy who had killed Bertie. No matter how desperate you get, you never leave a man down in the field. If anyone asked, I would say that I didn't know what happened and that it was an accident.

Clare would take about twenty minutes to get across to my house and I needed to get myself together. I had had nowhere near enough sleep and my chest felt tight. My eyes were red and I felt like one of those lost souls in a sci-fi film, the ones that Freddy talked about. I got in the shower, hoping it would make me feel better, but it didn't.

I could hear people moving around downstairs – the dreaded parents. But closer, there was a shuffling noise. Toby was in his room. I went over to his door and went in. What he was doing was so ridiculous it didn't even bear thinking about. He was dusting his bookshelves with a feather duster. On a normal day I would have taken the duster off him, thrown it out the window and told him to stop being so gay. But today I sat down on his tiny chair next to his tiny desk.

'Hi, Rich,' he said amiably.

'Toby, I want you to do me a favour.'

He placed a book back on its shelf.

'What?' he said.

'I want you to hit me over the head with a cricket bat.'

'What?'

I suddenly changed my mind – it wouldn't have made any difference anyway. 'Don't worry.' My mouth was dry. 'You carry on with your, er, cleaning.'

'What are you doing in here?'

For some reason his words really hurt me and I almost started crying again. 'I just want to be in here with you. Now carry on cleaning.' I actually shouted the last sentence.

Toby stared at me like he was scared.

I got up from my chair, that bad uncontrollable part of me coming out. I didn't want to be horrible to him so why couldn't I stop myself?

'Just fuck off,' I huffed and slammed the door behind me.

When I got outside the door, Clare was stood at the opposite end of the landing, at the top of the stairs. She looked a mess but it felt so good just to see her. I felt exposed because I was only wearing a T-shirt and a pair of shorts.

'Did you just tell old Tobe to . . . *fuck off*?' she said like it was amusing. She used to laugh her head off at Toby because he acted like such an old man.

I didn't share the joke. I found myself shaking.

'Hey,' she said, suddenly putting her hand on my arm. 'Are you OK?'

My mouth was filling with moisture and I could feel my face burning. I was going to start crying again. And in front of Clare as well. I couldn't let it happen.

'Let's go to my room,' I managed.

We went in and I locked the door behind me. I noticed her glance at the lock when I did it as if I was locking her in. I wasn't. She went over to my CD player and pressed play.

Damien Rice came on again. She skipped to the third track.

'What are we going to do?' I slumped on my bed and lay on my back.

'We won't tell anyone,' she said.

'Clare.' I didn't know what I was trying to say. 'I can't believe it happened.'

She had taken a seat at my desk. 'Did you do it deliberately?'

I so badly wanted to tell her that it wasn't me, but I couldn't. Do you think that's weird? Would you have told the truth about Freddy?

'It was an accident. It just happened. One minute he was flapping away, the next he was dead. We didn't do it on purpose. You know I could *never* do anything like that. Right?'

She stayed in the chair.

'I know you wouldn't.'

'I can't believe it. That poor bird.' I saw an image of Burlington prodding his oldest friend's dead body and tried to calm myself.

'So which one of you . . . you know . . . killed him?'

I had to turn away. I'm a superb liar, absolutely second to none. But I can't lie about serious things. I am completely incapable of lying when something important is at stake. That was one thing I had definitely learnt from my bad times. If you showed me the colour green, I could lie for ever and say it was red. But not with something like this.

'I don't know,' I grumbled.

'Was it you?' I thought she was being quite cruel, making me dredge up the memory.

I looked at her over the tops of my toes. Tell her, Rich, a voice in my head was saying. You can share this with her. But I still couldn't betray Freddy. What had happened was between him and me.

Quietly I said, 'I said I don't know. What don't you

understand about that?' I didn't have enough energy to argue.

'You're pathetic, you know that?' Her voice was high.

'Whoa.' I couldn't understand why she was being so harsh.

'Why won't you tell me what happened? I thought we were friends.'

I stumbled over my words. 'I . . . can't . . . remem . . . Why do you have to know anyway?'

'Because I need to know if I can trust you.'

'What?' I said. 'This isn't the CIA, Clare. We're not spies. What are you talking about?'

She looked solidly at me. 'You're not who I thought you were.'

I started to wonder if she was being dramatic. I decided not.

'I can't *re-mem-ber.*' I drew the syllables out like those paper men you cut out and pull apart to reveal a whole line of them.

'You can remember. I *know* what happened,' she said conspiratorially.

She didn't know. No way.

'Freddy told me.'

OK, maybe she did. Or did she? I started to panic that Freddy had turned the story round. If he had told her that I had killed the bird and then she came here and I was arguing that I couldn't remember the details, then that would make me look guilty as hell.

'What did he say?'

'He wasn't lying, *Richard*. Don't act like what he said was just a *version* of the truth.' She paused and I was reminded of our secret team we had made in the graveyard, just the two of us. It seemed so long ago – had all this really happened in one night?

'He said that *he* killed Bertie.'

That wasn't what I expected to hear. For some reason I

weirdly assumed that Freddy was plotting to bring me down. I stayed silent.

'He said it happened when it flew towards him. I *know*,' she finished.

'Did he say how it happened? To be honest, I couldn't see properly.' The trap was laid. This would tell me how much truth Freddy had really told. The wording was awkward but Clare didn't seem to notice.

'He said he must have grabbed it too hard.'

I nodded and threw my head back on to my pillow. Not the whole truth then, Freddy, I thought stupidly.

'And you . . . should have told me the truth, Rich.'

I noticed a spider web on my ceiling and I had to fight off a WCS about how the spider might have crawled into my ear and laid eggs in the middle of the night. They would have hatched and . . .

'I was just trying to stick up for my friend.'

'He's hardly your friend, Rich. You've known him for less than a month.'

'He's my friend,' I retorted, offended. I was slightly bemused when I said it so sternly. Why was I defending him after what he had done? Why the *fuck* did Clare saying that make me feel closer to Freddy?

She shook her head and rolled her eyes.

'Look, whatever. I'm gonna get outta here.' She got up and kissed me on the forehead.

When she did that I leaned up and quickly kissed her lips. I don't know why – sometimes my impulses get the better of me.

We looked at each other for a *long* time. She looked beautiful. I wondered what was working through her brain. Given the mood she seemed to be in I thought she might slap me. But she didn't. She smiled.

'Don't forget our team,' she said, and went to leave.

'Hey,' I called. She stopped. 'What's it called?' I asked. 'Our thing. What's its name?'

Clare thought for a second and her mouth took on a weird, thinking shape.

She looked at me and said, 'The Eskimo Friends. What else?' She opened the lock and disappeared.

I let out a sigh and asked myself why I had kissed her.

Then, all of a sudden, she was back in the room.

'And it's not a "thing", it's a team.'

Five minutes later the door opened again. Mum.

'Morning, honey,' she beamed.

I don't want to keep whinging about my emotions, but the guilt returned full-force when I saw her face. I didn't know how anybody could possibly find out it was us because the school was hardly going to fingerprint all of their pupils, but still, if my parents knew what I had done, I don't think they'd ever get over it. After all they'd been through with me, after sticking by me after what I did when I was fourteen, finding out about Bertie would destroy them. They had done so much for me and this was how I repaid them.

'Did you have a good time yesterday?' she asked.

I smiled, but only with my mouth. 'Yeah.'

'What are you doing today?'

I shrugged. 'Dunno.'

'Would you like to help me with the shopping this afternoon?'

'I can't,' I said. 'I'm going over to Matthew's house.'

There was a brief pause.

'You could make more of an effort,' she said.

'I'm tired.'

'We all remember what it's like to be a teenager, Richard. But manners don't cost anything.'

My mind was at breaking point. 'You remember what it's like to be my age? Oh, OK. But then . . . your parents didn't split up and humiliate you in front of the entire school, did they?'

Apart from it being an incredibly cruel thing to say, I knew I shouldn't have said it because my mother is one of those people who believe that matters can be solved by Talking Things Through. Usually I'm nice to my parents because I want to be a good son, but my façade was drooping like it had been injected with muscle relaxant.

'Do you want to say anything?' she said.

I let out a huge sigh. 'I'm sorry,' I said, just trying to get out of this conversation. I was starting to feel sick again with the thought of Bertie.

'Your father and I are trying to make it work,' she said. 'And we're very happy at the moment.'

'I'm glad you're happy.' I paused. 'Mum, do you think I'm well behaved now? Am I much better than I was?'

She smiled at me. 'Of course you are, my love. You know that. You're doing really well.'

Patronizing. I was getting annoyed with her again, my mood all over the place.

'I love you, Mum, you know that, don't you?' I cooed, not meaning a word of it. Although I did love her, when I said it I didn't mean it. If I really wanted to tell someone I loved them and actually mean it, I don't think I'd have the strength.

But, whatever. The words had the desired effect. My mother filled up, kissed me on the forehead and left, leaving me to stare blankly at my ceiling Craig Bartlett-Taylor-style.

11

We were caught immediately. On Monday morning, before first lesson, I was frog-marched through the corridors by a teacher who had never actually taught in one of my classes. It was silent all the way down apart from the ominous clicking of shoes on wood. I felt like one of those guys being led down death row.

The teacher was just ahead of me and, when he reached the headmaster's door, he opened it and I walked past. Of course I already knew that the game was up but, when I saw who was in the room with the headmaster, any remaining air of hope fizzled away. Sat in five chairs were Clare, Matthew, Jenny, Craig and, of course, Freddy. None of them looked at me as I took my seat.

The headmaster stared at us like he was somehow better than us. We didn't believe that to be true (apart from maybe Matthew) because we knew the truth about most people. Everybody has a secret.

I grabbed a glance sideways at Freddy, who was gazing out the window, no expression on his face. You would never have guessed that somebody with his outward appearance would have done what he did to that bird.

At last the headmaster spoke.

'So what have you got to say for yourselves?'

We all stayed silent. I got a few glances my way from Clare and Matthew.

The headmaster got up from his chair with one of those crushed-leather squeaky sounds and walked over to the TV stand like he was a high-powered detective from the Met. Far too much self-importance. He switched on the TV and pressed play on the video.

The screen faded in. It was a surveillance-camera shot of the falcon paddock. My gut turned to acid and sludge. It was dark but the moon was bright, and a crack of dawn was throwing a half-light in from the left. I had to sit there and watch as we all flowed into shot. We were done for, all lost at sea. My heart was beating hard as I watched the ghostly images of me and Freddy climbing over the fence and running over to the cage. The camera was high up and we looked small, like little matchstick men. But it was definitely and clearly us.

It didn't bring back memories of the event; rather I just watched it without any clear thoughts registering in my brain. All I felt was a kind of numbness. At least this would show that Freddy was the one who was guilty and I would get away with nothing but a rap on the knuckles. It actually made me feel a little bit better.

I could sense the atmosphere in the room intensify, like the air was getting rarefied and more difficult to breathe. I found myself wondering what was going through Matthew's mind – I didn't want him to think bad of me.

On the screen, Freddy whipped open the cage and the bird came thrashing out, his wings all over the place. Jenny adjusted herself uncomfortably in her chair.

It was strange watching the event with no sound. The camera showed Bertie escaping my clutches and flapping towards Freddy. But then it all went wrong. Freddy suddenly turned his back away from the camera like it was the most deliberate thing in the world. Then I turned my face away from the camera and Bertie disappeared out of sight, obscured by Freddy's, and my, body. My throat went dry. The next thing you saw was the limp corpse of the falcon being put back into the cage, still. And there was no way you could tell who had done it. As Freddy shut the door of the cage, so did the door shut on my life.

The headmaster was back in his chair, hands steepled under his chin. Smug. He didn't care about the bird, I could tell. All he cared about was punishing us.

'I'm sure I don't need to tell you what this means.'

We were all silent.

'Sir,' I said at last. 'We didn't mean to hurt it.'

'Save it, Harper. I don't want to hear it.' There was venom in his voice. He was genuinely disgusted with us. It was actually quite shocking. It kind of punched home how bad what we had done really was. He was especially disgusted with me and Freddy. He never liked me anyway. 'How can you say you meant it no harm? You broke its neck.' His face was going red and I could feel an explosion coming on. But it never arrived. He was deliberately hemming himself in.

The weird thing was that I wasn't feeling frightened, which is what I should have been feeling. I was, in all honesty, feeling anger towards the headmaster more than anything else. I'm sure my reaction wasn't rational, but that's the way it was. I felt confrontational.

'Well, gentlemen,' he said to me and Freddy. 'What have you got to say about this?'

I was only fifteen and I was already more intelligent than my headmaster, who didn't realize that he had just told me to shut up and was now asking me to talk. Long service can get you a long way, you know? I'm sorry for saying that, but that's how I felt. Something was stirring in me, and it wasn't good. I knew what it was. It was the old me, the acerbic, ruthless Richard Harper that had been so horrendously behaved when his parents split up. I didn't want him back. He was not welcome but he was still coming. I knew it.

'Sir, we didn't mean for it to happen. We didn't want to kill it.'

'Tell me which one of you did it.' His voice sounded menacing.

'It was me.'

Everyone looked at Freddy, who was fixing the headmaster's stare.

'I grabbed it and its neck just got caught and somehow . . . it happened.'

I was hugely impressed that Freddy had taken the hit. He knew I wouldn't have said anything so he could have got away with it if he'd wanted, but he did the decent thing.

'Sir, I swear I didn't mean to kill Bertie. I was trying to set him free.'

'What do you think your father will say about this, Mr Spaulding-Carter?'

Freddy's face looked a little afraid now.

'He'll be upset,' he said calmly.

I should say now before you get the wrong idea that Freddy's father was not one of those strict fathers. He didn't force him into doing anything that he didn't want to do, like military school or something like that. I never actually met him, but I know that none of Freddy's defects were caused by abusive parenting. Freddy was just plain nuts, I suppose. I guess you could say that everything he did tied in with his theory of motivation and how human behaviour can't be explained away by cold, unromantic science. There was no reason for killing Bertie. None. It happened and there was no reason for it. A lot of life is like that.

Then, out of nowhere, Craig Bartlett-Taylor burst into tears. Just suddenly started crying a torrent. He was inconsolable. His face was all red and I felt an arrow of sorrow pierce my heart. How long had this tear-storm been brewing in his poor fractured soul? Since Bertie, since the pill incident, before that even? His whole life maybe. I wanted to hug him and protect him from the world, apart from, of course, there's no protecting anyone from it – it will get you in the end, no matter what.

The headmaster's face simply went blank, like he'd had a lobotomy.

'Stop crying, boy,' was the best he could manage. Cruel bastard.

It showed me there and then that some adults live their lives behind a veil. As far as I can see, they pretend for all the world that they know what they're doing but they only seem so self-assured because they think they know what's going to happen next. They are planning two steps ahead and living within certain boundaries. But it is when things happen that are sudden and unexpected – when genuinely good people step up to the plate and come to the fore – that these supposedly 'confident' people flounder. My God, I sound bitter. But I'm not. And I am. I'm both. People think you can't have two feelings at either end of the spectrum towards the same thing, but you can. Why do people think that?

Clare and I both got out of our seats and went over to Craig. He wasn't bawling like a little girl, he was crying with a real fucking tragic POWER. I'm sorry to swear but that's what it was like. His entire body was aching up and down, heaving like an oak tree being uprooted. His pain was coming straight out of his skin. I noticed that his sweater was a bit too small for him and some of the scars on his arms were just poking out. I found myself holding his hand, which he gripped tight like a baby does. The headmaster actually got up and left the room. Not being able to deal with this amount of emotion, which I admit was intimidating, he had gone to fetch his secretary.

There was no way that he could have understood what Craig Bartlett-Taylor was going through. I could tell that he was the sort of person who had never known the deeper depths of the spectrum. He'd probably never even fallen in love properly.

I clutched Craig's hand tighter and looked at Clare, who returned the stare. A bond burned up between us for a second. Suddenly we were all around Craig, all grabbing him and comforting him, telling him that it would be OK. Lying to him that it would be OK. How could it ever be OK for someone like him?

'We're going to be with you all the way,' I told him.

Freddy was crouched down. He had put his hands on the back of his head and was staring at the floor. He lifted one of his hands and put it on Craig's knee. And then he started patting it, kind of in the same way that a child would try to reassure somebody. And that was when I forgave Freddy for killing Bertie. I sensed, in a searing flash of clarity, that I knew what had happened. He had made a stupid mistake. That was all. He had lost his head for a moment and done something terrible. I had to forgive him. God knows, I had to forgive him for doing something like that. How could I not?

He sighed and stood up.

'This is fucking bullshit,' he said. 'I'm getting out of here.' He strode towards the window, quickly.

'Freddy, hold on,' I pleaded. 'Don't go. It's not worth it.'

Craig had stopped heaving now but the tears were still pouring down his face and he was making this odd groaning sound. His head was slumped over his shoulders and I wondered if he was about to break for ever, or if he was feeling some sort of catharsis. An image of his old parents flashed in my brain and I hoped that this outpouring of emotion would clear the skies and make everything nice and fresh for Craig and his family. I knew that it wouldn't though. Nothing could change the fact that he wasn't quite normal. That was it for him, the beginning and the end.

Freddy was on the windowsill and looked like a super-hero, crouched and ready to pounce.

'I'll call you all at some point. I have an idea,' he said. And he jumped out the window, just as the headmaster came back in.

His face was a picture, you should have seen it. It was pure astonishment mixed in with what can only be described as *hatred* for Freddy.

'Get back here,' he screamed. And I do mean screamed. Even his voice was angry because the air from his lungs split either side of his vocal cord and came out far too high-pitched.

But Freddy was heading across the lawns. I hoped to God that the headmaster would get out of the window and start pegging it after Freddy. But he didn't. He let him go with a shake of his head. I assumed that Freddy was going to be expelled. Which he wasn't. Our crime was deemed so heinous that we had a far worse punishment awaiting us.

12

'Mr Harper,' said the headmaster. 'You come with me.'

I looked at my friends and saw four faces staring back at me like I was the Chosen One. I was being torn away from them and it was becoming apparent that it was me who was going to take most of the fall for Bertie. Which was, of course, the way it should have been.

My brain was blazing. I now felt *exactly* like I had when I was fourteen. I was the same person, all those months of hard work had gone out the window as I regarded the world with cold eyes. I felt the headmaster by my side and whereas I should have felt intimidated, I actually felt nothing.

I was taken out of the office and into the room next door, a room that I had never seen the inside of before. It was a conference room with a big meeting table and a load of high-backed chairs all around. Sat at the far end like the Godfather was a fat woman wearing a blouse that was absolutely horrendous. I took an instant dislike to her. Not because of her clothes but because of the way she looked at me. She looked at me like I was a victim.

'Richard,' the headmaster said calmly. 'This is Miss Bowler. And I'd like you to have a little chat with her.'

I thought she might have been a detective. The headmaster went to close the door behind me.

I sat down at the far end of the table, keeping my distance from Miss Bowler, still having no idea who she was.

She grinned at me and I thought her mouth was going to rip apart at the edges.

'Hello,' she said, her voice all waterlogged and flabby. 'I'm Sylvia.' Her voice was horrid and she had a terrible double chin. I'm not at all judgemental ordinarily, but something about this woman really gave me the creeps. 'Do you know why I'm here?' she asked.

I shook my head.

'Elucidate,' I said sharply. It was a bit too acerbic for me. The monster was growing inside.

Her eyes narrowed when I said that.

'I'm here to help you,' she hissed.

'Are you a counsellor?'

'Yes. I'm a psychotherapist.'

I sneered inwardly.

'How many A levels have you got?' I said cuttingly.

She fixed my gaze. I'm never this confrontational and I could feel myself breaking new ground. But I didn't like it, I wasn't being a nice boy.

'I don't have any A levels because I got my degree as a mature student,' she said, thinking that she had regained her composure. She should have regained her salad.

I smiled. 'Don't worry, I'll never get any A levels either because we do the baccalaureate here. Because we have a lot of American kids, you know?'

'Yes.'

It was obvious that I had offended her because I had let her know loud and clear that I was laughing at her idiocy. I tried to make it up.

'I'm sorry,' I said. 'How can I help you?'

But my remarks had struck a nerve.

'You make fun of me because I didn't have the

opportunities you have. But let's take a look at facts. No, I don't have any A levels but then, you killed an innocent creature.'

She sort of had a point. Apart from I hadn't physically killed Bertie.

'Look, I didn't mean anything by asking about your credentials.' I was on a roll. 'I've read some Freud,' I lied.

'What did you think?' Her guard was up. She was being exceedingly unprofessional.

I shook my head.

'I haven't really read any of that stuff. It's not science, is it? I mean, in a hundred years' time, people will look back at people like you in the exact same way that we look back now on the people who thought the world was flat. You think you know it all but you don't. People will laugh at you because your evidence doesn't follow the rigours of the scientific method.' I cursed myself for saying it because I didn't really mean it and also because I was being very rude. I immediately apologized and asked if we could start again. I also lied and told her that I didn't really think such awful things about psychotherapy and that I sometimes said things to show off. She liked that because I was scratching beneath the surface.

'Tell me what happened on Saturday morning.'

I went through the story of Bertie, telling her that it was *just an accident*.

When I was finished, Sylvia looked at me with condescension.

'Tell me about your parents.'

I sighed a little and went through the story just to keep her happy, making sure that she knew that I had fully forgiven them for what they had done.

'Thank you,' she said at last. 'Listen, I'm going to the coffee machine. Would you like anything?'

'I don't like tea or coffee,' I said.

'What about a can of Coke?'

'Oh, my parents don't like me drinking carbonated drinks,' I lied again. I like lying to people for whom I have no respect because it's funny.

She left the room and I was on my own. I considered, but only for a second, what I had said about my parents. About how I had forgiven them for my humiliation. I have forgiven them. I never tell them, but I love them. Normal teenagers never tell their parents that they love them, but that doesn't mean that they don't.

Sylvia returned and waddled back to her chair. She was carrying a plastic cup of coffee, from which rose a snake of steam.

'Would you like to hear what I have to say about you?'

'Sure,' I said. I really did want to hear. It would be amusing for someone of my intellect to hear someone of her intellect judge *me*.

'I think that you have forgiven your parents. But you haven't forgotten. You think that your fellow pupils still look at you and make fun of you behind your back because you were once part of a broken home.' She looked at me as though she was clever. She thought she had impressed me.

In fact she had done the opposite. She was plain wrong. I freely admit that my parents' temporary separation did mess me up, but not any more. The scars will always be there, of course, but scars don't actually *hurt*, do they? I decided that this woman had embarrassed herself for long enough so I started to make fun of her. I looked at the desk, pretending that she had struck a chord. I was play-acting. I can guess what you're thinking. You might be thinking that I was being arrogant, but I wasn't. Consider who was wrong: me, because I was being cynical, or her because she thought she had all the answers? I absolutely admit that I was being very, very horrible to Sylvia but then I didn't ask for help, and she didn't know me, so why did she think that she could just waltz into my life and 'cure' me of whatever it was I had? I know I was being harsh, but I didn't care.

'It's OK, Richard, I'm here to listen.'

She really did say that, I'm not making it up. And do you know what she did next? I was dumbfounded. She took an orange ball from her bag, got out of her seat, put the orange ball on the table in front of me, walked back to her seat and sat down. Let me just reiterate: this was an orange *ball*, not a piece of fruit. She then looked at me and said something so incredible that, as soon as she said it, I couldn't wait to tell my friends so we could have a good laugh at the stupid fat bint.

She said, 'Peel the orange, Richard.'

'I'm sorry?'

She made the motions of somebody peeling an orange. 'Peel the orange.'

I had to nip this in the bud straight away.

'Look, Sylvia, I have to tell you this.' I picked the ball up. 'This is an orange ball. I don't know what you mean, but I'm not going to pretend to peel a ball as if it's a piece of fruit.' I couldn't exactly have said it any clearer.

She wrote something down in her book.

I put the orange ball back on the table.

'We've had a good talk today,' she said. 'I'll see you next week.'

She went back to her book. This was the end of this session.

'Can I ask you a question?' I asked.

'Of course you can, Richard.'

'Um, this is awkward, but, you know you said you'll see me next week?'

'Yes.'

'Does that mean that, sorry, that I'm . . . not . . . going to get in trouble for killing the bird?'

'I'll see you next week,' she said.

I left the room and the headmaster was waiting outside.

'Take this home with you, Mr Harper,' he said. He was holding an envelope. I took it from him and tried to look timid.

'Sir,' I said. 'How's Craig?'

'His parents are coming to collect him. He'll be fine.'

I smiled a little.

'Can I just say something?' I said.

'What?'

I looked at the floor.

'You know I'm sorry about Bertie, don't you, sir?'

I was serious that I was sorry about Bertie being dead – of course I was sorry, I'm not disaffected. But that didn't change the all-important fact of the matter; that, although I was sorry about Bertie, when I said I was sorry to the headmaster I only said it because I was making fun of him.

13

I knew what was in the envelope. It was a summons for my parents. The headmaster would like them in to talk about their son – me. This would be the worst part of it all. I had to somehow explain to my parents about Bertie. This bird was kind of like a local celebrity and now he was dead. They were going to see that all of their efforts had gone to waste and that their son really was a bad egg.

By the time I got home that evening, I was numb. The envelope from the headmaster was in my hand and I desperately didn't want to give it to my parents. But I had decided to face the music like a man so I went into the kitchen and sat at the table with my mum and dad whilst they read the letter.

The initial reaction wasn't explosive because they were in shock. How could their son have done this? My father looked at me like I was a stranger, and that hurt. My father was always supportive of me, but now I feared I had lost him for ever. My mother stood up from her chair and walked out of the room, carrying the letter in her hands.

That was a bit of a let-off. I was glad that she had taken the time to cool off before speaking to me. But I was not going to be so lucky with my father.

I really love my father. After he left he stayed in constant contact with Toby and me. We never spoke about whether or not he was seeing another woman, or who she might have been. And that suited me fine because I knew nothing was going on.

I always knew that my mother would forgive me for anything and I could sort of get away with anything, but my father was different. If I, for example, murdered somebody, he would turn me in. Because that would be the right thing to do. And now I was on trial and in jeopardy was his approval of me.

'I can never forget this, son,' he said coolly.

His calm voice chilled me. I knew that he wasn't going to go off his nut at me because the nature of my crime was *so* horrific that scolding me would be meaningless. But the way he was speaking was not nice. My mouth got even drier than it already was. I knew what he was thinking – he was thinking, Richard hasn't changed. My chest was actually experiencing physical pain and my head felt light.

'What the heck were you thinking of?'

'I . . . I . . .' I wasn't being dramatic.

'Christ, be a man. Stop crying this instant,' he said sternly.

I looked at him through my bleary eyes.

'I'm not going to shout at you just yet. Did you do it deliberate—'

'No.' The word rang out. 'Of course not.' I couldn't help but let water leak out of my eyes, although I wasn't *sobbing*. 'It wasn't me.'

'What would you think if you were me?'

I didn't know what to say.

'I mean, after all we've been through with you, and we forgave you for it all. If this was an isolated incident then I could believe you. But what do you expect me to think, given your past? Do you think I should believe you?'

'But I've tried so hard,' I cried. My voice shook and broke. I couldn't help it. I guess it was the Straw that Broke the

Camel's Back. Everything that had happened had caught me by the throat and I was broken. My dad just sat where he was. How could he not believe me? I had been so good. It was like the end of the world for me. The bond between me and my father was being severed and it was unbearable.

'Listen to me, son.' He leaned forward over the kitchen table. 'Let me talk to you as an adult. I think I owe you that much. You see, I have to look at this from two sides. On the one hand, I have to have sympathy for the school. This is the institution that is educating you and, if rules are broken, then the transgressors have to face the responsibility. As a parent, I should support the school because they only have the best interests of their pupils at heart.'

Hearing my father use words such as 'transgressor' was awful. Because it meant I had lost my innocence. I was no longer a child if he was using big words.

'If you've done this thing, then I have to see it from the point of view of the school. I'm not going to be one of these parents who can't see the facts.' I could feel his soul standing tall. 'But on the other hand I'm also a parent.'

His voice was kindly now; I had never heard him speak quite like this, addressing me like I was an adult.

'If you say that you didn't do it deliberately, then I'll trust you. The school could be wrong.'

'They are wrong,' I pleaded.

'Are you sure?'

'No, yes. It was . . .' I tried to breathe. 'We didn't plan it. It was just an accident.'

'But, Rich, you've lied to me before.'

When he said that it was like a soap bar wrapped in a towel had been smacked into my chest like in that movie *Full Metal Jacket*. My father had just revealed to me an irreversible truth. He thought I was a liar. Or at least capable of telling lies. Which I'm not. Not any more. I can't lie about serious things.

He was talking about the time I went off the rails, he was talking about my Bad Thing, the incident that set me apart. I should tell you it now. You should know what happened. It's only fair.

I had been with an old group of friends (who refused to hang around with me after what happened) and I kind of threw a brick through a shop-front. We went to run away but an old man had seen us and stopped his car. My adrenalin was pumping so hard I thought my veins were going to burst. He came towards us and he was on his phone to the police. I was really drunk and got really scared all of a sudden so I picked up a piece of metal that just happened to be lying on the pavement. It was kind of like a pipe but there was no hole in the middle; it was solid. I paused. My mind said, Go on, Rich, take this as far as you can. My brain was howling at me. Just see what it is you are capable of. In one awful moment I swung the metal pipe at his head and just at the last minute a piece of common sense opened up in me and I changed my swing, smashing the phone out of his hand. I could feel the crunch of metal on bone. The man gasped and swore at me, and said that I was evil but his voice was scared and shaky so I pushed him in the chest and he fell backwards on to the pavement. I towered over him and the look on his face was awful. It was like he was looking at the devil. I walked past him quickly, towards his car. The door was still open and I ran up to it and, with the sole of my foot, smashed it closed. I felt the metal cave under my blow as the door slammed shut. My chest was going up and down, up and down. I turned back to my friends with a smile on my face, looking forward to seeing how impressed they were. But all I saw were six frightened children looking at someone they didn't recognize. I remember the metal pipe feeling heavy in my hand just before I dropped it to the ground.

I don't tell you this expecting any form of forgiveness – I

know that I can never be forgiven for what I did. I tell you it because it happened. I was drunk and I did something that 99.9% of the population would never even consider. I can't say it could happen to anyone, or that it was a terrible mistake, because it's not true. Only a certain type of person can do something like that. Only a certain type of person can go to such extremes purely to see what would happen. It was a true act of evil and most people cannot perform such acts. It is as simple as that. I despise myself because of it and whenever something good happens to me I remember what I did and my happiness drains away. The police were called in and I told my father that I didn't do it. But I did do it. And I was found out.

'Dad . . .' I said. I was sniffling now. So pathetic.

'Son, I want to believe you, I really do. I know you've been trying very hard to get back on the right track, and I have to say that as your father I *do* believe you. But this . . . *killing* a helpless animal—'

'It was an accident.'

'I'm going to take your mother and your brother out for dinner. You'll stay here. And not go out. All right?'

I nodded.

He got up from his seat. As he walked past I expected him to ruffle my hair as a show of solidarity. He always ended things on good terms. But he didn't do it. He left without even looking at me. I could feel that he *couldn't* look at me. I felt sick. I couldn't believe what my parents were going to have to go through again; all of the worry and fear.

When he shut the door it was like my mind had opened the floodgates. Inside my head was like a war zone. I felt like the line in the song where I could blow through the ceiling, you know? I was literally devastated that they were going out for a meal and I wasn't. I hoped that they wouldn't tell Toby what I had done – it would break his heart, which

I imagined to be vulnerable in the first place because he was so frail.

But at the same time I was glad, which I know sounds stupid because how can you be sad *and* glad at the same time? Well, I was. I was glad that my father had spoken to me in the measured way that he had. I felt more respect for him than I ever had before. And that just made me feel worse about Bertie because it must have been such a let-down for my dad. I was in a cold sweat and I dried my eyes with the sleeves of my school sweater that I sometimes wore beneath my blazer in the winter.

I suddenly had a Worst Case Scenario in my head, a really bad one, roaring out of the darkest corner of my brain. My parents were driving to the restaurant and they took a corner too fast. A car was coming the other way. It was too late. When the two cars hit, Toby's body was thrown clean through the windscreen. I saw his face get sliced apart by the glass, his outstretched arms not saving him. He always wears these stupid sandals with grey socks and I saw them hurtle past my dead parents' heads. So tiny, so small, rounded like bulbs over his child's toes. His skull smashed into the other driver's windscreen and his neck got snapped like it was made of balsa wood. His eventual resting position was with his head stuck backwards at a sickening angle, almost ninety degrees, to his neck. The driver's windscreen was shattered where Toby's head had hit, and looked like a spider had spun a web over the surface of the blood-smeared glass. Toby was face down and his arms were by his side. If you were hovering low in a helicopter, you could see the soles of his stupid fucking sandals. And if you looked closely, you could just see the side of his face, all covered in blood. And his eyes, do you know what they were? Closed. He was still, oh so still. My whole family was dead. I was alone, a broken man with nothing but pain, just like Craig Bartlett-Taylor.

★

Freddy got sent back to his parents and so when I was asked to go to the headmaster's office to watch the video with my mother and father, I had to go it alone. I knew their appointment was at two thirty and when that time arrived I was summoned. This was a shock as I didn't know that I was going to be in attendance. My father had requested my presence because he wanted me there when they were shown the tape.

It was an uncomfortable experience for all of us. We watched on as I saw my back turn away from camera on the headmaster's television set. Then we saw the dead bird in Freddy's hands and the footage was just as ambiguous as I remembered.

When the show was over, the headmaster told my parents that I had been very well-behaved during this school year, and that this sort of activity was abnormal.

'I think it might be prudent to keep Richard and Freddy separate for a while,' he said at last.

'I don't even know who this Freddy is,' said my mother (who was still ignoring me), her eyes burning into me as though I should tell her about everybody I knew.

In fairness, the headmaster went on to explain that Freddy had come clean about killing the bird.

'He's been sent back to his family until he can accept what he's done. I haven't suspended him officially, but he won't return to this school until at least next week. And like I say, when he does come back, Richard and he should stay apart.'

'Oh, you don't have to worry about that,' Mum said. 'He won't be seeing anybody for a while.'

I listened, not really thinking much. My mother was talking as if I were a child, and she was being a bit stereotypical. If she was going to react like this, then I wasn't about to start caring what she thought. At least my father had treated me like an adult.

When the meeting was over I was returned to my lesson. I sat next to Clare.

As the teacher spoke, I whispered, 'Freddy's been kicked out.'

She looked at me. 'I know. I heard this morning.' She paused. 'My mother says—'

'Clare!' The teacher had heard us. 'Have you got something to say?'

My God, why do some teachers have to use such awful clichés?

'No, sir,' she said meekly.

I loved her for that.

She started writing on a piece of paper: *My mother says I'm not allowed to speak to you anymore.*

I took the paper from her. *Are you going to listen to her?*

We glanced out of the sides of our eyes at each other. Her black hair was the entire background. In the last two days, since Bertie's death had become public knowledge, Clare had sort of distanced herself from me. She had gone back to hanging around with her old friends all the time. My old friends had also distanced themselves. Jenny simply hadn't spoken to me at all. Only Matthew was still on my side and things were all going bad. I was glad to have the chance to sit next to Clare. I waited for her to write her reply. Finally, she smiled at me and brought the pen down to the paper.

I looked at her scribble, and then looked up at her, and that was it. I was in love with her. With Clare. My heart started beating fast as I looked into her big wide eyes. I don't know what processes happen in your heart when you're falling in love, but they had just finished in mine. The machines had stopped. I was fallen.

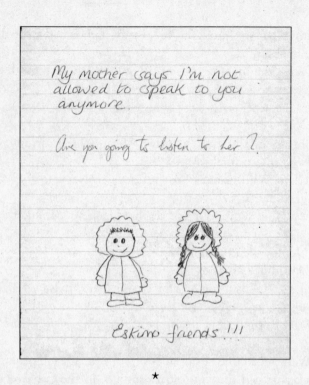

My mother says I'm not
allowed to speak to you
anymore.

Are you going to listen to her?

Eskimo friends!!!

★

I had been friends with Clare since I was eleven. We hadn't gone to the same primary school but I remember seeing her around town when I was a kid and thinking how pretty she was. So when I turned up for my first day at secondary school I was ecstatic that she was in all of my classes.

I can't really remember how we became friends, but we did. For a while we were the talk of the year because we hung around together so much. But we were always only friends. That was just the way it was with us.

Back in those days we were still innocent and we had some great times together. We'd go into the city and hang around over each other's houses and go into town to eat chips on the war memorial. We were so innocent that we even went for bike rides together. Sometimes we spoke about how the other kids perceived us, and we had a good laugh about it.

In our first summer holiday, we used to hang around in the park with the other kids our age and eat ice creams whilst the lazy sun dipped behind the hills.

After my first kiss, Clare was the second person I told after Matthew. She didn't have her first kiss until she was thirteen, the same year that she lost her virginity. That was our third year of school. At that time, Clare started hanging around with the older boys and, although we still spoke, it was far less often and we found ourselves drifting apart outside school. When we did go round to each other's houses, we would mostly listen to music. She had an older brother and it was from him we got our impeccable music tastes. Clare loved this band called the Smashing Pumpkins, from America. Her favourite song was theirs: '1979'. It's a beautiful song. My favourite song also happens to be by the same band, but mine is called 'Today'.

When she finally got her first boyfriend our friendship ceased to exist. I was a little hurt but we had been growing apart so it wasn't as bad as it could have been. It was roughly at the same time that I started going out with my first girlfriend. But whilst I was standing on corners and having a fluttering heart because I was in love, Clare was out having sex and smoking marijuana.

Then my parents split up and I joined Clare on the slippery slope to the loss of innocence.

It was strange how we both came out of our wild phases together. One day in school I remember Clare approaching me and we basically apologized for dissing each other for so long and agreed to go back to the way it was before. Of course it never got back to being *exactly* the same because we both knew that we had our secrets and they were irreversible.

Because we both had our dark pasts, they caught up with us emotionally. We were scarred from our experiences and, eventually, we slipped into playing our mind games. At first it was just a bit of fun, but as time went on it got to the point where we could not have a normal conversation without having it slip into Drama.

I think we both felt bad that we had got to such a point, but we were too afraid to back down because it would be too much like losing, even though I don't like to say that because I hate the 'games' that get played between boys and girls, when the power of unbridled love is a much better thing.

So, although we had a strange relationship, it was built on a foundation of solid rock. Why I fell so suddenly in love with her I have no idea – maybe it was because of the Drama with Craig on that day when he swallowed those pills, or maybe it had happened by degrees across the time that had elapsed since. I don't know. Whatever the reason, it happened and there was nothing I could do about it.

After school, me, Matthew, Jenny and Clare went over to visit Craig. None of them had been to his house before. I thought about warning them how weird his bedroom was but I decided against it because, if I had said it was weird, then I would have been judgemental.

On the way over, Jenny grabbed me.

'Hey,' she said. 'Can we talk?'

'Uh, sure.'

We dropped back.

'So what you and Freddy did to that bird was pretty fucked-up, Rich. I know it was Freddy who, you know, but still . . .'

I suddenly went all emo.

'I know,' I whispered, my throat too heavy for volume. I

didn't want Jenny to hate me. She was a good person, and I didn't want to lose someone like her. She was right, of course. She always was. Freddy had done it, but I had helped.

'Are you OK?'

I nodded.

'Rich?' She put her hand on my arm. 'It's all right, Richie. I was just going to say . . .'

I focused on a red postbox that was fastened to a lamp-post at the end of the street.

'. . . I forgive you.'

I didn't say anything because I didn't feel that I could. My emotions really were starting to fly all over the place. Losing many of my old friends after the Bertie incident was starting to catch up with me, and any sign of warmth towards me, such as that being shown by Jenny, was setting my feelings off like fireworks.

'You've been punished enough, by the other kids and stuff, and I know that it was an accident so I just want to say that it's in the past. I know you're one of the good guys.'

I closed my eyes for a second and opened them again.

'Thanks,' was all I could manage. I loved how American her forgiveness speech was.

We walked a little further, not saying anything, and I slowly regained my composure. Jenny went on ahead to talk to Clare, and Matthew slowed down so that I could catch up.

'I'm going to turn over a new leaf,' I said to him.

'What do you mean?'

'All this stuff with the bird has shown me that I've got to stop being such an asshole.' We often said the word 'asshole' like the Americans because it rubbed off from the kids on the airbase. 'If I'm not careful I'm going to end up like I did before and I really don't want that. To be fair, with this bird thing, I've sort of gotten off lightly.'

'Are you joking?' Matthew said. 'You have to see a counsellor.'

'So? That's better than detention.'

'What if the other kids at school find out?'

I had thought about that before but blocked it out of my mind because it was so horrendous. They would think that I was nuts. Not funny nuts, just regular nuts and that's not good. 'They won't find out. I've only got to do six sessions anyway.'

He sucked in air through his teeth.

'I just hope nobody finds out.'

'Nobody will find out,' I assured him. But I now had a sick feeling in my gut.

It was a shame that Matthew had said that because I felt like I was just coming out from the tunnel.

We got up to Craig's house and I could see everyone having a good look round.

Craig's old man looked at me like I was the devil and that made me feel terrible. Everyone knew about Bertie, but hardly any of them were aware that it was Freddy who was to blame for the actual snapping of the neck. As far as everybody was concerned, Freddy and I were one and the same. It was a shame because I really liked Craig's dad but now he hated me. It was the first time of many that people would look at me with absolute disgust. I'm surprised he even let me in. Let us in.

I sat in the corner of Craig's room and listened to the others telling Craig how much they'd missed him, and how Freddy was gone. Craig just sat on his bed with those glazed eyes of his and looked out the window.

I noticed on his bedside table that there was a fresh cup of tea and I imagined how it had got there. His father had probably shouted up from the bottom of the stairs. 'Craig, darling,' he would have called. 'Your mother and I are having a cup of tea. Would you like one?' There's no way that Craig would have answered, but his father made one anyway. I imagined how he had clambered up the stairs on his old legs and shuffled across the landing before taking the cup to his beloved and tormented son.

Suddenly I was on my feet.

'Craig,' I said. I pointed to the parrot poster on his wall. 'I've got a joke for you. Why is there no aspirin in the jungle?'

Still no response.

I delivered the punchline and nobody laughed, of course, but I felt like I had to try and lighten the mood. This visit was excruciating.

'I like parrots.' The words reverberated around the room. Craig was speaking. 'I like all birds,' he added. Then his head started turning. Towards me. He was looking at me. 'And you killed Bertie.'

Whoa. Of all the things that had happened since Friday – Bertie's murder, the guilt, being caught, facing the head-master, facing my parents, the counsellor – none of them were as bad as that. The worst thing about it was the simplicity and clarity of Craig's thoughts. He liked birds. I killed birds. It was childlike and undeniable in its logic and it nearly knocked me down.

'Craig,' I said, my voice all craggy. 'It was . . . Freddy.'

Suddenly he smiled at me and it was horrible.

'I know, Rich,' he said. 'I really appreciate what you've done for me over the last few weeks.'

This was totally weird. Really totally weird. His eyes were still glazed but he was speaking like he used to, before he had tried to commit suicide. Too friendly. I suddenly had an awful premonition: he was recovering. This, I hate to say, was definitely a bad thing. If he recovered he would turn back to his old weird self that nobody really liked. There was simply

133

no solution to his problem – every road was a dead end.

'So,' said Jenny to break the awkwardness, 'there's a disco on at the base this weekend for Thanksgiving.'

Thanksgiving is an American holiday that I don't quite understand. And I have no intention of learning. The others started talking about going to this disco but I, for some reason, started thinking about Freddy. It suddenly struck me that he had gone. I wondered if he would ever come back. I know I hadn't known him that long, but he had made a massive impression on all of us. I don't think that he would have ever become my best friend or anything like that because he was too crazed, but he was just so interesting. I still wanted to be a part of his great romantic adventure he had told us about on the very first day we met him, where life would be about poetry and love, nothing else. Even after Bertie, I still believed in him.

That night was Toby's birthday and to celebrate we went ten-pin bowling. Because he didn't have any real friends at school, it was just me, him, my mum and my dad.

The atmosphere in the car was frosty. My mother was still ignoring me and my father was driving. Toby was wearing a pair of red corduroy trousers and a bright-yellow shirt, tucked in. I remember looking across at him and thinking absent-mindedly just how tiny his body was beneath his clothes.

We got to the bowling alley and took our rink. I programmed in all of our names and my dad went first. We had to have one of those rinks with rubber tubes down either side because Toby couldn't reach but his face lit up whenever he hit over some pins and he'd come running over to me asking if he had 'done a good bowl'. Good old Tobe.

At one point my mother went to the bar to buy drinks and when she did my father grabbed my arm.

'Get over there and apologize,' he said quietly.

My heart instantly started beating. I didn't want to do this. I was too weak.

'If we're going to get past this,' he said, 'you're going to have to break the stalemate, Rich.'

He was right, of course he was right. I had to be a better person. I took the three low steps in a leap and went into the drinks area. My mother was at the bar, passing four glasses of Sprite on to a tray.

I went straight up to her.

'Mum.'

She turned to me but didn't say anything.

'I'm sorry.'

She slowly placed the last glass on the tray but still didn't say anything.

'You know we didn't plan it, don't you?' I considered adding, 'We were just supposed to kidnap him,' but luckily realized in time just how bad that would sound.

She lifted the tray with both hands.

'I need more time, Richard.' She turned and we went back to the rink. 'But I do appreciate your apology,' she said.

It wasn't going to be that easy, but I didn't really expect it to be. My mother thought that I had killed Bertie and it would take more than a quick apology to make things better. I hoped that I wouldn't let her down. Even though, I think I knew, I would do just that.

Craig wasn't the only thing that changed. It's funny how people can be so fickle, you know? My initial fame after the death of Bertie, after turning slightly sour, was now turning very sour. The 'do-gooder' girls had done a hatchet job on me and I found people giving me funny looks. Some of them actually said things to me but I just ignored them. One boy who I had been sort of friends with said, 'You think that just because you're clever you can do whatever you want, but that's not the way it is.' I was only halfway through my sessions with Sylvia and I had no intention of getting into a fight and having them extended. My secret was still safe for the time being.

Another change that took place was that myself, Matthew, Jenny, Clare and Craig found ourselves hanging around with each other even more than before. Although Clare had initially distanced herself she had now come back, despite the fact that her parents had strictly forbidden my company. You see, there was a reason that we were all hanging around more. Me.

A lot of the kids ostracized me. It upset me at first because I wasn't used to it but I knew that I deserved it. There were a few occasions where there would be a big group of people and I'd go over and everyone would walk off. Moments like that made me feel like crying. But Matthew and Jenny always stayed on my side, no matter what, and as a result, after a while, they became tarred with the same brush. I loved them for what they were doing, but I wished they had kept at arm's length so that they wouldn't be dragged down with me. I was OK anyway. I was strong and determined to be a better person so I knew that I'd get over this temporary blip.

There was also a second bond growing between us, born of the fact that we had been through so much together. Apart from the whole Bertie thing, we had been the ones to help Craig. We had smoked cigarettes at the lake that night. We had played tag in the graveyard. We had been there when Freddy had run away from the headmaster and because of that we stuck together.

I guess, after all of this, what I'm trying to say is this: Yes, I was trying to be good, that's one thing. But the second thing was, and I hate to say this, it . . . wasn't . . . working.

I realize now that we were cutting ourselves off. We must

have looked like a gang of kids who thought they were better than everyone else. Which, and this is where the acid kicks in, we genuinely were becoming. Even though I wanted to be a better person, I really did, the fact of the matter was that, after a while, I started not to care that the other kids in school were trying to mentally bully me because I had my small group of friends. That was all I needed. It's often the case that when you're in the middle of something very harmful, you don't realize it. We were the emo kids who had killed the bird and we thought we were special. We were unapproachable and intimidating. And you know what? I was beginning to like it.

14

It was the evening of the Thanksgiving party at the airbase. My MCR album still hadn't turned up, so I sent Play an email asking them what had happened. I was starting to get fed up with it all, to tell you the truth.

Anyhoo I called for Matthew and we walked to the base. We had agreed to meet Clare, Jenny and Craig there. The airbase is on the outskirts of town. It's surrounded by huge fences and the inside is like a town in itself. On a miniature scale. There are funny little suburban American streets with little white houses, clipped lawns and American flags fluttering from flagpoles in the gardens, all the sort of stuff that you would absolutely expect. There was even a little high street with little shops. We were going to be in the main hall that they have there – I think it's called the mess hall or something.

The night was bitterly cold and I was glad that I was wearing my fashionable new scarf. The gates up ahead were lit up like a piece of heaven had snapped off and landed at the entrance – incredibly bright. A few people were filing in and I wondered how the hell they could call this *security*. Clare was right there with Jenny and Craig. She had on a pair of jeans with a shirt, tie and a cool-looking tank top. Around her wrists were white bandages that made her look like a self-mutilator. Which she wasn't. She looked awesome; the quintessential little MySpace emo girl.

Jenny was dressed in a big winter coat and scarf which made her look tiny. She took us to the security booth where we were issued with passes and we headed in.

Beyond the security gates was a main thoroughfare where all of the shops were. It was a really bizarre place, but I liked it. It was like a microcosm of America right here in my English town. McDonald's, Starbucks, Gap, they were all here with their shiny shop-fronts. To get to the mess hall you had to walk through the residential area.

It was as we were walking past the houses that we heard a shout.

'Hey, Ricardo.' We all turned and looked down the street. It was empty. 'Up here,' came the shout again.

We craned our necks up to the bedroom window of a house to our left. It was Chad, an American kid who lived on the base.

'Come up and have a drink,' he called. 'All of you guys.'

'Aren't you going to the mess hall?'

'Sure,' he called. 'Later. Come on, get your asses up here.' He was such an American meat-head, but I still liked him. He was one of the few kids who were still talking to me after what had happened to Bertie. I could tell that he had a good heart somewhere beneath his muscles and efficient haircut.

Have you ever noticed how American kids seem so much bigger than us Brits? It's always struck me as odd and I put it down to differences in climate affecting our genetic make-up over many generations.

His house looked like something out of the fifties but I won't go into it because that would be pointless. We went up to his room, which was a little more modern, even though he had loads of dumb-bells and that sort of thing to feed his biceps, which he probably called 'guns' non-ironically.

'Sit down,' he said. I suddenly realized he was drunk. His

139

words were slurred and his eyes were a tad off-kilter. Upon closer inspection I saw a half-empty bottle of vodka on his desk sat next to a tube of plastic cups, which he used to pour us drinks.

I took a sip and almost choked with the heat of the vodka.

'I've got to show you guys this,' he said. His arm reached over the side of his bed and he opened the lowest drawer of a chest of drawers. When his hand reappeared I felt a shard of panic in my ribs. Chad was holding a gun. It was one of those quite old-fashioned pistols that have six chambers, you know the type. The metal was dull, dark-grey, and it looked really solid. My initial jolt of fear died away almost immediately and was replaced with curiosity. I had never seen a gun before in real life.

'Jesus,' said Clare, acting like Chad was a stupid little kid.

'Do you know where I got this?' he said, smiling and waving it around. As he washed it through the air, it criss-crossed the line between my eyes and the light bulb so my world was suddenly all light followed by dark shadow.

'Is it loaded?' I said.

'Hell yeah,' he said Americanly, like it was impressive. 'Do you know where I got this little puppy?' he asked again.

'Your mother?' Matthew said quickly.

'Hey, man,' he retorted, looking drunkenly at Matthew. 'What did you say about my mom?' He raised the gun and pointed it at Matthew's face. The atmosphere suddenly changed in the room and I could feel a cold sweat under my clothes. Everybody recoiled, even though Chad was clearly playing around.

'Chad,' said Jenny quickly. 'Put it down.'

'Ha,' he said. 'Whatever,' and he lowered his aim.

I breathed a sigh of relief. Really. You never know, the gun might have gone off of its own accord.

'I found it,' Chad said. 'I found it at the side of the road. Right on the sidewalk.'

'Don't you think you should hand it in?' I said.

He flopped back against his headpost. 'Nope. I think I'll hang on to it.' He took a swig from his drink.

'So if you found it on the base, how come there are no signs up saying that it's gone missing?' Jenny, being a resident of the airbase, was clearly talking about some sort of protocol that came into operation if a weapon was lost.

But Chad just shrugged. 'Like I give a fuck.'

'Can I hold it?' It was the first thing that Craig had said all night. I didn't think that giving a loaded pistol to a boy with clear mental problems was a good idea but it was in his hand before any of us could say anything. Now the room started to descend into panic again. It was a calm panic, just like what I imagine a plane crash to be like – nothing hysterical, just silent dread.

Craig was fingering the barrel of the small pistol.

'It's heavy,' he said hollowly. And then he pointed the pistol at me, held it square at my heart. 'Bang,' he said calmly.

I've got to say it, I had never felt anything like this before. I had a loaded gun pointed at my chest and my terror was turning loops in my stomach. I was getting the feeling that Craig really hated me. I guess he still blamed me for Bertie. His face, even though he was talking, had that indifferent glazed look of his. Everybody was silent. And then Craig did something that made my bones tighten. Slowly, purposefully, he lifted his thumb into the air and released the safety clip.

'Shit, Craig,' I said.

'Craig, baby, put it down,' Clare said. I'm sure she said it patronizingly so that he would be antagonized and shoot me. She was cunning like that. I kept my eyes on his trigger finger so that I could at least *try* to get out of the way of the bullet should it happen to get fired out of the gun.

'I'm not putting the gun down,' he said, neither calmly nor maniacally. 'Why shouldn't I shoot him?'

I hated the way he was talking about me like I wasn't in the room. He had probably forgotten that I was a person in his crazy brain.

'I could shoot him in the face,' he said.

That chilled me. The seconds dragged on like a shovel being scraped along concrete. I found myself physically unable to speak. My guts were loosening and I started to feel tired. I always feel tired when I'm in dire trouble. I'm just glad I didn't feel like crying.

'Craig,' said Matthew. 'Craig, please put it down. Stop messing around.'

He cocked his neck so that his right eye was aligned directly over the barrel of the gun. He was looking straight at me. I could feel the light bouncing off me and burning into his retina.

'Chad. Do something!' Jenny shouted.

It must have jolted something in Craig's brain because he suddenly brought the gun down and tossed it on to the bed. Nobody grabbed it and nobody said anything. I think we were all too stunned. Eventually Chad leaned over and took it in his hands, put it back in his drawer.

I didn't feel suddenly relaxed, I felt angry. Extremely angry. In fact, I was shaking and I sort of lost control, which I don't do very often. I was on my feet and on Craig in a second. I didn't punch him in the face or anything, but I pushed him up against the wall and started screaming at him.

'What the fuck are you doing, you fucking idiot!'

His face went blank like it always does and that made me even more angry.

'Don't you go inside your shell, you stupid bastard.' I

wasn't being too harsh – this boy had just threatened to murder me, for crying out loud.

Matthew and Chad pulled me off and the girls took Craig away.

I was kept in Chad's room for a few minutes so that the others could get to the mess hall without me going nuts again and trying to kill Craig.

'What the hell was he doing?' I said to Matthew.

'You know, he's . . . mental.'

I shook my head. I was feeling a little calmer now as common sense returned.

'I know, I know. Christ, did I go over the top?'

He didn't say anything but I suddenly felt a separation between us. Usually, Matthew would tell me exactly what he thought. But he wasn't doing that. I felt like he was holding something back that he would have normally said. I wondered if the murder of that stupid bird had left a deeper impression than he had let on. A terrible feeling was creeping into my gut. Was Matthew *afraid* of me? I could hardly blame him, given my past and how the old Richard seemed to be resurfacing. But I couldn't stand that thought so I stopped thinking about it.

'Come on,' I said. 'Let's go.'

'You're not going to do anything to Craig, are you?'

I breathed out. 'I suppose I should apologize to him.'

I felt like there was a great burden on my shoulders. No matter what I tried to do, things were thrown back in my face. I had tried to help Craig. After he had tried to kill himself it was me who had called for him to make sure he was OK, who looked after him, who brought him into our own little group. So why was it me he pointed the gun at? Was he really so upset about Bertie? Or was there something else?

An unbearable soul-cracking splinter shot through me with an idea: did Craig know the real me? People say that mental illness can give you an extraordinary insight. Did he know that deep down I was a really bad person? Evil. I was almost crying with how unfair this was. I didn't want to be evil. I wanted to be a good boy, but life was determined to stop me becoming that.

Inside the hall the noise was deafening. The roof was nothing but metal and the sound was crashing off it like cymbals. There was a line of disco lights that flashed around the room like spectres. The hall was full of people. Most of the adult men were All-American Heroes with steely haircuts. Most of the women were their wives. But the kids were a fair mix from all three of the town's demographics: Americans, locals, boarders. There were lots of little kids running around as well but I liked that because family values should be admired. And I love kids. I like to play stupid games like Cowboys and Indians with them.

'Here,' a voice whispered in my ear. It was Clare. Her face looked like an alien because the disco lights were shining all over it green, red, yellow. She was offering me a cup.

'What is it?'

'Just drink it.'

I took a sip, keeping my eyes on her. I think it was whisky and Coke because it really burned my throat. Whatever it was, it was very strong.

'I'm sorry for going so mental on Craig,' I said.

Clare smiled at me and then did something amazing. She kissed me on the cheek. 'You're so sweet.'

I had to bite my lip in case I broke down. Why was I apologizing for having a gun pointed at me? More importantly, why the hell was I feeling so emotional?

'Do you hate me?' I said to Clare.

'Rich, why do you say things like that? Why are you so sure you're evil?'

I frowned at her. 'What?'

'He pointed a gun at you. He's a twat.'

I smiled. 'You're right,' I sighed.

'We all know it. Jenny doesn't hate you either. We know Craig was wrong but, you know, we have to look after him.'

She was right. We did have to look after Craig. If we didn't then who would?

Clare left me and I finished my drink. My head started spinning. I looked into my empty cup, at the droplets of brown Coke running down the white inside. The drink was so strong. I placed the cup carefully down on a table near by and headed shakily outside for some fresh air.

The air was cool and refreshing, the clouds low and threatening rain. The wind was up and it felt like the whole atmosphere was writhing with life, like it was desperate to, I don't know, *do* something. Like it was restless. Just like me. It was probably because I was drunk, but I felt I had come to a point where something had to change. I either had to let myself go and embrace the person I really was, or decide once and for all that I was going to be a good person.

I was sitting on a crate, looking down at my Converse trainers, when the universe made the decision for me.

'Richard?' said a voice.

There he was, standing before me, the wind blowing his hair wildly and romantically, a scarf tied tight around his neck.

'Freddy? You're back?'

He looked sad, looked like how I felt.

'I guess so. I got back this afternoon. How have things been since . . . you know?'

I wanted to tell him that everything was OK, but I didn't have the heart to lie to him.

'Not so great. I mean, pretty much everyone's cut me off, apart from Matthew and Jenny and Clare.' I shrugged.

'What about Craig? How's he?'

I didn't want to go into the whole gun thing.

'He's OK. The usual.'

Freddy nodded and we looked at one another. For a long time.

'Rich, about Bertie,' he said at last.

I thrust my hands into my pockets and looked at the floor.

'I don't know why I did it. It wasn't an accident. I killed him deliberately.'

The wind blasted across the tarmacked ground, picking up some of the plastic cups, rattling them against the wall.

'Why?'

'Because . . . I don't know.' He was on the verge of tears. 'All my life I've just—' He stopped himself.

There was a brief pause, during which we shared our whole worlds. I felt in him what he felt in me, this sense of . . . doom.

'It's OK, Freddy.'

He had turned his head to one side, looking out across the sparse base towards a patch of grass on which sat an old Second World War fighter jet. A powerful floodlight under its fuselage lit up the plane brightly so it stood out in stark relief against the flat terrain, a circle of bright-green grass around its base.

'It's not OK.'

'Yes it is. It's in the past.'

He looked at me. 'You don't understand.'

I adjusted myself on my crate to make room for him to sit down. We both sat there for a while in silence.

'I do understand,' I said at last. 'I've done some bad things

146

as well. After my parents split up I . . .' I composed myself. I had never told anybody this story before. Saying it out loud just reminded me of what sort of a person I was. When it was in my head I could lock it away. I felt Freddy's body warmth next to me. 'We're not different,' I said. 'We're the same.'

'What did you do?'

An image of Mrs Kenna, my history teacher, suddenly flashed in my head. She was alone now that her husband and son had died so she was almost certainly asleep by now. Tucked up in her old bed with old sheets, sleeping her life away.

I pulled my knees up together and rested my forehead on them. I wanted to tell him. He was feeling sick because of what he had done in the exact same way that I had, all those months ago. I knew what he was going through. I knew the cramps in his stomach. I knew the searing flushes in his face. I knew the dark, terrible flashes in his brain that made his heart pound. It was just something bad that he had done. A moment of insanity. All he wanted was for someone to say that it was in the past and that one day his soul would be wiped clean. That was all he wanted, for another human to tell him it would be OK. That was all. So I told him all about the old man and the metal pipe.

15

'You know the corridor at the far end of the mess hall?' he said.

'Yeah.'

'There's a room on the right. Can you get the others and meet me in there?'

'What for?'

He shrugged and stood up from the crate. 'I want it to be just us.'

This was the first time we had all been together since Freddy had jumped out of the headmaster's window. A lot had happened since then. The world had attacked us but we were still standing. Having Freddy back only served to tighten the rope we had slung around ourselves.

Seeing him again gave everything a sense of completion; everything was back to the way it should be. We had been knocked out of orbit but now we were back. He had lit four candles that were now stood in holders. Ordinarily I would have said that such a setting was overdramatic, even for us, but on that night it didn't feel so. There was a kind of increased gravity in the room; a weight. Shadows cut across our faces as we sat down in the chairs we had found.

There was a big window on the far wall and the first drops of rain were clicking against it. The wind rattled its frame.

Freddy had brought with him a bottle of Smirnoff Blue, which he shared with all of us, handing it around for us to swig from.

Sat in a circle, feeling slightly drunk, I noticed that Matthew and Jenny's little fingers were touching sweetly. Now, that image of young love burns like acid across the rivulets of my brain.

'I'm so sorry about Bertie,' Freddy said. The sound of music coming from the mess hall could be heard only as a low, dense beat coming through the walls. 'I didn't want to ruin everything. My first night here, the night we went to the lake, it was . . . you know. And now it's spoilt.'

'Stop,' said Matthew.

Freddy looked up, his concentration knocked.

'All I hear about is that stupid bird. We killed it. It was an accident. The end. It's over.'

'Nothing's spoilt, Freddy,' Jenny said gently.

Freddy looked around the room, at each of us.

'I want us to do something. Together. I've been thinking a lot about what happened at Halloween. And, you know, how the headmaster reacted. Actually' – he paused – 'I've been thinking about stuff like this for longer than just a few weeks.' His voice was flat.

We listened intently.

'You know how people get treated if they do something that people don't agree with? I don't mean the bird thing, I mean other things as well. Like whenever I do something good and other kids just put me down because they're jealous.' I guessed he was talking about his old school. Although I did know what he meant. Whenever I did something amazing like one of my stories for English, I was almost ashamed of it because of the way the kids looked at me. 'I hate all that crap,' he said. He started gesturing towards the mess hall, to the party. 'And I hate all that stuff too.'

I was shocked to hear Freddy say this. It was the first time he had been openly angry about something.

'All those people in there patting each other on the back because none of them have amounted to anything and they're glad that they've all stuck together.' He stopped. 'Have you ever noticed how there's something not quite right with the world – like it's not quite what it should be?'

I knew. I knew exactly.

'I could never tell what it was. But I think I've worked it out. And you know what? It's people's attitudes towards people like us. The fact is, we're talented. But whenever we do something good, people always congratulate us and say how great we are but then they always have to wreck it by turning serious and saying something like, "But you must keep your feet on the ground." Why?' His voice was still as calm as a lake. The words were powerful, but the delivery was soft. 'Why should I keep my feet on the ground when I'm trying to get to the stars? All my life I've had it and I know it sounds bitter, but I believe it's because they're jealous. They don't want us to be all we can be because *we're* living *their* dreams. I hate it.'

I recoiled at his suggestion because it was such a cliché. But do you know something about clichés? They only get there because they're true. Right?

'They're angry with us because we killed Bertie, Freddy,' I said calmly.

'I know that. This has nothing to do with Bertie. If they're upset about him being dead, they should try going inside my brain for a while. I fucking killed him – I can hardly even eat any more.'

Clare had the bottle of vodka now. I watched her as she drank. As she moved her neck back the shadows and light shifted on her face and my heart palpitated. I looked back to Freddy. This night was quickly turning into one of the weirdest of my life. First I had almost been shot, now this.

He took the vodka from Clare and brought it to his mouth. When he moved the bottle away, his lips glistened in the orange light.

'The world is run *by* the mediocre *for* the mediocre.' He went into the inside pocket of his blazer and took out a packet of cigarettes. He threw one to each of us and lit his own. I don't really like smoking but it felt right to take one.

Matthew gave his back.

'Thanks, but I don't feel like one,' he said. My respect for him soared and I felt jealous. Matthew was turning into a man. He had his girlfriend and he had a healthy lifestyle. He would be Great and leave me behind. I knew it but I was prepared to let him go because, deep down, I loved him. Not in a gay way, you understand.

'Think about it,' said Freddy, his voice still not quickening at all. 'None of the world's geniuses fit in, do they?'

'But we're not geniuses,' I said, my head whirling from the vodka.

Freddy looked at me.

'What I mean is we're in all the best classes of one of the best schools, and we're near the top of those classes. Even Matty.'

I smiled. Matthew gave an arrogant purse of the lips. It was true what Freddy was saying. We were the most intelligent kids in the school, though I don't really like to mention it.

'And what are we? Everyone hates us. They probably always have, but they haven't shown it because we've always been nice to them.' He took a drag from his cigarette. I suddenly noticed how long his fingers were. 'But now that we've killed the bird they think that they've been proved right about us. They think we're actually *evil*. Us. We're the good guys. We can't really get on with other people. We can talk to them, but not as equals. I know how terrible this sounds, but it is a fact that we're *better* than the rest of them. We really are. Not because we're more intelligent, or funnier, or better-looking. That doesn't matter. It's because we're *nicer* than them. All they do is try to drag us down. We don't go around being horrible to people, getting our kicks at the expense of others. We love, absolutely love, life. They just exist, we live. And they don't like that. These people don't go to graveyards to play tag, you know?'

'What are you saying, Freddy?' Matthew asked. He seemed to be caught in Freddy's words.

As, I hate to admit, was I. Ever since Bertie things had changed. I'm not sure if I *actually* believed what Freddy was saying or if I just *wanted* to believe. I felt that if I believed it meant that I was part of something special, that my life had some sort of meaning.

'I'm saying that we don't stand a chance in life. The whole world is totally cynical and we still have the innocence of children because we're . . . incorruptible. The whole world is mediocre, and we're exceptional. We want to excel and make the world a better place. The rest, just because they can't, want to hold us back and rubbish our ideals as naive and childish. We could change the world, but *they* won't let us. They won't even listen to us. Every *normal* person resents us. We've got no chance. Whatever we try to do in life, we'll be held back by other people's mediocrity, cynicism, stupidity and envy.'

There was a resounding silence after these words. I don't think I had ever heard anyone speak like this before, so flowingly, like the exact kernel of what was in their brain was being perfectly articulated through words. Whenever I try to say what I mean, it always comes out with only half of the meaning because I can never express what I'm trying to say. But that wasn't the case for Freddy. He knew exactly how to say what he meant.

His words hit home hard. I did feel like others were holding me back, telling me that my ideas and opinions didn't matter, that I was no good. Like the time my short story about the artist who cut his eyes out was taken away from me by the headmaster. I was choked by what Freddy had said.

And more than that, he looked insanely cool in the candlelight. He delved back into his inside pocket and took from it six cream-coloured envelopes. They had been sealed with red wax and each one bore the name of one of us. They were handed around and, as I took mine, I noticed the texture and quality of it. It was sublime. A new wave of curiosity got up in me. I knew by this time, as did everybody else, that this moment of our lives was seminal. A line was being crossed. For me, I knew that these friends would last for ever. I didn't care about my other friends who had ditched me because this group of people, with candlelight on their faces, were *special*.

We opened our letters and, as we did so, Freddy spoke again.

'I think we should all enter a pact,' he said.

I now held the sheet of paper gently between the second and third fingers of each hand. It hung in the air and glowed in the light. I could feel that golden bond-rope wrap itself around our souls and scream out of the ether between us; linking us, binding us, encasing us, imprisoning us to each other for ever.

'I think we should stay together for eternity,' he said, his emotions starting to creep into his throat. 'We can show our solidarity. The world can stop in space and we'll all get off. We can show everybody that we won't take it any more. We can stop them from holding us, and everyone like us, back.'

I started to unfold the paper and looked at Clare one more time. She looked at me and nodded, smiling. She looked so, so, so sweet I can't even handle thinking about it.

'What I propose is the founding of a club,' Freddy said. 'A club that the whole world will know about, but which it can never join.'

His words were so lucid they flowed over me like syrup. All of the others were now staring at their sheets of paper like they were in a trance. I took my friends in, one by one, a turn of the head for each of them. Their faces flickered in the candlelight, each in their own little world. My head spun a little with the vodka and nicotine. I forgot that I was holding the lit cigarette in my left hand and, as I looked at its sulphuric embers and at the smoke washing up, out, twirling, spinning, pirouetting into the sky with the cryptic symbolism that I would never *know* but would always *feel*, I looked upon the opening line of Freddy's paper: *The Official Charter of the Suicide Club*.

<u>The Official Charter of the Suicide Club</u>

We, the founder members of the Suicide Club,

   (i)   understanding our exceptional nature,
   (ii)   understanding the non-exceptional average of the
          masses,
   (iii) understanding that the world is run by the mediocre
          for the mediocre,
   (iv)   understanding the will of the masses to bring good
          people down to their level,
   (v)   understanding the ideals of drama and romanticism,
   (vi)   understanding that words are non-effective,
   (vii) understanding and holding dear the brilliance and pure
          joy of life,

hereby state that in order to effectively articulate our
thoughts we must end that which we hold most dear.

For you, we have this message: All we wanted was to keep our
dreams. That was all. We didn't want to hurt anybody, we
didn't want to hate anybody. We wanted to be left alone. All
we wanted was to stick together, the lost and the gentle.

But it is not possible. We see that now. The exceptional are
to be crushed. We didn't understand this and thought that
perhaps our lights could shine forever. But you will not allow
it because you take your hate and your envy, and you throw it
into us. Well it found its mark. We do not want our souls
crushed and hardened into shapes that we do not know. This is
your fault.

We are exceptional not because of what we have achieved; we
are exceptional because we are not... like... you.

We take our lives from the world because we love them too much
to simply hand them over to you and yours. From the bottom of
our lungs to the top of the mountains we scream. You drove us
to this. That is all. This is a pact.

Signed,

Frederick Spaulding-Carter

Frederick Spaulding-Carter

Clare Forster

Clare Forster

Jenny Hannon.

Jenny Hannon

M. Grange

Matthew Grange

Richard Harper

Richard Harper

Craig Bartlett-Taylor

Craig Bartlett-Taylor

16

Let me just get something straight. When I signed the Charter, I had no intention whatsoever of killing myself. I don't think any of us did. Not even Craig with his history of mental illness. You see, we all knew that killing yourself has more than one victim – it rips entire families apart. We even had a good laugh about how bitter Freddy sounded in his writing. But in the candlelight, with vodka in our throats, we each took Freddy's pen and scribbled our signatures above our typed-out names on each other's sheets of cream paper.

A lot of people have asked me since whether or not I thought Freddy actually expected us to kill ourselves when he wrote the Charter and I can only answer the question honestly: I don't know. I've thought about it loads but I just can't come up with an answer. I don't know what he was thinking.

The following Monday was my final counselling session before Christmas with the dreadful Sylvia Bowler. Our last few sessions had descended into ridiculousness because I couldn't take her seriously. We had a healthy dislike for each other. As far as I was concerned, the only good thing to have come from these sessions was that nobody in school had actually found out about them.

However, when I went to see Sylvia on that day my mouth almost dropped to the floor. Instead of Sylvia, sat at the head of that big meeting table was a vision of sheer perfection. There was a woman, or maybe she was girl, of about twenty. I could try to describe her but I don't want to sound clichéd by saying that she had olive skin and perfect features, so I won't. But that was what she looked like. She was amazing. One thing was for certain: I would not want to beat this woman up like I sometimes wanted to do to Sylvia the fat old hag (I'm showing off – I would *never* hit a woman).

'Hello,' she said. She got up from her chair and went over to the unit at the side of the room where a coffee pot had been added. She poured herself a cup and I saw that her body was amazing as well, and I would not usually say something sexist like that so it must have been excellent.

'Hi,' I said. 'Uh, where's Sylvia?'

'Sylvia's gone.' She didn't say it mysteriously. Her voice was beautiful and I *never* use that word because it's become so passé.

'Gone where?' I sat down.

'Would you like some coffee?'

'Yes please,' I answered.

'Sylvia told me your parents don't like you drinking coffee.'

'Yeah.' I paused, looked at her. 'I didn't really like Sylvia. She was a know-all.'

The new girl went back to her seat.

'I guess there's not much point talking in depth,' she said. 'You'll be breaking up for the holidays soon so we can start properly next term, if that's OK with you.'

I was pleased that I was in my last session before Christmas but I was also looking forward to my next one in the new year if it meant that this woman would be my counsellor.

'What's your name?' I asked.

'Emma.'

I liked the way she wasn't too friendly with me. No doubt

Sylvia had had a part in that. I used to ridicule her intelligence by researching a psychological trait the day before a session and then pretending to have that thing wrong with me, getting Sylvia to think that she knew what was going on in my head. But then I would explain to her my game. She hated it, I could tell.

'My mother's name is Emma,' I beamed.

'Really?'

'No.'

She laughed. I didn't expect her to laugh because she was an adult and I was still, basically, a child, and adults and children don't operate on the same level because of the idea of respect, you know? Telling jokes like that might have come across as precocious.

'Can I ask you a question?'

'Of course you can.' She still wasn't friendly.

'Sylvia once gave me an orange ball and told me to "peel the orange". What does that mean?'

Emma smiled. Her whole face changed when she smiled. She was radiant.

'Why don't you look it up? I hear you're into that.'

Now it was my turn to smile.

'Do you think I'm going to ask you about your qualifications?' I was sort of seeing how far I could push her. I was flirting with her and must have looked like a complete idiot.

'Maybe.' I never did find out how many A levels she had, but I knew by the very fact that she refused to answer my question that she had done well and gone to a good university. 'Now let me ask you a question,' she said.

I sat there and listened.

'Do you feel that you've got anything out of your sessions with Sylvia?'

I sighed.

'No,' I said honestly.

'You don't go in for us social workers then?'

'Don't say that word.'

'Social workers?'

'It's so meaningless. You must know that.'

She just smiled.

'You know what, Rich? You might find this hard to believe but there are good people in the world who genuinely want to help. I have chosen this career to try and put kids back on the right track. Do you think there's something wrong with that?'

'I'm not disaffected,' I said right out. 'I know that there are good people in the world. My all-time hero is Bob Geldof. What he has done is mind-blowing. But for every good person, there's a know-all like Sylvia. There's a difference between the two. She's not a good person. She's a busybody.'

'Tell me what you want to do with your life.'

'I want to make cartoons,' I said. I had never told an adult this in my life, not even my parents, mainly because I knew how far-fetched it sounded. Only a handful of my friends knew what I wanted to do. When people asked me, I would say that I wanted to be a vet. But here I was blurting it out.

'Cartoons?'

'Yeah. Kids' cartoons. I want to write the scripts. I can't really draw very well, but I can come up with ideas and stuff.' I felt like I was unshackling chains from around my chest as I spoke. 'And I mean cartoons for kids, not ironical things that can be enjoyed on "two levels", I mean cartoons *for* kids.' I paused. 'I want to make a cartoon that parents and kids can enjoy together on *one* level, you know? I want it to be completely innocent.'

She seemed impressed by what I had said because I could feel her warm to me.

'Have you got any ideas?'

'I have but I don't like talking about them.'

159

'You can tell me.'

'No,' I said. 'I'm not embarrassed – I just haven't fully formulated what's in my head. If I told you about my ideas, they would sound terrible because they're all over the place. When I write everything down in an order, I'll be able to tell you.'

'I look forward to that.'

I paused and leaned forward on to the table. I had to tell her something important. And when I said it, I *meant* it.

'Emma. I didn't mean for any harm to come to the falcon.' An image of Freddy flashed in my head, his face all aglow in candlelight. He was signing the Suicide Club Charter. Whoa! That felt . . . sinister.

Emma was smiling at me.

'I think I know that,' she said.

17

I left the counselling room feeling a little better. At lunch, I sat with Freddy and Matthew. Freddy, I remember it well, was eating a plate of salad and fish. He was probably the only boy in the school who wasn't gay and ate salad.

'So,' I said. 'The Suicide Club.'

Freddy pushed a lettuce leaf into his mouth, kept looking at the table, and nodded.

We sat in silence as he ate. When he finished he picked up his glass of apple juice and took a swig.

'Yup,' he said.

At the doors to the dinner hall I saw Clare waft in with some of her old friends. She had her fringe clipped up above her head with a clip that had a butterfly on it.

'Jesus, why does she still hang around with those?' said Matthew bitterly.

Freddy and I stopped chewing.

'Did those words just come out of your mouth?' I said.

'They're so vacuous.'

'Whoa, Matthew,' I said. 'Easy.' I was shocked.

'What? They are,' he protested unapologetically.

I agreed with him, I hated Clare's friends, but it was still unexpected coming from Matthew.

'Yeah, but . . . don't be so bitter.'

'I'm not being bitter,' he laughed. 'They're a bunch of dicks.'

161

'They're OK,' said Freddy, popping a piece of tomato into his mouth.

'This coming from you,' Matthew snorted. 'The founding forefather of the Suicide Club. The hater of mediocrity.'

'I don't hate mediocrity,' answered Freddy. 'The masses might be deluded, but so what? They've still got to live. They've got to go to their jobs.'

We all laughed cynically, which was unlike us. This whole conversation was unlike us. We were supposed to be nice kids, not these monsters sat at the lunch table. But there we were.

By this time, Clare had her lunch on a tray and was paying for her meal. Her friends were chattering about something or other and cackling. You know how girls kind of like, scream when they laugh, well, that's what they were doing.

They all filed past us and everything went silent. I looked at Matthew and Freddy, who were quietly eating their meals. I shook my head. Clare and her friends chose a table three away from ours and sat down.

Just then my mobile phone buzzed in my pocket. I took it out. It was a message from Clare: *Come over to my house tonight. I have a present for you.* I looked across at her. Her phone was on the table next to her plate. I half expected her to look over and smile but she didn't. She was holding her drink in her left hand, her straw resting gently on her lower lip, as she listened to one of her friends say whatever it was she was saying. She knew that I was looking at her.

When the school bell rang at the end of the day, I practically ran home. I needed to get ready to go over to Clare's. She told me that her parents had finally lifted the ban on seeing me and so I was allowed back. I hadn't even known I'd been banned in the first place. I decided that I'd go over at about seven. Not because it was too early to look keen, or too late to look as though I was deliberately being late because I was 'cool', but because that was the time I wanted to go over. I didn't feel like playing games.

I went online for a while and spoke to Matthew. He started slagging off one of our old friends. The way in which this stalwart of humanity was loosening made me feel bad. He was still a great guy, don't get me wrong, but he was definitely on the turn. His parents were still moaning about him because they thought he went out too much. They had even told him that they were *concerned* and *disappointed*, the two words used by these stupid modern parents who don't think it's right to give their kids a quick slap. Not that you should smack a fifteen-year-old. In fact, I don't even know what I'm talking about any more.

At about six o'clock I had a visitor. It was Toby. My mum had told him to call up to me to tell me that dinner was ready, but Toby was far too much of a gentleman to shout across the house. Instead he took it upon himself to climb up the stairs, which took him about twice as long as most people because he was short with short legs. He then knocked on my door.

'What?' I called.

Nothing. *Knock, knock, knock.*

'What?!'

Still nothing. I had to get off my bed to open the door. I then did my little joke where I look around and don't notice him because of his height and went to close the door.

'Don't be such a silly,' he said.

'Jesus Christ, Toby. What the hell are you doing saying things like that? Do you know how stupid you sound?'

'What do you mean?' And he looked at me with his clear eyes.

'What are you trying to do? Make my heart bleed? It's made of stone, my friend.'

I grabbed him under the arms and hoisted him into the air. He was giggling like a little girl as I spun him around on the landing outside my room.

'Put me down,' he laughed.

So I did.

'Listen, Tobe,' I said. 'You're special. Do you realize that? Because you've got innocence.' I paused. 'How about this for a plan?' I looked at him with his curly blond hair. 'How about a trip into the city?'

His face lit up. I could see happiness shooting out of his flesh like the stardust that came out of the Big Bang and made everything.

'Really?'

'Sure. I'll be breaking up for Christmas soon. We'll go on the first day of the holidays. But only on one condition.'

'What?'

'Two conditions, actually.' I crouched down so that I was at his height. 'One. You don't wear a tie.'

He agreed.

'And two. You have to give me the picture you drew. The one with the people skating on the iced-over lake. Deal?'

I knew how happy he was because my stomach was buzzing away like a power station. He ran to his room, came back, and thrust the drawing in my face. I took the picture, which was really excellent, and told him to tell Mum that I couldn't eat dinner because I was going to visit Clare and that I'd grab something on my way.

Clare is rich. Not rich like my family, I mean *filthy* rich. That's probably why she's so into Nirvana. Her house is this mansion with white pillars spilling into sky and those windows that come out of the roof.

I knocked on the door and was shown into the hall by her disapproving father, who was something to do with heavy industry. I think he was like, an oil baron, something to do with the petrol trade, I think. Whatever he did, he earned enough money to cover his hall floor in disgusting marble. It was opulent and hideous. He was not a man of style. Nor was her mother, who chose to drive around in, can you believe it, a banana-yellow Porsche of all the dreadful things.

Clare stood at the top of the spiralling staircase that I swear existed, and smiled at me. She looked great. She had on a pair of baggy jeans with a pink studded belt and a pink T-shirt that she had made herself. On the front she had sewn little black letters. You know those French Connection T-shirts that read:

$$f \quad c \quad u \quad k?$$

Well, Clare had sewn:

$$f \quad u \quad c \quad k$$

She was a very clever girl. She was so lovely there in the surroundings of her parents' mansion that she so abhorred. Her wrists were covered with Stars and Stripes sweatbands.

'Come up to my room,' she said. As she turned around I couldn't help but notice her pink underwear climbing over the top of her belt.

Let me describe her bedroom. It's about forty feet from one end to the next and she's got a sofa at the far end with a massive plasma TV and DVD player with surround sound. I first saw *The Matrix* on that TV. Her bed is a double bed and is pink. Most of her room is pink or purple. It's like the bedroom of a teenage girl who could have it the exact way she wanted. Being a designer-type she had already decorated for Christmas. All of the overhead lights were switched off and the illumination was coming solely from hundreds of coloured fairy lights that she had strung up all around the walls.

I went over to the sofa and slumped into it. Matthew popped into my head.

'Do you worry about what's happening to us?' I said.

'What do you mean?'

'I mean . . . this whole Suicide Club thing. I sometimes think it's a bit too intense. I feel like it's frying our minds.'

She came and sat on the sofa next to me, but not too close.

'Frying our minds?'

'I just think we're becoming cynical.'

'Speak for yourself. I haven't even got a clue what you're talking about. So how am I cynical?'

'When was the last time you went down to the homeless shelter?' Clare used to visit the homeless people every couple of weeks, either helping out in the kitchen or repairing their clothes. She didn't particularly enjoy it, but it was the right thing to do. One of the guys there had once tried it on with her, but she still carried on going.

She flipped her hair in front of her eyes, grabbed a handful and inspected it.

'I'm not allowed to go down there any more.'

'What?' I said. 'What do you mean?'

'Since all that stuff with Bertie, my parents have stopped me going down there.'

'Your parents have stopped you going down there?'

She shrugged like she didn't care. But she did. I knew she did.

A thought suddenly struck me. Clare's parents had stopped homeless people having nice food and having the rips in their clothing sewn up in order to punish their daughter. But what about the homeless people? I was genuinely bewildered – surely her parents weren't that stupid.

'So now who's cynical?' she said.

I think a bond came up for a second but it wasn't full-blown. Not yet.

166

'Anyway,' she said. 'I've got you a present.' She jumped up from the sofa and danced over to the side of her bed. She picked up a wrapped package and brought it to me. It had a red bow tied around the centre.

'What is it?'

'It's a new car,' she referenced.

It was clearly an item of clothing. I tore the paper away.

'I made it myself,' she said.

I held it up to the light. It was a white T-shirt and, when I saw it, there was a catch in my throat. She was such a loving person. When she wasn't being a bitch. Up the shoulders of the T-shirt she had sewn on epaulettes. Stitched into the cloth, alternating colours all the way up, were yellow and black stripes. It was exceptionally cool-looking. And sewn across the chest, in the exact same way that she had sewn *f u c k* into her own T-shirt, she had sewn, again in alternating black and yellow:

t h e   b e e s   k n e e s.

I didn't know what to say. So I said nothing and looked at her.

'It says "the bees knees",' she offered.

I felt like we were young lovers untainted by experience. We were nervous and excited and like two pieces of substance on the quantum level – all crazy and vibrating. I wanted to tell her how much I loved her. But I couldn't do it. I just wasn't ready.

'I love it,' I said. 'I really love it.'

I stood up and pulled my sweater and T-shirt off so that I could try it on. It fitted perfectly. She knew my size and had made it slightly too small because that's always the best way.

'So you love it?'

I could see on her face that she was beaming inside and that made me feel so good, knowing that she was happy.

The rest of the evening we spent lying on her sofa watching TV. She had her head on my chest and I played with her hair, just like the old days. We talked sporadically about nothing in particular apart from the book *1984*, which, coincidentally, we were both reading at that time. I can't remember exactly what we said but I think we spoke about how the main guy and the main girl had the best relationship ever. It was just like our Eskimo Friends team that we had set up – nobody knew about it. There were a lot of great things about that night: the closeness of it, the sheer joy of being alive, the sense of intense easiness. But the best thing about it by a long, long way was the texture of her skin when we joined our hands and made steeples.

Many times I wanted to tell Clare how I had been feeling about her lately but every time I thought I was close I couldn't quite find the courage. I was, in truth, a little scared. I liked her but I had no idea whether or not she felt the same about me. With all of the rules and tricks and games we had set up over the years I felt like I had just entered a minefield. What I considered a signal could just as easily be a joke. I was sure that she liked me but just how much was anybody's guess. I had a WCS where I told her I loved her and she started laughing and saying, 'Oh my God, just wait until I tell my friends what you just said.' I was going to have to tell her eventually but not having any idea whatsoever of what the reaction might be was not good. You see, it wasn't like asking out somebody I hardly knew. Clare wasn't just another girl. If I messed it up I could lose the special bond we had, and I didn't want to do that. In fact, the thought of it, coupled with my WCS, started to freak me out a little bit.

'OK, I have to go,' I said at last.

She lifted her head off my chest.

'What?'

'Yeah, I've got homework.'

She shook her head as if she didn't understand.

'Homework?' For some reason she was upset. 'Are you serious?'

'Um, yes.'

All of a sudden she jumped up off the sofa.

'You are a fucking dick,' she said.

It was like the scene in my bedroom all over again.

'What? I have to go home,' I said, drawing the words out like I was talking to a slow child. I hated the way I had to destroy perfect moments.

'I made you a T-shirt.' Her voice was warbly and I could see her chest going up and down.

I didn't know what to say. I froze.

Clare looked at me very deeply indeed.

'My friends were right about you.'

When she said that another WCS burned into my brain. A bad one.

'Wh . . . what?'

She rolled her eyes.

'God.' She folded her arms and her eyes went up to the ceiling. 'Just go.'

What had she meant? The idea of Clare talking about me behind my back didn't bear thinking about. The WCS got bigger and bigger and bigger. 'So I'll see you tomorrow?' I said.

She deliberately looked at the wall to her left, dramatically ignoring me.

I walked past her, said, 'Thanks for the T-shirt,' and started to feel sick because of how much I had fucked everything up.

18

'Do you know what? If we did go ahead with the Suicide Club, I bet there'd be a special place for us in heaven where we could spend all our time together. I can just imagine it. You get to heaven and it's all in the clouds and most people go through the main gates, but we'd find a way of skipping the queue because, just round the side of heaven, there's this porthole of cloud that leads to a secret chamber where it would be just us. Heaven would be just on the other side, but before we went there we'd wait for each other.'

We were all sat around the war memorial when Freddy said that. This was what he did best: painted pictures. He'd build up these little worlds in his head that you could totally buy into. That was his talent.

I looked at all of my friends. Jenny, her nose red in the cold, had a faint smile on her lips and I noticed that she was wearing mittens on her hands. Matthew could have kissed her sweetly on the cheek and it would have been perfectly natural. Craig was sat on the bottom step next to Clare, looking blankly ahead as per usual, but we all knew he was listening to us. Freddy was sat on the highest step of the memorial, like he was the King. And I think that back then he probably was.

I started to get a mental image of bright clouds and angels and light, trying to imagine what Freddy had just been saying.

'And what do we do while we wait?' Clare said.

'Whatever we want. Because on one of the walls is where our dreams come true. Whatever we can imagine, we can jump into the wall and our wildest dreams become real.'

'Oh yeah,' drawled Jenny. 'Like what?'

'What would you want to do?' he said.

'I don't know,' she said. 'Have a picnic?'

'Exactly,' he chirped. 'We'll go and sit in sunny fields by a stream and eat apples from an apple tree.'

I noticed that he was looking at Craig and that jolted something in my gut. Was Freddy trying to persuade Craig to do something bad? I wondered. It was a complicated thought that I couldn't really deal with right then.

'What about you, Rich?' said Freddy. 'What would you do?'

I shrugged.

'I'd become wrestling champion of the world.'

Everyone laughed and that made me feel great because it wasn't that funny. I glanced at Clare but she was looking in the opposite direction. She wasn't laughing.

'Let's make a pact,' said Matthew of all people. He must have been struck by this idea of Freddy's mystical heavenly chamber. 'No matter how we go, or when we go, when we get to heaven, we'll all go to this chamber and wait for everyone else. Whoever goes first, even if it takes fifty years for the last one to arrive, we wait in the chamber.'

Freddy held out his hand and offered it to Matthew, who placed his hand on top. Next to join the pact was Jenny with her mitten. Then there was Clare. Then it was my turn. I looked at Matthew, who was smiling at me innocently. I placed my hand on the pile of other hands. When Craig put his hand on to complete the pact, I noticed Freddy give himself a little grin, which was a bit chilling, to tell you the truth. In that moment I could just tell that his evil streak had come to the surface. But I also noticed something else – something brand new in Craig's blank eyes. And it kind of chilled me even more. Right in the corner, only recognizable because the light was shining off it from the street lamp, was a tiny, round, glistening teardrop.

19

Christmas was just around the corner. The air was stingingly cold and the clouds were dense and silver. A few weeks had passed and you know what? Things were getting better. In school everything seemed to have settled down after the whole Bertie thing and, even though I still pretty much hung around with only those of us who had signed the Suicide Club Charter, life was not too bad.

It was a Saturday afternoon and I had gone into town to do some Christmas shopping. It was whilst I was out that, out of the blue, I saw Jenny.

'Hey,' I beamed enthusiastically. I loved it when I accidentally bumped into people I knew. Back in the old days, before all my old friends deserted me, this sort of thing happened all the time.

'Hey you,' she drawled.

I noticed that the sleeves of her hoody were rolled up and that she was wearing bright sweatbands with rainbow stripes. She was carrying her camera, attached to a tripod.

'So you're on a photography outing,' I said.

She looked at her camera and lifted it.

'I guess so.'

'What are you taking photos of?'

'Freddy wants some pictures to take home with him in the summer so I said I'd do it.'

'Really?'

'Uh-huh,' she said, and nodded quickly with wide-open eyes and a smile.

'So what, you're just taking pictures of people?'

'Yup. And the buildings in the background. I've got a long shutter-speed so, you know, the buildings will be still and the people'll come out all blurred and weird.'

'I love blurred and weird.'

'You are blurred and weird, Richie.'

It didn't surprise me that she would do something like this. She was such a kind person. There was nothing contrived about her kindness – it was just an innocent, naive outlook that resulted in doing nice things for people.

I smiled.

'So what's a shutter-speed?'

'Oh,' she said, happy that I was taking an interest in her hobby. 'Shutter-speeds are like, how long you have the shutter open on a camera?'

I nodded, not really understanding, to tell you the truth.

'OK, when you take a photo you push the button on the top, yes?'

'That's the technical term? The "button on the top"?'

Smiling, she said, 'Yes, Richie, that's the technical term. So anyway, when you press the button, the shutter is opened. When that happens, light is flooded on to the film inside the camera, right? If you let too much light in, the film gets overexposed and is ruined so the camera has automatic settings so it can't happen. But if you keep the shutter open for just a *little* bit longer, you let more light in and whatever's in your frame will be taken over a longer period, you know, just a second longer or so.'

'So, what, normal shutter-speed is a fraction of a second?'

'Right. But what it means is that if you photograph something that's moving while you have a long shutter-speed, the photo will come out with that movement.'

174

'What?'

She laughed.

'You know when you see those photos of roads at night and there's bright-red lines running down the roads from the car tail lights? Well, those are taken with long shutter-speeds. Because the car is moving while the shutter is open, the light hitting the film is *changing* and the red lights are caught as one continuous line. Get it?'

'Not really.'

She blew out air in exasperation and put her hands on her hips.

'I'll show you what I mean when I get my pictures back.'

'I look forward to it.'

'So what are you doing?'

I pushed my hands into my pockets.

'Christmas shopping.'

Jenny was squinting to see me because the sky was so bright. I had never realized how short she was before. She only came up to my neck.

'Have you done yours?' I said.

Our eye-line was suddenly broken and she looked down.

I had inadvertently said something that had made everything awkward.

'What? Tell me.'

'It's nothing, it's stupid.'

'Just tell me.' I crouched a little so that I was just below the level of her eyes, up into which I looked kindly.

'My family don't buy each other presents.'

I laughed.

'What? What's wrong with that? So you don't celebrate Christmas, who ca—'

'No,' she interrupted. 'We do celebrate Christmas. It's just that my parents have got this idea that it's become too commercialized and has lost its meaning.'

I made a bemused face.

'Why is that embarrassing for you?'

Jenny sighed, still looking at the floor, clearly uncomfortable.

'I don't know. They're just . . .'

'Weird?' I offered.

She laughed.

'I was going to say opinionated.'

Her dad was one of those military nerds, you know, like a normal nerd but more of a twat. A Strong Disciplinarian without really understanding anything about anything. Her mum didn't work because her father believed in 'stay-at-home-moms'. I'd seen him once before and he had a flat-top haircut. Seriously, he did. 'Sometimes going to war is necessary for the greater good,' I could imagine him saying from the head of his family dinner table as he helped himself to a spoonful of mashed potato. It was amazing that someone like Jenny had managed to come out of his household.

I didn't really know what to do. Jenny was embarrassed by what she had just said and that was just stupid. Far be it from me to offer advice, but I did anyway.

'Why don't you just buy them something anyway? It's nice getting presents. Get them an Easter egg.'

She laughed.

'I'm not joking,' I quipped. 'Or get them one of those blue elephant gods with eight legs.'

Jenny tapped me playfully.

'You're an idiot.'

'My grades would suggest otherwise,' I retorted arrogantly.

This time she laughed really loudly and even kind of snorted.

'Ugh,' I said. 'How disgusting.'

She was laughing madly now like the awkwardness of a moment ago had heightened her senses. She punched me in the right-hand side of my chest.

'Why don't you just ask Clare out?' she said.

I gasped. What the hell kind of a direction had this conversation just taken? It was like we had been driving through a dense city, turned a sudden corner and now we were in a beautiful forest. Was it that obvious that I liked her? My God. I stared at Jenny and thought, Fuck it. Before now I had never told anyone how I really felt about Clare but now was a time for honesty. She had just shared something with me so I was going to reciprocate. 'It's difficult.'

'What's so difficult about it?'

I don't normally like saying pathetic things, but I said this anyway.

'Do you think she likes me?'

'Honestly?'

'Yeah.'

Jenny shrugged.

'I don't know. I have kind of asked her for you—'

'You what?' I said, shocked.

Jenny smiled.

'You're welcome. But she never gives me a direct answer. So, honestly I don't know.'

'We had an argument about a week ago. She hasn't really spoken to me since.'

'Really? She hasn't said anything to me.'

This didn't actually surprise me. Clare had her other group of friends and Jenny wasn't a part of that. They had never really hung around together, apart from when it was with us. I looked at the sky and put my hands in my pockets.

'I think she probably likes me,' I said jokingly. 'Who wouldn't?'

Jenny laughed.

'Richard Harper,' she said. 'You'll be the end of me.'

20

On the night of Monday, 20 December I was looking for my iPod but couldn't find it anywhere.

Toby was sat in the living room watching TV so I went to ask him about it.

'You haven't seen my—'

'Ssssh.' He held his hand up, keeping his eyes on the screen. On TV was a wildlife programme about those little desert-rat things called meerkats. They were all up on their hind legs looking out over the desert.

'I was just going to ask if you were still available for a trip to the city on Thursday,' I said. The end of term was just days away.

'I'll be there,' he said flatly.

It knocked me out of kilter. I expected him to have done something excited when I said that, not kept watching his documentary.

I sighed and left the house. As soon as I got out into the night the cold hit me. My ears suddenly froze so I pulled up my hood and headed across town. I was going to try the war memorial to see if anybody was about.

When I got there Clare was with her friends, which I didn't like at all. I thought about turning round and walking away but I was sure they had seen me and so I had no other option but to head into the vipers' den. As I approached they started giggling but I just shook my head. Some of them were lounging on the steps like lions after a meal.

I had to go through the process of receiving a load of 'Hiya, Riiiiich' taunts from the girls, but there's no point in getting annoyed with people like them. They had always been childish and talked to me in this way, even before the Bertie incident. These were the same girls that had led her to say, 'My friends were right about you.'

I looked up at Clare. She was sat on the top step. I noticed that she had pulled her sweater sleeves right down over her hands so that only the ends of her fingers were visible and between those I saw that she was holding a cigarette. That made her even more attractive. She skipped up and bounced easily down the steps before throwing her arms round me and kissing my cheek.

'Hi,' she cooed.

'Hey,' I said warily. Something was up. This was the first time she had spoken to me since the night in her house when we had argued, so why was she being so nice? 'What are you doing?'

'Just playing a game,' she answered. The other girls laughed at that.

'Listen,' I said. 'I have to speak to you. Will you come with me?'

'Where?'

From where I was standing, it felt like I was looking at a perfect photograph; one of those weird photos where every level is in sharp, crisp focus. In the foreground was Clare, and then her friends and the war memorial made up the middle ground, whilst the Christmas lights and passing cars filled the background. It was like reality had got sharper. Exquisite. When she said, 'Where?' it was like it was in slow motion, but not really. It was more like something surreal, difficult to articulate. I guess it was like the neon from the lights were

179

fusing with my reality and making it all fake, but good fake. Like artificial lights. Do you know what I mean?

'I don't know where,' I said. 'Can we get a coffee?'

There are a lot of ornate coffee shops in my town, with crusty old books on shelves, because there are a lot of pseudo-intelligent people living there who think it's sophisticated to drink coffee. Which I guess it kind of is. But not if you go there thinking you're sophisticated and then talk about *shopping*!

Clare thought about it for a second and nodded. In a way I was glad of this coincidence. I had to try and clear the air and Mr Fate had said there you go to me.

We walked away from the group of girls. I wanted to ask Clare why she even bothered hanging around with such nasty people, but I didn't want her to flip out on me so I just grabbed a hold of her hand and made sure she didn't get run over when we crossed the road. Amazingly, she didn't pull away.

We went to this little place that has big windows so that we could look out on to the street. We both ordered a coffee and I looked at her.

She was slumped down in her chair.

'So, Harper, what's up?'

I shrugged.

'I just wanted a coffee.'

From where I sat I could still see the war memorial. The girls were still milling around, and messing with each other's hair and all that sort of thing.

'That T-shirt you gave me is great,' I said. This was more awkward than I had thought it was going to be.

Clare didn't even answer me, her good mood having dissolved now that it was just us.

'It's cold out?' I said it as a question to let her know that I was making an effort.

'Are you looking forward to the Christmas party?' Clare said suddenly, and in a chipper voice.

It was turning into one of our games. I wondered if she was being like this to me, kind of distanced, for the same reason that she had had sex with a large number of boys – whatever that reason was.

'This Wednesday? I suppose so.'

'Are you going to dance with me?'

I closed my eyes and sighed.

'You know how I hate that stuff.'

Clare shrugged.

'But I like dancing. Don't you want to make me happy?'

The conversation was already over.

'I'll make you happy when we get married. I promise,' I said.

She looked at me. It could go either way. Now that I was onboard with the game she might turn it around and become sullen again. All I could do was wait.

'Will you buy me a castle?' she said.

'I'll buy you a castle that goes up into the clouds and we'll live in a chamber at the top.'

'I'll want a moat around it.'

'Of course. I'll fill it with acid.'

Her eyes went wide with excitement. 'And we can invite our friends round and when they turn up, you can take your bow and arrow and shoot them all from the tower, one by one.'

I laughed. 'I'll grow roses in window boxes and do you know what will surround the castle for miles and miles?'

'What?'

'Ash. Nothing else will grow around us.'

We both started laughing, but I was hollow. I didn't want this sort of conversation at this point. It was a brilliant idea, killing all of our friends and living in an evil castle, but it wasn't exactly healthy. In a way I was relieved that I didn't have to go through another argument, but in another way I felt bad because it was so fake. There was definitely something in the air between us, something unspoken, a heaviness.

Suddenly I saw a figure heading for the war memorial and my heart froze. Freddy. A mass of thoughts started piling through a bottleneck in my brain. Clare had been with Freddy and they hadn't called me? Did he see me coming and hide?

'That's Freddy,' I kind of coughed.

Clare turned in her seat coolly and stared out across the dark street. I just caught a glimpse of the birthmark on the back of her neck, the one that we don't mention. I wanted to ask her about Freddy then, but I couldn't. I just . . . couldn't.

After our coffee I went back across the road to the war memorial. The girls saw us and started whispering and laughing.

Freddy had a magazine rolled up into a tube in his hands, and when he saw me he waved it in the air.

'Richie,' he called.

'Freddy,' I shouted back, pretending that nothing was up, even though I was being eaten up inside.

The next day, Tuesday, all the talk in school was of the Christmas party. There were only two days left until we split up for the holidays and I couldn't wait. The day passed quickly and most of the lessons consisted of quizzes and puzzles and Christmas-card making, which is always fun, even when you're fifteen. My Christmas card was a rip-off of Toby's idea with people skating around a lake. I'm always disappointed when I draw, not because my pictures are pathetic (which they are) but because drawing is one thing that I would love to do but can't.

That night I left my house and headed over to Freddy's. I just had to ask what he had been doing out with Clare without asking me. It had been playing on my mind all day, niggling away at me. Surely they weren't having some sort of relationship behind my back. Freddy must have known how I felt about Clare. Surely.

It's about a half-hour walk over to the school dorms and Craig Bartlett-Taylor's house is on the way. I walked down his street, but had no intention of calling for him. In his drive, though, was his father. He was clearing frost from the windscreen of his car with one of those plastic scraping things.

'Hello, Mr Bartlett-Taylor,' I said nicely, because I liked him.

He looked up and adjusted his old glasses. He saw it was me and scowled before returning to his windscreen.

I knew why. It was because of what had happened to Bertie. Everybody knew about what we had supposedly done and everybody pretty much hated me.

'Is Craig in?' I asked.

'He's gone to see his friend,' he said coldly.

His friend? He didn't have any friends. He had us, the Suicide Club.

'Freddy?' I asked.

'That boy who lives over on the airbase. The American lad.'

I nodded my head, even though I didn't have any idea who he was talking about.

'Well, can you tell him I called by?'

He stopped scraping the ice off his windscreen and sighed.

'I don't think so, Richard.'

I paused and my gut churned because I knew what was coming.

'I don't think that it would be a good idea for you to see Craig any more. I don't think that you and your friends are a good influence.'

I bit my lip. Not a good influence? This was a perfect example of what the Suicide Club was all about. The mediocre trying to stop the exceptional – this old guy (who I still liked) was taking Craig away from the only thing that could save him, just because he didn't understand. It hurt because it meant even those who you think are OK can turn out to be snakes. I didn't want to feel this way, but it was like I didn't have a choice. The fact of the matter is that we weren't a bad influence on Craig. We loved him and had helped him after his suicide attempt. But because of the bird thing our die was cast. I hadn't killed the bird, yet here I was completely guilty in the eyes of Craig's father. It wasn't fair and I had had enough.

'Mr Bartlett–Taylor, I don't—'

'Please, Richard.' He held his hand up in the air. 'What you and your friends did to that bird . . .' He trailed off. 'You're all trouble.'

I just stood there and took it. He wasn't going to listen to me.

'I know all about it. And don't think I don't know what else you get up to.'

I looked at the old man and my opinion of him changed. Not in an instant, more like over a period of about three seconds, like a landslip running down a hillside and revealing the truth. He wasn't such a good old guy. He judged people just like everybody else.

'Well, I'm going to go now,' I said. 'Make sure you don't go sliding around on the ice – it's a cold night.'

He didn't say anything back, which I sort of wish he had.

I carried on my way and shook my head. I hope he didn't mean what he said about not allowing Craig to see us. I hadn't seen Craig outside school for a while, now that I thought about it, and I wondered if that was the doing of his father. I also realized that I didn't like the idea of Craig having friends outside the Suicide Club. It was us who had taken him under our wing after he tried to kill himself with the pills and I didn't want to share him.

Anyway, there was no point in letting it get me down and I was soon at the old, ivy-encrusted school dormitories that were sickeningly old-fashioned.

I skipped up the stone steps and went into the foyer. There was a bunch of kids milling around wearing baggy jeans and hoodies, sitting on their skateboards and using their feet to gently roll back and forth on the clean stone floor.

I went up to the desk and signed myself in. As I made my way up to Freddy's corridor I tried to calm myself. I wasn't angry at Craig's father (actually I kind of was), but I was both nervous and excited because of what I was about to ask Freddy. It would be just me and him so there wouldn't be any distractions.

I was running by the time I reached his corridor because sometimes you can't even waste fractions of a second from your life. I rapped on his door and, after about five seconds, he answered.

He was wearing a Nirvana T-shirt, which I thought was a bit of a cliché and not in tune with Freddy's personality because Freddy was no nihilist. Not that Nirvana were nihilists.

'How's it going?' he asked.

'Not bad. I just ran into Bartlett-Taylor's father,' I said.

'Oh yeah? What did he have to say for himself?'

I shrugged and explained.

Freddy sighed.

'It's a shame. I should very much have liked to have had him on our grand romantic adventure.'

We went inside his room. The posters on the walls were mainly of sports teams and clearly belonged to his younger room-mate, who I remembered was called Anthony. Freddy slumped down on to his bed and rolled his desk chair over to me with his foot. I sat down and spun around in it for a second.

'So what's up?' he said.

'You are,' I answered honestly.

'That's good because you also bother me.' He paused. 'Deeply.'

'Listen, Freddy. I'm sorry to ask you this because it's pointless, but' – I sucked in air (not really) – 'is there anything going on between you and Clare?'

'Me and Clare? What?'

'I don't know, it's just, you know, I thought you two might be seeing each other or something.'

He laughed a little.

'What?'

I adjusted myself uncomfortably in my seat.

'Why, um, were you with her last night without asking me?'

'What? You think boys and girls can't be friends? How weak.'

I nodded and breathed through my nose because I knew what he meant. He meant that shallow people can't be friends with members of the opposite sex. It's weird.

'It's not that. You can't deny that you're . . . very . . . close.'

'Why do you ask? Do you like her?'

I looked at him. Before I had met Freddy, my life had been nowhere near as colourful as it was now. I admit that my emotions were all over the place nowadays after everything that we had been through but at least I was at the end of the spectrum, whatever end that may have been.

'I'm in love with her,' I said, slowly and deliberately.

Freddy made it easy for me. If it had been Matthew I had been speaking to, then he would have ribbed me for ages, but Freddy knew that love is a serious matter. As if.

'There's nothing going on between me and Clare.'

You have no idea how good those words sounded. The last day had been strange, doubting Freddy. I didn't want to feel like that because I wanted Freddy to be perfect. He *understood*.

'So, my friend,' he said. 'You knock yourself out.'

'Do you think this is the point where I should ask you what you think she thinks about me?'

We both laughed.

'I'm going to ask her out tomorrow night,' I said.

'At the Christmas party?'

'Yup. You going?'

'Of course I'm going. My mother wanted me to go home but I told her to go fuck herself.' He closed his eyes, like he was cursing himself for being so teenagerish. 'No, she said I could stay until Thursday morning and get the train back then.'

'She's not coming to pick you up?'

I remember very clearly that he didn't flinch at all when he said, simply, 'No.'

I became suddenly aware that the floor was tiled and not carpeted.

'Doesn't this floor get cold?'

Freddy shrugged and looked at me.

'So how long have you liked Clare?'

'I don't know. Always, I guess. I think I actually fell in love with her that day you saved Craig's life.'

'She is amazing.'

I paused.

187

'Do you think she likes me?'

Then we both paused. And then started laughing.

'Jesus Christ,' said Freddy, 'some people are just so pointless.'

21

The next day in school my head was in a blur. I had decided that I was going to ask Clare out at the Christmas party. This had gone on long enough. I kept getting extremely nervous and my palms would get all clammy. My heart would go crazy with palpitations and my field of vision would burn white, as though someone had turned up the brightness-levels in my eyes. It's those teenage hormones that are the best – the ones where there's so much *feeling* in every pore that you think you're going to collapse.

Because it was the last day of school before we broke up for Christmas, it was a non-uniform day so we could wear whatever we wanted. I wore my bees knees T-shirt with a scarf, and I felt good. My dress sense was more pretentious nowadays; I will concede that.

When I was sat in class I couldn't stop my legs shaking. I tried not to think about what she would say if I asked her out because it would make no difference to the outcome anyway. I saw Clare here and there, but I wasn't in any of her classes that day so I didn't manage to speak to her until lunchtime. She was with her friends who, as usual, laughed when I went over.

'Do you like the game, Rich?' one of them said. This was a girl called Darlene, for Christ's sake.

'Let me just remind you of something, Darlene,' I

said quickly. 'I had five As and six A-stars in my continuous assessment, whereas you only had seven As and two Bs, so why don't you make like a tailor . . . and button it?' I said the last part of the sentence in an American accent so that every-body would laugh. Which they didn't. I guess what I said was a bit harsh. But she was a bully so I think it was OK. I had had enough with people like her, manipulative people, so I decided to stand up for myself. That's all.

'You're bad,' Clare said, coming over to me and dragging me away from her friends.

'Yeah, well.'

'Are we dancing tonight?'

I lowered my voice.

'So what's this game? You said something about it the other night at the war memorial.'

'The game?'

I tried to absorb all of her features in my brain so that if, for whatever reason, I never saw her again, I would be able to remember what she looked like.

'You want to know about the game?'

'Yes,' I said.

'But if you know about it, the game is wrecked.'

I sighed.

'Whatever.' To be honest, I didn't really care about their game because her friends were stupid and soon Clare would leave them behind and just be with us. 'I'll see you tonight,' I said.

The afternoon went fairly quickly with quizzes and sitting around talking about Christmas. I heard some of the boys talking about – oh God – fingering girls and I actually went red because it was so crass.

When I got home I tried watching TV and listening to CDs but nothing was any good; I couldn't get Clare out of my head.

At one point Toby came into my bedroom, and I cursed myself for not locking the door. He was carrying a notebook.

'Richard,' he said, pen in hand. 'I just need to confirm what time we're going into the city tomorrow.' He wasn't even looking at me because he was looking at his notepad.

I stared at him incredulously and left a dramatic pause.

'Half ten,' I said at last.

'Hmm,' he answered, as he wrote something in his book. 'That's excellent timing.' I noticed that he was still wearing his brown leather sandals with his grey school socks.

'I'm getting you a pair of Converses for Christmas,' I said. 'Here, give me that.' I took two quick steps forward and pulled the notebook out of his hand and looked at what he had been writing. That boy is the living end, I swear to God. This is what he'd written:

> 7:00 Wake up, shower and change.
> 7:20 Prepare breakfast – Cornflakes, orange juice and one slice of bread.
> 7:30 Eat breakfast and watch Spongebob Squarepants.
> 8:00 Help Mum clean living room.
> 9:00 Go to Tesco with dad to wash car.
> 10:00 Get home and read book.
> 10:30 Go into the city with Richard.

And I'm not even making it up. He'd written it all down in his book.

'Tobe,' I said. 'Why do you do stuff like this?'

'Like what?'

'Like this.' I held my right hand over the book, which was resting in my left. 'You've written what your plans are.'

'So?'

'Well, what's the point?'

Toby looked at me and crumpled his face.

'I find it useful.'

'Well, I think you and I need to play some cricket.'

I knew his face would light up and he ran off to his room to get his bat and a tennis ball. In our house we have quite a long landing that makes a great cricket pitch. Toby doesn't really like sports but he'll do anything if I'm involved. I played for about five minutes (I declared not out) and decided it was time to get ready for the party. Toby was upset that I had only played for a short time, but I didn't mind too much because I'd be spending the whole day with him tomorrow anyway.

I got showered and went online. I checked my emails and something incredible had happened. Play had emailed me saying that my My Chemical Romance album had been posted, which made me feel awesome. At last it would arrive. And it was about time too.

Matthew and Jenny were both on their computers so we quickly exchanged schedules for getting to the party. After that I ran downstairs and ate a couple of packets of crisps.

'Don't eat those, your dinner's almost ready,' my mother said.

I wanted to make a witty quip and sweep out of the house but things were still frosty between us after Bertie so I said, 'I told Matthew I would meet him in five minutes. I have to go.'

She didn't say anything but her shoulders slumped. She

clearly wanted to say something but didn't. A few seconds passed and I left the room.

By the time I got to school, music was blaring and the disco lights were laser-blasting everywhere. The whole place was stuffed full of eleven- to eighteen-year-olds. The first years were all skidding around on their knees, just as you would expect, of course.

I couldn't see Matthew or Jenny, or Craig or Freddy. Or Clare.

'Rich,' somebody called. 'Hey, Rich.' It was Phil, one of the boys who had once liked me but who had now followed the herd and deserted me after the Bertie incident.

'Hey, how's it going?' he said, grinning.

I found myself doing something very odd. I was judging him. I looked him up and down. I had been friends with this boy up until just a few months ago. But now I felt like I didn't know him at all, like he was an embarrassing memory from my past. I know that what I was doing was a bad thing, but I don't want to lie and pretend that it didn't happen. Freddy's mediocrity theory was seeping into me slowly but surely. This boy in front of me would never do anything exceptional. He would get a job for which he would be well paid, but he would hold people like me back. Was I really thinking this? I was disgusted by myself. But that's how I felt.

He was drunk. Completely off his face, in fact. He stumbled over to me and put his arm over my shoulder. He was a good foot taller than me.

'What's your problem lately, Rich?'

I could smell the alcohol on his breath.

'What do you mean?' I said diplomatically.

'Why don't you hang around with us any more?'

'What?' I said. 'It's not me. You lot have totally snubbed me since Bertie died.'

'All you do is hang around with that fucking faggot Freddy,' he said, ignoring me.

I immediately removed his arm from around my neck.

'Get off me, you fucking loser.'

I pushed him away. He looked at me with contempt.

'You're a prick.'

'You know what, Phil?' I said. 'You're pathetic. What sets are you in now, anyway?'

He just looked at me with glazed eyes.

Then I said something quite bad.

'You're going to end up just like your father – a *fucking* manager. It doesn't *mean* anything.'

We both looked at each other. Whatever had gone before, I was now cutting myself loose of my old life. After saying something like that, there was *no* going back. I didn't really expect him to do what he did next though, which was to try and punch me. I felt bad as I stepped to one side and pushed his back. I stuck out my foot so that he tripped and went sprawling over the floor. Basically, I removed all of his dignity.

He got to his feet, but some of the other boys held him back. There was a wall of them, the people I used to know, and they all looked at me like I was a disease.

'You're all mental,' I said to them and walked off.

'How's your counselling going, Rich?' somebody shouted. I stopped where I was. My heart went thud in my chest. They knew. Fuuuuuuuck!!!!!!!!! I turned round and saw that everybody had smirks on their faces. Something suddenly hit home. Everybody knew. Everybody knew about me being in therapy and must have been laughing at me all along behind my back.

A nausea suddenly came into my throat and I felt my ears heating up. I was a laughing stock. Me. And I was so much better than all of them, I told myself blindly. So why was I getting so angry? Why were my hands balled into tight fists? My existence was crashing in around me. I wondered where Clare was but couldn't see her. I looked at my old friends, who had all turned against me. Who were they anyway? What would they ever do with their stupid fucking lives? Nothing. They'd get jobs and fade away into the mediocrity of life. They were completely pointless. A hundred years from now, nobody would even know they had existed.

'Why don't you all fuck off?' I shouted, a little too emotionally. My voice cracked and the last part of my sentence went way too high. I closed my eyes as everybody laughed at me. Now I felt really sick. All along I had thought that everybody laughed at Craig Bartlett-Taylor because he was nuts, but it was me they were laughing at.

My thoughts suddenly strayed to the Suicide Club – to Freddy, Jenny, Matthew, Clare, even Craig. Had they been laughing at me too? Had all of my bad thoughts about humanity been totally misplaced? Was it *me* who was wrong and evil and mediocre? My body felt like an empty eggshell. Was this what it was like to be unpopular?

Suddenly the music stopped and the next song came on. Music cranked out of the speakers and do you know what song it was? It was 'Teardrop' by a band called Massive Attack. It's probably the most beautiful song you'll ever hear and now here it was cascading over me as I was being humiliated in front of everybody. I wanted to scream, cry, hit out, buck against it all, but I stayed where I was, my feet made of concrete.

'We've known all along, Rich,' said one of the boys.

As I stood there, helpless, flailing, I knew exactly what Freddy meant. This was how the mediocre took down the exceptional. It was me against them, and there were more of them. It was they who had cruelly cut me out of their lives, yet still they did this to me.

I had to do something to stop this. I had to make a decision. So I did.

Deliberately, I turned away from my old life and, across the dance floor, saw Clare. She looked up and our eyes met. The first line of 'Teardrop' kicked in and my destiny came crushingly to life and I took my first steps towards my love. All thought of my humiliation was gone because I was about to show everybody how life *should* be lived. Clare was heading for me as well, and my arms went weak. I saw Clare's friends look up at her as she walked away from them. Their eyes followed her path and saw me at the end. They put their hands over their mouths. I could feel the eyes of the other kids behind me burning into my back.

Still the music poured out into the hall and then I was only ten feet away from her. I lifted my right hand ever so slightly, so that I could brush her hair away from her face when I reached her. She didn't smile at me because she was nervous and I could feel her energy. The golden rope came up between us and reeled itself in around our souls as we got closer. It was pure magic.

We finally reached each other and stopped. The song percolated into us and would for ever be etched into our memories. I took her right hand in my left and moved her hair away with my right.

Here it was. We looked at each other for no longer than a second and then came that most amazing plunge where all fear and doubt retreats and you tilt your head. Our lips met and I suddenly realized just how much in love with her I truly was. More than I knew. We stood there for about thirty seconds, our jaws moving up and down in tandem as we tasted each other properly for the first time. I think in that kiss I experienced pure being; that physical joy where you forget *everything*.

I could feel a circle of people around us but I kept my eyes closed. I had won. My secret about therapy was out and I had been completely humiliated, but here I was kissing the girl I loved. The song just carried on and on and I remember it ringing in my ears as I kissed her. We pulled away together and looked at each other.

I have to admit that after kissing I never know what to say and I usually say something to embarrass myself. Which I did this time as well, but what I said was quite sweet, I guess, even though it was very cringey.

'Now am I playing the game?' I said.

I saw for the first time everybody gathered around us, looking on in near disbelief.

Then something happened. Clare looked me in the eye and took a step back, just like she had in the graveyard that night when she refused to free me.

'No, Rich,' she said coldly.

A shiver went up my spine as I noticed her friends were laughing and high-fiving.

'Don't you get it?' she said as she took another step back. She brought her hand up to cover her mouth, but not so much that I couldn't see the emergence of a smirk.

My sweet Clare was leaving me. I felt like I was in Hades or whatever it's called and was saying goodbye to her. She was being taken away across the water in one of the boats, wearing only a white gown. And she wasn't looking back. The mist and the night finally dissolve her.

She lowered her head and looked out at me through the tops of her eyes. Her mouth opened.

'You *are* the game.'

22

I stood there as Clare took three or four further steps backwards and I thought I was going to dissolve into the spaces between the atoms. Chest swelling with too much oxygen in my lungs, my feet became stuck to the floor and I started to sway. I wanted to be physically sick right there. My mouth filled with moisture as my glands secreted saliva to line my throat. I felt like somebody had hit me over the head with a chunk of iron. I don't know if you've ever taken a blow to the head, but right after it happens your brain just empties and you can't do anything. I knew what the problem was, just as surely as I knew that there was no cure. I had had my heart broken.

Clare had just hurt me more than any person had ever hurt me before. Even more than when my parents split up. Somewhere in the distance of my mind a switch clicked on and I heard the end of the song. Suddenly the place was silent, apart from people laughing. Not even Drama could save me now. If I collapsed into a ball on the floor, it would make no difference this time. It was all over.

She had even kissed me. I still can't believe how cruel it was to do that. She could have just told me that she wasn't interested. But for her to go through the motions of that kiss, which had meant so much to me; it was just too cruel to bear.

I couldn't believe what had happened. I felt so empty and helpless.

I hate the way I let my emotions get to me so much. I wish I could control them so that they didn't hurt me as badly as they do. I'm glad I still feel the pain because it re-inforces the fact that I'm still human, but I don't feel any happiness any more. That end of the spectrum is closed to me now.

All because of Clare and my unrequited love. Unrequited love is a terrible thing. I don't think many people know it as deeply as I do, but it can tear a man apart at the seams. If you get a bad dose of it, you can't recover. I loved Clare so much that for about four months I had thought about little else. Even now, years after everything, I'm still in love with her. When I tell people about it they laugh and shake their heads and think, What a fool, but that's only because they don't *know*. They think I'm being dramatic and childish and some of them are even worried about me. I tell them not to worry, but the fact of the matter is that I'm a bit of a wreck. How can you move on from something when all you want is that one thing that you can't have? What's the point in moving on? It's unhealthy, yes, but it's all that matters to you. Jesus Christ, I'm really mining my soul here; I must sound like a lunatic.

The first person to come and speak to me was Matthew. He sat down and handed me a can of Coke, which had quite a lot of vodka in it. I gulped it all down because I knew the alcohol would make me feel better.

He said some pretty cool stuff to me about how he thought I was a great guy, and how I had once pulled him out of an icy lake (which I had) and how I had given him my entire collection of WWE wrestling figures when his brother had been run over (he didn't die), and how I used to help out at the homeless shelter with Clare more than anyone else. I guess he was right that I had been a pretty good kid, but now things were different. I didn't see life in the same way any more. The world had crushed my spirit out of me and now I was nothing more than the school psychopath who had killed the falcon and was seeing a shrink because I had mental problems.

It was sad, but it was the state that things had reached. Matthew gave me his hip flask of vodka and, even though I was just fifteen, the drink was gone in under an hour and I was on my way home alone.

I'd be lying if I said that on the way I didn't take a detour into a side street, sit down on a kerb and stare at the ground for about half an hour. I didn't cry because I was numb. My social life was gone but I was OK with that because I was sort of trying to cut myself loose from my old friends anyway. But losing Clare was like getting cancer on the surface of my bones. Every time I moved it would rub up against my muscles and sinew and leave my entire body raw and tender.

I was fairly drunk and I stopped at the twenty-four-hour garage, where I bought a packet of cigarettes and some matches. I went to the park and sat on a swing.

I lit a cigarette and only smoked about half because my head started spinning crazily and I whitied out, which usually happens when you smoke too much marijuana and pass out, but it can also happen with cigarettes if you're not used to them, which I wasn't. I managed to get to the bushes before vomiting. My stomach came up in thick waves and scratched at my windpipe as it came. I dry-heaved about ten times before I collapsed on the freezing grass and lay there in a cold sweat, shaking.

It was only ten thirty when I got to my front door and my parents were still up. I scrambled inside and couldn't even be bothered to hide the mess I was in.

When my mother saw me, she said, 'Oh my God, what have you done?'

I could feel remnants of vomit mixed with saliva between my fingers and I looked at her bleary-eyed. I couldn't focus.

'You haven't changed at all,' she said.

That would have hurt so much if she had said it at any other time, but after what had happened I just didn't care what she said. I smiled and felt a little bit of dribble bubble up on my lip.

'You've got sick all down you,' she said. 'How clever.'

I just sighed and fell against the wall and started laughing my head off. My mother went crazy and said that I had to get out of the house for ever, which was shocking coming from her, but I just slumped further down the wall until I was lying on the floor, laughing.

'Why don't you just re-laaaax,' I sneered disgustingly.

'Don't talk to your mother like that.' I didn't even see my father come into the hall.

The whole room was turning like those slow-motion cameras that photograph the stars wheeling in the sky over the course of a whole night. I started feeling hot again as a feeling of impending sickness consumed me. I got on to my knees, crawled to the downstairs toilet and emptied my stomach again. I think my mother was crying, but I'm not sure. I grabbed the toilet door and slammed it shut before sliding the lock across. I then took my top off like I imagine a spastic would and let the cold vinyl of the floor fuse with my skin.

Through the door my father told me not to fall asleep as I might choke on my vomit but my fringe, damp with sweat, was caressing my face and his words meant *nothing*.

I didn't really fall asleep. Rather, I drifted in and out of oblivion. My existence was made up of fractured bouts of sweaty subconsciousness and hyper-reality. I was physically, mentally and emotionally fucked. Everything was gone. My family hated me, my old life had disintegrated into a void of hatred, the girl I loved not only didn't love me back, but had taken pleasure in humiliating me, and I could see no way that I could ever be happy again.

At around two in the morning I finally got up to my bedroom. The house was cold, quiet and dark. I looked at my mobile and had received ten missed calls, all from Matthew and Freddy. I threw the phone into the wall and it smashed apart, but not as satisfyingly as I would have liked. I lay on my covers and fell asleep, covered in my own vomit.

Somebody was banging at my door.

'Go away,' I croaked, my throat raw from vomiting and drinking no water.

But the banging continued. I eventually realized that it was Toby and that he wasn't going to go away so I rolled over and opened the door.

'What?' I said.

'Are we going into the city today like you promised?'

My eyes were closed so I could just hear his voice. I sighed.

'What's the time?'

'Nine o'clock,' I heard him say.

I shook my head, which hurt like hell to do.

'I thought I said ten thirty.'

'I thought I should get you up so that you won't be late.'

'Christ, Tobe, what difference does it make if we're late?'

'I've got it written in my book,' he answered.

That was just too much so I shut the door and went back to bed.

'Wake me at ten,' I called.

'OK, I'm going to Tesco to help Dad clean the car,' his voice said. I heard his feet walking away and down the stairs.

I suddenly remembered the events of the previous night. For about a minute, I had completely forgotten what had happened. But now it all came back to me. It was so hideous that I just smiled and shook my head, but that hurt so I buried my face in my pillow instead.

There was a layer of sweat over the surface of my mattress. My hangover was the worst yet. I must have drunk more than I thought. My stomach was tender and my throat stung. My head was pulsating. Before I knew it, my door was being banged against again.

'What?' I shouted into my pillow.

More banging. For five minutes. I struggled off my wet mattress and opened the door, reaching for the door handle from my bed. It was Toby again.

'What now?' I growled.

'It's ten o'clock,' came his voice through the crack in the door.

I looked at the clock next to my bed. I had lost an hour to fever and torment. My head felt even worse now and I tried to slam the door.

'Call me at eleven,' I said.

But Toby stuck out his foot before it shut. He came into my room.

'What the hell are you doing?' I slurred.

I felt his hand grab my ankle and his feeble body try to pull me off my bed.

'Get up,' he moaned.

It was like a fly was on my leg, not a human being. I kicked out, mildly amused.

'You promised me, Rich.'

When he said that I suddenly felt bad. I was such a bastard I couldn't stand it. How could I do this to him? I opened my eyes and looked down the end of my bed to where he stood. And you'll never guess the sight which greeted me. Not only was Toby not wearing a tie, but had clearly had my mother buy him his first pair of jeans and a yellow hoody, which had a picture of a smiling dinosaur on it. His hair was gelled ridiculously into a Mohican and his feet filled a pair of skater shoes. The country-gent clothes were gone. All this and he was still probably less than three feet tall. The effort the poor kid had put in was insane. All he wanted was for me to be his friend. But here I was hungover to hell with the worst broken heart in human history and a humiliation from which I would never fully recover.

'Mum told me not to get my hopes up,' he muttered sadly.

I had never heard Toby say something like this before and it almost made me cry. His childishness was leaving him and he was beginning the hardening process that Freddy told us about. He was just a kid and here he was feeling upset because of something that *I* had done. Me.

And what the hell was my mother doing anyway? How dare she say that to Toby. She didn't *know* me. She was manipulating Toby for her own gain. She wanted Toby on her side just because I had thrown up and laughed at her last night. Bitch. I should have told Toby that I'd get ready and be down in a minute – that would have shown her. But I didn't. Rather, I decided that if my mother wanted to play games then I'd play. I'd show her that, if she wanted to play with Toby's feelings, then I'd hit her hard. I can't really explain why I said what I said next, but it made sense to me at the time.

'I'm not going into the city with you, Toby,' I said.

He stopped tugging at my leg. I looked at him. The stupid dinosaur on his sweater, I noticed, was actually doing a thumbs-up and winking as well as having that stupid grin on its face. Some dinosaur. I looked at Toby. My head hurt so much that I could barely keep my eyes open, but I couldn't help but keep looking as I saw my little brother start to cry.

He rushed out of the room, not quite having let go of his emotions, like he didn't want me to see him burst into tears. He pulled the door shut behind him and I heard him scuttling around in his bedroom, no doubt looking for a fucking cravat to pull around his neck or something.

I closed my eyes and almost died with the badness inside me. I felt like my history teacher Mrs Kenna – like I was having layers of tragedy poured down my neck and filling my body from the feet up. Toby was just the latest addition. My own mother was starting a war with me and we were throwing Toby's emotions around like a rag doll – this was a boy who tried to look cool and ended up wearing a sweater with a smiley, happy dinosaur on the front.

The room to my door opened and it was Toby again. This time he was fully crying. Seeing his emotions laid bare like that was a rare sight. Light reflected off his tears that had run messily all over his stupid cheeks and his lips were quivering.

'I'm not going to listen to you any more,' he said.

With some reserve of energy that I didn't know about I bolted upright. All my rage was in me now, like nuclear fuel, my monster full, and I jumped up off my bed. Everything had finally caught up with me.

'Don't you ever talk to me like that, you little fucking shit,' I screamed at him.

I grabbed his dinosaur sweater and lifted him bodily off the ground and threw him through the open door on to the landing. The force with which I threw him scared even me. His feet hit the floor but he was off balance and he fell backwards on to the carpet. My chest was heaving up and down and I found my whole body shaking uncontrollably as I loomed over him. I could have ripped his head off right there and then. I was having flashbacks to the night before, to all those kids laughing at me, to Clare ripping my aching heart out through my splintered ribs. And then further

205

back . . . to the old man in the street. I saw the fear on his old face, fear of me, as I reached down to pick up the metal pipe . . .

I took a malign step towards Toby and he shuffled back towards the top of the stairs, a look of terror on his face.

I stopped myself right there. We looked at each other for a second. What the fuck was I doing? I didn't start crying, like I should have done. I did something worse, something for which I can never be forgiven. More than anything I wanted to pick him up in my arms and tell him that I was sorry, that I was a prick, that my whole world had been torn apart by the atomic bonds that tie everything together. I wanted to tell him that I loved him more than anything in the world, even more than Clare, but I didn't. I didn't do any of that stuff. Instead of doing the right thing, purely because I couldn't stand to do anything else, I leaned over him and spat into his hair before turning round, going back to my room, and locking my door.

23

It was because of our strong and lengthy history that Clare's humiliation of me was so distressing. She had torn our friendship in half. So many years together and they obviously counted for nothing. Over the Christmas holidays, she rarely left my thoughts and it was the mental image of her laughing at me that made me feel like I had an anchor strapped around my lungs.

Christmas was miserable. My mother had calmed down slightly because she didn't want to spoil her own Christmas by being mean, so that was one good thing. But nobody called me and I didn't call anybody either. Freddy had gone home for the holidays and I hadn't spoken to him since before the school disco. I would have loved to have talked to him and messed around with him, but he was gone – disappeared.

Jenny had gone back to America for Christmas. Back to the old US of A.

I didn't even speak to Matthew over the holidays, which was completely weird because it was the longest I hadn't spoken to him in my whole life (apart from when one of us went on holiday). This may have had to do with me not having a phone because I had destroyed it. Over the weeks I expected him to call me on the house phone but he never did. I assumed he was missing Jenny and that he wanted to be on his own, or that he wouldn't know what to say to me because what had happened had been so horrendous. I don't know why I didn't get in touch with anybody – probably because I was scared.

So the whole holiday was spent in my house. It was awful. Toby ignored me the whole time and my father told me that he was terrified of me. Whenever I came into the lounge to watch TV and he was in there, he'd stay for about five minutes and then leave without saying anything.

In the nights I'd be up in my room listening to music or watching a film and my dad would come and sit on my bed. I wouldn't say anything to him and he'd eventually go away. I'd hear my mother prowling around upstairs, tidying things. At one point I felt incredibly sorry for her. I thought about what it must have been like to be her. She had a nutcase for a son. Despite all of this, I still acted frostily towards her because I blamed her for my outburst on Toby, which is completely pathetic.

For Christmas, Father Christmas brought me a book on screenwriting. I had no idea why I had been given it because I had never once mentioned to my parents the fact that I wanted to write cartoons when I was older. The only reason they could have had for buying me the book was that they had been snooping around my drawers and come across my notebooks. Because I had been starved of company, I went completely mental and made my mother burst into tears. She started screaming that I had ruined Christmas but she should have thought about that before she started looking through my personal things. I was really starting to lose my grip on sanity at this point and doing and saying things because I knew they would make matters worse.

On one cold, cloudy afternoon I was stood in my bedroom looking out the window at the silver birch tree in our garden. The latticed, spindly branches near the top were swaying in the wind. I sighed and went over to my desk, where I opened the bottom drawer. I took out the Suicide Club Charter that I had hidden underneath a pile of old *Empire* movie magazines. As I read over it I thought back to the night on the airbase, when we had been sat in the candlelight. I kept getting caught on the words, *the world is run by the mediocre for the mediocre.* A sudden thought that I was cut off from the world struck me. It didn't make me feel emotional; I felt cold, like I had just learnt a fact in science class. I simply didn't fit. A square through a circle. I was trapped. I recalled signing the Charter, sitting in that room. I remembered feeling good being hidden away whilst the rest of the world was going about its business in the mess hall. I remembered looking at Freddy, at his face. I remembered the headmaster's office, us huddled around Craig. I remembered how linked I had felt to my friends. We had skimmed away from everyone else, been sent on a different trajectory, but where could it possibly lead? Freddy's idea of life being an adventure couldn't really come true. We'd soon get old, get jobs, die. The whole idea of living a life of romance led to one place: a brick wall. You weren't allowed to live like that. People would not allow it. They would hold you back.

I returned to my window and looked down to the patio. I wondered what would happen if my skeleton fell limply on to it. It would only take a few seconds, perhaps less. The act of jumping would be instantaneous – that's all it would take; a snap decision, over in an instant. I had no intention of actually doing it, of course, but it started me thinking. Is killing yourself a slow steady climb, a decision reached by degrees? Or just an opportunity meeting a circumstance – the right place at the right time? One moment of madness or clarity and it could all be over, surely. I looked long and hard at the patio, at the lines running at right angles to one another between the slabs. I suddenly wondered what

Freddy was doing at that precise moment, hundreds of miles away. Then a very odd question popped into my head: would he be proud of me if I did it? I could feel myself setting on to tracks that would take me to a bad place and so I took a deep breath, a step back from the window, and said, 'Stop it,' out loud.

There was a knock at my door. It was unlocked. I quickly folded up the Suicide Club Charter and stuffed it back under the magazines in the bottom drawer of my desk.

'Come in,' I said.

It was my father.

'Hello, champ,' he said. 'Fancy going for a drive?'

I got into the passenger seat alongside my father and we drove in silence out of town. I didn't even want to speak because my throat was heavy and laden with antimatter. My life was a wreck and I could see no way out.

We reached this forest on the edge of town that my father used to bring me to when I was a kid. He drove me up a dirt track and parked under a canopy of pines. He killed the engine and looked straight ahead. There was nobody about and it was quite serene.

Just like my father, I stared straight ahead. I guess if you were secretly filming it and the camera was looking in through the windscreen, it would have been quite moving; father and son staring ahead, not speaking because the son had hurt the father so badly.

We looked into that forest for about five minutes that, not surprisingly, felt like longer.

Eventually he spoke.

'Don't you know what you're doing to us?'

I couldn't look at him. I could see from the corner of my eye that he was staring at me.

'We're so worried about you, Rich.'

'I know,' I muttered. He was breaking through my walls. I wanted to tell him everything. All this time I still hadn't spilled my heart out to anybody about Clare, and I felt like bursting.

'Is there anything we can do?' There was a pause. 'You're going to destroy yourself. You know we love you, don't you?'

'Don't say that,' I said.

There was all this emotion in me but, because I knew myself so well, I knew that I wasn't going to let it out.

'We'd do anything for you, Rich. You're such a talented boy.'

I kept looking ahead.

With genuine sincerity, but with not enough strength to turn my head, I said, 'I'm sorry.'

'Come on, let's go for a walk,' he said.

We got out of the car and traipsed off into the woods. It was very cold, but it was Christmas and I was in a pine forest so that suited me fine. For a while the fresh air started to cleanse my insides, and I think I started to recover. It's funny how people say that, to get over something, you have to take a course of action *yourself* to get over it – like conquering your demons or something. But here I was, in the middle of the woods, and mother nature was healing me and I had nothing to do with it. It was pretty great, even though we didn't say anything to one another.

We found this brook running through the forest and we paused at the bank. We would have to get our feet wet if we wanted to get across. I thought to myself how amazing it was that I was here in this place doing something so joyous and *nobody* knew. We jumped into the water and the cold started attacking our feet immediately.

My father gasped.

'Jesus shits,' he shouted.

I looked at him and we started laughing. He had no idea

how much good he was doing – parents can always turn it on when they need to.

We waded across the three feet of water, which came up to our ankles, and clambered up the other side. It was muddy, but my dad made it up OK. I started the climb but the mud was more slippery than I had realized. I lost my footing and was about to fall back into the water. Instinctively I reached out and my hand grabbed on to the nearest thing that came to my touch. Which was the spindly outshoot of a bramble. My palm closed over the thorns and I gripped tight, not under-standing what I was doing. As the thorns punctured through my skin and into my flesh, I screamed out. The sudden shock made me stop thinking about my footing and I lost control. Electronic signals made my hand involuntarily squeeze the branch tighter and, as I slid backwards, my palm and the inside of my fingers were drawn along a gauntlet of thorns jutting from the main stem of the bramble. Each one stabbed at me and tore along the fleshy parts of my hands.

I released my grip and slid back into the water. I stumbled back but didn't fall. I looked down at my hand in horror. Flaps of skin were loose like those little thin flags you see on castles; tiny triangles of torn skin. The blood was flowing like a river delta over my palm. The agony was unbearable. It was like the thorns had decapitated the nodes off the top of my pain nerve endings. My hand was throbbing and I was getting bile in my gut. Why me? I asked.

I looked at my father. A real man would have borne the pain and carried on. A real man would have put the pain in a box in his head and locked it up. But I was having some sort of crisis inside.

'Are you OK?' said my father. 'Let me see.'

I held up my palm and the blood ran down my wrist into the sleeve of my sweater. I could have cried right there, but I wasn't *that* pathetic.

'I want to go home,' I said.

As we stumbled back through the forest, shattered and broken like a dream, I was overcome with an impending sense of dread.

Clare's game had broken my insides, being so horrible to Toby meant that I had passed a critical mass point that couldn't be redeemed, my mother hated me, my father did not trust me, I had no friends and now, after all of that, I was suffering intense physical pain. This was the end.

That night I read the book on screenwriting that my parents had bought for me. In it, it said that most screenplays are constructed in three acts and that at the end of a second act things get so bad that you can't imagine anything working out OK. I felt like I was at the end of Act Two in my life. I couldn't see how things could possibly get any worse. Everything had turned to dust.

But there was one thing left for me. One bright star in dark space. Emma. My counsellor. She would understand. The day before school started again, I couldn't get the thought of her out of my head. With everything gone I had nothing better to do than fall in love with her. Which I kind of did, I guess. You always need to find hope somewhere, right?

That night I couldn't sleep. I lay in bed sweating, my sheets getting caught up in my legs and my shorts riding up my thighs, making me restless. It was like I was in hell. As I finally drifted off to sleep and the real world faded to black, I could see four words in the blackness, as if they were on a page, and they made me feel better:

END OF ACT TWO

24

My first session with Emma was on my first day back at school after Christmas. The whole morning was spent trying to avoid people glaring at me and laughing at me. It was quite horrible but I didn't really care that much because they were headed on the road to shitsville.

I knocked on the door to the meeting room next to the headmaster's office and suddenly my malaise lifted. Emma looked even better than I remembered. Today she had her hair tied back behind her head so I could see her ears that stuck out and made her look like an elf. One of the elegant elves like in those *Lord of the Rings* films, not Christmas elves. She looked up with her hazel eyes and I almost died.

'Hello, Richard,' she said. She seemed too young to be talking in such an adult way. 'How are you?'

'I'm OK,' I said, trying to act cool.

I went to the table and sat in my chair and we looked at each other for a long time. I guess we were staring each other out and it felt like the right thing to do because we were both assessing one another; she was looking for certain reactions, I was just drinking in her beauty.

But I broke first.

'Did you have a nice Christmas?' I said.

'Great, thanks,' she said quite coldly, which I liked because

I'm drawn to that sort of stuff. 'Did you have a nice Christmas?'

'Not really,' I said, holding my hand up and showing her my bandage.

'I noticed that when you came in. What did you do?'

'I cut it on broken glass,' I said for no reason.

'Did it require stitches?'

'Yes.'

'How many?'

'One.'

'I didn't know you could get just one stitch.'

I just shrugged.

'It got infected.' This was true. My hand had basically turned green by New Year's Day.

'How was Christmas apart from what happened to your hand?'

'Not very good.'

'Why not?'

'My parents told me Father Christmas doesn't exist.'

Emma didn't respond because I was being arrogant and ugly.

'What's happened, Rich?'

Everything bad from my life flashed through my head but there was so much crap that I couldn't focus on anything. My neck was feeling heavy.

'Some bad things,' I choked.

'Do you want to tell me?'

As the conversation was moving forward, I felt myself opening up. My emotions were boiling up and bubbling over.

'I'm glad you're my counsellor and not Sylvia.'

'And why's that?'

'Because I like you,' I said honestly. 'And I didn't like

Sylvia.' I stopped for a moment. 'You're young and I feel like I can talk to you.'

'Do you think that our sessions will help you?'

I brought up my good hand and, with my second finger, scratched the top of my forehead, just below the hairline.

'No,' I said.

'Why not?'

I didn't feel like I could explain without offending her so I lied. And besides, if I told her about Freddy's theory of motivation and how it doesn't exist, she wouldn't understand.

'My friends found out that I'm in counselling,' I started. 'Do you know what happened to me?' I stared her right in the eye as I spoke. 'In the school disco, I had about thirty people stood around me in a circle' – I knew how bad this must have sounded, it *was* bad – '*laughing* at me because I was crazy.'

I could see that she was shocked. If you think about it, if you imagine it had actually happened to *you*, think how you would feel.

All Emma could say was, 'Children can be cruel sometimes.'

'You have no idea.'

I looked at her and, right there and then, and without prior knowledge, I poured out my heart to the girl in front of me. As I spoke I was determined not to start crying but it was just so hard. I won't start getting all metaphoric about how it was like a waterfall pouring out of me, but let me just say that it felt great to finally speak about this stuff to somebody who might understand everything. Life is *so* hard sometimes that you have to share your bad stuff with someone or you'll collapse.

When I think about it now, I reckon I probably said all that stuff about Clare, about my humiliation, about Toby and my mother, about hurting my hand, because, in some weird way, I thought Emma might feel sorry for me and fall in love with me. How crazy is that?

When I had finished my tears had gone back into their ducts and I felt *amazing*.

'Richard, listen, let me say this to you as a person, not a counsellor.'

I sat there, deflated and exhausted.

'I think that you are going to be fine. I know you've done a lot of bad things, but I also know that you've done a lot of good things as well. Shall I tell you what I think?'

'Don't bother, you're just going to say that I'm a self-loather. But I'm not.'

'Actually, Richard, you are. You've got two sides to you. One is the good side, the side that helps people and is kind and sensitive. The other side is the one that does the bad things, such as what you did following your parents' split, and the side that you say you can feel returning.'

'OK.'

'But you've also got this hinterland in between the two.'

I didn't expect her to say that.

'That's the place where you have these deep-rooted emotions. It's the place where you think too deeply about everything, and where you beat yourself up over everything. What you said about you being a self-loather? That's interesting,' she said.

'Why?'

'Because most people don't think about that sort of stuff.' She sighed. 'There's no doubting your intelligence, Richard, but intelligence and being a good person do not necessarily go hand in hand.'

'I know that. I know I'm intelligent, but I still try to be a good person as well.' It felt strange to talk about this sort of stuff, because I kind of hated psychoanalysis.

217

'The very fact that you think about self-loathing means that you have it in you.'

I rolled my eyes.

'But don't worry, it's healthy to question yourself. You're lucky because, although you think deeply about things, you can still act in the real world. You still put yourself out there. Let me explain. When you were at the school disco, and you kissed that girl who you thought you loved, that was a brave thing to do. A genuine self-loather would never do something like that. They would never put their innermost emotions on the line like you did. For all you knew, that action could have led to you and her going out. You could have been happy. Self-loathers don't usually give themselves a shot at happiness, even if it's right there in front of them for the taking.'

'So what's wrong with me?'

She smiled.

'There's nothing wrong with you, Richard. A lot of people would love to be you. You seem to attract drama.'

A tingle ran up my spine when she said the word 'drama'.

'But this emotional hinterland that I mentioned also houses a strong self-destructive part of you. You like to experience exciting things and at the same time you don't like to hurt people. So the only way you can get a rush is to hurt yourself.'

I stopped listening at that point. Maybe because she was getting too psycho-analytic, maybe I was bored, or maybe she was getting a little too close for comfort. I already felt better now than I had since before Christmas, so that was enough for me.

She kept talking and I just used the time to look at her. She was so pretty it was almost unreal. I don't think I was ever actually in love with her or anything like that, but I was infatuated with her. I imagined having sex with her, which I know is crass but I think it's important to say because you should know the sort of relationship we had. As I've said before, I'm quite good-looking, well, I'm not horrendously ugly anyway, so my thoughts of having some sort of affair with her were not totally unrealistic, even though I was fifteen and she was, I guessed, twenty-one.

But, nevertheless, I'd had enough. The screen doors came down.

I left the room feeling a little bit like a soldier who's near a bomb going off. My body was going hot and cold. It seemed strange that a person I had only met a handful of times was able to know me as well as Emma. In truth, it freaked me out a little. I didn't want somebody to understand my head through textbooks and lectures. It wasn't special, or human.

I wandered up the staff corridor in a daze. The bell hadn't gone for morning break yet and it seemed like I had the whole school to myself. I looked down the corridor ahead of me and listened to my shoes on the floor. The fact that I was soon going to have to face my classmates was numb in my head. It was there but I couldn't think about it for too long.

I made my way to the boys' toilets and hopped up on to the wooden table at the end of the washbasins. The toilets looked smaller than usual. I started wondering if Jenny was back from America yet, and what she would think about what had happened, and just then the bell started ringing and I jumped with shock. My back faced the door and I dramatically put my head in my hands, waiting for the first of the kids to arrive.

'He's in here,' a familiar voice said behind me.

I turned around and climbed down from the table.

'We thought you'd be in here.'

It was Matthew. His hair had grown over Christmas and he looked much scruffier than normal. He had always been so neat and tidy, ever since I had known him.

'I didn't feel like going outside,' I said in a flat voice.

'How are you feeling?'

I shrugged.

'I've just been in counselling.'

'So I heard.'

My breath jumped out of my mouth. How had he heard?

'I'm joking,' he smiled.

I did a big sigh. 'I don't like this new sense of humour of yours.'

Matthew laughed.

'Sorry.' He looked into the corridor and smiled to someone who had come into the toilet.

Freddy looked incredibly healthy. There was colour in his face for the first time ever and there was a sense of, I don't know, *cleanliness* about him.

'Hello, Richie,' he chirped.

There was ten feet between them and me.

'Hello, Freddy.'

'So, Clare feels bad for what she did.' He came right out with it.

I didn't like the way that Freddy had clearly talked about me to her when I wasn't there but I was too deflated to think about heavy things like that at the moment. I looked at my shoes, at the lace that had started to come undone.

'My life is a mess,' I said suddenly. I instantly felt small and pathetic for having said it. I could feel them pitying me.

'It'll be OK,' said Matthew.

I climbed back up on to the table and watched my feet dangling in mid-air.

'I can't believe she did it, Matt. I can't believe how cruel it was.' I didn't realize at the time that I hadn't called him Matthew.

The atmosphere was unbelievably depressing and heavy. Freddy jumped up next to me and Matt stood opposite. A couple of first years came in to use the toilets.

'I suppose you heard about the kids finding out I was in counselling,' I said.

I felt his hand on my shoulder, his fingers gripping.

'Fuck them. We don't need them.'

Matthew agreed. 'They're just sheep. And I'm not just saying that to make you feel better, I'm saying it because it's true. They're a bunch of pricks.'

I looked at him, at Matt, and couldn't think of anything to say. Was this figure standing in front of me really my best friend? The boy who I loved because he never had a bad word to say about anyone?

'So what are we going to do to get Richie his cred back?' said Freddy, trying to lighten the mood.

'My cred?' I looked at him out of the corner of my eye and smiled.

'Cred is OK to use.'

'We should turn into the trench-coat mafia,' Matt laughed.

Freddy took his hand away from my shoulder. 'The best thing we can do is carry on as normal, show them that we don't care about them.'

'Yes!' Matt exclaimed. 'Your mate's band are playing in the Egg and Train on Saturday.'

'Johnny?' I said, starting to feel sick. He hadn't told me about any gig.

'Yeah, there was a poster in the window for it.'

'Right, we'll go to that,' said Freddy.

I shook my head.

'I don't know.'

'What do you mean, you don't know?'

'I mean I don't know if I fancy it.'

Freddy sighed, exasperated.

'Come on, Rich. You're starting to sound like Craig.'

I saw what he was getting at. I was being a little bit emo. I was moping.

'I haven't seen Craig in ages.'

'He's OK,' said Freddy. 'I went to his house last night.'

I was glad to be off the subject of me.

'What? His father let you in?'

'Yeah,' he replied, surprised that I would say that.

'But he hates you. He hates all of us after what we did to Bertie.'

Freddy smiled.

'Yeah, but I spoke to him about it and grovelled for forgiveness. He's OK.'

'So what did he have to say for himself? Where's he been?' I pushed my hands into my pockets because they were cold.

'Nothing, he's pretty much the same old Craig. I think he's a bit better. He's started hanging around with that boy from the airbase. Chad, is it?'

'Hang on,' I said with a slight laughter in my voice. 'Craig prefers that moron's company to ours?'

Freddy just shrugged.

'I guess so.'

After that, there was a bit of a pause as we all digested the atmosphere in the room. Although Matt and Freddy were trying to act positive to cheer me up, there was an obvious sadness in the air. It was freezing and the rusty old pipes and cold tile flooring mirrored the way I felt.

'You know what?' Freddy said. 'Maybe we should try and push the Suicide Club along.'

Matt and I looked at him.

'What are we? Two months down the line? Let's try and push Craig into doing it,' he said matter-of-factly. His voice was still chirpy when he said it. He was grinning. I couldn't tell if he was being sarcastic. It was kind of evil.

222

I suddenly started to realize something. Deep down in my belly something dawned on me.

'Come on,' he said. 'We don't need him any more. He's with Chad now. Let's see how far we can go.'

Is he being serious? I thought. But there was no need to ask myself the question because I already knew the answer. The façade had cracked. The real Freddy was finally with us. My skin went all clammy. Something in my head seemed to click into place. I looked at Freddy but he wasn't there. The boy I knew wasn't there, at least. I saw the mask on his face again, the same mask I had seen when he had killed Bertie. A stupid voice said, What is this monster I see before me?

'Freddy, you shouldn't say stuff like that,' Matt said.

'Look,' he said. 'Craig would be better off dead. He's fucked for life and we all know it, so what's the point in him?'

Something started to lift in my gut. A pressure was being relieved. I should have been feeling terrible because of what Freddy had just said, but the opposite was true. I was feeling better. Suddenly everything was clear.

I jumped down from the table, my thoughts having now resolved into a solid idea. Freddy would not manipulate me this time. This time I had had enough.

'Well,' I said loudly.

Freddy and I were face to face. His blank stare and insincere smile just confirmed what I thought. He was a desert underneath. I waited for a second, allowing the moment to mushroom around us.

Then I said, slowly and deliberately, right into his mask, 'I've . . . got . . . to . . . go.'

My meeting with Emma, me telling her about all of the things that had happened to me, had loosened something that had been stuck inside me. Freddy's words had dislodged it completely. Suddenly everything made sense. Everything bad in my life was *because* of the Suicide Club, not despite it. Freddy had pulled down a screen with his version of the world on it, and I had fallen under his spell. The world wasn't the bad place that he said it was. I had believed him because I had wanted to. I had believed that Freddy was showing me the way, but he wasn't.

My fall from grace had actually taken place *since* meeting Freddy. I thought he had come in and changed my life for the better. But that wasn't the case at all. He had wrecked my life, but had done it with style and a smile on his face.

Before Freddy, I hadn't been the best guy in the world but at least I respected things. Now I didn't. I had been moving away from my bad side but Freddy had steered me back round to face it, said that it was OK to embrace. It was easier to follow him because he knew my insides and knew what appealed to me and I had been too stupid to see. So I made a decision right there and then, as I walked away along the corridor full of kids, to pull myself out of the quagmire and back to the real world.

I wouldn't have had the strength to act had nothing forced me into action. In my screenwriting book it said that the main character had to have enough resolve to keep trying to get over his problems. But I wasn't in a story, I was in real life and real life isn't so easy. I would have kept getting lower and lower had it not been for what Freddy said in the toilets about trying to get Craig to kill himself. I guess in that respect, he had sort of saved me.

Break was almost over. I made my way to my next lesson, which I remember being geography. It would be the first time I had seen Clare since the Christmas party. The other kids were still in the yard and I was the first person to arrive at the classroom. I took a seat right at the back, as far out of the way as possible. Through the windows I could hear all the kids talking and laughing. Their voices were being filtered through the silence of the empty room. The bell rang to signal the end of break and I started to feel nervous as I took out my books and pens.

I pretended to be reading as the first of my classmates bowled into the room. They were talking loudly about something but stopped suddenly when they saw me sat at the back of the class. I pretended to carry on reading as they went to their seats but I was watching them through the tops of my eyes.

As more and more kids arrived I could sense them looking at me and thinking, What a freak. I think the worst thing about it was the way in which none of them said hello to me. Not one. I had known them for years but here I was being ignored, an outcast. I realized that it was going to be a long way back but I had done it before and I was sure I was strong enough to do it again.

And then I saw her. She drifted into the classroom on her own, her bag slung lazily over her left shoulder. She glanced around the room and suddenly our eyes met. My heart leapt into my mouth. Her lips formed into the tiniest of smiles and I looked down at my book again. A few seconds passed before I felt a presence approach and stand over me.

'Can I sit here?' she said.

My heart was beating like mad. Her black hair looked lank.

I moved across so that she could sit down. I wanted to tell her that I no longer wanted anything to do with her, and I wanted to do it like a man, by having a conversation. After what she had done to me at the Christmas party, there was no going back. But when she sat down a waft of her scent spiralled up my nostrils and I was catapulted back to the acid kiss that she had delivered to my lips. I knew then that I was doomed because, even though she had done that to me, I was still in love with her. I was weak.

'I can't believe I did it,' she said. 'I can't believe I did it to you. I'm so sorry.'

'It's OK,' I said pathetically.

She sat next to me and I went back to staring at my book.

'Rich . . . I will *never* do something like that again.' Her words were naked and honest. We weren't playing our little games any more.

We said nothing for a while.

'I love you,' I said. I had to say it. At last I wanted her to know. I looked at her.

Her face changed, like she had never been told it by some-body before. Or maybe she had never been told it by somebody who was genuinely close to her, not like the guys who she used to have sex with. When I saw her face like that, I caught shattered glimpses of a vulnerability that I hadn't seen before. She was just a girl. Everything that had happened since last October had crumpled our relationship into an un-recognizable shape. In that instant I think a bond burned up between us, but it was sad and remote. A melancholy and infinite sadness separated our bodies now, just like the Smashing Pumpkins album that housed her most favourite song in the whole world. After I told her that I loved her, she didn't say anything. The moisture on the surface of her eyes said enough.

I detached the heart part of my brain. I had to. I had had practice doing it before and I was glad for it. I don't think I could have done it without my experience, without my ability to make myself cold.

'But I don't want to speak to you any more,' I said.

We stared at each other. The teacher came into the room and shut the door behind him, ending the conversation before it had really begun.

The tear broke in Clare's eye and she turned away from me. She picked up her bag from the floor, got to her feet, and ran out of the classroom.

For all the world I wish that it didn't have to be like this, but I didn't own all the world and so my wish did not come true. It *was* like this. It was cold and hard, but I felt better. All I knew, all I cared about, was that I felt better. Deep, deep, deep down, right in amongst it all, *I felt better.*

25

After school that night, I knew that there was something I had to do. Rather than take my usual route home, I called by Craig Bartlett-Taylor's house.

His mother answered and gasped when she saw me. She went to slam the door, but I held up my hand.

'Wait,' I said. 'Please wait.'

God bless that woman, she did wait.

'Please let me see Craig. I have to speak to him.'

The way she looked at me made me feel ashamed.

I spoke like a child would speak.

'Mrs Bartlett-Taylor, I didn't do anything to the peregrine falcon. None of us did. It was Freddy who killed him, and we covered him because we were his friends. But not any more. I'm trying to put things right. Please let me speak to Craig.'

The edges of her lips moved but I couldn't tell if they moved up or down. Whatever, she opened the door and let me in.

'Thank you,' I said as kindly as I could. I wasn't trying to be like an adult, I was trying to be like a child because that was what I was. I didn't want to appear as a precocious youngster, because that wasn't me. I knew my place. I didn't want to pretend to be more grown-up than I was.

The stairway suddenly didn't look as depressing as I remembered it. I bounded up there like a rabbit and headed for Craig's room. I knocked but there was no answer so I went in anyway.

I automatically looked at his bed, expecting to see him lying there, staring at the ceiling. But he wasn't. Looking up, I saw him leaning on the back two legs of his desk chair, his feet up on his desk, a copy of *National Geographic* in his hands.

'Hi, Rich,' he said warmly. 'How's it going?'

There was a bizarre pause because his reaction was straight out of left field. I suddenly started to think that maybe Craig could recover and lead a normal life.

'I'm fine,' I said. 'Were you in school today?'

'No. I don't go to that school any more.'

This nearly knocked me off my feet.

'What?'

'I've changed to the local comprehensive.'

I had to blink and shake my head.

'What?'

'I know. I really like it there.'

'Did you tell Freddy this last night?' I asked.

'Why would I tell him? He's one of the reasons I left.'

I smiled. I think Craig knew a lot more than I had realized. I was speechless.

'I didn't like the old school because you all think you're special,' he said. 'You think that you're better than everyone else. Well, now I'm the one who's in the best classes.' He wasn't ranting, he was speaking truthfully and it made me feel great. 'You guys don't understand what the rest of the world is like.'

'I know,' I said quickly. 'Craig, that's amazing. I feel the exact same way as you. I've been a prick, but now I think I can see where I've been going wrong. This Suicide Club idea, and hating everybody? It's bad for you.'

Craig smiled and lobbed his magazine on to his desk.

'Don't take this the wrong way, but I don't want to speak to any of you any more.'

You see, I should have been offended by that. I should have screamed at him and cursed at him because we had been the ones who had been nice to him after he tried to kill himself. But I wasn't angry at all because I realized that he and I were the same. We had both realized the truth and we needed to stay apart.

'You're right, Craig.' I got up and walked over to him. We shook hands and I went to leave. Just as I got to the door, I turned round.

'Just promise me one thing,' I said.

'What?'

'If Freddy tries to speak to you, if you see him anywhere around town and he tries to say something to you? Promise me that you won't listen to what he says.'

Craig chuckled.

'I've never listened to anything he's said.'

And with that I walked out of Craig Bartlett-Taylor's life. The sneaky little monkey might not have been so stupid after all. I couldn't believe that he knew the truth all along. My respect for him shot through the roof and I smiled all the way home. Yes, he was gone, but at least he was safe from us.

When I got home I decided to run the vacuum cleaner over the living-room carpet to try and please my mother. She told me that it wouldn't be so easy, that I couldn't buy her forgiveness, but I didn't mind too much – I could wait for her to come round.

Jenny came back from America on the Thursday. I found it difficult to comprehend how she and Matthew had fallen under Freddy's spell as much as I had. I had my bad side and Freddy had preyed on that, but they were so normal. It wasn't until the Friday that I spoke to Jenny.

'Rich,' she called. She had in her hand a notebook with a metallic spiralled spine and was smiling massively. 'I've got something to show you.' She skipped over to me and started to open the book. Inside were a series of photographs. 'I had the film developed that you saw me taking before Christmas, remember? When we were in town together? The photos for Freddy.'

'I remember.'

She showed me the photos, and I was startled by what I saw. The people in the pictures were blurred and out of focus whilst the backgrounds, the shops and lights, were crisp, focused and bright.

'This is because of a long shutter-speed?'

'Yup. It's cool, right?'

'Yeah.'

It was more than cool. The photographs were superb. They just sucked your eyes into them as though they had magnetic powers. The photographs she had up outside the art room were of bowls of fruit and horses, not cool stuff like this. She was really opening up her talent.

'Rich, I heard about what happened to you at the Christmas party.'

'Yeah, well,' I said.

'I'm sorry.'

'How was California?'

'A lot warmer than this.' She lifted her arm up slightly to the sky.

'Did you miss Matt?'

She smiled and nodded her head like a little girl.

I felt a tingle.

'So. Are you going to the Egg and Train tomorrow night to see Atticus?'

'What, are you kidding? You try and stop me. Matt, Freddy and Clare are coming to my place beforehand. If you want to come, you're more than welcome.' Her American accent was quite sexy when she said things like 'more than welcome'.

'I'm OK,' I said.

She seemed taken aback by this.

'You sure?'

'Yeah. I don't really want to do this Suicide Club thing any more.'

Her face was now just bewildered.

'You don't want to do it?'

I moved my head left and right.

'I need to take a break from it. It's just . . . a bit too intense for me at the moment.' I was really trying not to hurt her feelings.

Her face shifted ever so slightly, just a few muscle movements, and everything changed. Her features now told of being torn between offended and disgusted.

'Whatever,' she said. 'Well . . .' She slammed her book shut. Actually, she didn't slam it, she closed it harder than normal. 'I'd better go.' And she walked off.

'Jenny, wait,' I said. She stopped, her back to me. 'Don't you see?'

Her head turned and she looked at me over her shoulder.

'See what? That you don't want to spend time with your friends?'

'No,' I laughed lamely. 'Freddy . . . he . . .'

She came back over to me, her notebook under her arm.

'Don't you realize what we've done for you, Rich?'

'I'm sorry?'

She pinched her lips together.

'I just don't get you sometimes. I've gotta go.' And she walked away.

I watched her cross the yard, her blonde head bobbing up

232

and down. I kicked a stone and sighed. Of course I felt bad, but I really did have to make a clean break. I knew that one day she would understand. As I watched her disappear behind a group of schoolchildren I thought, She'll see it in the end.

I could feel myself moving out of the doldrums and as I got ready that night I felt an energy in my bones that I had thought was long since gone. There was a party at Johnny's band-mate's house – he lived on his own – which I had agreed to attend.

I filled a bag with a sleeping bag, towel, spare clothes, toothpaste and stuff so that I could sleep over there.

I listened to The Shins to get myself into a happy, fun mood and by the time I bounded out of the house I was the good child Richie Harper, ready for anything. I was on the up and up!

I got to the house at around seven. I could hear the band thrashing away from outside. They were getting some final practice in for the gig tomorrow night. The front door was open so I walked in. There was a long hallway with a bicycle leaning against a wall and a massive Canadian flag hanging off it. There was noise coming from every direction. The band were upstairs, but a stereo was blaring out of the living room. That's where I went, just to see who was there.

I wasn't quite expecting to see what I did. The room was stuffed full of girls of all shapes and sizes, the type of girls that go to art college, you know? The room was thick with smoke. I could hardly see but it was awesome. I was particularly impressed because they were listening to a singer called Willy Mason. He's got this song called 'Oxygen' that you have to hear when you're down in the dumps. It's so up it's unreal; all about how if we stick together we can make it through and save the world.

When they realized that I had entered the room, I got a few smiles rather than childish giggles.

'Hi,' said one of the girls, who had brown hair in one of those cool bobs.

'Hello,' I said. 'Is Johnny here?'

'He's upstairs.'

I smiled at her as best I could and she smiled back. She tilted her head a little bit and her hair caught the light. It was then that I realized that her hair wasn't brown at all. It was that blondey sort of colour that was a little bit brown but I don't know what you call it. Mousy, maybe. I got a small tingle in my belly.

'OK.' I turned to leave and totally embarrassed myself. The door had swung shut because it was one of those fire doors and I almost walked straight into it. They all saw it. I stopped where I was and smiled inwardly. It was OK.

I jumped up the stairs, still happy. I slammed through the door to where the band were practising and grinned like a canoe at Johnny. He saw me and motioned with his head to the table, where there were four crates of lager. I pointed at the cans and raised my eyebrows questioningly. He nodded his head. I went over and took a can. Apart from the band, I was the only one in there. There was a beanbag against the far wall so I slumped into it and admired the band past my Converses.

I didn't need Freddy and the others any more. This was great.

The band were good, but I hate it in books when people talk at length about music just to show off so I won't say any more about Atticus.

When they stopped playing I said, 'Do you realize that the downstairs of this house is full of beautiful women?'

★

234

It was late and we were all in the living room listening to music. Johnny's friend didn't have any light bulbs in the overhead sockets so all of the light came from lamps in the room and they smoothed out any hard edges.

The scent of marijuana was all-conquering.

'This is great,' I heard somebody whisper in my ear.

I turned around. It was that girl I had spoken to when I had come in. In the dark, I could hardly see her face apart from two bright specs of light in her eyes.

You may think that what happens from here on in to the end of this chapter didn't happen. For those of a more cynical persuasion, you may say that my story comes off the rails here because nothing so amazing could possibly happen. But if you're a dreamer, a real romantic who's willing to go out on a limb and embrace beautiful ideas, then you will *know* that it did happen. And I say to you now that the way I recount these events to the end of the chapter is completely accurate.

'I've never been to a party like this,' I said to her. 'It's amazing, isn't it?'

She came and sat next to me.

'So you're having a good time?'

'What, are you kidding me?' I said Americanly, because I sometimes slip into that frame of mind when I'm drunk. 'I love it here. I just wish I had gone to your school.'

She smiled. 'We're OK.'

'So what's your name?' I said quietly.

I missed her reply.

'What?' I said.

She moved her mouth up to my ear and cupped her hand over it.

'Sam,' came her voice.

I nodded.

'Hi, Sam.'

'So you're Johnny's friend?'

'Yeah. I went to primary school with him but then I went to Atlantic High and he went to the comp.'

'He talks about you a lot.'

My heart suddenly leapt. Was that true? I don't think I had ever received such a massive compliment.

'Really?'

'Of course. He loves you.'

I started feeling nervous because I had some idea of what was going to happen, and I always get nervous when things are about to happen with a girl. I think everybody should; it's part of the buzz.

'Do you want to burn one?' she said.

'Burn one?' It was obviously a saying of theirs, but I didn't know what it meant.

'Burn one,' she said. 'A joint.'

'Ohhh,' I said. 'Riiiight.'

'I thought that's what the American kids called it.'

I made a confused face.

'I don't really hang around with the Americans.'

'What?' she almost shouted. She became suddenly animated. 'If I went to your school, I'd love to hang around with them. They're hilarious.'

'Really?' I said. I didn't mind the Americans, but I would hardly call them hilarious.

'They're so stupid,' she laughed.

'Yeah,' I laughed back, even though I didn't mean it. Americans aren't stupid, they just wear their hearts on their sleeves and cynical people don't like that. I hoped that Sam wasn't a cynic.

She reached over to the coffee table and picked up her bag. From it she took a Marlboro Light cigarette packet and from that she took a joint of cannabis. She lit the spliff and took a few deep breaths from its end. She opened her mouth and, even in the dim light, I saw the smoke swirl inside like a vortex. Eventually she closed her mouth and, when she next breathed out, there was hardly any smoke left. She took another drag and passed it on to me, before flopping back into the chair and looking at the ceiling.

Just as I moved the joint to my own mouth, I saw a boy placing a CD into the player. He waited for a second, pressed play, and you wouldn't believe the sound that came out.

As I breathed in the smoke from the joint, a xylophone started singing into the room. The tune was so simple, like a little child had written it. All of a sudden a guitar and a bass and soft drums kicked in and the room fell into absolute silence save for the music. I sucked the smoke into my chest and felt the effects right away. I passed the joint on after about four tokes and sat back.

The music washed right into me like my skin was a dry beach as the tide moved in and saturated the sand totally and inevitably from below. I turned to Sam. My mouth was dry and my head was purring.

'What's this song?' I said so quietly that it was almost a whisper.

She had closed her eyes. I thought she was asleep. Her face looked so pretty. Clare didn't even cross my mind.

'Velvet Underground,' she said from her state. 'It's called "Sunday Morning".'

I touched her hand with my little finger.

'It's amazing.'

She suddenly opened her eyes and lifted her neck up from the chair.

'It's my all-time favourite song,' she said, staring me right in the eyes.

The spliff had made its way about halfway round the room and I could feel something amazing in the air, like an electric storm. Everybody was just sat there, listening to the music, glad to be alive. I kissed Sam lightly on the lips.

After about five minutes, she got up from her seat and turned to me, held out her hand. Can you remember at the start of the book when I said that I had never experienced life in slow motion? Well, right then, in that room, I did. Her hand moved towards me whilst the other one picked up her bag. I took her hand in mine and we walked out of the door. The music swelled inside my head as if it was suddenly being piped right into my brain. My heart was thundering because I knew what I was doing. I was crashing through barriers. I was nervous, but I knew that I had to do this.

We went up the stairs and I had to let go of her hand because the stairway was too narrow. We went into a bedroom with the lights turned off. An orange glow came in through the window from the street lamps. Sam went into her bag and took out a personal CD player. From its belly she removed a disc and popped it into the machine. The same song that we had been listening to downstairs started playing and I looked at her and smiled. I was sat against the headboard of the bed. She came over to me and my heart suddenly slumped down an inch. She brought her face in close to mine and I could see her eyes reflecting the amber light. Some people's eyes really reflect light, just like Sam's, and it makes you think that they have a better soul than most people. She was breathing on me and it made me crazy with buzzing before I saw her head tilt slightly, her lips part, her hair flop lazily across her face and her eyes close.

I won't say any more about it because I cherish those memories and you can't have them. I wouldn't know how to write about that stuff anyway because it would either come out as cheesy, or cold and nihilistic. And it was neither of those things. It was perfect.

About an hour later the bedroom door was thrust open

and the light was switched on and I was back in the real world away from the warmth.

I squinted at the person in the doorway. It was Johnny.

'Have you seen outside?' he shouted. His excitement was always contagious.

Sam and I looked at each other and then out the window and, not for the first time that night, things got a *lot* better. Huge flakes of snow were drifting down out of the sky.

'Holy shit,' I said.

Sam let go of this shriek and grabbed her clothes. I pulled on my jeans and went to the window. I looked down on the street and saw all of the kids from the party running around, snow lying thick on the ground, being balled in their hands, and being thrown at anybody who got in the way. They were loving it, loving life, just loving *snow* because there's nothing better. This was being alive, I suddenly realized. One night. One night away from the Suicide Club and look at what had happened. I got a sick feeling in my stomach because I started to think that I may have wasted my life up to this point. But I shook that feeling clear because I wanted to enjoy this moment because everything in life is made of moments. Don't ever let an old moment wreck a new one. Please don't do that.

There was a tug at my arm. I turned around and Johnny was holding out my shirt. He was such an amazing friend. So full of life and nothing bad inside.

'Are you coming?' he said.

26

The next morning I awoke on one of the settees in the living room. Cold, grey light lasered in through the window. My clothes were soaking wet from the melted snow and I was freezing. But I felt alive. Each cell in my body was tingling with a new energy. I felt like I was a little kid again.

Looking around the room I saw it was empty. Crushed cans and half-full glasses had been left on the tables and arms of chairs. I sat up and rubbed my eyes. I found my bag, jumped in the shower, cleaned my teeth and got changed into my spare clothes. By now I felt even more refreshed than before.

When I went back downstairs, Johnny was watching TV with a bowl of cereal.

'Are you nervous about tonight?' I said.

'Not really. I'm a professional.'

I sat down in the armchair next to his.

'Yeah, right.'

'You and Sam seemed to be having a good time last night.'

I looked ahead at the TV, trying to avoid the question.

'Is she going tonight?'

'I think so.'

I knew that I didn't love Sam, but I did like her. I hoped that we could be friends and never mention what had happened the night before. I don't know why I felt that way and in that respect I guess I was a hypocrite because I don't like it when people have sex just for the sake of the physical sensation, which is a self-righteous thing to say I know, but it's just the way I feel. Actually, that's not entirely true. What I should have said is that I don't like it when people have sex just for the physical sensation and then brag about it to their friends – that's what I don't like because it means they don't get how deep human emotions can go and that makes me sad. And on that point I was not guilty.

The afternoon was bitterly cold. I was glad that Johnny had lent me his scarf and gloves to cart the band's equipment from the house to the pub. The sky was a deep, deep blue because there was no pollution hanging in the air – that had been washed out by the snow, which was now clinging to the insides of kerbs and shady walls. Little cotton-wool balls of cloud were in the sky and I knew that the day was going to turn into one of those days that you look back on because something magical happens and it gets ingrained into your memory. Nothing ever happens on such days; there's just something in the air, you know?

I spent the afternoon drinking cans of Coke whilst the band did their sound checks. I even smoked a few cigarettes, which was totally unlike me, because I wasn't drunk. But they made my head feel great.

The day disappeared beneath me, like the road when you're riding your bike and you look straight down.

By eight o'clock the pub was packed and that's when I caught my first glimpse of Freddy. I saw him just as a flash as he moved into a gap between two groups of people before disappearing again like a shark. When I saw him I got a sudden jolt in my upper body. I couldn't quite place the feeling at first. I hadn't seen him since that day in the school toilets when he had said that he wanted us to talk Craig into

241

killing himself. I suddenly knew what the feeling was: dread. I dreaded Freddy.

I moved in the opposite direction to that in which he was moving.

'Rich,' I heard a voice call. I looked up. It was one of Johnny's friends. He was stood in a group of boys, some of whom I recognized, some of whom I didn't.

I went over to them but couldn't follow the thread of the conversation because I was thinking about Freddy. Why did he have to be here? Why couldn't I have this time? Why did he have to push in on it?

I kept looking over my shoulder, expecting to see him standing right behind me with that smile of his all over his face. Suddenly the jukebox kicked into life and I jumped. My skin started to crawl when the music came on. It was that Green Day song that has those lines about being alone, and lonely streets.

I hoped to God that the song wasn't symbolic for the moment. I had been feeling so great lately but now I was receding into a malaise. Just because I had *seen* Freddy. I hadn't even spoken to him.

My frame of mind switched in my head and I started looking at Johnny's friends. I can't explain it, but something changed. Emma, my counsellor, had told me that I had two sides to my personality; one was the nice kid and the other was the self-destructive kid, and I think I had just flicked the switch. My skin went clammy and I hated myself for thinking too deeply about things when there was life out there to live. So why did I have to hit these troughs where everything seemed so black? Why couldn't I be the nice kid all the time? How could I change so instantly?

I turned to move away from the group of kids and saw, straight ahead of me, staring at me, Craig Bartlett-Taylor. My heart froze when I saw him. He had his vacant stare on his face. I could tell that he had reverted to his old depressed self. I could tell instantly. He had receded with me, like our souls were intermingled and dependent on each other. I took a few steps towards him. As I got closer, I saw that his face looked swollen somehow. It was darkish and I couldn't really see him in the low light. As I got closer I saw that he had a black eye.

'Shit,' I said. 'What happened to you?'

'Hey,' called a voice.

I swung round just as a pair of hands pushed into my chest and knocked me backwards. I almost lost my footing but my good balance prevented me from falling. I looked at who had pushed me. There he was, haircut and all. Chad. The American kid from the base.

'What the fuck are you doing?' I said, sort of offended. I only wanted to help.

'Get away from him. He doesn't need you, man.'

'What the fuck would you know, Chaaaad?' I looked at Craig. 'Who hit you?' I said.

'What the fuck do you care?' Chad snorted.

I felt somebody on my left flank. I knew who it was immediately.

'What's going on?' he said.

'This moron just pushed me,' I said.

Matt looked at Chad.

'Why did you do that?'

'You can fuck off as well, Matt. You used to be a nice guy and now look at you.' Chad pointed to the scarf tied around Matt's neck.

Matt just sneered at him, like he was a lower life form.

'Are you OK, Craig?'

Craig looked at Matt.

'I'm OK. The kids from my new school don't like the *exceptional*.'

Whoa! I didn't like it when Craig said that. I didn't like it at all. When I had spoken to him in his bedroom, he had seemed to be thinking so straight, but now here he was speaking like Freddy.

'Come on, man,' said Chad. 'Let's get out of here.' He threw one of his massive arms around Craig's neck and pulled him away from us, cutting the golden ropes from that rancid bond that had burned up between the three of us when he said the word 'exceptional'.

And then, just as sharks can smell the scent of blood from miles away, they had all swarmed around me. Freddy was grinning at me, but his eyes looked cold. Clare had her hands in her pockets, her face ashen. Jenny was there with her warm colours but her insides were all twisted up and rotten. I was trapped.

'You OK, Rich?' Freddy said.

I looked at their faces.

'Why are you standing so close to me?'

'What do you mean?' he laughed. There was a pause. 'What happened to Craig?'

'I don't know.' I couldn't understand why my heart was thumping so hard.

Jenny folded her arms. She had on her rainbow sweatbands. 'Tell them what you said to me,' she said.

'What?'

'Tell these people, your *friends*, what you said about them.'

I was even more nervous now. It was like I was being hunted. I wondered if this was how people had felt when we had spoken to them. I wondered if I had ever been this intimidating.

'I don't know . . .' I trailed off.

'Why did you say that stuff?' His voice was like a drone, like he was a zombie. Freddy's grin had gone. 'Are we not good enough for you any more?'

244

There was that brewing, undefined craziness in his eyes. I thought he could lash out at me any second like a tentacle thrashing out of a sea monster.

'I didn't say anything,' I said, searching for some inner strength.

'You said you don't want to hang around with us any more.'

A new song came on the jukebox now. I didn't know it. It was alien. I was detached from the rest of the pub. All there was now was me and the Suicide Club and the wooden floor on which we stood.

'I didn't say—' I didn't know why I was being so pathetic.

'You said it,' said Freddy. 'I just want to know why.' He took a step in, even closer.

I glanced at Clare, who I expected to have a smug grin on her face. But she didn't. She was almost crying. I knew her well enough to know that.

I looked Freddy in the eye.

'I didn't say that, Freddy. I said that I didn't want to hang around with *you* any more.' And I pointed at his face so that he knew exactly what I was saying.

The surroundings suddenly re-emerged out of the ether and I was back. I took a step away from Freddy and looked at Clare. She broke the eye-line and looked at her shoes. I almost died when she did that, but instead I turned around and walked off into the crowd.

'Hey,' I heard from behind me. Freddy's voice sounded angry. I stopped and swung back, expecting him to hit me. 'You're not what I thought you were,' he shouted across the ten yards between us.

The jukebox died out and instantaneously there was a squeal of feedback from the PA speakers. I winced as the noise drilled into my skull.

Then I heard Johnny's voice.

'Good evening,' he shouted into his mike.

I looked at the stage. The whole band were up there, lights singing out from behind them like heaven, cutting five heroic silhouettes out of space. The crowd cheered.

They were ready to go.

'We're Atticus.'

And then the guitars raged into the room like the SAS storming a building. The drums were crisper, the bass louder, the guitar seething with divine angst.

I turned back to Freddy.

'I thought you *meant* it, Rich.' I caught a strange look on his face as it flashed across his features. Sorrow. I shook my head, confused. Was I witnessing vulnerability? For a second I saw the Freddy who I had fallen in love with, the little lost schoolboy sent away by his parents.

I went to say something but my words caught. I didn't know what I wanted to say to him.

Suddenly, there was a commotion near the stage and feedback ripped out into the room again like a snaking electrical wire spewing blue energy in incandescent sparks. My head snapped around quickly. Something was happening. I didn't get a forewarning of doom, I just knew that something was happening. There was a sudden unity of screams from the crowd at the front of the stage. The drums were still banging and the one guitar was still thrashing. I craned my neck. Craig Bartlett-Taylor was on the stage. The spotlights showed everybody how puffed up his face was, his eye purple and black. Tears scored his cheeks like acid. Something metal glinted in his hand as he raised it to his head.

I had stopped breathing. There was another scream, a frantic, chaotic, atomic mass of distributed shock. Johnny moved in for Craig but he stepped to one side and looked out into the crowd. Whispers of smoke were in the air and time moved so fast that there was nothing that anybody could do. Craig moved something underneath his thumb. A third scream crashed from the front of the stage to the back of the room like a tsunami and then, right in front of everybody, and in an act that sent into oblivion all of his pain and anger and sadness and indifference, Craig Bartlett-Taylor pulled the trigger and blew his brains out.

27

His body went instantly and sickeningly limp. His face kind of crumpled on the side that he shot himself in and the bullet ripped out of the other side and took with it an explosion of blood and skull. I watched it all in vivid reality, unblinking. Absolutely nothing went through my head when it happened. For the first second, I just watched his body topple sideways.

I found myself pushing through the crowd, heading for the stage. Freddy was right behind me. Everybody else was too shocked to do anything. I got to the front, where lots of girls were crying. Johnny had turned away and was crouching on the stage, seemingly unable to comprehend what had just happened. I turned my head to the left-hand side of the stage where Craig's body was lying. I jumped up on to the low platform and tried to pick him up.

I can't say that the thought that he might still be alive went through my head because it didn't. I knew he was dead because his body had gone from being *something* to being *nothing*, like his essence had left him and the thing on the stage was just a slab of meat.

Smoke was coming out of a crisp hole in his head where the bullet had gone in. I thought there would have been a lot more blood but there wasn't because the bullet was so hot it had sealed up the wound with searing heat. The other side of his head was a complete mess; a white mushy material that I guessed was his brain was poking out through the brilliant red of his blood.

Why I tried to hold him in my arms I have no idea. He was certainly dead. Freddy stood between me and Craig and the crowd so that nobody could look at his corpse. The way he was staring at him was crazy. He was just completely expressionless. I'd like to say that he gave himself away by letting an evil grin creep out from his mouth up his cheeks, but that didn't happen. He looked like he had looked when he'd killed Bertie: cold. But not cold in that he didn't care. More like he'd been hit over the head with an anvil that severed all the connections in his brain and made him a picture of confusion. I felt sorry for him. But then his face changed. Like it was suddenly full of dread. He was looking at something on Craig. On his knees, he leaned in and took something from Craig's pocket. I recognized what he had taken immediately. It was a folded sheet of yellow paper. Freddy looked at me and slipped the paper into his pocket. I felt like somebody had drawn a sharp blade across my chest with tremendous force, slashing my clothes, opening my flesh and scoring into the surface of my ribs. A yellow sheet of paper.

My mouth went dry and it was then that the doormen arrived on the stage. One of them told me and Freddy to move aside (he said it really kindly, 'Watch out, lads') whilst the other one lifted Craig in his arms like a sleeping child, as light as a feather. That's when I suddenly lost feeling in my legs and stumbled backwards. Behind me was the drum kit from the band and I sat on the bass drum, my head in my hands.

In my head I heard the noise and screams die down. People were filing out of the pub, following the doormen, trying to get a look at the show. The show that *I* had orchestrated. I was feeling sick. I now knew that Craig's death was because of me. Not just me, but because of me, Freddy, Jenny, Matthew, Clare, all of us. We had broken him in two like he was a twig. Christ, I thought, his poor fucking parents. I WCSed it and it was the worst one I had ever had because *it was going to come true*. At some time in the next hour, Craig's parents were going to be told that their son had killed himself; that he had put a gun to the side of his head and pulled the trigger. They no longer had a son because he was *dead*. He was fucking dead. I don't know how you use words to describe that feeling you get when someone dies. It can only ever last for a few seconds because it's so huge and complicated that if you think about it for longer than that your head will explode. It's that feeling that you just *get* – that sudden knowledge that death is final and irreversible and you'll never talk to that dead person again. And Craig's parents would get that feeling in waves over the coming months and years, probably for ever because he had done something Not Natural. Oh my God, how the hell were they going to go to bed tomorrow night? They'd have to climb those old stairs with horrible carpet knowing that they wouldn't be saying goodnight to their son because he was crazy and had killed himself. Oh my God, how do you even start to comprehend their grief? I wished that they would have a car crash and die so that they wouldn't have to go through it. I really did. They were too old and good for all this. I just could not imagine it because it was so very, very sad.

And it was my fault. Our fault. It was a fact, as undeniable as the spinning atoms. I knew it, Freddy knew it. I'm not being guilt-ridden for no reason – my knowledge was evidence-based. Because Freddy had taken that sheet of yellow paper from Craig's corpse. He had taken the Suicide Club Charter, which was probably the last thing that Craig ever read. It was the last time his eyes absorbed the light reflecting off a piece of writing that was decoded in his brain – the last message. A message that told him to kill himself. And he did. Jesus. We had killed him. Craig may have been unstable, and he may have tried to kill himself in the past, but we had told him that it was OK, that it was to be encouraged. I had gone over to his house, befriended him, dragged him into this utter mess. Without us, he would probably still be alive.

The bright-blue lights of an ambulance fractured my mind, here to take Craig away again, just as they had come for him at the very beginning of it all. Those lights had returned for him as if the dimensions had opened up to swallow his soul. Those blue lights. Now, whenever I see them flashing past me on the street, I wonder if they can carry substance in their beams, I wonder how many people's essences are trapped in between the photons.

The pub was practically empty now so I tried to regain my composure and went outside. As I passed through the doors into the night I didn't even see them load Craig's body on to the ambulance. All I saw were two white doors slam shut, sealing the world away from the tragedy.

We watched the lights recede into the distance, blue echoes shimmering back off the buildings even when the ambulance was gone.

As I tried to breathe, I felt a hand tap me on the shoulder. My sweet Clare. She wore a hoody and her neck disappeared into the rolls of fabric. In a fury of emotion, the incident in the school disco now utterly *meaningless* to me because I loved her, I suddenly grabbed her and she grabbed me and we hugged tight, tight, tight, like if we let go we'd fall off the world into outer space.

She started crying into my shoulder, but I was going to support her. We had once been in a team, a secret team that comprised just me and her, and I think she was back there then, back in that time that seemed so long ago when things were *not like this*. Now everything was over because Craig was dead.

A lot of cars arrived at the pub. Parents with concerned and saddened faces jumped down from their people carriers like they knew Craig. Girls were crying and I looked at them and do you know what I thought? Hypocrites. They didn't *know* Craig, they didn't care about Craig. When he had tried to kill himself, it was they who had made fun of him and laughed at him because he was crazy. They weren't the ones who had actually donated chunks of their life to help him. I had. I had helped him, and even though he had killed himself (and even though we were responsible), we were still his friends and I know that what I just said sounds contradictory but I don't care.

As I held Clare close and realized how much I still loved her crazily, I went right back to square one – I was a member of the Suicide Club once again. As Clare entered me through osmosis I suddenly got shunted to the point where directly in front of me was the truth: the Suicide Club were right.

The night before I had had sex for the very first time and it was with a girl I had only met that night. How could I have done that? That girl was now nothing but a memory and I knew even at the time that I would never fall in love with her. I had told Clare that I loved her but couldn't be around her because it was unhealthy – that's not what a romantic would do; we embrace only emotional storms because we crave the deepest feelings because that's the only place where you can *live*. By sleeping with that girl I had skimmed the surface of the human spectrum because I 'didn't want to get hurt'. I was disgusted with myself.

And then my father was coming towards me. Clare was taken away from me, still crying, and I was taken back to my house. It was the last place I wanted to go. I wanted to stay with my friends; they were all I had in the whole world. But they took me home.

The place seemed even quieter than normal and the walls seemed grubbier. I hated being there, hated it with every piece of me. The books in the hallway had dust all over them and they insulated the heat and I hated it. I went straight up to my bedroom and locked the door. I wanted to be on my own because one of my best friends was dead and I would never see him again and I had been washed over by one of those instantaneous waves of understanding that I told you about. He was gone. Craig was gone. Gone.

There was a knock at the door and I opened it straight away because I didn't have any energy to fight any more. But it wasn't my parents. Do you know who it was?

It was Toby.

'Mum and Dad told me what happened to your friend.'

I went over to my CD player and put on my Damien Rice CD and let it play from track one before flopping down on my bed.

'Are you all right, Rich?' He was talking to me like I had never spat in his hair; all that was gone now because he wanted to tell me that everything would be OK.

I fell back and rolled on to my side so that I wasn't facing him.

I heard Toby shuffle on my carpet.

'I just feel so sorry for him,' I said at last.

I felt the angles of my mattress shift as Toby sat down.

'It'll be OK,' he said comfortingly.

'Do you think he's OK?' I asked.

'I think he's probably gone to heaven.'

I breathed.

'Me and my friends said that when we die we'll all wait for each other in a secret chamber in heaven. And when we

253

get there, we'll do all the things we ever dreamed of before going to see our families.'

Toby was silent for a second.

'He'll be waiting for you,' he said at last.

'I hope so, Tobe.'

And that was it. Our conversation ended just like that. I don't think I could have said any more even if I'd wanted. Not because I would have broken down in tears, but because I didn't have any energy left in me. I just lay there in an L-shape on my bed, my legs stretched out over the edge and dangling in open air. Toby sat there for a while with me, up until the end of the song 'Aimee' in fact. And then he fell asleep. I got up and folded the bottom half of my duvet on top of him so that he would stay warm and then I curled up on the bottom of the bed like a snail's shell and fell asleep with all of my clothes on, where I encountered no dreams, no breaks in my sleep, no discomfort, just deep, deep rest.

28

When I awoke the next morning I felt like lying in bed for ever because I couldn't find a reason to get up. I was empty inside. Craig's death was starting to sink in deep and it was all but unbearable. I felt like my senses were flatter, like something had left me for ever. And there was this other thing as well; this weird *boredom*. My mother and father came into my bedroom at about eight o'clock. They too sat on my bed, next to a sleeping Toby, so that our whole little family was there. I was awake already, but I couldn't move because it was too hard.

'Son,' my father said, 'do you want some toast?'

Ten minutes later, all four of us were sat around the kitchen table eating warm toast slowly and in silence. I could only manage one mouthful. Outside was all grey and the little light that came into the kitchen was weak. I saw my mother and father glancing at each other and I knew why; it was because they were concerned about me. They loved me and I loved them. I truly appreciated them, but in truth I wanted to be left on my own. Toby reached for the marmalade in the centre of the table and clumsily spread some on to his toast in the way that little kids do. He had that tired look on his face like little kids have when they have to concentrate like crazy on the most mundane of tasks.

I knew what was happening. My family were supporting

me in silence. They were just there. With something as traumatic as what I had gone through they knew that it was best not to say anything so they didn't. It was the sweetest moment. My mother, who was so tormented by my behaviour, had forgiven everything I had done because, in the end, she loved me.

As I sat at the table and looked at the grain of the wood in front of me, I experienced something quite extraordinary. A dense feeling sat in my stomach, a feeling that had come from the sadness of Craig's death. But directly on top of that was the help that my family were channelling into me. There were two incredibly strong, polar opposite emotions in a tight space. They fought with each other, adjusting themselves for position inside me. But rather than cancel each other out they did something different. The two emotions actually magnified each other so much that I thought my torso might split apart. Emotions exploded through my veins like fireworks with nowhere to go but down the fleshy corridors. It felt like the nodes at the tips of my nerve sensors were being filed down and lubricated with gasoline. I sort of couldn't bear it any more and, even though I loved my family for being there, more than I'd ever realized, I had to get out.

I stumbled out of the kitchen and collapsed on to the settee in the living room. The cool material soothed my skin, but not my insides. I didn't know what to do with myself. Whatever I did wouldn't change anything because what had happened last night was irreversible. That was the first time I truly understood what that meant.

As you go through life you do good things and you do bad things. You can feel yourself moving along a timeline as you go, but you're always safe because you can always undo things. If you have an argument, you can apologize. If you steal something you can give it back. But when somebody dies, you pass a marker to which you can never return. No amount of anything can bring someone back – death is for ever and that for ever is such a terrifying prospect that I can't even think about it for long.

The next morning I didn't want to go to school but my parents made me. They said it was the best thing for me. As I walked down the dark, depressing corridors, alone and cold, I felt myself going and it was all I could do to stop myself from crying. There was a tangible difference in the air, but not as much as I would have expected. I thought that the whole place would be more respectful, but the younger kids carried on with their games of football whilst the older ones rushed to complete their homework on the school benches. To them, it was just like nothing had happened.

In assembly the headmaster came on to the stage and started telling us about Craig and how if anybody wanted to talk to a counsellor then they should go to his secretary. That was the sickest thing of it all. This was the man who had lost control when Craig had broken down in his office. He had offered him no support; that task was left to us.

I wished I had had Craig's gun on me so that I could have put a bullet in his heart.

I had only ever been in one of Craig's classes, which was history, and when I went that day, his empty chair seemed to have its own gravity field that was sucking me in.

It was in history that I spoke to Freddy.

'How are you feeling?' he whispered.

I just shrugged because I was having trouble speaking.

'What did you do yesterday?' he said.

'Nothing,' I croaked.

'I had my mother on the phone to me most of the day.' I don't know why he said that. 'Telling me that her and my dad are proud of me,' he whispered, and even laughed a little.

I tried to understand how he could be so cool about all

this. I thought that it might have been his way of dealing with things. Maybe he was just nuts.

'Have you seen Clare today?' he said.

Clare was conspicuously absent from history. I shook my head and felt the blood drain from it.

At lunchtime there were about four vans parked in the school yard. One of them had a BBC logo painted on to the side and people were milling around with TV cameras slung over their shoulders or mounted on tripods whilst suited presenters dragged microphones with long dark leads trailing into the backs of their vans. I watched with a detached mind.

It was strange to see people at my school who would later appear on the TV, all because somebody I had been very close to had shot the side of his head off. I still couldn't speak to anybody. Apart from one person.

When I found her I grabbed the top of her arm. When she saw it was me, she seemed to have relief on her face.

'Oh God,' she said quickly and she grabbed me and hugged me, but there wasn't the electricity that there had been on Saturday night after Craig had killed himself – this hug seemed forced somehow. 'Have you spoken to Freddy today?' she asked.

'I saw him in history.'

'Did he say anything to you?'

'About what?' I said.

She smiled awkwardly, like she was hiding something.

'About Craig.'

'What are you talking about?'

'He's just so . . . cold. Like he doesn't care.'

'It's just his way of dealing with it.'

'Ha,' she spluttered. 'Please.' I noticed that there was a sheen of water across her eyes. She wasn't looking at me, she was staring off to one side at some kids sat on the ground.

The cold, dry wind howled across the yard and caught strands of her hair, blowing them into the air like electricity in one of those glass orbs. Her hands were in the pockets of her coat. The unbroken tears may have been because of the cold, I couldn't tell, but she seemed upset. 'It's not his way of dealing with it,' she spat. 'He's glad he did it.'

'You mean Craig?' I said, disgusted.

'Of course. Craig signed the Charter, didn't he?'

My skeleton suddenly breathed in my flesh, tightening over my bones.

'Don't be so ridiculous.'

'Well, did Freddy seem upset to you?'

'Sure,' I lied weakly.

Her eyes went suddenly wide and her look told me that Freddy was coming. I stayed where I was and waited for him to arrive.

'Hello,' I heard his voice say behind me.

Clare looked at me desperately. What did she want me to do?

'I've got to go. I've got homework,' she said, and walked off.

'Jesus Christ, what the fuck is wrong with her?' he said loudly so that she could hear. Clare didn't even break stride, such was her magnificence.

I was taken aback by the way he said it. He wasn't usually so teenagerish. He kept looking at her, burning laser holes in her skull.

'Look at those fucking ghouls.' He pointed to the camera crews at the other end of the yard. I hated the way he was swearing. It was unlike him. It was creepy.

The wind gnawed painfully at my ears. His heavy hair swayed. The clouds overhead let in hardly any light and flashes of red sprayed across the yard – the last leaves. I wanted to go home and see my mum, lie on my settee, run my hand through the living-room carpet. Hollow, I looked at Freddy.

'So, he did it,' he said.

My chapped lips stayed closed.

'I didn't think he had it in him.'

I finally mustered speech. When I spoke, my voice didn't sound like my own. It sounded like it had been filtered through something viscous like amniotic fluid or something.

'Are you glad?' I said slowly.

Freddy shrugged.

'What else could he do? We all know he didn't stand a chance.'

I didn't answer.

'Richard, listen to me.' He looked at me very, very deeply. 'We are going to stick this out together, all of us. We have to see it through. We're in it now.'

I should have been chilled by what Freddy was saying, how he was so calm, but I wasn't. So what did that make me? I remember actually finding it hard to believe that Freddy was being serious, acting like Craig's death was all part of the big plan. I didn't really know what to make of it. He wasn't making me angry because his attitude was just so ludicrous. Maybe it really was his way of dealing with it. Who could tell?

When I got home that night I watched the news for the first time in probably my whole life. Craig's death was the third item on the national news, and the first story on the regional news. As I sat in my living room, my left leg kept shaking with restless excitement. Weird. I was a part of this story and my grief made way for a feeling of, what was it, happiness? For a second a thought flashed across my mind that I had to push to one side because it was so abhorrent: I was glad Craig was dead.

But no matter how much I tried to ignore the thought, it

kept digging away and digging away until I couldn't keep it out any more and it got inside my head and ripped through it like a fire storm. My mind soared with possibilities. All my life I had wanted to be a part of something genuinely dramatic in which everybody else was interested, and now here I was, living it out. I had entered a suicide pact and the first member had gone through the barrier. Five left. I wondered if anyone else could do it. Matthew? I doubted it because he had always been so stable, despite his recent changes. His parents were strict, but not so strict that he would kill himself. I was pretty sure that Jenny wouldn't kill herself, for the same reasons as Matt – she was too normal. The only scenario I could imagine was if they crept into a car together and carbon-monoxided themselves into oblivion. They would be found together; grey faces, blue lips, hands joined. I felt a shiver.

There was no way at all that Freddy would do it because he was more like the evil architect of it all. It was all his idea and I knew that he would try and talk to us in time to try and get somebody to make the next move. Maybe I was going crazy thinking about this stuff but, if somebody else were to kill themselves, all hell would break loose.

The most likely person to go next, I reasoned, was Clare. She had always had an eye for drama and she was always heightened emotionally. This whole mess would have affected her deeply and I could easily imagine that she would see the only way out as being at the blade of a razor. She'd probably go for pills though because she wouldn't want the fear of it all. With pills, it's pretty simple. The right pills.

I suppose she could do it in the bath with candles lit all around, real emo, which would have been contrived but at least it would have had a symmetry to it artistically. She could draw a blade across both wrists and bleed her life away. You'll hear people who think they're clever and dark saying that if you want to slit your wrists you should go *up* your arm. But that's not the case. The chance of you slicing an artery by going up is smaller than if you go across. The secret is to cut *deep*. As long as you get through the artery and you don't get found too soon after, you'll be fine. Yes, I saw Clare as the most likely candidate for the next death.

This must sound crazy to you, thinking like this, but that's the way it was. If you think it's shocking then I'm sorry. I wasn't exactly in a normal state of mind.

Seeing the headmaster saying what a wonderful, bright boy Craig had been made me realize that the world was fundamentally messed up and nothing I did would change that because horrible people will always rise to the top. That's just the way it is. The headmaster hardly knew Craig, nobody did. Not like us. I hated the way that everyone had suddenly become his best friend now that he was dead. People would see the headmaster on the news and think he was a Great Guy. They would never know how evil he was. Basically, the news report had changed everything.

As soon as the news finished I stepped into the back garden and went into the shed. I unchained my bike for the first time in over a year and yanked it out through the flimsy wooden door. I went out through the back gate into the lane behind my house, started a run, threw my bike down and jumped on board, gravel crunching underneath my wheels.

I sped across town as fast as hell, dodging in and out of cars, jumping up and down kerbs, wind thrashing in my hair, oxygen rushing down my arteries. I pedalled like my legs were powerful pistons, like I was a machine.

The whole dark world came alive in the neon of the town centre as I sailed past the war memorial. Cars beeped their horns at me because I kept pulling out in front of them to slice seconds off my journey and in less than ten minutes I was throwing my bike down outside the school dormitories and gliding up the steps, past the security desk and on and on to Freddy's room. My heart was pumping because I finally understood. In the final corridor, I rounded the corner and there he was, already coming to meet me.

We looked at each other.

'I saw you coming from my window,' he said.

'You were right, weren't you? About what you said. About people. About everything.'

'I think so,' he said. 'I'm pretty sure I am.'

That was a big moment. It was when I truly left normality behind and plunged completely into the mindset of the Suicide Club. Freddy had me now. Craig's death, and people's reaction to it, had finally shown me the way. People simply weren't very nice. They were dishonest and selfish, trying in some way to get involved with a situation that was nothing to do with them. Everything that Freddy had talked about seemed to be coming true. He had been right all along – Craig's death had shown me that. I was now completely under his spell.

We went to the park and climbed the trees. They had powerful lights underneath, which made them look astoundingly weird and creepy. In a way, just like we must have appeared to the outside world. We found comfortable sitting positions in an old tree and smoked a cigarette each. We were like leopards in those trees that you see in wildlife programmes about Africa.

'Do you think anyone else will kill themselves?' I said to him.

'Sure.' He blew out some smoke into the air.

'Who do you think will do it?'

'What do you mean?'

'I mean, who do you think will do it?'

'All of us,' he said simply.

'Just answer the question, moron.'

'I'm going to do it.'

I felt like a sudden surge of liquid nitrogen had been spliced into my genes. I was only joking when I asked. I thought he knew that I was joking. I didn't want anyone else to die and I didn't want to continue this conversation. It was too frightening, too disenfranchised. I turned my thoughts away from something obvious that I wasn't prepared to accept.

'You know it's a mortal sin,' he said, smoke coming from his mouth as he spoke.

'Suicide?'

'We'll go to hell for it.'

I watched the lights of an aeroplane cross the clear sky.

'What about our chamber in heaven?' I said.

But Freddy didn't answer.

I still felt a tiny amount of *something* in my gut. It was a little bit rotten and I think it was echoes of the grief from Craig. It was still weird to think of him as being a dead boy. But he was and that was that. We talked about his funeral and how sickening it would be to see all the kids from school turn up pretending that they knew him even though they would only be there to get time off school and lament the fact without even realizing it that they were selfish and had never taken time out to think about the poor boy who shot himself in the head. No doubt the headmaster would be there too, dark overcoat with lapels turned up and polished leather shoes that would click all the way into church. Horrific.

29

In assembly the next morning the headmaster particularly embarrassed himself because he made us all observe a minute's silence in memory of Craig. So we all stood, pretending to be solemn, and bowed our heads. I was next to Freddy and he kept nudging me and it was all we could do to not collapse in hysterics. Clare, who was further along our line, saw us and was disgusted.

I'm not saying that we weren't devastated about Craig, I'm saying that we simply couldn't believe everybody's reaction – that was what was ridiculous. Maybe we should have been more sombre, but that's not the way it was.

'Now then,' said the headmaster, clearly relishing his newly found celebrity. I noticed he was wearing shinier shoes than normal. 'I'd just like to reiterate that if you need to talk to anybody about anything, you can see my secretary and she can make you an appointment with our counsellors.' He shuffled a little in front of his lectern. 'The police will be in school today and they might want to talk to some of you. So if you get called out of any lessons you don't need to worry because there's nobody to blame in tragic times like these.' He really did say 'tragic times like these' – can you even believe it?

When we got out of assembly, Matt came running up the corridor. His hair was all over the place and his shirt was untucked.

'You're not going to believe this,' he laughed. I was glad he was laughing. It meant that he was having a similarly weird reaction to this thing as me. I wasn't alone. 'Have you heard about Chad?'

I looked at him and raised an eyebrow.

'What about him?'

'He's only been arrested.'

'What?' chimed Freddy.

Matt was grinning like he was about to crack up.

'Yup. Do you know where Craig got his gun?'

'Oh my God,' I said in a high voice. So that's why Craig was friends with Chad. So that he could steal his gun. It made me wonder how long Craig had been planning his own death. He must have been planning it even when I spoke to him in his bedroom and I thought he had put his psychological problems behind him. It made me respect him even more. I started laughing. 'So they've got Chad? That's awesome!'

We all laughed and I suppose it was a bit evil and we also knew at the time that it was a bit evil, but then Chad was a moron so what did it matter? He should have handed the gun over instead of keeping it like a typical American. I was ecstatic that he had been held responsible for it because it was so typical of everybody. Somebody had to take the blame because that's just the way it is. Nobody could accept the fact that *they* were to blame, that it was *society* that had killed him. They had to have a scapegoat. It's hilarious.

'How can you laugh like that?' We all turned to see Jenny looking at us. She had bags under her eyes, ringed in red, and bloodshot whites. I think she had been crying.

Suddenly she bolted forward. Looking up I saw that she had been physically barged by one of the American kids.

'Get out of the way. Fucking freak.'

And then he headed for us. I stepped into his track even though he was older, taller and bigger than me. He didn't even reach me because Matt leapt forward and punched him across the face. His speed and ferocity really surprised me. It might have scared me a bit if I hadn't been in such a mangled state of mind. Instead, when Matt grappled him to the floor, I jumped on and swung two punches, left and right, into either side of his head. I hated doing it because it's not a good thing to do but I was possessed and I just did it. Then Freddy was there too, his face in a creased rage as he let go about a million kilojoules right into this kid's skull. If the American kid had looked up he would have seen three monsters seething at him: the crazy kids who had killed the bird. We were one. But he didn't look at us because he was covering his face with his forearms. He shouldn't have barged one of us like that. He was a bully and now he was getting what he deserved.

His friends grabbed us and I felt a fist impact my face and was sent sprawling across the corridor into a bunch of younger kids. I got straight back up and felt blood trickling over my lips from my nose, which must have looked incredibly cool. I lowered my head and stared at the boy who had hit me.

'You're a fucking basket case, man,' he drawled.

I heard a teacher shouting about thirty yards away and I knew that I didn't want to get into any more trouble than I was in already so I unfolded my fists and wiped my nose. My hand came away red and I had no idea why I started thinking about my My Chemical Romance album that still hadn't turned up from Play even though they said it had been posted.

We were taken to the headmaster's office and the American boys told the headmaster that we were Craig's best friends and that they thought we were witches and that we had made Craig kill himself. I sat back in my chair and sniffed through my bloody nose. My knuckles were really hurting.

'That's a very serious allegation,' the headmaster said. 'A *very* serious allegation.'

'It's what I think, sir,' said the American.

The headmaster looked at all three of us.

'Do you boys think that you're going to Mr Bartlett-Taylor's funeral tomorrow?'

We just sat there. I was horrified to hear him start talking like this – he really was an embarrassment.

'Why should I let you go?'

'I'll tell you why,' said Freddy gloriously.

I started to get tingles in my fingers.

Freddy's cool hair hung with drama.

'Because you're a fucking moron,' he said calmly, 'and it has *nothing* to do with you whether we go or not, you abominable cunt.'

Jesus Christ, you would not believe how amazing it was to witness something like this. Freddy had just planted a flag on Everest, drunk from the Holy Grail, put a boot through the gates of heaven. The headmaster's face dropped when he said the 'c' word. I don't think anyone had *ever* said something like that to him. Freddy inflected the words in such a magical way that the headmaster must have known instantaneously that what he had said about not allowing us to go to the funeral was completely idiotic. Freddy had just held up a mirror to this man and the reflection was unbearable.

But do you know what? Such was his weakness, he would not accept Freddy's reproach.

'Well, Mr Spaulding-Carter,' he said, trying to act calm, even though it was quite obvious that he had lost it. 'You don't understand that it has *everything* to do with me. I suggest you apologize for your outburst.'

I watched Freddy deliberate for about three seconds.

'Ordinarily I would.' He paused. 'But not today. I just can't. If I did, I would be letting Craig down.'

He really was superb when he wanted to be.

'Sir,' said Matt suddenly.

'Don't start, Matthew.'

'Sir, I'm sorry. But how can you use our friend's funeral as a bargaining chip?'

'Matthew, you keep your mouth shut, or you won't be going either.'

Matt looked at his feet. So that was that. Freddy was not going to the funeral.

'And what about you, Richard?' he said, turning on me. 'Have you got anything to add?'

Here was my chance.

'I have nothing to add,' I said coldly, like I was in court.

'Good lad.' He paused. 'Go on then, off you go. And don't let me hear any more about fighting or anything like that.'

We all got up to leave.

'Not you, Mr Spaulding-Carter.'

Freddy sat back down without even looking at us. I was the last to leave and I pulled the door shut behind me. It was a dramatic moment as the slit in the door got narrower and narrower until Freddy and the headmaster were cut off from the rest of the world.

First lesson, maths, passed uneventfully but, as I sat there and listened to the teacher talk about angles or something like that, my dread unrolled in me like a tapeworm. I really didn't want to see Emma today. I would much rather have skipped school and taken Clare to a riverbank somewhere, where we could throw pebbles into the water and kiss each other whilst the rest of the world washed by, blissfully ignorant that we were even by that river. I guess I just wanted to be innocent again but I had gone well past that point now and so I went to the meeting room and met with Emma.

The session started with five minutes of silence.

She spoke first.

'So you've been in a fight.'

I just sat there and looked at the glass of water in front of me.

'Rich,' she said, really kindly in a way that made my stomach lurch. I was going to crack, I could tell. I tried to reel myself in before she continued. 'It's OK, Rich. Tell me about Craig.'

I kept looking at the water in my glass. There were two bubbles stuck to the bottom. I watched them closely. At last one of them set itself free and headed for the surface. As soon as it went, its friend joined it and they scorched for the surface, wobbling as they went to their inevitable deaths.

'What do you want me to say?' I said, very, very calmly.

'Did it make you sad? Angry? Tell me how it made you feel,' she said professionally, which was repellent.

'You never did tell me how many A levels you had,' I said coldly.

'This isn't about me, Richard. If you don't talk about what happened to Craig, it will sit inside you and eat you from the inside out. You have to talk about it.'

'What do you do when you feel sad?' I asked. 'Do you have your own shrinks? You people?' My head was spinning. I hated her because she was a psychotherapist and I loved her because she was so pretty.

'The police wanted to talk to you but I didn't allow it.'

I couldn't look at her. I was right on the edge.

'Richard, you held him in your arms after he died, didn't you?'

I shrugged. Just for a second I was back on the stage, Craig lying dead in my arms. It knocked the breath out of me.

'You have to talk about this, Rich.'
I sighed.
'I don't want to talk about it.'
'It will haunt you for ever if you don't.'
'Good,' I said.
'You think that's good?'
'Yes,' I said childishly, but what else was I supposed to do?
'Richard, studies have shown—'
And then I stopped listening.

30

The weather was almost too perfect for the funeral. It was windy and cloudy and shards of rain licked against the air. My parents gave me a lift to the church. I had never been to a funeral before and I wondered how I would react. I waited in the churchyard, amongst the graves on my own, because I was the first of the Suicide Club to arrive and nobody else wanted to speak to me, which suited me fine. I wandered over to a little corner full of colours. The headstones had little white picket fences around them about six inches high. You know those little windmill things that kids have that you stick in the ground and they spin in the wind? There were dozens of them whizzing around and humming away. And then there were little statuettes of cute bunny rabbits and frogs. Set up against the side of one of the graves were about ten action figures that had been faded by weathering. None of the living kids had stolen them, which moved me.

My throat caught. I closed my eyes, but not out of Drama. I closed my eyes because I was sad. So sad. Imagine the mothers at these kids' funerals, putting the thing that grew in their womb into the mud. You think you've got it all sussed out, but then you see something like that and there's a moment of dread when you realize that there's no meaning in anything.

I was standing in front of children's graves and I knew

then that it was the end. In that corner of the graveyard, right up by the fence and underneath one of those trees whose seeds fall to the floor like helicopters, a poet might say that because of all the colours, that little section of the cemetery was still alive. A poet might say that in the colours live the souls of those poor little children. But that's not the case, is it? It might seem alive, but it's not. It's dead. Those colours? They were put there by people who assumed that their kids could still see them after they were gone. As if little kids would visit their own graves if they were ghosts.

That little chamber in heaven where we had agreed to wait for each other seemed a long way away.

I could feel the congregation of people up at the top of the graveyard looking at me. They were looking at that weird kid who killed the bird, made his friend shoot himself, and who was wandering around the graves of the dead. But I simply didn't care. I knew that it didn't matter because heading my way, drifting over the grass between the graves like spectres, were Matt, Jenny and Clare.

I felt Clare next to me, just felt her presence. I loved her so, so much. All I wanted to do was to go to that river with her and throw pebbles. I didn't want anything else in the world.

I saw the headmaster looking fake-solemnly into the bare trees. He was wearing, just as I had predicted, his overcoat with upturned lapels, trying to get some Drama into his hair with the blowing wind, but failing miserably.

We went into the church and everything became hollow and echoey. I hadn't been to church in years and I had forgotten what it looked like on the inside. No matter what you say, there's something magical about those places.

We sat on the pew furthest from the front. The church was heaving, its walls expanding out with all the fake people

273

pretending they once cared for Craig. But I won't keep repeating myself about that any more.

I sat in the back row and thought about Craig as everybody filed past. I remembered the day I had seen him in town just after he had taken the pills. Another image popped into my head of a kid taking his ice cream when we were kids and throwing it into the side of the church in which I was now sat saying goodbye to somebody I had known since I was three.

I looked towards the aisle and saw his ragged old parents ache down the centre like their joints had rusted over. Horror crunched through me, or rather I crunched through it. I suddenly let my mind wander and something very weird happened. I started to come away from reality and now, although my body was still in the church, my mind was not. My mind was at the top of the world, falling through clouds. As the awfulness of what was happening encroached on me, I took a secret exit.

As my mind plummeted through the clouds I watched them part. Layer upon layer peeled away, as if they were trying to show me something underneath. Some sort of answer. The answer to everything. Through the clouds I went and they suddenly took on a soft yellow glow. Pinpricks of light dazzled in the midst of the cloud and then there was just one thin translucent sheet left and as it moved away I caught my first glimpse. A glimpse of the answer, the truth . . .

'We are gathered here today,' said the Vicar, and my mind crashed back into my skull and I was in the church again. I looked about me. I could see the backs of Craig's parents at the front of the church. I felt shaky, like when you don't have enough sugar.

The Vicar started talking about Craig and I started listening. Because he had that white ribbon around his neck, I was enchanted by this man. He would never lie. He started by saying that he didn't really know Craig and that was the best thing he could have said from my point of view. He spoke about how Craig was a deeply troubled boy, but had a good heart. Apart from his voice, the church was totally silent.

But then he started reading passages out of the Bible and that stuff's a bit boring so I looked at Clare's leg underneath her black skirt and prodded her thigh with my index finger.

She looked at me sadly. I left my index finger held out to her and she took it in her fist and we both faced forward again.

The last sentence the Vicar said, was, 'And now Craig's father will say a few words.'

An instant, blazing WCS scorched across my brain where his father broke down in tears and started wailing embarrassingly. Everybody would feel awful apart from the schoolkids, who would love it because they can be pretty evil sometimes. I had to do something to stop this. But what was I going to do? Stand up and make a spectacle? Come on.

It was too late anyway, he was up there. He took from his top pocket a few sheets of folded A4 paper. I wondered if he'd written it in the middle of the night, in the silence of his lonely house.

'Craig was my only son,' he started, and I felt Clare grip my finger tighter with despair. I looked at her and tears were streaming over her cheeks, making her make-up run. 'When he was six, we took him to Longleat Safari Park because he had the strangest fixation with monkeys.'

A sad laugh cracked across the transfixed congregation. I pictured the pile of *National Geographic* magazines in his bedroom.

'We drove into the middle of the enclosure, where the monkeys live and, although we had been warned not to, we stopped the car. As soon as we did a whole group of these little beggars came bundling over and started jumping on

275

and hitting my car. One little blighter even tore my aerial off.'

Again, a laugh yawned out.

'I'll never forget my son's face. The little critters were destroying his old man's car.' He paused and there was a silence. 'He'd never laughed so much in his life.'

Again, everybody laughed, a little louder this time, less stale.

My respect for this man went through the roof. I could not understand how he could be so strong at a time like this. I would have collapsed into a ball by now – I guess that's the difference. He was a Great Man. He had spent a career in the Army, for crying out loud. His job was to protect us all.

'And I know he's gone, and I know that times will be hard, but I, and my wonderful wife Margo, are just *so* grateful for the happiness he gave us.'

Now I was welling up. How could this man say that Craig had brought him happiness? I thought he must have brought them nothing but torment, but I guess I was wrong.

'We'd like to thank everybody for coming today and, although he didn't have many friends, we'd like to thank those children from Atlantic High School who are here today.' He looked at the large group of kids down at the front and smiled at them like he had smiled at me on that day in town when he was queuing for food with his wife. He did not look at us, Craig's real friends. Craig's real killers. At this time, of course, nobody knew about the Suicide Club because Freddy had taken the Charter from Craig's pocket on the night he killed himself.

Suddenly Clare let go of my finger and ran out of the church, the back of her hand covering her mouth. She was trying with all her might not to explode until she got outside.

I stood up and followed her as quietly as I could, which, in all truthfulness, wasn't very quiet.

Outside the church was a gravel path and Clare was crouched down in the middle of it, facing away from me. I went over to her. She wasn't shaking and she wasn't making a noise. When I came round to her front I saw that her eyes were balled up tightly and her mouth was open and full of moisture. She looked like she was in agony. Her face was reflecting everything because of her tears, which had bottlenecked in her brain, stopping her from doing anything. And then they broke free and she rocked back and forth, inconsolable. I crouched down next to her and put my hand on her back because I couldn't think of anything else to do because I had never seen anyone act like this before. Actually, I had seen one person act like this, Craig. When he was in the headmaster's office after we killed Bertie. But he was dead.

I hated seeing her like this. I wish I could have been a demon and possessed her body so that I could suck out her pain for her. But that's not real life. She cried and cried. She fell to one side into the gravel and there was nothing I could do about it. I was watching her break and all I wanted to do was stop it for her. I know I'm an arrogant person at times and I sometimes think that I can do anything. I hate it when I'm reminded that I can't.

'Please stop crying,' I said.

But she couldn't even hear me.

It took her ten minutes to come round and then we hugged but there was no magic in it. Something had snapped inside her. The congregation started to come out of the church and we stood to one side and watched. I hadn't seen them carry it in, but when I saw them carry it out the sight of Craig's coffin almost made me throw up.

They lowered Craig into the ground and his father did a sterling job of it, just as I should have known he would. He didn't cry the whole time and I loved him for that. He would have wanted to cry, he wasn't cold, but he was so strong that he wouldn't. He was like an old oak tree, I guess.

Outside the church, Matt came up to me.

'Rich,' he said. His voice was quiet.

I couldn't answer.

'I'm scared,' I heard him say. 'I just . . . can't believe this.'

I still couldn't find any words so I just put my arm around his shoulder and we looked at the damp grass and gripped each other tightly. All of the bitterness towards the people who were fake-mourning Craig was gone, and for the first time I really started to grieve.

The blame was already on us. The kids knew that we were the only ones who spent any time with Craig, us, the bird-killers, so it must have been our fault. It can't have been theirs. It's funny how things work like that.

On the way back to school from the church, we had to pass through this weird little alley. It's like a little oasis of trees with a path running up the middle. It's lodged in between two tall buildings, neither of which you can see because their walls are covered in ivy; it's just a tunnel of green in the middle of the grey buildings. It always gave me the creeps because when there are no lights and it's dark, it's *really* dark in there.

That was the spot where a group of about twelve kids caught up with us and the hatred felt towards us by so many people finally turned into something real, something you could *feel*. They weren't from my school; they were from the comprehensive. As well as between eight and ten boys, there were a couple of girls with greasy hair. They snarled at us like they were animals, feral and savage.

This one kid came right up to us, hair glued to his red scalp, uniform ill-fitting – generally disgusting. He pushed me in the chest without even saying anything and I stumbled backwards but didn't fall because of my balance. I could have beaten him up with pure skill but Clare's fit of crying had zapped my energy and I couldn't do anything. This time, the bullies would win.

'You fucking pricks,' he said to us. 'We know all about you.' He was trying to be cool but it came out as a cliché and I felt genuinely sorry for him because he didn't understand. He would never know the depths.

Another three boys came up behind him. I looked at Matt. I caught his eye and noticed that he was standing directly in front of Jenny, which was really sweet. I looked at her and was shocked to see how white she was. Her face was really odd. She had been crying as well but she hadn't broken down like Clare. I wished we had Freddy with us.

I could feel Clare taking a few steps backwards, leaving me on my own. That was a complex and hurtful thing for her to do.

I looked back to Jenny just as her face changed, her muscles crumpling, her cheeks stretching tight around her bones.

'Why don't you just leave us alone?' she screamed. Screamed.

'Why don't you fuck off back to America,' said one of the stringy girls who were with the boys.

'You killed that poor little boy,' said another.

I sat down. Sat down on the floor in the alley. Just sat there. I had to do it because if I hadn't I would have fainted. The fact is I was terrified. I was terrified of these kids because they were dirtier than the kids in my school and I know that it's a crappy thing to say but that's how I felt. I didn't want to get hit any more. I didn't want to be punched ever again. I didn't want any physical pain any more. I didn't want any more of my best friends to kill themselves. I didn't want to feel the exhilaration of the news on TV because of something I had caused. So I sat down.

'Get up,' said the first kid. He took a step towards me and went to grab me but I just rolled away from him, my black jacket that I had worn for the funeral sinking into the wet mud.

I saw out of the corner of my eye that Matt had now stepped between me and the boy but then he disappeared into a mass of teenage bodies as they took him into their midst. I heard him grunting as they attacked him. I looked back down the corridor of trees from the direction we had come and saw something that I never wanted, nor expected, to see. The comprehensive-school girls, with all their greasy hair and crass jewellery, had jumped on to Clare and Jenny. Those girls were pure horror. They were thumping the back of Clare and Jenny's heads because they had lowered them to protect their faces. It was just so brutal. My beautiful girls were being beaten up. Those comprehensive-school girls looked like monsters with their faces folded up in rage.

My strength returned when I saw what was happening. I got up on to my knees but was pushed back into the mud.

I tried to think if these kids would feel remorse in the future for what they were doing to us. Of course they wouldn't. They'd justify it to themselves by saying that we deserved it because that's what a mediocre person does for 90 per cent of their lives; justifies the bad things they do.

We didn't deserve it. We had lost our friend and look what was happening to us, just half an hour after his funeral. It was not in balance with the order of things. This should not have happened. I lay on the ground and just let the punches sink into me. I felt a weird leathery sound from where the kids had totally lost control and were kicking me in the skull with their hard shoes. I felt my skin split on my cheek but I just let the mud wash in because there was nothing I could do.

When they were finished they didn't even run away. They simply walked.

So what do you think? Are you glad I took that beating from those kids because I was getting my comeuppance for being so weird? If so, stop reading because I don't want you coming with us on this final leg of the journey. But if you're feeling sad because these kids were punching me and my friends because they couldn't handle who *they* were, then read on, come with me, come with Matt, Jenny, Freddy and Clare, we'll point the headlights into the night and follow their silver lines and we'll go to the dark places hand in hand because, if you know what I mean, we're all going there in the end anyway.

31

I didn't go back to school that day. None of us did. By the time the kids had left us alone we were too badly bruised and upset. The girls were crying and Matt's face was all lumpy. I was probably the least injured. Apart from the cut on my face and some aches on my body and head, I was fine. On the outside at least. Inside, I . . . I don't really know how I felt. I wasn't upset, or angry, I just felt . . . beaten. Like there was no hope left.

By the time I let myself in through the back door of my house I simply felt numb. Both of my parents were at work and Toby was in school so the house was empty. I picked up the mail, going through normal motions, trying to stay in control, when I noticed that there was a letter for me. My name and address were handwritten on the envelope.

Sat at the kitchen table, in my silent house, I opened the letter. Inside was a sheet of notepaper. As soon as I saw the words, 'Dear Rich', I knew that I was reading Craig's suicide note. The bottom dropped out of my world:

Dear Rich

I'm going to do it.
Freddy was right.
I thought I was
going to be okay
in my new school
but it's worse.

Don't tell my parents
about this letter.
Make sure the others
know that I did
this for them. For
the club.

I hope I'll see you
again, in that chamber,

Craig

I felt a tingle in my stomach because, at last, there was a bond. That gold rope had finally come up between me and Craig. I don't know when it happened, when it was that I made the connection, but the fact that he had written his note to me was proof. All of the time I had spent trying to be nice to him, to help him, had finally paid off. I noticed a few tears had dropped on the page and smudged some of the letters. I dried my eyes with the sleeve of my muddy jacket, sat back in my chair and looked at the ceiling. My whole body was coursing with pain but at last I knew that I had, in some way, helped Craig. I know he was still dead, but at least for the last few months of his life he had had real friends. He had never had that before and I was glad that we had been able to give him that gift.

As I sat at the kitchen table and tried to pull myself together I pictured Craig's glazed expression one last time. I saw him sat at the edge of his bed staring at the parrot poster on his bedroom wall whilst his parents brought in a plate of tea and scones. His mother set them down on the desk and buttered the scones. They had to pass the plate to Craig but that was OK because he was their son and they loved him more than anything.

Craig was never going to live longer than his parents because his mind didn't fit in this world. No matter what his parents had done, they could never have saved him. What we did, how we befriended him, it hadn't made any difference because Craig was doomed, whatever. He was sentenced to an existence inside his head where the outside world could only knock at the window – it could never come in. I finally understood this. Even his suicide note was cold.

My house phone started ringing, jolting me back to the kitchen table and reality.

It was Matt.

'Hello?' I said.

'Can we come over?' he said.

'Who?' I asked, drying my eyes again.

'Me and Jenny.'

'What for?'

His voice sounded almost bored.

'I don't know, we just want to see you.'

I sniffed.

'OK. Come over.'

'Are you OK?' he said.

There was a silence at both ends of the line and I closed my eyes.

'Yeah.'

'We'll be there soon. See you.'

The brief conversation made me feel happier. Just a little.

I loved Matt so much because he always knew when I felt at my worst and always made it better. Before they arrived I called Clare to ask her to come over as well, but her mobile was going straight to voicemail.

There were a few cans of Coke in the fridge so I took them out and went back into the living room. I set the cans down on the table and almost broke down in tears again.

'Fucking hell, Rich,' I said. 'Pull yourself together.'

Outside I heard voices and then the doorbell rang. In the empty house, it seemed to resonate more than normal.

'Through here,' I called, trying to clear my throat.

Seeing their heads pop round the door shocked me. They both looked as if their faces had been kneaded like putty. Two black eyes were already forming under Matt's eye-sockets that were going to be hideous.

'How are you feeling, Jen?'

Her eyes were glazed over dangerously like Craig's. She didn't answer.

I glanced at Matt as he nodded slightly and put his hand on her shoulder.

'She's OK. She's just scared.'

'Don't be scared of them,' I said, passing her a can of Coke. I felt myself trying to be strong for her.

Jenny sat on the settee at the far end and watched the silent TV. She held the can of Coke in her hand, unopened.

'I found out about Freddy,' Matt said.

'Yeah?'

'One of the boarders said he was allowed to go to the funeral but only if he apologized for calling the headmaster a . . . you know . . . cunt.'

'And he didn't apologize?'

'Obviously not.'

I could just imagine Freddy sitting cross-legged, refusing to back down, staying strong for Craig.

'Jesus,' I said.

Jenny had turned her attention to what was happening outside the window, which was nothing but an empty street on a workday afternoon, peaceful and still. I didn't like the way she was reacting to the fight, to everything. Her silence was scary because it wasn't her. She would always have *something* to say, even if it was some American nonsense. Her expression was as blank as a sheet of paper unwritten and I got a feeling of sorrow mixed in with the terrible thought of will-she-be-next-to-take-the-plunge. I didn't like that thought because it's completely evil but that's what I felt and I'm just trying to be honest. There's no point in me trying to sugar-coat anything from here on because things are about to get a lot worse and just writing about it is making me tired and all I want to do is tell you things exactly as they happened because if you've got this far, I love you and from those that you love you should never hide your deepest truths. And so I won't hide anything from you, I promise.

'Jenny,' I said to her. She slowly turned her head towards me. When she looked at me I had to stop myself grimacing because her face was so pulped. 'Have you seen your parents?'

'Not yet,' she said quietly.

There was a pause.

'If I ever see those kids again,' started Matt, suddenly getting angry, 'I'll rip their faces off their skulls.' He said it so deliberately that if one of the kids had walked in just then he probably would have.

'What should we do about it?' I said.

'Nothing,' Jenny whispered.

We both looked at her.

She continued, quietly, balefully.

'This is what Freddy has always said would happen.' I hated the way she was so calm. 'It's just normal people pulling us down like they always do.'

Me and Matt looked at each other, and then at her.

'Freddy's a fucking idiot,' I said quickly. I could sense that Jenny was going down a bad route and I needed to stop her before her thoughts got away from her and she was suddenly hanging from a lamp-post or something.

This time it was they who looked at me.

'Come on,' I said. 'You don't *really* believe what he says, do you?'

'Why not?' said Jenny.

I stumbled for words.

'Because . . . because it's rubbish.' She must have known I was lying. I didn't believe that what Freddy said was rubbish at all; I believed every last word of it. I was only saying it to Jenny because I was scared for her.

She gave me a weird look.

'It happens every day,' she said slowly. 'We can't do anything about it. I hate being bullied like this.'

Bullied? What the hell was she talking about?

'You're not thinking about committing suicide,' I said straight out.

Jenny looked at the TV again. She was becoming upset. Matt held her hand but he wasn't trying to talk her out of anything, which was fucking insane of him. I'm sorry for swearing there.

'We signed the Charter, Rich,' she said finally.

I hated hearing her say that. I know for a FACT that she did not sign the Charter with the intention of killing herself. But now, with a seed planted so firmly in her mind, roots were starting to tentacle out into her brain.

'I signed the Charter,' I said. 'Do you think I'm going to kill myself?'

She shrugged and looked out the window again, like I had actually hurt her in some way.

'My God,' I said, 'you did? Fuck.' I looked at Matt and, to

my horror, he shrugged too. 'So how's it going to be? Back of a car, carbon monoxide?'

They still didn't say anything.

'Matt,' I said. 'If you kill yourself, I swear to God, I will desecrate your grave. I'll smash it up with a hammer. I promise. Imagine how your parents would feel.'

'They'd be pretty pissed off,' he said with the most sinister, crooked, jagged smile you could imagine. He would never have been capable of such a smile a few months ago. He didn't like his parents. That was a problem for me because it gave him motivation for his own suicide, even though we didn't believe in motivation. Things were snowballing, spiralling, collapsing, whatever. I couldn't believe what I was hearing. Was I missing something?

'Just . . . think about it,' I said, without really knowing what the hell I was talking about any more.

All of this bad talk had made me forget about Craig's suicide note in my pocket. It suddenly crept in at the back of my brain.

'Oh,' I said, and took it out. 'You're not going to believe this.' I handed the folded-up paper to Matt.

He took one look at it and passed it to Jenny. I couldn't make out what he was thinking.

Jenny, though, reacted badly.

'Oh my God,' she said and covered her mouth. She got up and ran for the door.

'It's by the front door, on the left,' I called after her.

We heard the toilet door swing open and her heave into the bowl. The plunging of vomit into the water made me shake with revulsion.

Matt sat back in the settee.

'Rich,' he said. 'I don't think this is Craig's handwriting.'

'What?' I paused. 'What?!' We were both thinking the same thing. Freddy. But surely not, right? No way. 'No way.'

'I reckon Freddy wrote this.'

I sat up and he handed back the paper. I looked at the writing. I realized that I had never seen Craig's handwriting, nor Freddy's for that matter. I ran up to my room and fetched the Suicide Club Charter to see if I could find out more from the signatures.

Matt and I huddled around the two sheets.

'It's hard to tell,' I said.

He squinted at the papers and held them up to the light.

'The 't's look the same as Freddy's, slightly angled to the right,' he said, as if he was some stupid detective from one of those TV dramas. 'Although, it could easily be Craig's writing as well.' He paused and studied some more until he became aware of me staring at him, incredulous. Since when did he become an expert on handwriting? Answer: never.

There was a quick beat and then we both realized how totally moronic we were being before completely cracking up into hysterics and throwing the bits of paper to the floor. It was so strange, us laughing like that, like the good old days. But it felt wonderful, a pure release of pressure that we both needed so much.

Just then my mother came through the door. She was home early and I wasn't in school. I was going to get in trouble. I was so glad that Matt and Jenny were there because then she would see that we couldn't have gone back to school because their faces would tell her the full story.

When she saw me sat in the living room, she actually did a double-take, which I had never seen anybody do in real life.

'What are you doing home?' she said. Very angrily.

'Hello, Mrs Harper,' said Matt suddenly, and to my rescue.

She popped her head around the corner and saw his pulpy features.

'Oh my—' she gasped. 'What have you done?'

'Some kids beat us up on the way back from the funeral,' I said, trying to sound shaky. 'That's why we're not in school.'

My mother stood in the doorway for a moment.

'What is the world coming to?' She went back into the hallway and picked up one of the cordless phones from the receiver. 'Who did it?' she demanded.

'Who are you calling?' I said faintly.

'The school. Who did this? Give me their names.'

'Jesus,' I whispered. 'Mum, leave it. We don't know who it was. They weren't from our school.'

She looked at me like I was lying.

'Honestly,' I said. 'They were from the comp.'

Just then Jenny returned from the bathroom and my mother's face went white. Symbolically.

'Oh my God.' Now she was really angry because she liked to consider herself a 'strong woman' so she hated it when women were victims. 'What kind of animal?' she stammered.

Jenny gave her a timid look and slid past, back into the living room. She gave Matt an 'I want to get out of here' look.

'Hello?' said my mother. 'Yes, put me through to the head-master's office, please.' She looked at me. 'Hello? Is that Mrs McKinsay? Yes, this is Helen Harper . . .' She left the room and went into the kitchen.

I walked them down the hall towards the front door, which was still open. I could see the top of Toby's head through the glass panel. Just seeing him made me feel better. If he was around, everything would be OK.

We walked past him and I said, 'Hiya, Tobe,' but he ignored me so I pushed him playfully into the shrubbery.

But, because he's so frail, he tripped and fell into the mud. I covered my eyes and shook my head because I was such a bastard but also because I hadn't meant him any harm and it was, I'm sorry, funny. He slowly picked himself up by sticking his backside into the air and walking his hands backwards until he could stand upright. Then he dusted himself down and, without looking at me, went inside and closed the door quietly behind him. Not a word had been said.

I went back inside, just as Toby topped the last stair and disappeared around the corner. I chased him up the steps to say sorry.

His bedroom door was closed so I just barged straight in there. I was just about to apologize when something bad happened. Toby started screaming at me. SCREAMING.

'Get out! Get out! Get out!'

I stepped inside and shut the door, hoping my mother wouldn't hear.

'Tobe,' I said, so shocked that I was suddenly afraid. I was scared because this was Toby and this wasn't like him. I didn't think I was going to be able to handle this. It was only supposed to have been a joke.

He picked up the tiny red plastic chair that he sat in to read and hurled it at me. I stuck out my arm to block and the bottom of the leg caught me on the elbow. The pain shattered up my arm and I doubled over.

'Get out of my room,' he squealed.

My heart sank when he screamed that way because I knew he was crying.

'I'm so sorry, Tobe, I didn't mean for you to fall—'

'You killed Bertie,' he screamed at me.

Time stopped. I was in stasis, the universe was in stasis.

'Who told you that?' I said calmly, my heart racing, elbow throbbing, sweat oozing out of my pores, terror sucking my marrow out.

'James O'Donnell,' he shouted, like James O'Donnell was some great sage. And then he threw himself on to his bed and started bawling his eyes out.

I took a step forward and put my hand on his back but he

just went crazy. He jumped up like my touch was electric and started trying to punch me. But he was so slow and weak that he either missed me completely or I just blocked him.

I didn't know what to do. Just like I do to everyone in my life, I had broken him. I had finally broken old Toby. The one thing that was a constant source of good was finally corrupted. I had pushed him and pushed him until I had found his limits and then I had pushed him again. He was exceptional and I had dragged him down. And now here he was, down at the bottom. His brother, his idol, had killed an innocent bird. He wouldn't be able to stand it and I knew it. His illusions were shattered like when kids find out there's no such thing as Father Christmas – it's just the worst thing that can ever happen to anybody. Never would he return from this because he had passed one of those life markers that I told you about. I had done to him what I thought everybody else had done to me. Only he didn't deserve it. He cried on the bed and I left the room. Toby was effectively dead.

32

The next day at school was really bad. Everybody hated us. You could feel people's anger beaming out of them like ribbons of energy surging from their chests. Groups of kids huddled together, covered their mouths and spoke about us with their eyes not leaving our own. We had to stay together because, if we didn't, something bad might have happened. I don't know what. I had had enough of fighting. In two days I had been in two fights and sandwiched in between that had been Craig's funeral. We were lucky that the kids were utterly insignificant to us and we didn't care about them. I was so glad I had the Suicide Club to keep me going.

Clare's face wasn't as badly beaten as Jenny's and Matt's, but she was still shaken by the whole thing. I told her that I would never let anything like that happen to her ever again. And I meant it. Up until Craig's death, Clare had kept her old friends but now, after Craig, they were distancing themselves, leaving her alone and vulnerable. It was like some of her wonderful essence had been drawn out of her.

Wherever I looked, there were faces staring back at me, but I didn't care. I hated these people. Now there was a clear line: our side . . . and theirs.

At lunch I saw Freddy for the first time since the headmaster's office. I was with Matt and Jenny when he came over to us.

Freddy immediately picked up on something that I hadn't. 'Are you OK, Jenny?'

She looked at him and I shook with the look they exchanged. Matt didn't seem to see it, that quick glance that told me instantly that Jenny was totally under his spell.

Jenny smiled, but only with her mouth.

'I'm OK.'

'Don't let anything get you down. I wasn't even allowed to go to Craig's funeral, but I won't let them beat me.'

Jenny nodded and looked past Freddy's shoulder. I thought she was going to start crying.

'What happened in the headmaster's office after we left?' Matt said. His black eyes were starting to bruise out on to his cheeks. They actually weren't that bad – they looked kinda cool, like he had goth make-up on.

'He said I had to apologize but I just couldn't do it.'

'Didn't you want to go to the funeral?' said Jenny suddenly. She was glaring at Freddy, as if his non-attendance was a personal attack on her.

'I—' He didn't know what to say. He looked lost. 'Please don't talk like that, Jenny. You know that—' He cut himself off.

Jenny's teeth bit her swollen lip, restraining her tears.

This was unbearable.

'I'm sorry,' she said. And then she started sobbing.

Matt grabbed her and hugged her, but she pulled away from him. She used her hands to cover her face, but she was standing on her own. Matt looked at me, as if I could help in some way, but what could I do? That act had made perfectly clear that, although Matt was her boyfriend, she was dealing with this on her own. She was not using Matt for support in any way. Everything that had happened had encroached on her heart and pushed downwards, and she had no one to share it with. Her parents would certainly not have helped, her old friends had all but deserted her because she had stuck up for me after Bertie, and now, as she had just demonstrated, Matt couldn't help either.

'Jenny,' he said, and put his hand on her shoulder, one last effort. But she shirked him off again and carried on sobbing into her hands.

I glanced at Clare. She grabbed my hand and pulled me away.

'Come on,' she whispered, 'let's give her some space.'

We wandered some ten yards before turning back to see what was happening. All there was was Jenny, her head bowed and Matt standing in front of her, a metre away, not saying anything.

'Did you see the way she looked at me?' Matt said.

I didn't know what to say. What could I say to him?

'She doesn't love me.'

Things were reaching a point now where everything was descending into chaos. We as a group were supposed to be tight, but it wasn't seeming like that. Things were disintegrating. Jenny was fracturing away from us. It was like we were all on a raft out at sea, each on our separate piece of wood, the pieces bound together by rope, keeping us whole. But Jenny's wood was loosening and her section of the raft was drifting away. We were trying to pull her in but she refused to help herself. The gap of water was growing larger, waves were coming up between us and she was disappearing and reappearing from sight. Why wouldn't she listen? 'Hold on,' we called to her, but she didn't want to. She had given up. For her, holding the raft together was just too hard and she was just too tired. Overhead, it started raining. Everything was geared towards us losing her. 'Stay with us, Jenny,' we screamed but the sound of the storm was too loud and she couldn't hear us any more. As we watched her piece of wood drift away to the ocean, we kept looking at her because that was all we could do. We maintained eye contact.

That was how I saw the situation.

But what about Matt as well? Jenny had just broken his heart. Now his rope too was starting to unravel.

'What can I do, Rich?' he asked.

We were passing the art department, on our way to the first lesson after lunch. The bell hadn't gone yet so the corridors were relatively quiet. It seemed that things couldn't get any worse, but it's funny how the world can always find something to push you even further down. To this day I believe that what happened outside the art classroom was the trigger for Jenny's death, that final event that snapped the twine that had wrapped itself around her heart.

'Oh my God,' she breathed, just behind us, putting her hands over her mouth. I turned around and her face was in mine; we almost bumped into each other. I watched her eyes swell with water as she looked past me to the wall. I turned to look and the breath left my lungs.

Somebody had ripped her photography project off the wall. She had always been so proud of her photography on display. I remember the day when she found out about it; she hadn't been able to keep still. But now there was nothing but a patch of white paint, a blank void where her pictures had once hung. It was never revealed who had pulled it down, it may even have been the teachers, but whoever it was I hold responsible for what happened to Jenny.

'Jenny,' I said.

The bell suddenly sounded and kids started trooping in through all the doors like robots. The mass of bodies swarmed past us like bees, the occasional sting coming from somebody's tongue. I saw Jenny getting knocked forward and back, mostly deliberately. How could the kids be so cruel? Somebody called her a stupid American cunt, but I couldn't see who it was, there was so much abuse, aimed at all of us. Any restraint that had been shown before was now gone. Everything had bubbled over. It was like a feeding frenzy. Jenny's eyes closed when they said that, like she was trying to compose herself. I was hardened to it but I could see Jenny's defences were taking a battering. She was such a gentle soul. She wouldn't be able to take something like this. I wanted to reach out to her but couldn't. Nobody could. I had to stand by and watch as she fell apart, which she did practically in front of our eyes. I was amazed by Matt's reaction. He was just standing there, looking at some first year's crappy pictures of unicorns.

There was a gap growing between me and Jenny as more and more kids jostled for position. I felt like I was being pulled away from her.

After she died, of course, we all got blamed for her death, but it wasn't our fault at all. We hadn't been the ones who had ripped her pictures off the wall, we hadn't been the kids who beat her up in the alley after Craig's funeral, we hadn't been the kids who had shouted malevolent, spiteful abuse in the corridor, we hadn't been the teacher who shouted at her later that afternoon, and we certainly hadn't been her friends who refused to speak to her at all after Craig's death because somebody had to be blamed. Whoever it was, it . . . wasn't . . . us.

33

That night we agreed to meet up after school. Jenny told us that she wanted to take some photographs of traffic trails and we didn't want her to be on her own.

And so it was that on that night I threw on my red hoody and pulled it over my head. The air was warmer than usual for that time of year. It was one of those nights where the air seems heavier than normal, like it's pregnant with rain. I trekked across town in silence because, inexplicably, I had forgotten my iPod.

We met at the war memorial and made our way silently up to the motorway bridge on the edge of town. Not even Freddy was speaking much.

Jenny set up her tripod and clipped her camera to its mount. She played with some dials and, for the last time, I saw her rainbow sweatbands beneath the sleeves of her overcoat. She didn't say a word as she adjusted the settings.

'Are you taking one of those long shutter-speed photos?' I asked.

She nodded.

'So that the car headlights will come out as lines of colour on the picture?'

She nodded again and looked at me, her face like a ghost. When I returned her stare she looked away. Matt didn't seem to notice.

It was all so unreal, like a blanket was filtering out normality for us.

Underneath us the cars drummed past. They always look bigger from above. I went to stand by Clare, whose hair was blowing in the wind like it was alive. Jenny looked into the viewfinder and moved the tripod around a little to compose the frame. At last she stood up slowly and stepped back from the camera.

I still wish Matt had said something to her to make her feel better because she was clearly in torment.

Then Jenny clicked the button on top of the camera and the shutter was released. Light flowed in through a needle-prick of a hole and on to the film. It burned into its surface to leave that moment scratched into history. Jenny stepped in front of the camera and leaned against the railing. The sound of the traffic was like a hissing. She stood where she was for about five seconds until enough light had reflected off her body so that, when the photograph was developed, her ghostly image would be there, see-through and ethereal.

She turned and faced out over the river of cars and light. I can't remember if the stars were out.

We all looked at each other and Matt finally took a step forward.

'Jenny,' he said. He stepped into frame. Photons of light were pinging into him and bouncing off – into my optic nerve, into Clare's, into Freddy's, on to the photographic film. 'Are you OK?' he whispered like a lullaby.

Which I guess it was. One last soothing sound for her ears. She didn't look back, she didn't say anything, she just threw herself off the bridge.

Clare looked away and I grabbed her, not fully understanding what I had just seen. Below us and out of sight I heard a screeching sound and a loud thud of bones on metal. Matthew was leaning over the barrier, looking down on to the road, whilst Freddy . . . Freddy stood right where he was with *that* look on his face.

Something inside my head, like a little bell ringing, told me that I had to see the road. I had to see what had happened. I released Clare. The sound of brakes screeching and clashing metal did not register any more. A snake of traffic had already built up, all lanes static.

Sound was nothing any more, the past, the future, all nothing because in that moment I was alive. I was so wired into the universe that I thought I was going to explode outwards as shards of divine light. I could hardly breathe but it didn't matter because I had no lungs, my blood stopped but it didn't matter because I had no heart – I was purely . . . just . . . there.

I had no sense or feeling as the slow reveal came to me. The barrier receded and inching itself into my field of vision was the road that opened up like a panorama before me: crumpled cars that had ploughed into the back of others, steam rising from their insides, horns sounding, folded steel like a newborn mountain range. And then, just a line in the road, lit up for all the world in the headlights of the first car, bonnet bent into an inverted 'v' from where her body had hit, a line of blood running under the bridge, out of sight, where I could not see.

Matt came into view for a second. He had climbed down the embankment to the road, to the bridge, into its underbelly and gone.

Sound came back into my ears, the whooshing of cars, the trees swaying in the wind, Clare screaming wildly and uncontrollably.

Me? I stepped lightly and slowly over to Jenny's camera, unhooked the door on the back and took the film, slipped it into my pocket. I then folded her tripod away so that nobody would ever know that the whole thing was on a photograph. Jenny's moment was ours and nobody else's.

Then I called the police on Clare's phone.

People started coming out of the houses across the road to see why Clare was screaming. As soon as they saw the jammed motorway they knew that something was badly wrong and they ran over to us like people run across wheat fields towards the lights of a flying saucer.

I could hear the sirens approaching and those blue lights came to collect her soul, just as they had come for Craig. The police asked us what had happened and when we answered Freddy and I kept glancing at each other, but not smiling.

I guess if you pushed me to describe how I felt when that whirlwind danced around me I would have to say serene. I felt serene. In some twisted way I loved Jenny for what she had done. She had taken us all to the next level. She was the first person to kill herself when she didn't have to (Craig didn't have a choice). She didn't have mental problems, she would have overcome her troubles but she had been strong enough to do it. She had had the guts to say 'Fuck it'. It was amazing.

Do you know what I mean? What I mean to say is that, before Jenny jumped off the bridge, we had got to the point where we were in love with the idea of the Suicide Club but we couldn't actually do it because there was an invisible barrier in our way. Suicide was not the important factor. We loved the idea of killing ourselves to teach the rest of the world a lesson, but we were scared at the prospect of actually being dead. Jenny had smashed through the barrier and left a big hole in her wake.

I remember, when I was a kid, there was this big mansion near our town. This horrible old couple lived there who were in league with the devil. One night we all cycled out there with the intention of climbing over the wall, pegging it across the lawns and diving back over the wall at the far end to safety. We all huddled and crouched behind the first wall. All we wanted was for someone to go first and then, at last, Matt had made the break and that set us all off. Well, that's what Jenny had done. She was on the forbidden lawn right now, sprinting headlong across it at full speed, the wind blowing in her hair, free. We just had to follow.

I knew that this time round, I would definitely be taken to the police – there was no escaping it. But that was fine with me. This time round the media and the questions would be ramped up to a new level. Because this time round, it had been only us who were present – the Club. If people had hated us before, they were about to reach new levels. I felt like I was in a spaceship about to blast off into chaos.

The police took me home and I had to sit in the living room with my parents as they explained what had happened. My mother gasped.

'Oh my God, she was in my house just yesterday,' she said.

My father kept fidgeting in his seat, clearly not entirely sure what I was involved in but worried sick none the less.

'Are you sure you don't know anything more?' the police-man asked.

I shrugged.

'I guess she was fed up with the way everybody treats us,' I said, making fun of him. His face was all concern. 'And, you know, with what happened with Craig . . .' I trailed off dramatically.

The policeman's eyes shifted across to my parents.

'Will you be all right?' he asked them.

'Yes,' said my dad, 'we'll be fine. Thank you.'

'We'll contact you again soon.' And the policeman left. I heard the door close behind him.

My parents came back into the living room. I sat back in my chair and stared at them.

'What's going on, Rich?' my dad asked.

'What do you mean?'

'Rich, you know you can tell us anything.'

'What is there to tell? She's dead.'

They looked at one another. An unspoken urgency linked them, a sense of confusion, fear, a growing unsettling panic.

'Can I go upstairs? I need some time to myself,' I said, making fun of them, of course.

I got up and went to leave.

'Rich,' said Dad, 'don't lock your door tonight, eh?'

I smiled.

'OK.'

My room looked alien when I got in there. Like my version of reality had been warped. The colours were not as sharp and I could take everything in with an all-consuming expanse of detached, soulless brain power.

I lay on my bed and tried to get my head straight. Was she really gone? Had I just seen that? I knew that she'd been feeling bad lately but I really didn't think that she would actually kill herself. Not Jenny. Out of all of us she and Matt were the most grounded. Freddy had said that he didn't believe human behaviour could be explained away and now, with Jenny, his words had burned up bright and clear.

The house phone started ringing. Something told me it was for me so I bolted up off my bed and answered without looking at the caller ID.

'Jenny?' I said, which was incredibly weird.

'Rich?'

'Johnny?' My voice wasn't full of joy this time.

'I just heard about your friend.'

He paused, waiting for me to speak. But I couldn't get anything out.

'Are you OK?'

I didn't answer. Because I suddenly realized something. I wasn't OK. Something awful was happening. Jenny had died and I wasn't feeling sad. I was feeling flat, maybe even, what? Happy? No, not happy. I don't know. Whatever I was feeling, it was Not Natural and I knew that I was not being a good boy.

'Johnny,' I started. 'I can't be friends with you any more.'

Static.

'What?'

I swallowed and closed my eyes.

'I can't do it. You don't want to be friends with someone like me,' I said.

'Rich, what are you—' He stopped himself.

'Please, just . . . leave me alone. You're one of my best friends and I can't wreck your life for you.' I knew that I had to do this. Everything I touched became poisoned. I couldn't let that happen to someone innocent like Johnny. Matt was already destroyed and I couldn't face Johnny being broken as well.

'Rich—'

I hung up.

He tried calling back but I didn't answer. I went to the top of the stairs and told my parents not to answer. This was the only way.

34

There was a knock at my door. It was my mother. With a look of absolute terror on her face.

'What?' I said.

'There's a detective downstairs.' She swallowed but seemed to be having trouble doing it, like her throat was dry. 'He wants to talk to you.'

I went downstairs. My father was stood up against the door frame that led to the kitchen. He could hardly look at me. He wandered into the kitchen. I followed.

At the table was a slightly obese man of about forty with a moustache, thinning hair and dishevelled clothes. His moustache looked fake it was so lopsided. As it should have been, his top button was undone and his tie was loose. I dreaded to think how much coffee this man drank just for effect.

'Richard,' he said coldly. 'My name is Detective Berryman. Please sit down.'

I did as I was told. He wasn't messing.

'I think you probably know why I'm here.'

I felt numb.

'Jenny,' I muttered.

'Yes, the young girl, but there's more than that, isn't there?'

I looked at him. Sweat was glistening on his chin. I glanced at my parents, who had faces on that I had never seen before. Seeing your parents so filled with terror is scary.

'Tell me about the Suicide Club,' he said.

My heart seized.

'I don't know—'

'We found your little . . . charter . . . or whatever you call it. On Jenny's body.'

I sighed. That was so sweet of her. I didn't want to be here. I wanted to go and sit on the shore of that river with Clare and talk gently about the stars.

'It was just a bit of fun,' I muttered, knowing exactly how he was going to fly off the handle and say something like, 'Fun? Two kids are dead. Do you call that *fun*?' Which he did, of course.

'Do you?' he reiterated.

'No, the fact that they're dead isn't fun. The Charter was a bit of fun. We didn't expect anyone to actually do it.'

'But you knew that Craig Bartlett-Taylor had tried this sort of thing before, didn't you?'

'I guess,' I whispered.

'Your friend.' He flipped through his papers. 'Frederick Spaulding-Carter? He says that you wrote the Charter.'

I looked at the detective and, unfortunately, he saw a flicker of fear shadow-dart behind my eyes.

'He said it was all your idea because you didn't like Craig Bartlett-Taylor.'

I paused. This was a trick. Was this even legal?

His tone of voice softened.

'We know that it was just a joke that went wrong, but the justice system dictates that there have to be consequences.'

'I didn't write the Charter,' I sort of choked, a rush of blood going to my head.

'I know you didn't,' he laughed. Why was he doing this to me? Where was his compassion? He should have been trying to help me. 'Tell me who did.' He was a reptile. I bet he had a fork in his tongue.

'Can I ask you something?' I said timidly.

'Shoot.'

'Did your job crack your marriage in half?'

There was a pause as Detective Berryman folded his arms. 'You think you're big because you say something like that? Do you know the sort of people who act like this towards me? Like they don't care? Criminals.' He breathed loudly through his nose and stared at me. 'Criminals are always the smart-arses.'

I could feel him glaring at me, trying to intimidate me, and so I put on my doe eyes, which are excellent, and looked at him as if he had beaten me. I sighed sadly.

'I'm telling you this only because I want to do the right thing.'

'Just tell me.'

I breathed out.

'It was Craig. After he tried to kill himself we all tried to help him.'

His eyes gave nothing away. I couldn't tell if he believed me. I said it because I didn't want to get Freddy in trouble. This thing had caused enough misery for enough people already. I didn't want to add more to the list. The way I saw it, I had to protect my friends. They were all I had left in the whole world now.

'We spent loads of time with him, trying to cheer him up and stuff like that. He seemed to be getting better as well. And then he turned up with that thing.' I stopped.

'And?'

I shrugged.

'We signed it. We were only messing around. You know, trying to be nice to him.'

He shifted and the kitchen chair creaked.

'So Craig wrote it?'

I nodded. All of my efforts were going into not giving myself away. For Freddy's sake.

'You do realize that if you're lying to me you've slurred the name of a dead kid.'

'I'm not lying,' I said. He sat there and gave me the eye. 'You won't tell anyone . . . will you?'

He did something with his eyebrows.

'I'm sorry?'

'You won't say anything about Craig.' I was acting my head off, pretending to be distraught, having betrayed Craig's secret.

'We'll pick this up again,' he said. He slammed his notebook shut. 'I just want you to know that it's not my job to be Mr Nice Guy. We have counsellors you can speak to for that. Two kids are dead – that's what I care about.' He got up from the table and leaned in over me. 'If you think,' he spat, 'that we're not going to take this seriously just because you're kids, then you can think again.' I could smell the mint and coffee on his breath. It was embarrassing. 'If I find out that you have had anything to do with this . . .'

'Hey,' my dad said suddenly. He was grabbing the detective's arm. The detective looked at my father's hand and stood up straight. My father let go. 'I think it's time you left, Detective, but I have to tell you that the way in which you just behaved was completely inappropriate.'

They stared at each other.

'It's not my job to be . . .'

'I don't care about your job,' my father snapped. 'My son is clearly mixed up in something . . . awful . . . and you treat him like this?' He was shaking. My actions were making him shake.

Detective Berryman, to his credit, said, 'I'm sorry, Mr Harper.' And then he looked at me. 'And I'm sorry, Richard.

But in my line of work I see some terrible things. I just don't want this getting out of hand.' He had redeemed himself slightly; I have to say that because it would be unfair of me not to.

'Thank you, Detective,' my father said quietly.

My mother was leaning against the kitchen counter, like she couldn't stand of her own accord. I guess it was quite terrible, seeing the adults like this; so lost and confused, so helpless, their lives so out of control.

I sat in my chair; there was nothing I could do about it. The wheels were already in motion. Inside, bizarrely, I was laughing.

35

The police took my laptop and went through all my stuff. I stood right up in the corner of my room, out of the way, and watched as Detective Berryman and two uniformed officers who had been outside in the car during my interview rifled through my drawers and looked under my bed for I don't know what. They weren't very good at looking because they found neither my Charter, the note from Craig, nor the film from Jenny's camera. It was a farce.

Later that night my father called me downstairs for a chat.

'I don't know what you're playing at,' he said, 'but your mother's terrified that you're going to kill yourself.'

It was really weird, the way he just came out and said it so straight. It kind of shocked me. I didn't answer and we went into the conservatory. Next to the chair that my mother was sat in was a stack of books and something told me that I might have misjudged her. Maybe it was OK to like reading – it wasn't as if she had lived her life inside a cocoon or any-thing – so maybe there was room for reading *and* life. She looked so small, sitting in her chair.

'Rich, I'm sorry.' She said it so suddenly it almost knocked me flat because she had never been so wounded and open in front of me. It took me by surprise.

It's a bit of a cliché but you always see your parents as these infallible superbeings; even when they fly off the handle at something, they're still *better* than you. When my mum said 'I'm sorry' to me, that's when I saw that she wasn't this superwoman at all. She was just a person – skin and bones. A piece of life's magic slipped out of me when this painful truth hit me. I felt so sorry for me to have to suffer this sort of stuff so soon after another one of my friends had just died. The world can be so coldly scientific when it wants to be, you know?

'I'm sorry,' I said. 'But I can't speak to you any more.' I sat down in a chair. 'You'll have to talk to me through my assistant from now on.'

My parents looked at each other, half blankly, half horrifiedly.

'Peter will deal with all of your enquiries.' I looked at them, my monster completely in control now.

'What are you talking about, Rich?' my father said nicely, like he was scared to say anything bad to me. His hair was all scraggly.

'Peter, my new imaginary friend. He's sat right next to me,' I said, waving at thin air to my right.

'This isn't funny, son,' said Dad.

I held my hand up to silence him and eased my head to my right as if Peter was talking to me.

'What's that, Peter? They don't think it's funny? Think what's not funny?' I said, and looked at them.

What they saw was a son they had brought up from birth and who was now dancing perilously close to the edge of sanity. They must have been terrified.

'What did I just say to you?' my father suddenly shouted. 'And now you come in here with this shit? What the hell has happened to you?' he roared.

'I said,' I seethed through gritted teeth, 'to talk to my assistant.'

That set my mother off crying and I shook my head at how pitiful it all was.

'Why are you crying?' I said jarringly.

She couldn't answer because she was ashamed of herself. She suddenly got to her feet and bolted for the door. But it was too late. Chunks of vomit spewed out of her and smattered all over the carpet. My father tried to help by grabbing her round the waist and taking her out through the door that led to the back garden. These were my *parents*. She threw up again, this time into her potted rose bush. Because her son was treacherous.

I wanted to feel sorry for her because she was my mother and I was supposed to love her but, on the other hand, she was throwing up on a plant. I got to my feet and went over to the door, trying to think of something funny to say that would make everything OK. I didn't want to apologize because I hadn't done anything wrong.

So I went to the door and said, 'Looks like you've completely embarrassed yourself, doesn't it?' And I said it with a bit too much nettle.

I remember thinking at the time that my behaviour was way too much, that I was being unbelievably cruel to my parents, yet I couldn't stop. Maybe it was Jenny, maybe it was Craig, maybe it was because I was having a breakdown. Whatever it was, I just didn't care any more. As far as I was concerned, the worse things got, the better.

Her reaction was crazy. She lumbered to her feet like she had arthritis and then quickly lashed out at me. There was sick all over her chin, tears coming out of her eyes and snot running out of her nose on to her lip. It was monstrous.

'You're evil!' she screamed. I'd never seen her act like this before, not even when I went off the tracks. Even when she and my father used to have secret arguments before they split up. This was a whole new level.

My dad stopped her reaching me but her fingers still clawed at my face.

'I don't know where you came from! I don't know what I've done!' She leaned over so that she could get enough air out of her lungs and through her throat. Her mouth was wide open, like it might rip apart at the edges. Her neck was red, veins popping out purple and bruised. 'What's happened to you?' The pitch and volume of her shrieking actually hurt my ears physically. Then she started crying in my father's arms, sick going all over his sweater.

'Jesus,' I said.

'I hope you do kill yourself. So I don't have to look at you any more!!'

I stormed towards the door, barely able to hold in my tears when she said that. My mood had flipped 180 degrees just like that. I suddenly recalled being eight years old and going home at lunchtime from primary school. My mother had made me poached egg on toast and as I ate my lunch she sat and asked me what I had done in school, whilst holding Toby to her chest. The sun shone brightly through the window and on to her face. It had been such a close experience, just the three of us in our kitchen. I found it hard to think that our family could have come to this moment of insanity because of me.

I always thought that I could do anything and she'd always stay on my side but now it suddenly occurred to me that I might be wrong. Oh God, I was thinking, was I about to lose my mother as well?

'Rich, wait,' she cried. 'I didn't mean it.'

I stopped.

'Promise me you won't do it,' she wailed. It was really horrendous, seeing my mother implode so utterly. 'Promise me you won't kill yourself,' she cried.

I turned round and smiled evilly, oblivion scratching at my brain. 'I promise nothing.'

I lay on my bed and looked at the ceiling, trying to decide if Jenny's death just hadn't had time to sink in, or if I really didn't care that much. I was in one of those restless moods where you can't concentrate on anything and nothing seems particularly important. More out of a sense of duty than anything else I tried to think of the times I had spent with Jenny. There had been Halloween night so long ago when we had played tag in the graveyard – that had been pretty great.

Then there was that one time when I had seen her in town and she had been taking pictures of all the people for Freddy using long shutter-speeds. That was also a happy memory of her, although I did feel a pang of jealousy that Freddy had that spiralled notebook of her photos to remind him of her whilst I had nothing.

Then there had been that one time when she had told me about her little town in America. It sounded like the neighbourhoods in films like *ET*, you know? American suburbia. As a girl she and her friends would cycle around the valleys there, which were full of vineyards. Once she had even seen a puma – how cool is that?!? I remembered that when she had told me about it her eyes kept going wide with excitement, then normal again, then wide again.

I tried to think of other memories. I remembered the times before I knew Jenny and she didn't know me, before she started going out with Matt, when she first arrived from America. We were anonymous to one another and I remembered how she used to take long, deliberate steps to get to wherever it was she was going.

One final memory came to me. It was only a small thing, so I don't know why it was in my head. One day I had been in the yard with Jenny during lunch on one of those sunny winter days. She asked me out of nowhere about Clare's birthmark on the back of her neck. She had caught a glimpse of it whilst they had been changing for PE. She said that it made her feel really sorry for Clare because she would never be able to get her hair cut short. And I had told Jenny never to mention it to Clare because it would upset her.

I was suddenly exhausted. I was just drifting off to sleep when I got that image in my head again, the image I had weirdly got at Craig's funeral – the image of me falling through the clouds at night. I was dive-bombing straight down like an arrow returning to earth. Once again I knew that when I passed through the last cloud I would see some sort of eternal truth – like the meaning of life or something.

As I thundered through them, the clouds swept away, clearing a path for me. Then, suddenly, there was that final layer again, just a veil between me and the answer. I headed for it at a billion miles an hour but I didn't gain any distance. Pinpricks of light burned in the cloud once again but I couldn't reach it. I desperately wanted to stay awake to see what was beyond that last cloud, but I was no longer conscious. I had passed a critical barrier and there was no turning back. I fell asleep.

36

The next day at school all hell broke loose. There were about twenty news vans and probably a hundred photographers. Smelly, greasy journalists dressed in black were milling around clutching Dictaphones and notepads, living the cynical dream.

News had spread that a terrible tragedy had struck this sleepy little town in the heart of Middle England – a schoolkid suicide pact was unravelling. I could see one news reporter, a woman, with a microphone in her hand. She was filming a report and had her head tilted to one side to emphasize just how tragic it all was.

I drifted past them all like I was *just another kid*. They had no idea that it was I who was at the centre of this horrendous maelstrom. As I glided past I felt sorry for how pathetic they all were.

But then I looked ahead of me, in the direction I was walking, and my heart leapt. Clare was walking towards me, looking like one of those amazingly feminine women you see in films from the seventies wearing berets. Her features were sallow, her eyes deep in her face.

'Hey,' I said.

She didn't stop, she kept walking straight up to me and threw her arms around my neck. I rested my chin on her shoulder. The other kids were looking at us like we were freaks, either pulling evil faces or sniggering – they knew all about the Suicide Club now. It was all over the news. I felt a crushing desperation as I held on to that girl for dear life, not because everybody thought that *I* was a freak, but because they thought Clare was a freak. I didn't want to be a freak, but if I was then it wasn't the end of the world; people could think what they wanted about me. But for Clare . . . she wouldn't be able to handle this.

'I didn't think you'd be in school,' I whispered into her ear.

'My dad made me come.'

I went to let go but she held me tighter.

'Just hold on to me.' I did as I was told. Just held on. 'Remember the Eskimo Friends?' she whispered.

'Of course I do.'

And then she said, 'I'm so sorry for what I did at the disco.'

I don't know if she wholly meant it – maybe she felt she had to say it again to keep me next to her, where she wasn't alone. Whatever the reason I wasn't going to desert her now because to do that would have been indescribably cruel, so I did the only thing I could do and kept hugging her. But there was no magic in it, not like there had been outside the pub on the night that Craig had killed himself. I still loved Clare and throughout all this it was still her that pervaded my thoughts even more than the suicides, but I knew that something was forever lost. Something that can't be articulated had burned out and although I can't say it in words, I know you know what I mean. Right?

So we stood there and hugged each other in front of the cynical eyes of the schoolkids and our embrace just cemented our position of eternal teenage outcasts. The kids swarmed past us and, if there had been an infrared camera over the yard, we'd have glowed up like nuclear fallout on the film with everything else remaining a sterile, cold grey.

There's this line in the song '1979' by the Smashing Pumpkins – Clare's favourite song – that talks about this girl called Justine who used to hang around with the freaks and ghouls because she didn't realize that that's not what you're supposed to do. That line always snagged on me because I always thought I could empathize with what it must have been like to be a freak, even though I never was. And now that it was happening, I realized that my original thoughts were correct. I felt isolated and alone and cut off from everybody but as well as that I knew, just as all freaks must, that it was only because everyone else didn't *understand*. And because of that, I didn't care what they thought.

By now the Suicide Club was fodder for the school hive mind and I could just imagine clandestine corners of the cloakrooms where all the girls, eyes popping out their heads, lids surgically sucked back into their eye-sockets, hands gesturing, decried how weird we were.

Instead of first lesson I was supposed to see my counsellor for an emergency session. So I trudged off to the meeting room, knowing that Emma was going to ask me about Jenny.

To my surprise, she wasn't alone. With her were three other people. One was an old-looking, bald, pointy-headed guy with a rim of hair, tweed suit and smugness smeared all over his face, which was, to be frank, embarrassingly ugly. The second guy, who was also an ugly man, was wearing a leather jacket with a black roll-neck sweater underneath because he thought he was hip because he was only in his mid-thirties. The last person, who made me feel sick, was the horrendous Sylvia Bowler, my original counsellor.

As I sat down I said, 'You must be loving this . . . Sylvia.'

She just looked at me with fake-doleful eyes. I was in no doubt that she *thought* that she was being sincere; that's how far gone she was, poor thing.

Seeing those people there hurt me, because I wouldn't have thought that Emma would have put me through this humiliation.

'Rich,' she said. She looked genuinely sad. 'This is Doctor Kramer from the university.' She pointed to Pointy Head. Then she gestured to the fat slug. 'You already know Sylvia.' Finally she indicated the hip guy, who was introduced to me simply as, get this, Roy.

I sighed loudly with the sheer pointlessness of it all and put my outstretched arm on the table whilst bringing my other one across my chest, because these people would think that my doing this was a display of defensiveness because they thought they had all the answers.

'You know why we're all here, don't you, Richard?' said Pointy Head in a nasal voice that was almost as bad as his face.

I didn't answer because I felt like Emma had betrayed me and I was too upset to speak. It was funny how, now that I was involved in a suicide pact, everybody was clambering over each other to get the inside scoop on the circus act. All these people wanted was to make themselves feel important. But Emma was supposed to be my counsellor and I couldn't fathom why she was letting them into my world. She knew that I would hate being subjected to this crap. She should have been protecting me.

For the next five minutes, whilst the panel of experts told me why they were right and I was wrong, I did nothing but stare at Emma. She could barely look back.

And so it was that I listened to theories on group mentality, peer pressure, positive reinforcement, inferiority complexes, superiority complexes, all that stuff that's just a part of the big human fuck-up that's the glory of existence and should be encouraged, not 'cured'. When I asked Dr Kramer how old he was when his hair fell out he told me that I was engaging in a process known as transference. God, I wish I could be as sure as him about what's correct and what's not so that I could live in a spacious house and have a nice car and sleep easily at night.

The three of them all chipped in dramatically but Emma didn't say anything because, I realized, she knew that I wasn't listening to these people and that she had hurt me badly by letting them talk to me. Unfortunately for my panel of experts they were so pompous and all-knowing that they could never get back to real life and real people, where all the living gets done, and for that I felt bad.

After about fifteen minutes of their babble I thrust my head back and groaned, feeling my Adam's apple stretch.

Then I snapped my head back up just as quickly and said, 'I'm sorry. Do you think I could talk to Emma on my own for a minute?'

The experts looked at each other and nodded like they had any say whatsoever. I got to my feet, she got to hers, and we walked out of the room, me ten feet ahead. On my way out, I tried as hard as I could, but I couldn't help crying. Not real crying, just stinging, watery eyes.

Emma pulled the door shut and looked up at me. I had never realized it before because she had always been sat behind a desk, but I was slightly taller than she was.

'Why have you let them do this?' I said, trying to stop the tears breaking off my eyeballs.

'They can help you, Rich.'

I could tell that she was scared of me killing myself, and not because she would be losing a patient – but because I think she liked me. She didn't want me to die. I knew that she had never been involved with a case as heavy as this, a case which had at its centre, you know, a runaway teenage suicide pact.

The corridor was silent. Fuck it, I thought, I'll never get a better chance than this. I leaned in quickly and stole a kiss off her mouth. It lasted for about a second before she pulled away.

'No,' she whispered.

'I'm in love with you,' I breathed.

I took her by the hand and led her into the headmaster's office, which was empty, and closed the door. My heart was fluttering like a baby bird was trapped in there. We turned and faced each other and started kissing. Wildly and un-controllably. My hand was in her hair whilst one of hers started to unbutton my shirt and with her other hand she undid the button at the top of my trousers, her breathing hard and warm, and she started panting and if you haven't realized by now that I'm lying then shame on you.

Instead of that, after the first kiss Emma stepped back with consummate professionalism and told me that I had been wrong to invade her personal space and that nothing could ever happen between us because I was a fifteen-year-old boy. She also said that patients often feel this way towards their counsellors and I told her that nobody had ever felt this way towards Sylvia. My humiliation was so complete and embarrassing that I didn't even let it register in my head because if I had I would have had to have left town or some-thing. I was still upset at having been betrayed by her, but this embarrassment sort of diluted my anger and made me feel *nothing*. My tears got sucked back into their ducts and I was icy cool.

'Come on,' she said. 'Let's go back inside.' And she didn't even hold my hand.

She had won, that was the truth. I don't like to think of human relationships as games because that's just disgusting. But she had still won.

I had had enough of counselling, I had had enough of school. It was all too much for me. I was trying to act cool about my dying friends, but I couldn't handle this school any more. I couldn't handle forever being the boy who was crazy, who had cruelly killed the peregrine falcon, driven two kids into killing themselves, the freak, the ostracized.

I went back into the den of social workers and psychiatrists with only one purpose. To escape.

I sat down in my seat and politely said, 'Thank you.'

'Are you all right?' said Sylvia.

'I *am* going to kill myself and there's nothing you can do about it.'

Silence. I thought that one of the women would have gasped when I said it but neither of them did. I looked at Emma just to make sure that I wasn't making a mistake, and then I knew that I wasn't. I had only seen her as my equal in the past because she was so pretty. Underneath it all, I now saw, she was exactly the same as the others. She should have seen the drama and the romance that I had just offered her outside but all she saw was some theory she had read about in her textbook at university once. She didn't *get* it.

'You realize,' said Pointy Head, 'that if I think you are going to harm yourself we can put you in a psychiatric unit.'

What felt like a snake slithered up my back. It scared me when he said that. Surely he couldn't lock me up if I hadn't done anything wrong. They couldn't lock me up on the strength of this embarrassment's opinion, could they?

'But I don't think that that is the case,' he continued, light from outside shining off his scalp. 'You have some problems that need ironing out but I think that what we are seeing from you is merely a' – slow motion – 'cry . . . for . . . help.'

That was the trigger, all that was needed for me to realize that everything he had said was nothing but hot air, a fact which I had of course known all along. I got up from my chair and walked out. Roy followed but I was already out of the door and running. At the end of the staff corridor was the secretary's office. I swung into it at full speed only to be greeted by the headmaster and his secretary, Mrs McKinsay. He was leaning over her desk and showing her something in a booklet. They both turned their heads to me. I crossed the room quick as a flash. All I wanted at that exact moment was to be expelled and free of this hellhole. So, with a perfectly clear mind, like a beach at dawn, I disguised myself in a whirlwind of chaos that ripped apart what my headmaster thought that I was capable of. I rushed over to the desk and lifted her monitor off it like it was a toy. I took four quick steps back and yanked all the leads clear. The base of her PC shuddered across the carpet and smashed into the leg of her desk as the monitor lead got torn out of the back, socket and all. I hoisted the thing over my head and threw it as hard as I could at the wall. But the school was so crap that it wasn't even a flat-screened monitor so it was heavier than I thought and it only got about six feet across the room before heading downwards. It fell limply to the floor and faded from the world with a whimper instead of a bang, which is a phrase I once heard somebody use when describing how the world would most likely end.

37

I got my wish. I was expelled from Atlantic High School that day. My father came to collect me. We drove away and not a single photographer noticed my leaving. The headmaster didn't even allow me to say goodbye to any of my teachers or old friends. I was forced to wait in his office whilst he lectured me. He told me that, despite my angst towards what was happening in my life, my behaviour was not good enough for a school of this class. He told me that the way a person reacts in times of crisis is what defines a man.

My apparent outburst of insanity in the secretary's office only terrified my parents even more than before because they thought that I was genuinely crazy. After the incident that had happened between us the day before in the conservatory when my mother had thrown up, we found it difficult to talk about my expulsion. My mother, who had come home from work early, plain refused to see me at all, which I didn't mind because I just wanted to go into the living room and watch the news channels' coverage of my suicide adventure. My father just said something about sorting everything out later so I went into the living room and flicked on the TV.

The news reports weren't as extensive as I would have liked because I wanted 24-hour blanket coverage with news choppers all over the town, live satellite feeds to every corner of the globe, a frenzy of outraged parents roaring in the streets like it was the apocalypse.

At around half three the BBC news channel had an expert in the studio talking about the nature of suicide pacts and how once one person does it the rest usually seem to follow. According to him, people who would ordinarily never kill themselves on their own often do it if they are part of a pact, kind of like a chain reaction. The news report was good because as he spoke they kept showing pictures of my school. There were a few kids I recognized milling around the yard and then the camera suddenly panned round and zoomed in right on . . . me and Clare. We were holding each other in our arms and I almost choked when I saw it. My heart skipped and a sudden surge of happiness coursed through me. I was on TV! And I looked cool, even if I do say so myself. But then the camera panned to another group and my heart sank once more.

Since Jenny had died I hadn't even spoken to Matt or Freddy so I had no idea what they were thinking at this point. I had been thrown out of school before first lesson had even finished.

Inside I was in turmoil. I was happy because the school was on TV and I had even been given a brief cameo, and not just on the regional news; this story would get all over the world. But on the other hand it was me and my friends who were the stars of this story but our names weren't getting mentioned. I know it must sound weird, and it wasn't my strongest wish at that time, but a bit of recognition would have been nice.

I know that if it was another school and I was just an observer, I would want to know how many kids were left in the pact so that I could count down the deaths. And I would want to know *who* the kids were and their backgrounds so that I could guess how likely it was that they were going to commit suicide. I know it's what's called gratuitous but it's true. At least for me.

As I sat in the living room I wondered what my parents were doing. They were being very quiet. I assumed that a big lecture was coming up about how I was throwing my life away, but you know what? It never came. Ever. After the way I had behaved in the conservatory, our relationship had broken and, though you could tape it up, it could never be fully repaired because what had happened was Not Natural and you never come back from something like that.

So I sat in my room doing absolutely nothing. I could hear Toby shuffling around on the landing every now and again but I didn't feel like talking to him because I knew I wouldn't be able to handle it if I made him cry, which I almost certainly would, seeing as though everything I was touching lately was turning to shit.

At ten o'clock I watched the news on TV (I only have terrestrial channels in my bedroom). Our story had been promoted to the first segment and we totally dominated the regional news, which made me feel a little better. The editors at the TV station must have had time to put together a better report by this time because in this one there were shots of Jenny's house on the airbase and of her parents getting out of a car, her mother doubled over in agony, her dad in his uniform looking like the toughest guy in the world. The airbase was described by the reporter as having been 'rocked' by the events.

I remembered how Jenny had told me that her parents were 'opinionated'. Other than that all I knew was that they were from just outside San Francisco, from a town called San something. I suddenly realized just how little I actually knew about Jenny and her background. Right now, as I was in my bedroom, her parents must have felt like their world was over. Which it was of course because their daughter was dead after being smashed to bits by a car after jumping off a bridge. There was a gold rope of bond running between Jenny's parents and Craig's parents and they didn't even know it. It probably never crossed their minds that just a mile of space away were another grieving couple being drowned in the same river.

At least Jenny had done it dramatically. Thank God for that. Her death was probably better than Craig's if you asked me to choose. Just. If you think about it, you could never have imagined Jenny killing herself in such an explosive manner. She was the most normal of us all. She was definitely capable of killing herself, everybody is, but to do it like that? I would never have said she could have done it in such a dramatic fashion. But then again, she was very artistic.

The next morning I woke up with so much sun coming through the curtains that I thought that it had exploded. It was not normal for February. If it hadn't been that sunny I would have probably stayed in bed all day but how could I miss out on a day like this? I had been expelled yesterday and so this was like that song, the first day of my life.

The water in the shower fed me energy. Everything was going to be OK. My feeling wasn't based on anything real; nothing had changed, I could just *feel* it. In reality, of course, so my counsellors tell me, I had gone crazy. By this point I was so far gone I had no idea that my view of the world had warped so badly. I hadn't even noticed any discernible difference in me.

I wanted to see my parents. Not to bury the hatchet and start anew, that was impossible; I just wanted to be around them. I got changed and pulled back my curtains. The sky was so blue it was like neon and there were absolutely no clouds. The world was alive. I was alive.

I ran downstairs like one of those crazy winds that wash into France off Africa, ready to scream out how happy I was – only to find the house empty. I opened the front door. Mum's car was gone. Surely they hadn't all gone out without telling me, right? I looked at the floor and picked up the mail. My heart skipped when I saw my name written on a brown envelope. Don't worry, it wasn't another suicide note, it was one of those browny-yellowy padded envelopes that Play send out. My MCR album! There's nothing quite like the feeling of seeing one of those brown envelopes on the doormat, is there? I tore the wrapping off frantically, excited that at last I was going to get my CD. The envelope slipped away and my heart sank. I almost started crying right there and then. I had to sit down at the kitchen table to get my breath back. In my hands was a classical music CD. They had sent the wrong CD. I had waited for so long and they had got my hopes raised and now here they were slapping me in the face. How could they do this? I was on the verge of giving up on everything, finding a rope and hanging myself from it, but a little voice said, Just give it one more chance, Rich.

Hands shaking, I put the CD back into the ripped envelope and went over to the kitchen cabinet to fetch some sticky tape so that I could send it back.

It was when I was stood at the kitchen counter, reaching up to the cupboard for the tape, looking out of the window into the back garden, that I saw Toby holding a two-litre plastic bottle with the top sawn off. I got a twang in me because I thought about me lying in bed whilst he had been going about his business in silence, just walking around the garden with a bottle in his hand. I sighed. I wished he had more friends because he was such a great little kid. I couldn't even imagine why nobody wanted to hang around with him. If I had been a little kid I would have definitely hung around with someone like Toby.

Anyway, it was while I was having this very thought that Toby started talking to someone. Whoever it was, they were out of sight. Curious, I craned my neck round and couldn't believe what I saw. There was another little kid in the garden with him. A sudden sense of dread came out of nowhere and thudded into me. He had a friend. I watched Toby's mouth move, even though I couldn't hear what he was saying. Then I looked at the kid, and *his* mouth was moving in silence. They seemed to be having some sort of conversation. He didn't need me any more. Over the coming months and years I was going to be phased out. I had a terrible WCS about it where I was crippled in bed and he never came to see me because he was too busy playing some awful game with his friends.

Since he was born, Toby had been the weightiest constant in my life. No matter what happened, he was always there like a rock. Whenever it was raining on a Saturday afternoon it was never that bad because I always had Toby and he would do pretty much whatever I told him to because he idolized me. But that tide was turning. If he was going to turn into Mr Popularity then I would become the follower and he would become the idol. Now that he was all but gone, I felt it so hard that I almost collapsed.

Anyway, this kid. He had thin black hair, was quite tall and had on a matching red tracksuit jacket and trousers. And you know those zips that you have at the bottom of tracksuit trousers that run down the side of your calf? Well, he had zipped them all the way to the bottom so that above his bright white trainers was a hideous bulge of cloth. I'd say he was about nine. I instantly despised him.

Under his arm he held a shoebox covered in black masking tape.

I went into the conservatory and out through the French windows. I was more timid than usual because I was a little bit afraid. I knew that whatever was about to happen was going to be incredibly bad. I could just tell.

The air was so cold that my warm breath condensed into clouds.

'Hiya, Tobe,' I said cheerily, even though it came out with no middle.

'Morning,' he answered coldly.

'How come you're not in school?'

'School's closed. The pipes got frozen. Mum said I had to call her mobile phone when you got out of bed. She's just popped to the shops.'

'I've just spoken to her,' I lied. 'She's on her way back.' I sort of couldn't decide if I was upset or happy that my mum had to take time off work to look after her crazy son.

I stood just in front of the door, on the patio. Toby was in the middle of the lawn.

'Alan, pass me the box?'

Alan walked like he had springs in his shoes, all bouncy. He handed Toby the box. Tobe took it and placed it carefully on the lawn. Then he took his bottle with the top cut off and placed it inside. From his pocket he produced a roll of masking tape and unravelled it around the bottle. Then he pulled the tape away from the bottle and used the rest of it to secure the bottle to the box, if you know what I mean. Next, he looked at Alan expectantly. Alan took some scissors from his pocket and snipped the tape.

I watched on, incredulous.

The bottle was now securely attached to the inside of the shoebox and the two boys stood up simultaneously and awkwardly to admire their handiwork.

'Not bad,' Alan said.

'What the hell are you doing?' I called to them from across the garden.

Toby didn't answer immediately.

At last he said, 'Building a weather experiment.'

'So what's that?' I asked, pointing at the bottle and shoe-box. 'A rain gauge?'

They both nodded slowly.

'So how are you going to tell how much rain has fallen?' I crossed the lawn and picked up the box and tilted it in their direction. Toby looked scared, like I was about to smash it up and humiliate him in front of his new friend. 'This bottle doesn't have any measurements on it.'

Alan and Toby looked at each other sheepishly, realizing their mistake.

'Come with me,' I said at last.

Thankfully, they followed. I took them to my bedroom and lifted a geography textbook off my shelf. Finding the page I wanted I threw the book on to my bed so that they could see.

'Do you know what that is?' I was pointing at a photograph of what looked like a white bird house with slatted sides, mounted on a sturdy central post a metre tall.

The two boys said 'No' at the exact same time and thought nothing of it.

'It's a Stevenson Screen,' I answered. 'It's designed for measuring the weather. You put your instruments like thermometers and barometers inside. Because it's white it reflects the sun's rays so the temperature you get is always accurate. Did you know that official temperatures are always taken in the shade, usually in one of these Stevenson Screens?'

They didn't.

'And they're always kept on the top of one of these poles, which are always a metre tall exactly. That way, no matter where you are in the world, your recordings are consistent, which is exceptionally important in good science.'

They had blank looks on their faces.

'Come on,' I said. 'Let's go to the hardware store. We'll buy some wood and some white paint and we'll make one.'

Their faces came alive and lit up like Christmas trees when I said that.

'Really?' Toby said excitedly.

'Sure,' I beamed, feeling great. I needed this.

We set off right away. I took all the cash I had in my cash box, which amounted to nearly £60. I left my mother a note explaining where we had gone and we set off.

It's nearly two miles to the hardware store and we took the river route because if we had taken the road my schoolmates might have seen me and shouted things at me in front of Toby. I hadn't been down that muddy path for years and I had forgotten how peaceful it was; one of those places where you can hardly hear the cars. It was like the place I imagined going with Clare in my daydreams.

Alan turned out to be a delight. He was almost as bad as Toby for his country-gentness but at least he liked sports.

It was an amazing day. It took us about three hours just to get to the shop because the river turned out to be much more fun. We tried damming it in the narrow parts but it never worked. It was just like being a kid again, or maybe like being a father, I don't know. At one point I took off my shoes and socks even though it was the middle of February and freezing and was giving them piggybacks whilst they cracked up in the way that kids crack up when it's not even that funny.

Toby had forgiven me for Bertie and I hadn't even had to apologize. I could have apologized but it would have been so awkward there was no point. It wasn't because I paid him off with the weather station, it was because kids aren't as stubborn and they don't hold pointless grudges. They haven't hardened. By taking Toby to the hardware store and building him a Stevenson Screen (which is still in my garden, by the way) I had shown him that I wasn't such a bad person after all, and that was good enough for him because he was Toby, he was my bro. If he had made me apologize, it would have been the end because apologies are just words that people are forced to speak to make other people feel superior. If you're really sorry about something, you don't have to say it because you and the person you've hurt just know it. That's all.

Alan turned out to be the first in a long line of friends that he would make. Soon, Toby started to tell jokes and act cheekily in front of people, instead of being naturally funny by just doing stupid things. His dress sense sharpened and I remember the day that my mother finally put his red corduroy trousers and his other country-gent clothes into a bag for the Salvation Army. His bedroom got messier and he started lying on the sofa more often. Pretty soon he wasn't drawing pictures at the kitchen table any more because there were better things to occupy his time. It was sad for me to see because all that stuff was what made him Toby, but it was good for him because he was finally becoming normal. I guess that's just the way life goes.

38

The amazing sunny weather lasted through to Sunday. I heard a weather report saying that it was set to last for at least another week and probably longer because there was this rare weather condition called a Blocking High which sinks down from Russia and stops all the rain and wind and stuff coming in from the Atlantic, which was awesome news because I love the sun.

I didn't eat breakfast or lunch and I found it difficult to think back to the last time I had eaten a meal. It was a *long* time ago, literally months, but I definitely didn't have an eating disorder or anything like that so I didn't care.

I was in my room when something smacked into my window. I sat up on my bed, where I had been lying. Then something else smacked into the glass, this time with a loud *crack*. It took a few seconds for me to realize that somebody was throwing stones. I jumped off my bed and went to the window. My heart soared when I saw who it was.

Freddy and Matt were out there on their BMXes. They looked like the kids from the film *ET* in their colourful hoodies pulled over their heads. I smiled massively and waved like a madman.

Incredibly, I hadn't spoken to Freddy or Matt since Jenny's death. My computer had been seized and my phone was smashed up so there was only the house phone, which would have meant me calling Matt's landline and running the risk of his parents answering. Which I couldn't have faced.

I crept downstairs and snuck out of the back door of the conservatory. I tore across the lawn and wrenched my bike out of the shed with pure being.

'Let's go,' I breathed and we burned down to the bottom of the lane where my parents wouldn't be able to see us.

We pulled up at the end of the lane and looked at each other for a long time. Matt's black eyes had all but gone. All that was left were two red crescents under his eye-sockets. There were so many things that I wanted to say to him, my best and longest friend. But I couldn't articulate any of my thoughts. My mind was going so fast that I couldn't keep up with it.

'I'm so sorry about Jenny,' I said. What a pathetic thing to say. This one chance I had of saying something beautiful, and I blew it.

He smiled a little.

'Matt,' I said, trying to make up for it. 'I don't know what to say.' I was having difficulty saying anything as I looked at him, just a fifteen-year-old boy sat on his BMX. So much of his old life was gone. It wasn't just Jenny. It was so much more. Even his goodness had leached.

'It's OK.'

I think that what I wanted to say was that Jenny was amazing, that she had killed herself and opened the door for us, that she was so brave. But I found myself holding back. The thought was too radical to speak aloud, even for us. Matt needed more time before we started talking like that.

Apart from that though I wanted to tell him that I was there for him, to help him through this, just like he had been there for me countless times in the past. But I couldn't. I didn't like the way that I couldn't tell him how I felt deep down. If he was my best friend, I should have been able to tell him anything. Instead, all I could do was look at him with a stupid smile on my face because all of my words had jammed.

Freddy interjected.

'So. Expelled.'

I waited for a moment, trying to order my thoughts.

'Expelled,' I confirmed, glad for some normality to return. If expulsion can be called normal.

'We all heard what you did. You know that everybody thinks you've gone nuts.'

I huffed.

'Well.' That was all I could offer.

'I thought it was awesome.'

I sighed and picked at some of the rubber that was coming off one of my handlebars.

'I couldn't handle that school any more.'

'Have you heard about Matt?' Freddy asked.

Matt was sat on his saddle, one foot on the ground, the other on a pedal at the top of its arc.

'My parents have taken me out of school,' he said.

'You have got to be kidding.'

'Nope. It's good though because it's just what I need after my true love just threw herself off a motorway bridge,' he said sarcastically. 'Anyway, whatever, as of Monday morning, I will be an official student of the comprehensive.'

'Holy shit.' I laughed at the horror, trying to cheer him up. 'They'll tear you to bits.'

Matt nodded. He was trying to put on a brave face.

'Hopefully. My parents reckon they don't want me to hang around with you lot any more.'

We all laughed because he had already broken their wishes.

'Well,' I said. 'Fuck it. If you're going to have your life torn apart, you might as well do it right, right?'

Matt was undoubtedly going to get beaten up at that school. His parents probably thought that they were doing the right thing for him by keeping him away from us, but they were wrong. They had basically thrown him to the lions.

Freddy sat on his bike with a slight smile playing on his mouth.

'But that's not all. You realize that we're not going to Jenny's funeral, right?'

'What?' I coughed.

'Her parents have said that they don't want us there. Not even Matt. Can you believe it?'

'I haven't heard that,' I whispered, reeling. If Jenny would have wanted anyone there, it would have been us.

'The school will call your parents soon.'

This was so wrong that I thought that the world was going to stop spinning and we'd all turn into monkeys or something. I felt like I'd just been stabbed.

'I can't believe it. What are they doing? *Trying* to get us to kill ourselves?'

'You can't believe it?' said Matt. 'What about me? How do you think I feel about it?' He laughed a little when he said it because what was happening was so ludicrous. 'I was in love with her.' I saw his eye-line shift to the floor.

'Fucking idiots,' Freddy laughed. 'I love the way everybody's blaming us.' He was speaking in his calm voice again, the one he used when he tried to get a point across. 'Just because we signed the Charter. If they actually *read* the thing they'd know that it's *their* fault, not ours. It's all there in black-and-white but nobody can accept it because they're too stuck in their ways.'

'They'll never get it,' Matt sighed. 'That's the point, isn't it?'

We all digested that.

'So where's Clare?' I asked.

'She's not coming,' answered Freddy quickly.

'Not coming where?'

'With us.'

'With us where?'

'The forestry,' he said with a smile.

'The forestry?' I moaned. 'Jesus.'

'What's wrong with that?'

I huffed.

'It's just so . . . uphill.'

Freddy laughed and patted my back.

'Come on.' And he zipped off up the street, the bright sun shining off his back.

Now that Freddy was gone I could talk openly to Matt. The atmosphere turned melancholy, the unspoken presence of Jenny weighing down on us. When Freddy had been with us the mood had been lighter. But it was fake. This was real.

'Are you OK?' I said.

His voice snagged.

'Not really.'

'Matt, you do know she's waiting for you in the chamber, don't you?'

He couldn't look at me and I buried a thought that had crept into my brain – Matt didn't believe. If Matt didn't believe in the chamber then I had lost him. If he didn't believe in the chamber then he didn't believe in me, didn't trust me. My best friend. I had to change the subject.

'Where's Clare really?' I said, knowing that I would get an honest answer out of him.

'He wouldn't let me ring her.' He looked down the road to Freddy.

I thought about this for a second. I knew what Freddy was doing. He was isolating Clare so that she'd be next. If she found out that we had gone to the forest without her she'd be really upset and then Freddy might try something else, something more, to push her further, to force her into doing something stupid and I couldn't bear thinking of her like that.

'Give me your phone,' I said, looking up the street, seeing Freddy as a black speck a hundred yards away.

I dialled the number. When she answered, her voice sounded just so beautiful that all of my feelings suddenly burned up inside me. Her voice was all crackled and distant.

'Clare, it's Rich,' I said enthusiastically, trying to make her feel better because I could tell she was down just by the way she answered.

'Oh,' she said, surprised because I was calling from Matt's phone. 'Hi.' Her voice actually perked up when she found out it was me, it really did.

I was hopelessly gone for her. I hoped all this could fade away so that I could tell her I loved her, she could tell me that she loved me and we could live happily ever after.

'What are you doing?' I asked.

'Nothing.'

I switched hands.

'This might sound a bit weird but we're going for a bike ride up to the forest. I don't suppose you'd fancy it?'

'Who's going?'

'Me, Matt, Freddy.'

There was a pause. She was reticent, which I think means hesitant.

'Please come,' I said genuinely.

She thought about it for a second more.

'OK,' came her voice and I pictured her up in her bedroom, devastated like a smouldering crater, cross-legged on her bed, alone.

'I know it's childish,' I started.

'I want to go,' she interrupted. 'I'll borrow my brother's bike.'

'OK.' I didn't know what else to say. There was a lump in my throat that I didn't understand. 'We'll come and get you,' I recovered.

'No,' she blurted. 'If my father catches you near the house he'll kill you.'

'Not if I kill me first,' I said, trying to make light of the fact that we were in an active suicide pact. 'Shall we meet you at the war memorial?'

She paused.

'No. I don't want to see anyone.'

I felt bad when she said that because what she meant was everybody hated her. Everybody.

'Well, what if we meet at the bottom of your drive, where it meets the main road?'

'Yeah, that'd be good.'

'Can you be there in ten minutes?'

'Sure.'

I looked up and panic fizzed into my chest. Freddy was coming back.

'OK, I've gotta go.' And I hung up. It was a weird reaction because it wasn't really founded on anything other than a feeling. It was difficult to picture Freddy as a monster, even after everything that had happened, so why did I feel like this? That's instinct, I guess.

'What are you doing?' he said.

I was suddenly nervous.

'Asking Clare to come.'

'What?' He raised his voice. 'What for?'

'Why not?' I asked, trying to be brave.

Freddy shrugged and wheeled around the back of me where I couldn't see him. When he was behind me I held my breath, expecting I don't know what. He seemed to be behind me for a long time, during which I was genuinely terrified. He reappeared on my other side, standing on his pedals and leaning over his handlebars.

'Whatever.' He started pedalling. 'Come on.'

We were soon at the entrance to the drive that led up to Clare's house, which was at the top of a steep hill. She was wearing these pink sandal-things with white socks, reminding me again of the harsh reality – we were still kids, even though her shoes were a fashion thing.

Weatherwise it was still insanely bright but the air was death cold. We snaked through town like we were all tied to a piece of long thread, and reached the forest in about fifteen minutes, which I was happy with because when I was a little kid it used to take me about an hour to get up there.

We were all shattered when we reached the narrow road that leads up between the pine trees. You know how you think of Transylvania? That's what the forest was like. Well, a mixture between that and the wildlife programmes set in Canada with all the bears and lakes, you know?

We started to climb up the steep, bendy road until we came to the bike track that we always take up to the top of the mountain. Matt sped up it like a dog off its lead, Freddy on his heels all the way. Clare had already dropped behind. She must have felt so left out it hurt and when I saw her round the shoulder of asphalt and head for me, still going, not giving up, a slick of tragedy leaked into my ribs. She had lost everything.

When she finally caught up with me, she said, out of breath, 'Can we stop riding these fucking bikes now?'

I instantly cracked up with the way her words had cut my melodrama in half, and a few seconds after that a smile creased across her cheeks like it wasn't supposed to be there, like her smiles were finished but one last piece of joy had stolen out of her heart and shot into her face.

We hid our bikes in some trees and walked up the path.

'Are you feeling OK?'

'No,' she said softly. 'You know how it's been at school.' She paused. 'Does it seem weird? Not having her around, I mean?'

'Jenny?'

She nodded ever so slightly.

My hand suddenly exploded like stardust because Clare had taken hold of it.

'Can I be honest with you?' I asked.

She didn't need to answer.

'I don't know what's happening to me. When Craig . . . you know . . . I was devastated. I kept thinking about how he'd never do anything ever again, you know?'

She squeezed my hand as if to say that she didn't have the strength to speak.

'But with Jenny, I don't know, it's like I'm empty. I can't even feel sad. Just numb. I don't know why. I think I might be going nuts.'

I felt her head rest on my arm and my left shoulder slumped a little because she was leaning on me gently, a tiny redistribution of weight between us that meant the world.

'Let's go down there,' she said, her head snapping up quickly, reinvigorated. She let go of my hand and darted across the gravel path to a trail that led into some baby pines. I had never seen this trail before, which was weird because I'd been up and down that bike track hundreds of times.

'What about the others?' I protested, wary.

'We'll catch up with them later.' She disappeared into the trees and I had to follow her.

The track led off down the hillside. I had never been on this part of the mountain before. The little pines were so delicate, like gossamer spread over a mist, an unnatural greeny-blue. I could hear Clare ahead of me and whenever I went around a corner there was a flurry of pines floating to the ground where she had just brushed past. I quickened my pace a little, looking down so that I didn't fall, and finally caught up with her.

She was standing over a secret, hidden pool of creamy white water that nobody had ever seen before. That's how I saw it anyway. Secret and our own, like our feelings.

'Whoa,' I breathed, then, 'WHOA!' Suddenly the most disgusting stink stuffed itself up my nose. 'What the hell is that smell? Ergh!' It was like rotten eggs.

Clare smiled again, for the second time. Before today I hadn't seen her smile for an age and had totally forgotten how it made me feel.

'I know what this is,' she said, staring dramatically into its depths. 'This is the Egg Well.'

I made the few steps it took to get across the small clearing and joined her at the water's edge. On the far side, about ten feet away, a little stream gurgled in from a more ancient part of the forest, the underside of which was pitch black and primordial. The stream itself was only about two metres long before it disappeared underground into a carpet of mossy bracken.

'It's a spring from inside the mountain. That rotten-eggs smell is chemicals from the rocks dissolving.'

'It's disgusting,' I said crassly.

Her arm hooked under mine.

'It's magical,' she said. 'My dad used to bring me here. My God, I totally forgot about this place. The water has healing properties.'

I turned my head so that I was looking at her. Her hair had split in two around her ear. Her cheeks were red from the cold and exertion of the bike ride. I wondered if she was nervous like I was.

'I used to lie in bed and imagine it was full moon and all

the forest animals would bring out the sick animals and let them drink from the spring.'

All the world was bending over us, warping up and over to see the two of us by the side of the spring, talking nonsense.

'How do you know it has healing properties?' I whispered.

'Clive told me.' That's what she sometimes called her father.

Then she was looking at me and the whole planet was ablaze with the polyphonic colours that we used to drown in before everything went black. We were back from the dead and kids again.

'Shall we drink from it?' she said, excited like a little girl.

'From that?' I said, eyebrows up, disdainful finger pointing.

'We'll be immortal.'

'I already am.'

She punched my arm.

'Come on.' She crouched on the shore, her pink shoes sinking half a centimetre into the soft silt. Turning back at me and looking up, she said, 'Shall we do it?'

'I'm not drinking that. It smells like someone's shat themselves.'

She stood up and tutted, came close to me, eyeball to eyeball, mockingly threatening that if I didn't drink from the spring she'd do something bad to me. And then the threat faded, the meaning of her gaze changed, and everything was shifting. I thought back to our kiss at the Christmas party when she had sucked out my insides and I found myself wanting it again. As if I was submerged in water, my ears throbbed. How had it come to this?

'You feel free to take a taste,' I said.

'Not if you won't.'

'No,' I said. I suddenly jumped behind her and grabbed her round the waist. I lifted her up and dangled her over the water. She was strangely heavy, given how small she was. Extra gravity or something. 'I insist.'

'Agh,' she screamed playfully like girls do. 'Put me down.'

I did and we looked at each other like in a movie. Nothing would give me greater pleasure than to say that I put my hand on the side of her face, swept her hair to one side, made a tentative, nervous inward move, waited for her to respond, and then our lips met. But I can't say that because it would sound too perfect. And, more than that, it wouldn't be true. That's not what happened.

Instead, my eyes broke for the milky water and I said, 'I didn't even know this place existed.'

Clare nodded, maybe with a disappointed look on her face, I couldn't tell. Whatever, the moment was over.

'I think there's a quarry around here somewhere.'

And that was that. Without acknowledgement that it had ever happened, we changed the subject as if we were saving face or something bad like that. Like adults do.

'It's around here somewhere,' she said.

I saw a line of even newer pines near the far edge of the pool.

'What's that?'

We scrambled around the water, over the jagged rocks.

'It looks like they've planted over an old path,' she said Sherlock Holmesishly.

At the base of the trees were remnants of gravel mixed in with mud.

'Come on.' She went into the trees.

Even though it hadn't rained for over a week, the pine needles were wet and I could feel my hoody and jeans grow heavy as we plunged deeper. We moved quickly, like it was urgent, she in front of me. Our disturbance released the scent of pine all over us and I found my vision coming into sharp focus; the colours deeper and vivid, the world fresh, new, clean.

A tranquillity descended on me, like gravity had edged forward ever so secretly, like that feeling you get when the weight of a duvet sits on you in the night. I was happy. I had honestly forgotten what it felt like. Genuine happiness. I felt something spark up inside me: hope. I looked at the girl in front of me, thinking that nothing could spoil this sensation: Clare's back, her hair, her hood . . . the hood being pulled down her back, needles snapping at her, our heads dancing clear of branches, her hair glistening like silk, slipping to one side.

But suddenly a darkness came over me and my smile faded into my cheeks. A welling of tears crushed my throat and I thought I was going crazy to flip-reverse like this. But I couldn't help it because I was witnessing the world's end. I was looking at my Clare, the girl who was so amazing it made me numb, and I could see the death of all of us, including you, because we're all in this together. Her bare neck. Naked. Just there. She didn't even know about it being exposed. Or at least she did nothing to hide it, which was how she usually reacted when the wind got up and blew her hair away. But whatever, there it was – sour, malignant, devastating: her birthmark. It seethed out at me like it was alive – black, brown, indigo, bruised, spreading, burning, scarring, hurting, breaking, forcing her into loneliness for ever. It meant that she could never get through this, I just knew it deep, deep down where the bottom of my soul sloshes in the bile of my gut, I just knew it. Jesus Christ, stick another coin in my soul.

39

We came out from the trees and there in front of me was the most surreal landscape I had ever seen.

'God,' I gasped, non-ironically.

Apart from a rim of green pines hemming us in, the whole world was shiny and grey. Clare was right. We were standing on the site of an old slate quarry. There was something cold and sad about the place that told me that nobody had been here in years.

The quarry was like a perfect circle, not a semicircle, so I have no idea how they got the slate out. There was no sign of a road anywhere where the trucks used to come and go. It was like somebody had come along with one of those circular pieces of metal that you use to cut rounds out of pastry, a massive one, and taken out a chunk of the land. It was totally weird. I suspected that it was an alien landing site because the hundred-foot circular chasm would have been the perfect place to hide a craft. Probably the strangest thing about it though was that, when you peered over the edge, at the bottom, sixty feet down, was a green, green lake like molten emeralds.

'How crazy is this place?' she said and she stepped out towards the edge of the cliff.

Instinctively I grabbed her arm.

'Don't go so close.' I pointed to a beat-up old sign that said, *Danger! Loose rock.*

She took another step out, my arm lifting in the air. I took a step forward with her, my heart racing, an eerie detachment in my head. I didn't want her to jump.

From the cliff the green lake seemed to have a milky texture, all full of chemicals from the rocks like the Egg Well had been.

The walls of the quarry were sheer, lines scored into its sides running straight down into the water. If you fell in there, you wouldn't get out.

'It's so beautiful,' she whispered.

I couldn't argue; the shiny grey walls and the dense green water were like part of another planet. It was mesmerizing. I pictured the headlines: *Teenage Lovers Drown in Secluded Lake.*

'I have to tell you something, Rich,' she said, facing away from me.

I took a deep breath and, for the most terrible moment of my life, fixed my eye on her back, and thought about pushing her forward. It would be so easy, so poetic. I saw frogmen harnessing our sodden corpses to a bright-yellow helicopter and lifting us into the sky. I could do it right now. It would take just one moment of insanity, nothing else.

'What?' I said, my focus centred entirely on the small of her back. Was I really going to do this? If I was, then it would not be because I was evil, but because I was swept away by a moment. I didn't know if I was seriously considering it, or if I was fantasizing.

'What is it?' I heard my voice say again. My heart was still now, the lines between good and evil a fuzzy blur, not even existent, in fact.

And then . . .

If you asked me what happened next, I would have to say that I don't know. I like to think, have to think, that I *decided* not to push her, but the truth is I genuinely don't know. When Freddy placed his fingers in his mouth and let go of that whistle from the other side of the quarry I can't say that the whistle stopped me, or if it was me, myself. It still tears me apart, which I guess it should.

But there they were, Matt and Freddy, on the opposite side to us, their hoodies so colourful against the grey and green world.

'What did you want to say to me?' I asked half-heartedly, trying to put what had just happened out of my mind.

She was looking across to Freddy and Matt and waving, not smiling. 'Nothing,' she answered. 'It doesn't matter.'

I cursed myself. Maybe she had been about to tell me that she loved me and I had been too busy to listen because I was thinking about doing something so bad that just thinking about doing it meant that I could never be redeemed. But deep down I don't think that that was what she was going to say.

Clare and I, and Matt and Freddy started to make our way round to meet each other, the slate slipping away under our feet, some of it tumbling over the edge and splashing quietly into the lake below. We met halfway and all the way there I thought about who the bad guy really was. A sinking, lead feeling told me that it was not Freddy at all.

'Where have you been?' he said, looking at her, looking at me, almost as if he was jealous.

'Nowhere,' I said as calmly as I could. It was almost like a stand-off. I was glad it was me who was stood next to Clare and not Freddy.

'We've started a fire over there,' he said, in such a hurt way that I actually felt sorry for him. 'Then we heard you two through here.'

Matt picked up on the tension that had risen between us out of nothing.

'Come on,' he started, 'let's get over there before it spreads.'

★

Matt and Freddy's fire was pretty good. They'd cleared all the dead leaves away and made a circle out of stones, inside of which was a pile of logs and scraps of an old newspaper that they had found.

The forest was silent, the trees bent over us like a roof.

We helped each other drag some large logs over from a pile of timber so that we could sit and stare into the fire, each of us lost in our own thoughts. I don't want to go into mine because I was WCSing Clare's murder by me; thinking about what I could have done, wondering why I had thought about doing something so evil.

'I can't believe she did it.'

We all looked at Matt. Our attentions, wherever they had been, were now on him. In his hand, Matt was holding a long, thin stick which he used to prod some wood inside the fire.

Past the flames, I saw Freddy staring at Matt. 'She did it because she had no choice.'

My whole body shuddered. It seemed like such a cold thing to say. I knew he was trying to manipulate Matt. I hoped to God that Matt would stand up and storm off, tell Freddy that he was an idiot. At least that would show me that he was still strong and that he wouldn't kill himself. But Matt didn't react. He kept staring into the fire.

'You should have seen her body.'

A crackle of cold shuddered up my skeleton. I suddenly remembered seeing Matt climbing down the motorway embankment after Jenny had thrown herself off the bridge.

'It was like, not even her. It was just mush.' His words were slow and quiet and horrifying. 'She didn't even have a face.'

'Matt, don't,' Clare said quickly. 'Please stop.'

He glanced at her and breathed out through his nose. 'Sorry.'

The hairs on my arms were standing on end. The image

of Jenny, her face ripped off, was branding itself into my brain. I could feel bile in my stomach. It was too hard to take. Two tears fell out of my eyes, and I'm glad that the others didn't notice. I turned away and wiped them clear.

'Would you miss me if I was gone?' he said.

Clare gasped.

'Matt . . .' she spluttered.

He just kept staring into the fire.

I had to say something, I had to stop this.

'Matt, I know this is all fucked up but you can't talk like—' I stopped in my tracks.

Matt was looking at me and his stare was so terrible that I could not continue speaking. His eyes were looking at me like I was something alien, like I wasn't his best friend. I remembered the time on the airbase when Craig had threatened to shoot me and I had gone mental on him. Matt had looked at me in the same way then, like I was an animal. But this was more extreme, more concentrated. This was awful.

'Matt?' A shadow moved behind his eyes. 'Matt, Jenny wouldn't want you to do anything—'

'What do you know about Jenny?' he snapped. 'You didn't even notice—'

My heart turned to ice, my ribs liquid nitrogen.

'You think that because you're in this club that you're invincible, that we're better than everyone else. But it's not the same for the rest of us. You think' – he was pointing at me – 'that we're in the right. But the rest of us—' He stopped. 'Forget it.'

I felt like crying. We *were* better than everyone else, I knew this was true. I didn't like Matt saying that we weren't because it wasn't true. Everyone else was horrible. We were nice. We understood. I knew unfalteringly, as we sat around that fire in the woods, light dappling our faces, that I loved my friends. Even the dead ones who were waiting for us in our heavenly chamber that nobody else could enter. I loved that I was in this group of wonderful people and I didn't like the way that Matt seemed to be faltering. The Suicide Club wasn't about killing ourselves, it was about being nice people protected from the cold world by each other. I desperately didn't want him to kill himself. If he did, it wouldn't be anything to do with the Suicide Club. No, if he killed himself it would be because he couldn't stand life any more, not because he loved life. If any of us were going to do it, I thought that Clare would have been next, but now, as I watched shadows warp across his face, I knew that it would be him. Everything had been taken away from Matt – his friends, his school, his Jenny, his soul.

Across the fire we stared at one another and I think he felt sorry for me, like I had gone crazy and was in the wrong. But that's OK because I felt the same about him. I guess it was just his way of dealing with Jenny's suicide. We all had our own ways of dealing with it – Matt was angry, Clare was sad, I was numb. Only Freddy seemed to be *happy* about it. Or indifferent at least.

I caught Freddy's eyes moving back and forth between me and Matt and I never wanted to punch him in the face more than then. My heart was starting to beat faster and I was losing my grip.

Clare looked at me.

'Stop being such a fucking idiot and you' – she looked at Matt – 'you stop being such an idiot as well. You're supposed to be best friends.'

My lips were wet because the moisture from all of my emotions was getting the better of me again.

Then none of us spoke.

I felt bad because I didn't want Matt to hate me.

Jenny was dead and he was somehow blaming me.

But we were best friends and that was all there was to it.

That's why, after five minutes, and finally ending the stand-off, he said, 'I can't believe that neither of us are going back to school.'

I kicked a twig into the fire with my trainer.

'I don't care.'

Freddy adjusted himself on his seat.

'I don't want to say anything bad about your parents, Matt, but don't they realize what's going to happen to you in the comp?'

'I don't know.' He sounded deflated.

'They only want what's best for you,' Clare said.

Freddy laughed smugly.

I gave him a stern glare.

'What are you doing, Freddy?'

His eyes were lasers in my face.

'What do you mean?'

'Why are you trying to poison him?'

'Hey,' he snapped, but then recovered. 'Jesus, Rich.' His eyes and face went all emotional and I was lost because you could never tell what Freddy was thinking deep down. His expression would make you want to hug him like a father hugs his son, but at the same time you knew just how calculating he was. Just when you thought you understood him, had him pinned, he would slip away again. 'What do you think I'm doing? Engineering this whole thing? Planning your demises?' He laughed nervously.

I threw my stick into the fire.

'I'm sorry,' I said, making a decision. I had lost everything else; I couldn't lose my remaining friends. I had forgiven Freddy in the past because I saw me in him, but I don't know if that was still the case now. I gave Freddy the benefit of the doubt this time because, basically, I had to.

He sighed and gazed into the fire.

'We can't let everyone else get to us. We have to stick together, OK?'

'OK,' I repeated.

'OK,' Clare echoed out of nowhere.

Instinctively we all looked to Matt.

'OK,' he said half-heartedly.

It was all melancholic. Things were coming to an end and we all knew it. Matt and I were already separated from Freddy and Clare after having been taken out of school. After today, after we'd all gone missing together, we'd find it more and more difficult to sneak off and spend time with each other. The police, the school, our families would all be formulating plans to keep us apart. And soon the world would have its way with us and we'd go off to university, think of each other less and less often until, in the end, we'd be nothing but bad memories of an unhappy time. That was what the world had in store for us. Unless, of course, *she* were to return for one of us once again with beating wings.

Just like the daylight, our conversation got darker and darker and because we were with each other we had no idea how much damage we were doing to ourselves by going to these places. We talked about such fragile things with such mellow ferocity that all I could feel was my bone mass increasing exponentially whilst my body stayed the same. A million kids under a million stars had said this stuff before, stuff about feelings and the meaning of life and how there's so much sadness, but that doesn't mean that every time you say it it's any less important.

40

In the end we promised to meet up in the forest again on Friday whilst everyone else attended Jenny's funeral. She would be buried in America but there was going to be a special service for her friends in the local church – even though her real friends, us, weren't allowed to go. We decided that we'd get drunk and stoned in the woods like animals without a care, just one last time for us, for her; one last blowout.

By this time the twilight was dropping over the horizon and the canopies of the trees were sucking all the light so we made our way back home, single file. When we got off the mountain the stars were out and the sky was purple, with the last rays of sun spraying the western sky orange. We left Clare at the bottom of her drive, just a quick look back and a 'See you'.

When she was gone Freddy pulled up alongside me, the sound of our tyres gripping the road drifting quietly with us.

'You really do like her, don't you?' he said.

I stopped my bike. We were at the junction where Freddy would split away and head back to the school. He was going to get in trouble because he had been banned from leaving the school grounds but, just like in the song, he didn't even care.

'Of course,' I said. 'You know I do.'

For the longest moment Freddy stared at me. A few strands of hair in his fringe were caught in the wind.

'What?'

He shook his head.

'Nothing. It doesn't matter. I have to go. Say bye to Matt for me.' He wheeled his bike around and rode off.

'OK,' I said. To myself.

Now it was just me and Matt. We pedalled all the way to my house, Matt unable to bear even the thought of going home. He wanted to stay out for ever. I put my bike away and wiped my hands on my jeans.

'So, school tomorrow?' I said.

'Yup.'

It was unbearable. I tried to imagine just how messed up seeing Jenny's body was going to make him during the dark stretches of the night. I couldn't comprehend how awful it must have been for him.

'Don't go,' I said. 'Cut class. I haven't exactly got anything to do.'

We smiled but it didn't hide our true despair.

'We can hide out in the city.'

Matt sighed.

'Fuck it. OK.'

'Yeah?'

'I'll pretend to go to school and call you in the morning. Are your parents going to be at work?' I knew he didn't mean it. He wasn't going to call me at all. He was just saying it to be nice.

'I think so.' I felt incredibly emotional. Matt was my best friend and his life had stacked itself against him in such a way that it was all a dead end.

'Rich,' he said. 'You're a really good friend. You do know that I think that, don't you?'

'Why does this sound like you're saying goodbye?'

Pause.

'I'll call you at eleven,' he said. 'And we'll tear the world apart.'

Pause.

'Fine . . . so, do you want to hug this out?'

'Do I fuck,' he laughed suddenly, jumping on his bike and burning away like a meteorite. 'So long, sssssucker,' I heard him shout down the lane.

I laughed out loud. Just for a second there his old self was in him – that pure-of-heart child that could never be corrupted. It was so great to see it rise to the surface like that, so out of the blue. I watched him ride down to the bottom of the lane, round the corner, out of sight. That was the last time I ever saw him.

When I got inside it was like my whole house breathed a sigh of relief. My parents had been tearing their hair out, pacing up and down in the twilight.

'Don't worry, I'm not dead,' I said bitterly and needlessly.

'Where have you been?' said my mother, hardly able to stop herself shaking. She wasn't wearing make-up, which she *always* does, and she looked old, like her skull had shrunk and her skin had gone all saggy. She didn't even tell me off for saying flippantly that I wasn't dead. Rather she said, 'Where have you been?' flatly, as though if she had injected the slightest inflection of emotion into her voice I would have jumped on it and hurt her like I had hurt her before. She was now aware that she couldn't square off to me any longer because I would call her bluff. So, instead, she just showed me without meaning to that she still loved me.

'I've been out riding my bike,' I said, trying to apologize.

'Oh.' She sat down in her chair and looked at her knees as if I wasn't in the room any more.

Just then a policeman entered the conservatory. He was wearing the uniform and holding a glass of water, which he handed to my mother.

'Well, I'll leave you to it then.'

As he walked past, he looked at me with really reproachful eyes, like I was responsible for something very, very, very bad. I couldn't believe that the police had come round because I was missing. It seemed so surreal. I knew what this would mean though. It would mean that, after this, I was never going to be allowed to see my friends again. The adults, in all their wisdom, would see to that.

'Will you tell us when you go out in the future?' my father asked politely, thinking he was treading on eggshells.

I felt a bit ashamed.

'Sure,' I lied. I couldn't tell him that we were going to try and meet up the following Friday when Jenny's funeral was going on.

We all stayed still for a moment. I thought about what I could do next, like there were two roads in front of me, one dark, one light. To put it dramatically, I had to try and make a choice.

'Did you see what I built for Toby?' I said and I pointed across the room, through the window to the Stevenson Screen stood proudly in the middle of the back garden. I tried to bring myself to smile to show them that I was OK, but I just couldn't do it.

41

The next morning arrived and I awoke to the sight of my mother. She was sat on the end of my bed. Behind her, sunlight was blasting through the crack running down the centre of my curtains again.

'I need to tell you something,' she said, echoing Clare's words from yesterday.

My head was still muffled by sleep. I closed my eyes, my mouth dry. I knew what she was going to say; she was going to tell me that I wasn't allowed to go to Jenny's funeral. I felt sorry for her but it still didn't stop me getting annoyed at her having to tell me so dramatically – sitting on the end of my bed until I woke up, Jesus.

'Mum.' I opened my eyes a crack and squinted at her, the sun burning my retina. 'I know I'm not allowed to go.'

'Matthew's parents came here this morning.'

Jesus, I thought. He's dead. Suddenly everything went cold and I couldn't feel my arms and legs. My heart was throbbing like a pulsar, shooting shock waves out through my body. I didn't want my best friend in the whole world to be dead.

Oh God, Matt, I thought. What have you done? I remembered him up on that motorway bridge with Jenny before she killed herself; the image burning itself on to my memory. This was why he did it. My heart yawned open, a big hole appearing in its centre, visceral and exposed to the big bad world that had driven us all to this.

'Richard?' My mother had placed her hand on my leg. 'Are you OK?'

I couldn't answer.

'They gave me this letter,' she said.

I opened my eyes slightly and regarded her, the bright sunshine from the curtain crack lighting the back of her hair. In this strange light her face looked weirdly sallow.

'Letter?'

In her hand she held a white envelope. Delicately, she placed it on my duvet. I wiped the sleep from my eyes and squinted to focus. A letter? Brought by his parents? I ripped open the envelope and started to read.

Rich,

I'm sorry I didn't tell you yesterday but I didn't have the guts to say it face to face. I'm not really going to the comprehensive school. My parents are sending me to Boarding School in Scotland. My Mum and Dad think it's for the best. And, to be honest, so do I.

You were my best friend Rich and so I need to tell you this. You've changed. All along you thought we were the bullies and not the bullied. Although the kids in school were against us and had a go at us, you never cared because you thought they were morans. But that's not how we all felt. It's been tearing us apart Rich. You loved the Suicide Club because you thought we had our own little clique that nobody else could get into, but the rest of us were in the Suicide Club because we had no other choice. Do you see what I mean?

Jenny and Craig are dead and I can't handle this anymore.

So I'd better sign off. I do still consider you a really good friend and if you feel the same you won't try and get in touch with me ever again. I know how shitty that sounds, and I do really enjoy hanging round with you and stuff, but this is the best thing for all of us. I hope you can understand one day.

Over and out,

Matt.

A moment passed, my mother still sat on my bed, only there to enjoy the drama of my despair.

'Richard, are you OK?'

I had closed my eyes.

'I'm fine.' I swallowed. 'Just leave me alone.'

Silence. Her hand was still on my leg.

'This is the best way.'

'Please just leave me alone, Mum.'

'I can't,' she choked. She thought I was going to commit suicide.

'Mum, I'm not going to do anything stupid . . . today.' I winced when I said it.

'Richard . . .'

'Mum, please.'

She waited for a moment and then I felt my bed lighten as she stood up. And left.

My bedroom had that sci-fi silence in it, you know? So this would be how everything started to unravel. There was a darkness inside me, something bad; a thought. Was I really thinking that his non-death was an anticlimax?

I felt cold. Matt was a coward, a snivelling little rat. No, he was a snake. A fucking snake. He had succumbed utterly, capitulated entirely. How could he be so fucking stupid? How could he just fall in line with the mediocre like this? The whole point of the Club was *not* to fall in line, right? I resented him for being such a coward, for deserting us. Since Jenny's death, everything had been intense, melancholic and beautiful. But now, with this, all that had been zapped away. Matthew had wrecked everything. I didn't care that he was still alive, that meant nothing to me. All that mattered was that he had left me.

As usual, I knew that this anger, this one feeling that I had let through the barriers, was only there to take away the attention from the second, deeper feeling. There's no point in hiding it any more. The truth is, I do one thing, feel one way, so that I don't have to accept another feeling, a deeper, more painful experience. Maybe you've already picked up on this. When I was horrible to the counsellors in school, it was because I didn't want to listen to what they were telling me. This is so hard to write. When I threw the computer monitor and got expelled it was because Emma had rejected me. My God, I can't believe I'm about to tell you this but when I signed the Suicide Club Charter it was – oh God – because we had killed Bertie and I couldn't handle the fact that I was becoming unpopular so, rather than allow my friends to leave me, I left them. That's the truth, unblinking and deadly. You see? Shit. I'm sort of crying as I write this.

And here I was doing it again. I was pretending to be angry with Matt because the real truth was far too painful. I was not ready for that yet. The information that I had read off that letter, the *deep meaning*, was being carried by electrical impulses in the outer regions of my brain. It was pushing in on me like a planet trying to get through my bedroom window, so much gravity like a star in collapse.

The message was skipping from synapse to synapse, biding its time, encroaching on me, swimming around me. Circling sharks. But these neon-blue tadpoles of information didn't come any closer. Before reaching the centre of my brain they stopped, like soldiers in an army taking up positions in anticipation of a deadly, synchronized attack that could come at any time. But not yet – I wasn't ready. If they attacked now it would be too early. They knew that they could cause more damage later. So they waited.

Numb, I picked up the phone and called Clare, concentrating hard on each key that I tapped. I had to do something to take my mind off Matt. I had to speak to somebody who still loved me. At the other end I got ringing.

Click. 'Hello?' Her voice was tinny, distant.

'Hey.'

'He's gone.' Her voice was trembling.

'I don't care. He's a traitor,' I said half-heartedly.

'Don't say things like that.'

'Why not? I should have known he'd do something like this. He was never as good as us at anything.' I hated saying it, but I had to say it because the real truth would have hurt too much. 'Are you in school?'

She hesitated.

'No, I'm at home. My father won't even let me out of the house after yesterday. Not even for school.'

I lay in bed, my eyes closed as I spoke.

'Can I ask you something?'

There was silence at her end.

'Matt told me that you've felt bullied by the other kids in school.' I paused. 'Clare?'

'I'm here.'

'Is that true?'

The faint crackle of static sang into my ear. And then, through the electric hiss, I heard a sob.

'Clare?' My heart burned. Surely this couldn't be happening. Clare was in the Suicide Club – why was she letting normal people get to her?

'I . . . just . . .'

I felt unable to speak.

'They're just so mean to me,' she said, trying not to cry, her voice wavery.

'Is that why Jenny killed herself, do you think?'

She sniffled.

'I don't know.'

'So' – this was hard – 'did you only hang around with us in the end because you had nobody else? Not because you wanted to?' My skin felt hot.

There was a long pause.

'No . . . I don't think so . . . I don't know. Maybe. God, why do you have to say stuff like this?'

'I thought you liked me.'

Really quickly, she said, 'I do like you.' There was a slight delay. I was back in her bedroom, trying on my bees knees T-shirt, watching her face glow with happiness.

We stopped right there and recomposed. I hated that she was almost crying at the other end. Had I really not noticed the way that the others were responding to all this suicide/bullying/reaction stuff? Had the others been going through a whole different experience to me since Bertie, since Craig? Had they been going through hell? Some friend I was if I didn't notice that. We were supposed to be together for reasons of friendship and love, not desperation. If they had felt like that, then the Suicide Club had failed.

I suddenly remembered something that me and Clare used to do before all this mess. Back then, if I was feeling down, I would text her a sad face ☹, and she would do the same to me if something had made her upset. Then, we would reply to the sad face with a smiley face ☺. It showed that we were there for each other. To finish it all off, to show that the text had cheered me up, I'd reply ☺. That was how it worked. But not any more. I had destroyed my phone, just like everything else. There were no more smiley faces.

I suddenly heard a noise in the background of Clare's line.

'Who's that?' a voice said. It was her father, the evil oil baron. 'Nobody,' I heard her say before turning her attention back to me. 'Rich,' she sighed, 'I have to go.'

'Wait,' I said quickly. 'Clare, I'm always going to be there for you, no matter what. You're never alone, OK?' My heart was beating really fast but I just thought it was important that I told her that.

There was a brief pause at her end.

'I've really got to go.' And she clicked off.

42

I spent the next three days in a weird hinterland of existence, all of the colours bleaching to grey.

In the early hours of the morning, when I was in bed, my parents had started arguing again, just like they had done before they split up when I was younger. They would try to keep their voices down but occasionally they would explode and their hate would blast through my floor and into my head.

The police came round again to ask me some questions and my parents finally told me that I wasn't allowed to go to Jenny's funeral. They left it to the police to tell me that Clare's parents were going to take out a restraining order on me. How fucking crazy is that? I was only a fifteen-year-old, for Christ's sake. And I loved the way they thought it was my fault and not hers.

Because our group had been so utterly ripped asunder and I had no contact with anybody because the adults thought they knew best, I had no idea what was happening to Freddy. I was sure he was still up at the school because his parents were both working away and couldn't get back. Some parents.

An army of media had descended on our town by now because, although Jenny's death was a few days old, the whole nation had fallen in love with our tragedy and the news was still white hot. Though I didn't really read the articles, the newspapers had streams of words telling everybody how we had killed ourselves with apparently no motive. Even though the Suicide Club Charter had been found on Jenny, people still refused to accept responsibility.

The actual suicide pact of the Suicide Club had collapsed and seemed like a distant memory now. The media were two days behind real time. Inside the Club, none of us knew where the story was now headed; we were in uncharted waters.

I didn't care about any of the media stuff any more and so I let it all pass me by as if I was a tree at the side of a railway track. My parents tried to help me but they had grown cold towards each other and that made me even more cold.

Those tadpoles of electrical information holding the truth about Matt's letter had still not attacked and Clare had not called back and everything was like the final stretches of cancer; drug-addled and flat.

'Richard,' called my father.

'Yeah?' I called back.

'Can you come downstairs, please? Detective Berryman is here to see you.'

Jesus, why wouldn't they leave me alone? Couldn't they see that my whole world was in ruins? Why did they have to keep pushing me like this?

As I went to leave the room the phone started ringing. I had stopped answering the phone at that point but for some reason I answered it this time.

'Rich?'

'Freddy?'

Hearing his voice gave me the shivers. It suddenly dawned on me that he was my last remaining male friend. This boy who had come into my life and had left this trail of

367

destruction in his wake. Maybe I should have hated him for what he had done, but I didn't. I really didn't.

'I have to tell you something.'

He sounded very serious.

'What is it?' I asked.

A second passed.

'I slept with Clare.'

Just then my father came in through my door.

'Richard,' he said. 'Come on.'

I looked at him and bit my lip. It was the only thing I could do to stop myself crying.

On the other side of the line, Freddy was saying, 'Rich?' but I was gone. My head was scrambled so that it couldn't actually function. I thought I was going to collapse. I held the phone in my hand and was just looking at my dad. I wanted him to understand what I was going through, but how could he? He had no idea what had just been said to me.

'Rich, I'm so sorry,' said Freddy.

'Richard, we're waiting for you,' said my father.

Freddy was explaining to me what had happened. His words were going into my head, but they were indigestible at that point.

'We did it on the night Craig killed himself. I'm so sorry. She took me back to her house and it just . . . happened. Rich, I have to tell you this, I can't keep on lying to you. We didn't tell you because we didn't want to hurt you.'

I hated the way he was referring to them as 'we'. They weren't a 'we'. We were a 'we'. What did he want me to say? Did he want me to go nuts and start screaming, 'Was she good?' like a cliché? That's what I wanted to do but I wouldn't give him the satisfaction. I wanted him to stop speaking because he had just taken Clare away from me for ever.

First Matt, now Freddy and Clare. I had to stand there, so

small in comparison to the rest of the world, and experience my life unravel. Whilst my father was looking at me. He didn't know that, while he waited at the door, he was watching his son dying. I couldn't handle this, I wished I could be an innocent little boy again where my mum could save me from everything. I thought of Clare and why she would do this to me. Freddy had had sex with her and they weren't even in love. So that was the end of it.

Because my father was standing in front of me I couldn't say anything to Freddy. I couldn't tell him that she had only fucked him because she didn't respect him, that the reason I had never slept with her was because we loved each other, and she doesn't sleep with people who she loves.

I hate the way I let people get to me like this. I can't stand it because I want to be cool and aloof. I had almost made it to that point where I didn't care about anything and now here I was feeling my face growing red and my eyes stinging. I dried them with the sleeves of my T-shirt and followed my father downstairs, hanging up the phone without saying a word.

Berryman gave me this fake-sympathetic smile that almost made me throw up.

'Richard,' he said with an affected softness. I wanted to ask him why he didn't just throw himself off some balcony somewhere. He probably went on holiday to somewhere crass like the Costa del Sol every summer, so he could do it there. 'We'll do this here if you want.'

I sighed.

'Whatever.'

We sat at the kitchen table, the adults drinking coffee, me drinking nothing. I couldn't calm down. Terrible images of Freddy and Clare having disaffected sexual intercourse kept burning into my head, all fleshy and fish-cold.

369

'I think this has gone far enough,' said Berryman. He twitched his moustache and took out a notebook, breathing heavily through his nose like the air had to get past a tumour to get out. 'Don't you think?' He smiled at me.

'We're not even halfway,' I said calmly.

'Two of your friends are dead, Richard. Look what you're doing to your parents. Don't you care about them?'

'Of course I care about them, I love them,' I answered. That even shocked me. The words had just come out involuntarily. I felt a sudden release of energy in the room, a shifting of feelings, a loosening. I opened my mouth a little and drew in some air and focused on a fleck in the kitchen table, unsure as to what had just happened. 'But it's not that simple, is it?' I said.

'It can be.'

'You want simple? Who do you think is behind all this?'

He sat up straight.

'Tell me.'

I was so angry I just had to tell on him. He deserved it after what he had done to me. I didn't care about solidarity any more.

'You know who's behind it. Freddy wrote the Charter. You know that.' And there it was. I had betrayed Freddy, I had betrayed the Suicide Club, I had betrayed me. It was over.

'We've spoken to Freddy. Several times.'

Which was weird because Freddy had never said anything. 'What did he say?'

'He said that you wrote it. He told us yesterday.'

We sat there for a moment with slab-of-stone faces. Underneath I was like a hurricane. Would Freddy really have said that? I didn't think so because he had taken the blame for Bertie's murder. He had always been honest, he was incapable of not being honest. As he had just proved on the phone.

'Really?' I choked. The detective had tried this trick before but this time he was telling the truth. I just knew.

Detective Berryman nodded solemnly.

'My son didn't write that . . . thing,' my mother seethed from the kettle.

Berryman and I stayed silent.

'Rich?' she said.

'Freddy's had a lot of problems,' said Berryman.

I glanced at him. He was addressing my mother. Freddy didn't have problems.

'His mother died in the summer. His father sent him to Atlantic High because he travels a lot with work. The poor lad blah, blah, blah, blah . . .'

I feel still, inside my head like this. In here nobody can hurt me because it's my head and in here I am safe. No matter what, no matter where I go, no matter what they take from me, they can never get inside my head. Inside my head is where I keep everything that matters. Nobody can take my dreams away because they are inside my head. That is why I love it here, because they might take everything away from me that I hold dear in the outside world, but they will never take what's inside my head. And so if I live in here, they can never get me, because in here I am safe. And so that is where I will hide, in here, inside my head, with my dreams.

I started to get a cracking sensation in my skull, like giant boulders being dislodged in an earthquake. I could feel bile fermenting in my gut as something apocalyptic came over the horizon. His mother was dead.

What that meant was mind-blowing. It was all fake. The whole Suicide Club mentality was nothing but a lie that had cost Craig and Jenny their lives. I didn't bury the truth this time.

Freddy had never *meant* what he said at all. He wasn't a dramatist like me and the others, he was a nihilist. He didn't love life, he hated it. The whole point of the Suicide Club

371

was that there was no motivation behind it, that was what he had said, that human behaviour is magical and can't be explained. It was about being in love with life. We weren't abused or mentally ill (apart from Craig), or social outcasts. All it was was a perfect idea, crystalline. But it wasn't, was it? Freddy did have motivation. All along he had lied to us. We just didn't know it.

All of the things that we had fought against, he *was*. We railed against pent-up aggression, teenage angst, buried fury and he was all of those things. He was a Trojan Horse. I put my head in my hands.

'What did you just say about his mother?'

'She died, Richard. Why do you think he did it?' He looked at my mother. 'There's always a reason,' he said, all snide and content.

No! There's not always a reason – that's what I wanted to believe. Reality is what we make of it, not what is thrust upon us. I couldn't stomach the idea that Freddy had *motivation* because that wasn't the way I wanted the world to work. I wanted it to be magical, inexplicable – not cause and effect, atoms and genes. I wanted grass and poems and cigarettes and sun, not offices and concrete and family saloons.

The walls of my universe weren't crashing down, they were down. The colourful bricks that I had painted were in ruins at my feet revealing, for miles and miles, a cityscape of grey and smog, asthmatic visions of asbestos structures.

A huge tear dropped out of my eye and I felt it running down my cheek. In it were all of my hopes, all of my world, all of my energy, all of me. It was the end because the Suicide Club was not what I thought it was. Even the drama of hearing of Freddy's mother's death made me feel sick because it was like a twist at the end of a movie and I hate things like that because they're so cheap, and here I am writing in a twist

372

of my very own. But it's not a twist, is it? It's more like a conclusion.

I only cried that one tear. I lifted my head and looked at Detective Berryman, my heart split wide open, my soul lying on the floor in tatters.

'What do you want me to tell you?'

43

That was it. This might sound melodramatic, but I really could see no point in carrying on. Whichever way I looked was a dead end. I had had a cause, a belief that had driven the very centre of me. Having something like that is so powerful that if it ever leaves you you cannot recover. It's like when little children want to be astronauts. I believe that the first day that child realizes that he's not going to make it is the day he dies. That's when he joins the masses on the road to the Middle.

Freddy had built this idea in my head and I had happily absorbed it entirely, we all had, and now it was in tatters. We had fallen to pieces. When Jenny killed herself she had done it alone, not with us; Matt had surrendered and turned coat; Freddy and Clare had betrayed me worst of all. If one person could have saved me, it would have been Clare. I could have lived out my life in ecstasy if we had bought a cottage in the country and started an apple farm and I wouldn't have needed anyone but her. But that would never happen now.

As I sat at my desk that night, trying to make sense of what was happening and why it was happening, I kept coming back to the same conclusion: the Suicide Club had imploded because Freddy was a fraud. He had taken everything from me, taken my trust and my heart and squashed it up in his *motivation*. He had done all of this because his mother had died, and for no other reason. The strange thing was that at the time I was so furious that I didn't feel sorry for him. I didn't think, Jeez, his mother died. That is the normal reaction, and it wasn't in me.

So which way was I headed now? I had no idea. I had nothing left. Every bridge was burned. I simply did not know what to do, or what was going to happen.

In front of me at my desk was a sheet of paper and without realizing it I had drawn this picture:

how I saw me breathing

I think it's a picture of me getting sucked into a vortex with Clare trying to pull me out but I'm not entirely sure.

I started feeling tired, too tired to think rationally. Staring at the picture I found myself imagining what it would be like to get sucked into an oblivion like that. I must have fallen asleep because it was suddenly real and there I am, holding on to her hands for my life. Whenever I look behind me I see a swirling mist, gases like argon, xenon, all that inert stuff. Clare is trying to pull me out but my body is being stretched like my bones are elastic. I scream crazily but the scream gets sucked backwards into the vortex so all Clare hears is nothing. I can feel the nothingness pulling at my legs, a vast presence that I can't see.

And then, in a moment of pure release, I let go of Clare's hands. Ahead of me, in the point of space where the vortex had opened to bridge the two dimensions, I see the swirling mist close up as the hole between universes is sewn together by an invisible needle and thread. I am lost.

I am falling through space and I look down into the direction I am falling. It's familiar. I'm falling through the clouds again, heading towards the truth. I had been here when I was sitting on that pew at Craig's funeral and again when lying in bed on the night that Jenny died. I can feel that this time I am going to make it through to whatever it is that lies beyond that last cloud. Through and through I go and then I see that final veil between me and the answer. The cloud tries to sink away from me but I'm catching. I get closer and closer, those pinpricks of light popping up all around me. The wind howls through my hair and tears at my face. I am arriving. Closer, closer, closer. The last cloud stretches away north, south, east, west as far as I can imagine. The atoms that make up my body start to come apart, electron orbits growing ever wider. It doesn't hurt. I look at my body and I am almost transparent, like every alternate atom has slipped through a crack in the dimensions. I look down and suddenly lift my head up as I shoot through the final curtain.

All of my senses explode in a furious chain reaction and then, as fast as light, I crash through the other side of the cloud with a sonic boom and look down on the great secret, that elusive truth that always moves away when you're just about to unfurl the ends of your fingers and touch it. It takes my breath away. Stretched out all the way to the edges of infinity before my eyes is nothing but inky, empty darkness.

44

I gasped awake, sweating and clammy. I was actually out of breath. Somehow in the night I had made it across to my bed, where I lay, my chest heaving up and down. I was in that place between sleep and waking where you don't really know if a dream's real or not, you know? I brushed my hair off my forehead, my palm coming away damp. Could that really be the answer? Nothing. No meaning. Was there really nothing to save any of us?

I kind of started having what's called in psychiatry a panic attack. How was I going to get through the rest of my life if there was no point to it? The enormity and blackness of this question, coupled with everything else, loomed over me like a night sky would loom if it were sentient. It was so huge I couldn't handle it. I found myself hyperventilating, needing air, lungs not big enough. I thought I was dying. Searing waves of heat washed out of me like an earthquake at its epicentre. My chest suddenly tightened, wires being pulled taut about my ribs. I had never felt anything like this before. White stars started to materialize in front of me and I felt sick. My whole body went limp. I tried to call my mum but I couldn't get any sound out. I was in a state of pure, un-diluted dread; all sickle-cell and hyperglycaemic – no substance, all saccharin. Dusty air was in my throat and I couldn't swallow it because it wouldn't go down. I was in dread of there being no point in anything ever again.

I had to do something to stop this so I did the only thing I could think of which was to throw myself bodily off my bed and on to the floor, landing with a massive *thunk*.

I lay there for a second, cool and better. Down here the air wasn't so bad. Then I cracked up at how ridiculous I must have looked falling out of my bed like a spastic. I laughed and laughed and laughed like it was the end of the world and it was then, in my fit of hysterics, that I came under attack.

Those little electrical bytes of information, the little blue tadpoles lying in wait, the ones that were holding the true meaning in Matt's letter, the real reason why he had left me, had come to life. I could feel them swimming around the outside of my brain, their tales squirming slowly, mesmerizing. They came all at once, burrowing into my consciousness until they were inside my essence where their fragile bodies warped and folded outwards, their skin cracking open, exposing the monster that hid inside – desperate memories of an old friend.

Walking to school in the rain with hoods pulled over our heads; hanging around the park in the summer when the sky was like it was on fire; sitting on a wall eating Chinese food from cartons; nervously sat in a circle in a field with pretty girls; him laughing at me acting like an idiot, me laughing at him acting like an idiot.

Armies of memories vied for my attention, swamping me, smothering me, forgotten windows of bliss with Matt that I hadn't even known were happening at the time. From my neck to my belly button was like lead. I hadn't been able to grasp the concept of Matt's betrayal but now it was on me, unblinking and ferocious. On the floor, I dug my fingernails into the hard stuff that carpet fibre gets fused into and tried to bend my nails backwards, snap them off. My teeth clamped tight and I ground them down. I started making weird gagging, moaning sounds and my jaw hurt. I was in freefall.

Matt's disappearance was worse than death. All death is is a wall that you can't get past to see your loved ones. But Matt was still alive. He could still speak to me. But he wouldn't.

The reality was that Matt had left for boarding school because he wanted to get away from me because I was bad. He hadn't left because the mediocre had beaten him – that simply wasn't true. He had *chosen* to stay alive and cut me out of his life like I was a cluster of diseased cells and nothing more. That was the real reason he left. I had tried to deny it to myself but the truth had finally taken a hold of me.

I had thought that I could be a better person but it wasn't true. The boy who had attacked that old man had never gone away and never would. I *was* that boy; any approximation to being good was just that. Like when a robot wants to be human. It can never happen. Matt was right to leave me. He was right.

My breathing became forced again as I tried to comprehend this.

As I thought about it, images of Clare, her eyes closed in ecstasy underneath Freddy, his hair falling in front of his face, half damp with sweat, half dry, ripped at my imagination. I saw Matt on a train to Scotland, relief all around him. They were all gone. Gone, gone, gone. I was alone and I had been left behind because I was evil. That was that. I knew this now.

My heart wanted out, didn't want to be part of this faulty soul any longer. There was one option left to me; the only option.

I opened the door to my bedroom and padded lightly across the landing, a silver river of moonbeams leading the way. I went slowly downstairs and into the living room where, in the pitch blackness, I found a lamp and threw circles of orange light across the walls. I went to the mirror and brought my face up close. I dried my eyes because I wanted to look into them. I took in every facet; every fleck of colour in my iris, every red vein straggling across the surface near the duct, the deep, dark hole of forever that was my pupil. Finally I had seen enough.

I left the living room and went into the kitchen. I felt like my emotions were all gone, like the amount you are given when you are born is finite, and mine were spent. I had nothing left, nothing. I was just tired, busted up and hollow.

I opened the kitchen drawer and took out a steak knife. If I was going to do it, it had to be horrendous. I could have gone for a straight blade but I went for the serrated edge instead because I wanted to <u>saw</u>. In my head I imagined the steak knife running heavily back and forth, my wrists open and the flesh wriggling like it was alive with every thrust.

I placed the blade on to the surface of my skin and looked at metal on pink for a second, my heart rate slowing until I was ready. I could hear myself breathing and in my head I kept telling myself, Go on. The muscles in my right arm, the arm holding the knife, tensed as I pulled the blade down into my left wrist. The skin sank into the flesh and bulged out-wards until the seams failed and the first drops of red trickled out either side of the silver steel. Whatever happened from now, I would always have the marks.

I hesitated, waiting for the freight train of release that you hear self-mutilators talk about. It didn't come. I kept looking at my skin, the serrated edge of the knife out of sight under-neath the torn surface. I changed the angle of my right arm so that the blade was diagonal to the cut. My mind was working like a clock, mechanical and calm, no emotion. There was no feeling left, not even physical pain. I knew that all I had to do was cut deep.

'Richard?'

I whipped my neck around and looked at the figure in the kitchen door. My mother.

The feeling that pumped into my chest was like when an emergency generator kicks in during a power cut. First there's darkness, then there's that surge of power and the lights come back on and everything hums back to life.

The kitchen lights came on. I saw her eyes move down to my wrist, the knife still in it.

'Oh no,' she exhaled, extinguished.

My hand dropped the knife immediately. The blade held in position for a second before getting sucked out of my inner forearm, falling to the floor with a clang. The blood started to flow. The artery wasn't severed, the blood came from nothing but a few ruptured capillaries.

She was suddenly across the tiles and on me like she hadn't even had to move to get there. Pulling my arm up, she took me from the counter and over to the sink. Running the tap, she put her finger underneath to check the temperature for me. The hand that was holding my arm up she pulled towards her and placed my wrist into the flow of the water to wash away the blood. Not a word was said.

If you had asked me what her reaction would have been if she had caught me slicing my wrist up I would definitely have said that she would have flipped out, collapsed on the floor in tears. Not this. Everything she did was so methodical, like a field nurse in a war.

As the water thrummed over my wound I looked at her face. It was tired and drawn and all because of me. She saw me looking at her, turned her head and smiled.

'We'll find a way through all this, honey,' she said, with a voice that she used to use when I fell off my bike or got stung by a bumblebee when I was seven. She was my mum. My body buzzed with that weird security that only a mother can offer.

Just before, I had woken from a dream where I couldn't see any way out because there was nothing to save me. The story had run its course for me and I was utterly destroyed. Everything I had had before it all started was gone. My friends, my school, my girl, my family, even my beliefs. My parents were arguing again and I didn't even know if they'd get to keep each other after all this was over. Even though they had tried to save their marriage, it had never fully recovered.

But that night my mother bandaged my arm and made us both a cup of hot chocolate. We sat at the kitchen table in the depth of the night and forgave each other for everything we had done, in silence. Outside the window was the night but it couldn't get in past the glass because it knew it wouldn't beat her. Not my mother. I had obliterated my relationship with her and even though we would try to patch it together, it would always be broken. But even so, sat at that table, seeing her out of the corner of my eye, I knew that she was there and that was enough. Even though I had thought that there was no answer to anything, that nothing was there to save us, I saw then that I might just have been wrong. There was always my mum.

45

I would have thought that waking up the next morning would have been like, cathartic. The blazing sun was still with us but I still felt just so sad. It was going to take more than one night to get better from this, I realized. Which was depressing.

The story was all but over. I went downstairs and made myself some toast – four slices I was so hungry. I went through the whole process in silence, my parents watching me from the table. This was the first time I had eaten anything substantial in a long time. As I buttered my toast I couldn't help but notice how cool my bandage looked around my arm. I had to shake that thought clear. I dropped the toast on to the plate and sat at the table, all eyes on me.

'You OK, champ?' my father said.

I nodded and ate, not sensing that something was wrong.

'The police called us this morning.'

I stopped chewing.

'Richard, tell us honestly, do you know where Clare and Frederick Spaulding-Carter are?'

The saliva in my mouth suddenly retreated back into its glands and the toast turned to asbestos in my mouth. I couldn't swallow it.

'They didn't go home last night,' he added.

Jealousy tore across me. If they had run off together, I

don't think I could handle it. If they had killed themselves together it would be even worse. How could they leave me like this with nothing but a bland road to Healthy Recovery?

'I don't know where they are,' I muttered.

'You would tell us if you knew, wouldn't you?' he said.

'Of course,' I lied. 'I have to go and get changed.' I left my toast on the plate.

It was Friday morning, the day of Jenny's funeral, so I knew that they could only be in one place: the forest. I had to find them, even if I didn't know what for.

In my room I pulled on whatever came to hand, apart from my My Chemical Romance hoody, which I grabbed with purpose. With knowing, full-circle symbolism I pulled it over my head. I had worn this hoody that night way back when we had sat in the folly, the first night I had met Freddy.

I went through to Toby's room and opened the window, below which was the roof of the conservatory. The sill was slippery with grime and I almost lost my footing. Dangling my whole body down the side of the house I felt with my legs for the roof. This escape route was not a new one and I knew that the PVC columns would hold my weight. Dropping lightly to the dewy grass I danced across the lawn to the shed where I found my bike.

I reached the forest in ten minutes, my lungs burning. I hid my bike in the same place that I had hidden it last time with Clare, and found the gap in the little Christmas trees that led to the Egg Well.

As I ran I got the terrible feeling that Freddy had killed Clare. It was irrational but I couldn't get the idea out of my head.

The path was drier than before because there hadn't been any rain and I guess it was quite serene with the sun shining down, me wending my way through the foliage. Once I got past the Egg Well, the forest got denser and darker. I started stumbling over the roots, having to close my eyes where branches threatened to rip them out. And then, just as it had before, it ended and I was in the alien grey-and-green world of the quarry. The sun was blinding and I had to squint to see.

I looked around but there was no sign of Freddy or Clare. Maybe I had been wrong and they were on their way to California or something. Or maybe she was in the side of the road with stab wounds in her.

I skirted the edge of the chasm, occasionally peering over the edge into the green waters in case there were floating corpses in there. The lake was empty, at least on the surface.

When I got about halfway round I heard a disturbance up ahead and my heart instinctively started pumping blood faster and harder.

Freddy and Clare came out of the darkness hand in hand, from the same place that Matt and Freddy had come the last time we were up here. An instant relief smashed into me. They were still alive. But when I saw them holding hands the terrible realization that she would never love me like she loved Freddy hit me. It would have knocked me down but this is real life and things like that don't happen. Instead I got that feeling of desperation where you know that, no matter how much you want something, you're never going to get it. Just seeing them come out of the woods together, that sense of easiness between them, told me everything. She might have loved me in a sweet, teenage way, but it was Freddy she *yearned* for. He was the one who would get her lust and you can't beat that, no matter how Nice a Person you are.

They saw me immediately but didn't wave. They just headed over. I took a deep breath because it was clear that this was going to be the final confrontation. After this, there would be no going back. I found myself tensing my muscles, pumping myself up, getting ready in case a fight broke out. Freddy looked taller and leaner, more athletic, more animal. But he looked tired as well. Both of them did.

The air was unreal somehow, the atmosphere cloaked in something weird.

'Everybody's looking for you,' I said.

Clare's eyes were red and she was a million billion miles away from the full-of-life force of nature she had been a few months ago.

I stepped towards her.

'Clare.'

Her lips were shaking and I almost burst into tears because I could never be with her even though I wanted it more than anything.

I looked at Freddy. His hair looked different somehow, not as full. His skin was dry and a few spots had broken out around his mouth.

'Why can't it go back to the way it was, you know?' he said. He didn't say it sadly, he said it loudly. He had reached a point beyond sadness. He was in the final stretches of wherever his journey was taking him. I suddenly saw him in a new light. Now that I knew about his mother I was looking at a whole new person. So many questions had been answered now that the enigmatic last piece of the puzzle had been filled in. Freddy was like a magic-eye picture: suddenly I got him.

All three of us stood there in silence, a triangle.

'What are you doing up here?' I said.

Freddy glanced at Clare. 'We're up here for a reason.'

'There's always a reason,' I muttered to myself. I looked at Clare but she couldn't look at me. 'You're not going to do anything stupid, are you?'

'I'm not,' he answered. 'We are.' It was like the devil was in him when he said it.

I suddenly realized how cold the weather was, despite the sun. I was scared. We were miles from anywhere. Freddy's face was that expressionless mask.

'Clare?' I pleaded, hoping that she would say something to him.

'I'm sorry, Rich,' she said, taking a step towards Freddy and putting her arm around him. It almost crippled me to see that. It was an echo of that night in the graveyard playing tag, when she should have freed me but instead receded into the shadows.

'I don't want to live any more.'

I couldn't handle much more of this. The words were so clinical and to the point.

'Don't say that.'

'Why?' she said, trying not to cry. 'I mean it. Nobody likes me any more.'

'I do,' I blurted. 'I love you, Clare. I just . . . love you.' My face was pleading. 'Please don't.'

'Don't tell her what to do,' Freddy said.

It suddenly struck me that I had no idea how this was going to end. The most surreal thought entered my brain: was I living the last few minutes of my life? It seemed like a stalemate. Freddy had beaten Clare but how was he going to get her to kill herself and stay alive himself? Maybe he *was* going to kill himself after all. To be honest I didn't care. All I wanted was to save Clare.

'Please, Clare, just get away from him.'

'There's nothing left, Rich. Don't you get it?' she whispered.

'Of course there is,' I lied, thinking frantically. 'We'll run away,' I said. 'We'll go to London or Edinburgh and get jobs. We'll rent a bedsit and watch TV in the nights on our sofa. And nobody will know where we are, we'll just sink into the city.' Emotions coursed through every sinew, soaring like meteor storms. I actually believed what I was saying. It all came out of nowhere. 'We'll save our money and open a clothes stall in Camden Market and you can make all the clothes and all the cool people will come to buy your T-shirts and *only* cool people will know about it. Normal people will see your logo and wonder where they can buy them but they'll never know.'

'Shut up, Rich. We don't want to go on,' Freddy said, almost pathetically.

'Don't listen to him, Clare, he's not what you think. He's only doing this because his mother died and he's fucked up.'

The scene was at breaking point, chaos roaring at us from its secret dimension.

'What?' he said. 'My mother's not dead.' But he stumbled over the words. I was winning.

'Your mother is dead. That detective told me.'

'What? How can you listen to that greasy bastard?'

'Because he was telling the truth,' I said with unblinking certainty. 'You're a fraud. You don't love life at all, you're just a fuck-up,' I said harshly. 'And you told him that I wrote the Charter.'

'Well, I had to say something,' he smiled. 'I didn't want to get into trouble.'

Clare removed her arm from around his waist.

'Is that true?'

He looked at her, stunned.

'No,' he choked and I saw his face change imperceptibly. Something indefinable had slipped out of him.

'Your mother's dead?' She looked at him intensely. I saw her expression change to one of complete sorrow for Freddy.

He could barely look at her.

'Don't look at me like that,' he said forcefully.

Clare reached her hand out to him.

'Freddy—'

'Just fuck off!' he said, and took a step away from her instinctively so that she couldn't touch him. 'I'm not a fucking freak.'

Clare took two steps towards me and turned so that now we were stood against the trees and his back was to the quarry.

I felt guilty for what I had said to Freddy because he was my friend and I had just wrenched his guts out, but I had to save Clare. This was the first time I had seen him since he told me he had slept with Clare and I thought I was going to feel hatred for him, but I didn't. Seeing him in the flesh like this, and knowing that he had lost his mother, brought me the pity that I had lacked. Everything was so much clearer now. He was my friend, and he was in trouble.

Clare looked at Freddy.

'Let's just go home,' she said, still trying not to cry.

'What? No!' he shouted. A flock of birds shot out of the trees in shock. 'We can't go home. Don't you see? My home is a fucking school. That's not a home. Please,' he said. 'Please come with me.' There was no sign of a tear in his eyes but I knew that he was going through hell. 'I can't go on like this. Please. We had a *deal*. Doesn't that mean anything to you? Rich,' he said, looking at me with his big lost eyes, 'doesn't the Suicide Club mean anything? Were their deaths just a game?'

He looked so much smaller than normal. I thought about how he must have been a few months ago, when his mother died. I wondered what he was like before. He was just lost, that's all. He was a little boy without a mother. He thought he had protected himself from the grief of it all by making friends with us but now we were turning our backs on him.

'We're going home,' I said as kindly as I could.

Freddy looked at his feet for ages and then brought his head up, his face full of an exhausted rage. He reached around his back and pulled out from his belt a huge hunting knife. He wasn't like an evil psychopath, he was still a normal human being, just one that had crossed over to chaos. Whatever he was about to do, it would be out of love, not insanity. His own brain was torturing him to the limits. He was going through the exact same thing that Craig had gone through in the headmaster's office after Bertie had died, what Clare had gone through outside the church at his funeral, what I had gone through last night when I had slashed my wrist. Jenny must have gone through it as well at some point. The only one who hadn't done it was Matt, and he had gone anyway.

Freddy was going through what it's like when you are out of control, when everything hurts so bad that you're nothing. When you just want to ball up your fists, squeeze your eyes tight shut and scream until your vocal cords snap because you can't do anything else. That was Freddy.

'Whoa,' I breathed when I saw the knife, and took an instinctive step backwards. I grabbed Clare's arm and pulled her towards me. Behind us were thick trees and bushes that we couldn't get through and we wouldn't be able to get past him left or right. If we tried to push past him, he would easily be able to slash at us. And if I pushed him too hard he'd fall back into the quarry and I wasn't prepared to do that.

'Don't you realize that we *have* to do this?' he pleaded. 'All three of us.'

My heart was racing, getting ready.

'But I don't want to die, Freddy,' I croaked. 'I want to carry on.' I couldn't truly believe that this was actually happening.

'You're not my friends at all,' he suddenly screamed, his brain about to pop. His voice echoed off the inside of the quarry walls, ringing around like we were inside a church bell. 'You just used me like everyone else.' He took a step towards us and we took a tiny step back, the sharp needles of the trees pricking into our backs, not letting us into the forest. I looked at Freddy. Freddy looked at me. There it was. A tear. Two tears. One for each eye. He sucked in air through his teeth and his lips quivered because he was ended.

The world breathed in. This was it.

'Fuck it,' he whispered. He brought the knife up and, with the most force that I have ever seen come out of a human being, he ripped his throat out with the blade. As the knife came away a streak of blood spat out to the left and caught the sun. A lens flare burned into my eye.

Unable to move I watched Freddy drop the knife. He was trying to hold his neck together to say something. It came out as a gargling sound, guttural and horrifying. I knew what he was trying to say. He was trying to say, 'Push me.' He looked at me like I had been the only true friend he had ever had and tried to say it again.

I shook my head quickly, panicked, scared.

'I can't,' I coughed out of my dry throat.

When I said that, his face turned to that expressionless mask one last time. A lost, hurt desperation crossed his eyes. I had let him down. I suddenly got the impression that he was scared. He was dying. I wanted to push him but I couldn't. I was too selfish to do for my friend that one last thing.

After all we had been through, Freddy killing himself had finally shown me that he was not a fraud after all and that our ideals ran through him just as strongly as they ran through me. All of his ideas had come from a truth within. He had meant everything he said. The world would never get him. He refused to surrender his life to the Middle and so he surrendered it to the ether instead because that was the only other option.

But even though I now realized this, I still couldn't push him into the quarry, and those eyes he gave me will never leave my memory because they held in them every emotion you can ever experience in life. Not pushing him to let him know that I loved him is my biggest regret. Freddy took two steps back, looked into the chasm like he had a choice, and that was it. When he went over the edge, it was with sadness in his heart, not joy. And that was my fault. Because I didn't push him. Because I had betrayed him.

So . . .

And that's pretty much the end of the story. Just as I hoped it would be, Freddy's body was found by frogmen and lifted clear by a bright-yellow helicopter. It was even televised, although you couldn't see his bloated flesh. I'm sorry, I shouldn't say things like that because it's crass and I'm just trying to shock. And that's bad.

Following what happened at the quarry I was taken to what I suppose was a mental hospital even though they called it a Recovery Clinic. They gave me lots of tests, forced me to eat full meals and took me to see lots of people who tried to cure me of my illness. I even had a long chat with somebody who worked at the hospital who had a degree in philosophy. I told him about my falling through the clouds towards the meaning of life and finding only blackness and he told me that it wasn't such a bad thing. The blackness, he said, didn't represent nihilism, it just meant that the answer was so mind-bogglingly vast that it was impossible to visualize and that's why all I had seen was black. And I suppose that makes sense.

One day a local news reporter who I recognized off the TV crept into the hospital. He had somehow come across a copy of the Suicide Club Charter and tracked me down. He asked if I would do an interview but I was feeling tired so I said no.

At the end of the week I was sent home to my parents. I was told that Clare had gone to a clinic as well, and that she too had been sent home. After that week, and after the police had finished with all of their questions, I was released back to the real world where I had to try and go back to Normal Life. The whole process was hard.

My parents didn't make it. For the first month after it all they tried to be nice to each other for my sake but after three months they decided to split up and divorce. I felt sad for them but realized that it was in everybody's best interests. Toby was upset and when my father left the house for the last time he kept hugging his legs and crying like crazy, his face all red like sunburn.

Although it was decided that Toby would stay with my mum, they said that I was old enough to make up my own mind. I found it so difficult that I let a flip of the coin define my fate and so now I live in a flat with my father. I don't mind because I know he tries his best and I get to see my mum and Toby most weekends and I also go over there for tea once or twice a week.

I finished school through home-tutoring but didn't think that I was ready for university so I stayed at home. Nowadays I spend most of my time in the flat watching TV. Walking around town isn't as bad as it used to be because all of my friends went off to university. I don't feel I'm missing out on anything and I'll probably never go.

In my bedroom, hidden underneath the bottom drawer of my desk, is the roll of film that I took from Jenny's camera on the night she threw herself off the bridge. I want to get it developed but I'm scared that the photo-lab person will know what the picture is and give it to the police. I want to keep it for myself.

I only ever saw Clare once more. When we came back from our hospitals I didn't feel like calling her because the doctors finally made me realize that she was no good for me and they taught me to fight back the feelings whenever she popped up in my mind. And the same must have gone for her because she didn't call me either. The one time I saw her was in the mini-supermarket in town. I walked in and there she was, looking into the refrigerated section and picking up a sandwich, her face glowing bright like an angel from those powerful lights they have. If I had been as immature as I had been before, I would have grabbed her hand and whisked her away on the first train out of town. Instead I slipped into another aisle, out of sight.

Then, in the queue, she was about three people in front of me. All I could see was the back of her head and I thought about her birthmark and wondered if she would ever be able to have it surgically removed so that she could lead a normal life. The shopkeeper served her and Clare turned to leave. As she did we caught each other's eyes for one last time. We froze for a second but then blinked together and looked away as if we hadn't seen each other. As she left, the last thing I remember seeing her do was let the door swing shut after her. Later that week her family moved away and I never saw her again.

But I know that it's not a bad thing because Sylvia told me that if we had remained in each other's lives then we would have destroyed each other and she is right.

When I think of Freddy I guess he was just as doomed as Craig from the start but I've been told not to think about him if at all possible because he was a bad person who led me through a bad episode that's in the past now.

I sometimes wonder if Craig, Jenny and Freddy are up in that chamber we thought of in heaven, living their dreams just like we said we would. I never told anybody about that because I wanted one little thing for myself. I don't think that's so bad. I hope they are waiting for us because I think, I'm sorry to say this, that we will be friends again when we get to heaven and we'll terrorize the angels or something funny like that. Sorry. I've been told that whenever I say or think something bad I have to apologize immediately.

All in all I've learnt a lot from this experience. I know now that the world is what it is and there's little you can do to influence it. That's why it's best to put your head down, be a good person and make the most of your short time. If we all add just a tiny bit to the whole, then we can make it through OK. Sylvia has taught me that people aren't as selfish as I had once thought – all they're doing is looking after their own interests because nobody else will do it for them and so we all just have to do our best, I guess.

My MCR album never showed up and in the end I cancelled the order. I still buy stuff from Play.com and the service is always really good. I guess there must have been a glitch in their computer systems or something. A ghost in the machine. However, you'll never guess what happened. Six months after Freddy died, Johnny turned up at my flat and had bought me a copy. I had never told him that I was having trouble getting it from Play and when he gave it to me I almost hugged him because he's one of those people that can do things that make you get goose pimples.

In conclusion, I miss all of my friends, especially Matthew, but I know that our club was just teenage hormones running away with us. Each of them had their reasons for taking their own lives because there's always a reason. Everything I did was wrong but everybody will forgive me because I have seen the error of my ways and I'm going to be a normal person, just like them. I will soon be cured and I can start to think about a meaningful career where I can be successful. I hope one day that I can be a productive member of society. If I'm lucky I'll get married to a nice person and we can start a family together. If I try very hard I can erase Freddy and the Suicide Club from my memory entirely and life will be calm and easy, the way it should be. I know I can do it because anybody can do it. All I have to do is keep trying to be a good boy. And that is that.

I want to try and make this last chapter sound more hopeful, I really do. But, to be totally honest, I am having difficulty with that. Not because I Haven't Learnt a Thing, but because I'm still in my recovery period. So, although I can't truthfully cheer you up by saying something about me, I can show you this picture and that might make you feel better:

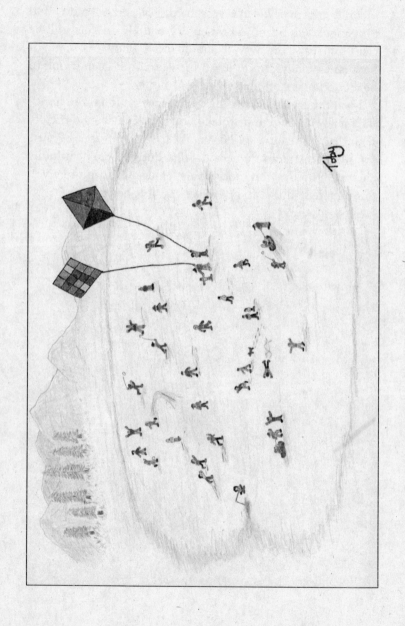